A Demigoddess' Guide
To
Interplanetary Parenting

By RL Andrew

JaCol Publishing Inc.

ISBN: **978-1-946675-17-0**
For information regarding permission, write to:

JaCol Publishing Inc.
195 Murica Aisle
Irvine, CA 92614
818-510-2898
Editor-in-Chief: Randall Andrews
Technical Editor: C.E. Hilburn
Illustrator: Katie Ketchum
www.jacolpublishing.com

ACKNOWLEDGEMENT

Without my husband Graeme, daughters Caitlin, Meagan, and Lauren, grandchildren Savannah and Elijah, son's-in-law Aaron and Nathanial, best friend Trace (and partner Lauch), and Jen (and partner Dave and kids), Sue, Tash, Michael, Eve, Max, Auntie Anne, Uncle Geoff, my other daughter Leah and her tribe Adam, Sebastian, Suzannah, Paul, Kirsten and kids, my brother, new friend Mickey, nieces and nephews, Marg and Ron, support I wouldn't be where I am. I thank you all from the bottom of my heart and bless your little cotton socks.

A special mention for my favourite twitter peeps: Marcee, Tanya, Ron, Don, Jake, Jim, Greg, Uvi, Jodo, Shaun, Shawn, Christina, Pratosh, Avni, Miss Quantum, Susan x2, Laurie, Bunny, Now what, Milton and countless other amazing people I've met.

A thank you to my amazing Facebook friends, fans, readers, and followers.

To Katie Ketchum, who brought her colourful art for my colourful work, and to Eva Hilburn who pieced together the title to make it beautiful.

A further huge thank you to my amazing Editor Randall Andrews, my doctors, specialists and medications, Lipton tea, Cadbury, Mars, my husband's bees' honey, and fresh fruit for your support and keeping me going.

Oh and to all of you in Simcity who left the Mayor's Club and me on my own, screw you. It's hard to win wars by yourself.

No matter what obstacles arise you can get past them. Never give up and never give in. Expect if there's a zombie invasion, then we're all frankenfucked.

TOC

Contents

Chapter 1
Weight Gain and Waist Bands
Jupiter City Central, Jupiter
& Yebu Township, Orion

Shayne's search for universal intelligent life disappeared into a black hole alongside a peaceful, god-like existence. With a protective aura extended, Shayne deflected the green beings' lasers. Their shots bounced off and hit the stone wall beside her and Annu.

Third time unlucky. Yet another place we've visited trying to find information on Annu's father and we're getting shot at—again.

Yep it's Tuesday. "What sort of fucked up shit is this? Yeah that's right. My kind." Shayne clicked her tongue and slapped her thigh. "Annu my love, this is not worth the aggravation. We've learnt nothing."

I say through gritted fucking teeth.

Heat consumed Shayne from inside out, an iced hand on her cheek offered little relief.

This is ridiculous. Why is it so fucking hot?

Ping, ping, zing.

In the distance, other military dressed beings fired weaponry at a black square hovering mid sky.

That's just weird, what the fuck? Blah. Who cares?

Bombs dulled Annu and wore Shayne's one nerve. "I didn't know this would happen beforehand, did I? What's going on with you lately? You've been extra—ah dare I say cranky and your powers unreliable. Please try a better mood for the meeting tomorrow and the rest of today. Your emotional requirements are exhausting sometimes."

The beings rolled out a bigger laser cannon, a red light hit the area before Shayne and Annu.

A dulled brain ached in time with rounds of ammo, Shane rolled her shoulders. "Thanks for that, my love. At least I show emotion. Let's see, why am I cranky? First up how about every time we follow information on your dad we end up getting shot at? On the positive side this way some people know we fucking exist."

Annu's tone sharpened, he physically and mentally shifted away. An inner darkness altered his features. "First of all just because I don't wear my moods on my sleeve doesn't mean I don't have emotions. Next, looking for my father is not open for discussion. It's something I must do to feel, I don't know complete. You may be all right with one parent but I'm not. So, understand and be nice about it or I'll go alone in future."

Admonishment climbed Shayne's spine and strangled her.

Shit, shit, shit. I've angered my chocolate hulk. I'm such a fucking bitch.

Shayne's shoulders tensed, her skin crawled. "I did—I mean I do. I'm sorry. You support me and of course I support you too. I didn't mean to say it like that."

Annu blinked a few times, the darkness abated. "It's all right. Forget it. I'm sorry. I haven't been right either. Among everything else it's bothering me we haven't heard from other planets by now. It's almost like they can't contact us, but then we haven't tried either. The problem is we're still in a rut, it's just a bigger, scarier, different one."

Shayne's nape burned, she turned away.

Fuck, fuck, fuck, shit, shit. Remember how Jacob gave me those messages months ago and I stuck them under the couch cushion and forgot all about them. And he distinctly reminded me not to forget and now...

Shayne kicked at a rock, her aura prevented contact.

In my bad memories and care factor's defence there's been none since. So it's probably not my fault?

Shayne's bottom lip quivered, she suppressed sobs. "Why are there still no rainbows and fucking unicorns for us? Only storm clouds, tornados, and mules. Motherfuckers need to respect our auth-ori-tay."

Annu's sigh added another layer to a cloak of disappointment. "Come on. That's enough negativity. It's not all doom and gloom. If the GC is ready to work with us Earth is next. It's some progress."

Mood change shrugged off the shroud, Shayne spat the words. "Hah. Yeah right. You're dreaming. The giant cockheads hate us, Earthlings can't stop blowing each other up long enough to hear what they should let alone completely change the religious and spiritual structure. It's more likely some black government would dissect us for their own evil means and more people will want to kill us."

Annu cocked an eyebrow. "That's a little paranoid blossom. Have faith it will all work out. I can't carry this life all on my own."

Shayne gave hope the finger. "Faith smaith, I've seen the conspiracy shows. I'm still with you though."

Boom, boom.

Grenades hurtled their way decimated Shayne's sanity.

They're not quick to work out none of it is hitting us. Morons.

To complicate matters, Shayne's waist band dug into her new paunch.

Why don't my pants fit and I'm so cranky? Mental note: search symptoms for fifth time at home and ask the doctor about it at my check up. It might not be cancer.

Shayne swept worry aside, undid the top button and opened another chocolate bar. Pudge poked over the hem.

Oh my fucking God. Why can't one of my powers be not gaining weight?

Kaboom.

Shayne dropped the chocolate, a flock of birds caught in the fray exploded, feathers and bird bits covered the area.

A torso landed a metre from Shayne, she swallowed vomit. "Gross. We're so, so, so trying a new approach on the next planet—like maybe not going at all." Zing, zing, zing. "Look can't you turn them into something else? They'd make great blocks of chocolate?"

Boom, boom, boom.

Stone structures on the left exploded, debris covered the bird mess.

Shayne's instinct kicked in, she ducked another barrage of shots and leaned against the wall of her aura.

Annu's sigh matched her own. "Yep. Walking out of a wormhole and into the middle of a busy farmer's market didn't help our reception, but you aren't giving up on something—again."

Sections of the wall centimetres behind them crumbled.

At some point they've got to run out of ammo surely?

Shayne's bladder tingled, she squeezed.

Not now.

"Hey what do you mean—again? My singing teacher said there's no more he can teach me, that I'm at the peak of my singing abilities. So let it go, let it—"

Zing, zing, zing. The shots hit the wall above them, Shayne flinched despite protection. "God dammit mother fuckers. I said we come in peace not pieces."

Annu moved closer, their respective bubbles merged with each other. "This isn't helping, and it isn't really the time to have an in-depth discussion about why you're cranky today."

Great he's noticed too, he probably thinks I'm a mean old fat cow. But so's he. Maybe it's spousal PMS.

"You asked me so too bad." Shayne picked up the chocolate and wiped off dirt. "Here's the second list—no money, no time for sex or anything other than this shit with you, Zeke hates me, Erin still hates me, Sam's being weird as fuck since he found out about us and Jacob's a huge pain in the arse spouting about that damned book thing all the time. Which I don't have time to learn more stuff and it gives me a headache. I'm pretty sure my brain's full."

Shayne tapped her skull.

Knock, knock. Is that an echo?

Annu's patient smile accompanied a side of guilt. "Silly me didn't realise I'd get the long version anyway. Look I get all that but I'm right here too so you don't need to get snappy all the time at me. There's been huge changes in my life I'm dealing with too. We'll talk about this later and try fit in some time alone. It might pay to stop eating so much chocolate too."

Ignore it, don't maim him before breakfast. It's not his fault. Wait, it might be his fault. It sure can't be mine.

Boom, boom, clang.

The end of Shayne's patience coincided with the walls complete destruction. "I don't care anymore. Screw this I'm going home. Are you coming? It must be killing you not to check the news."

Okay powers, no screwing around here, take us back to Orion. Enki island on Orion. Actually the kitchen in our house.

Crap that reminds me Annu needs to get food from Yebu later.

Shayne waved a hand, a pinpoint of light appeared.

Annu swiped through it. "One of us needs to keep updated. Look, we can't give up easily every time something gets hard Shay. I'm not going to find out anything if we never go anywhere. Trust me this pisses me off too. It's taking all of my strength not to kill them."

Shayne flipped her hand the opposite way, the light diminished. "Uh knowing your father's actual name would flipping help and I'm already at that point so you talk to them. I'm done."

Annu frowned and flew towards the beings. "We're here for peaceful reasons and I'm after information."

He's like so fucking patient sometimes. He deserves a medal. I'll make him one out of the empty chocolate wrapper. They have pretty paper and gold edging.

The gun fire lessened, one of the uniformed beings yelled. "You walked out of a twirling light in the sky similar to the portal over there. Since your arrival it's grown in size. Our people are terrified; many have been killed by the creatures coming out of it. Go back from where you came from and take the portal away or we'll continue until we kill you."

What the fuck is a portal thing? We don't have time for this.

Shayne levitated aside Annu and channelled inner calm from a galaxy far away, somewhere without angry purple fucks. "Look don't have a conniption."

Like I'm going to later inside the cupboard hiding, not sharing a huge block of chocolate and an ounce of weed.

"We are not here to hurt you and we've got nothing to do with that p-thing you mentioned."

The lead being tapped buttons on the cannon. "No. I repeat leave or we shoot to kill."

Annu's groan sealed the deal. "I admit this is going badly."

For one day I'd like something to go right.

"Whatever we do always goes badly. This is a fact finding mission and it's ended in weaponry being fired at us. We're never going to make changes for the better. We've still got nothing positive about our existence and mission to show the giant cockheads. Everything's frankenfucked."

Annu's ability to both parent and partner Shayne hurt her pride. "Shay it's only mentally challenging, we don't get harmed physically. You'll get where they're coming from if you think about it for two seconds."

In theory being a Demigoddess sounded fun, in fact pond scum lived better.

Bang, bang, bang.

Still beats meeting with Erin's in laws. You know I can't believe this shit has become so normal we have conversations in the middle of it. When will this get easier? Where is my glory?

Annu clicked his fingers at the end of her nose. "Shay, are you listening to me?"

Pay attention moron, time to focus.

Shayne yelled above the din. "Fuck it. I hate it when you're right. One day it will be me who is."

I swear you looking for your dad is going to drive us crazy or kills us.

"Not this week," Annu determination battled against Shayne's lost will, "all right, okay. If you stop and listen to us for a second we can work this out you'll realise it's not because of us. While we're not responsible for the portal, perhaps we can help regardless."

Ground fire erupted between bomb blasts from above.

Shayne searched for a joint and came up empty. She reopened the wormhole. "For fuck's sake. Fuck them and the weird shit they rode in on."

One foot inside and sound distorted, Shayne's physical self broke into molecules. Millions of stars, colours and blurred objects whooshed by. Shayne's sense of being split, shattered and distorted.

The tunnel ended, Shayne's feet touched obsidian not sand and people walked around them. "Fuck shit. We're on Orion. The cockhead's will be pissed." Mood change 666 took control. "Actually stuff them, it's time Orion knew."

People in mid-town Yebu froze, a child screamed, his mother and a group of others ran away.

Some fumbled with communicators, fear cloaked their movements.

Okay maybe not. No prizes for guessing who they're calling.

Annu hunched over and gasped for air. "Shit. You stuffed up coordinates again."

Shayne's enthusiasm evaporated as did having a wrinkle free neck. "Ah—fuck it." She flipped her hand, a light formed and flickered. "Let's try this again shall we?"

A news drone buzzed around their heads. "Huh, no need to guess the next report?"

A voice from behind shattered Shayne's enthusiasm and instilled fear. "You two stop right there and put your hands in the air."

Resignation lumped on Shayne's shoulders. "Fucking peace officers. Awesome way to end the morning. I repeat I hate my life."

Chapter 2
Ball Busters
Yebu Township, Yebu
Grand Council Building

Annu gripped the chair's sides, their 'caught red handed' position showed an ill-equipped hand.

Flark it Shayne and your screwy powers of late.

Flanked by other council members and swathed in robes, Councillor Igra leaned over the opposite end of the table.

Dread pumped through Annu's veins. Fury urged him onto his feet and out the door; little—aka no choice—plastered Annu in the seat.

A flat expression and folded hands offered no hints to Grand Counsellor Igra's state of mind. "Let's get right to why you're here earlier than scheduled. You've contravened our mutual legal agreement despite your pleas to the contrary. We've determined a way to fix this morning's fiasco but it's clear, such acts are deliberate attempts to circumvent our plans for disclosure, should we decide to do so, therefore are acts of terrorism against the Council and Orion itself."

I've had enough of this playing nice shit.

Annu lurched, the chair tipped backwards. "Now wait a damned minute. Again, it was because of a misjudgment in coordinates not on purpose and it certainly isn't declaration of war against you and Orion. Back up a bit. We do our best to comply and meant every word we've said. You're being unreasonable."

A woman on Igra's right raised a finger. "Sir, I must interject as Annu of Yebu rightly states thus far they've complied. Some consideration should be taken for this. Perhaps this once we can overlook this incident and continue on."

Oh hurray. At least one of them is on our side which is better than none.

Igra tapped sausage like fingers on the table top. "Thank you, Marguarite. Duly noted and subsequently dismissed—again. Remember the outcome of your suggestions during the meeting in chambers; you were voted out by a majority against and it does not need readdressing." He maintained eye contact with the tablet before him. "Which, brings us to the next matters of the Council's concern and the biggest one we've had from the start; the two non-humans living on our planet and one of which is also extra terrestrial. When combined with your ardent beliefs in a Creator entity which defies logic along with uncontrolled and unmonitored powers capable of massive destruction and death—"

Shayne's slap on polished wood vibrated. "First of all, don't call me names. I'm not one of those terrestrial things. Secondly, I don't understand why you won't just tell people the truth. Why the fuck wait? This knowledge brings security and joy to people's future. A spiritual existence they are unaware of, knowing for sure there's something bigger out there and we're all a part of it. Surely you see this?"

I love you woman but damned if you don't sometimes you confuse and excite me all at once.

Annu stroked her back and leaned against her ear. "Relax. Non Terrestrial means you're not originally from this planet."

Shayne wriggled back into the chair. "Oh, yeah all right then. The rest of what I said stands. Please continue."

Igra's consistent tapping scraped across Annu's patience. "Young lady, we only have your word on this supposed God and everything else. It's preposterous to expect us to make such drastic changes based on the word of two terrorists."

Shayne's breasts distracted Annu, her feistiness tingled his balls. "We are not fucking terrorists. Listen dickwad. I'm not a young lady and he, the big G, as in the Creator can't just pop over and say hi. Aside from being enormous, humans are not physically capable of being in his presence, it's incomprehensible. Hence why he needs us. You people are so fucking stupid."

You smell so good today. I love the way the little extra weight you're carrying fills out your curves more. Waking up next to you every day is heavenly.

How long has it been since we've fooled around?

A bulged vein on Shayne's temple muted Annu's desire. "This whole godly situation thing got sprung on us as much as all of you. We're aware of the implications this will have, which is why we agreed to your terms in the first place. This is a huge adjustment and opportunity for everyone but no matter what we say or do, you'll think badly of us. It's not fair or right."

Igra adjusted his robes and a matt of hair on his head. "Perhaps if it were only the two of you involved we'd derive an iota of comfort but the likely arrival of visitors from other planets whose motives are unknown is a definite threat we aren't prepared for. Conversely, an influx of beings from said planets would drain our recourses."

Counsellor Marguarite cleared her throat and opened her mouth.

Igra faced her and raised an eyebrow; Marguarite sank back in her chair.

We're pushing shit uphill here.

Tension gripped Annu's shoulders. "You're right, we don't know what might come, but it's just as likely to be positive rather than negative. Give people some credit; they'll adjust better than you believe."

Igra's sneer hardened his bloated features. "It's not simple. Our new policy stands. Orion is our domain and we won't hand it over to you. Who'd protect Orion from both of you, should you decide you're against us mere mortals or plan an intergalactic coup?"

Shayne's banged fists shook the table. "For fuck's sake. We're not going to turn on you—well on everyone else. You, I'm not so sure about you, fat fuck. I've more than proven my loyalty for this planet and its people, despite the fact it's tried to kill me a number of times. We're not pets who require monitoring. This is fucking stupid."

Annu's blood pressure rose, his internal thermostat soared. Small flames appeared on his hands, he stuck them under fire retardant pants.

Worse time ever to erupt. Keep your cool. There will be a way around this; we just need to think of it. Doing the right thing will pay off. Eventually.

Annu exhaled his angst. "We're not wanting Orion handed over to us. We're merely trying to work alongside of you for the greater good of all."

Not that it's done us any benefit so far.

Igra twirled his thumbs. "Which brings me to the only solution if you both wish to remain on Orion in conjunction with our demands, you'll do so under the supervision of a Counsel elected regulatory body designed to deal with otherworldly threats such as yourselves. Under Executive Order two-twenty-one, The Intergalactic Defence Intelligence Operatives and Tacticians Squad are now in force. In addition to being overseen, you're required to conform to further, stringent guidelines. Firstly, the woman is allowed one more trip to Earth under said supervision, which we believe is—"

Shayne scoffed into her fist. "Ha, you've compiled a bunch of idiots."

Annu kicked the chair out of the way. "Shayne focus. Firstly? What the hell? How many rules are there?"

Shayne pursed her lips, her chest heaved. "Oh yeah, I ought to freeze your balls off."

Annu imagined strangling Igra over the table.

I'll burn the flesh for your body. Oh that's a bit dark. Step it back a bit. Eyeball poking first.

"This is out of control. What are you playing at?"

Igra's sneer widened, his lips disappeared. "Secondly, in consideration of aforementioned Earth trip and Earth in general, the woman's children or other family members are not permitted on Orion. Thirdly, within forty-eight hours you must advise the Counsel of all your powers, resources, otherworldly contacts, technology, possible threats, treaties, full details of family members and other information we may request thereafter. Now passage between planets has re-opened, you're to operate a space watch program which integrates with the Counsel's and we must be notified of all incoming threats immediately. In conclusion no more off planet trips, uses of powers away from the island, or any other activities related to your demigod state without prior counsel approval. From here on the penalty of breaking any term is incarceration and death."

Annu's imaginary grip on Igra tightened, his eyes popped. "This is inhumane treatment. Are you serious? Up until months ago I was an ordinary Orion citizen, it must count for something."

Goop oozed out of Igra's empty sockets. "I assure you, we find no humour in this situation. We take this matter seriously. May I continue?"

Annu's jaw ached, he unclenched it. "What choice do we have?"

In Annu's mind, one of Igra's eyes rolled across the floor and under the table. "Absolutely none if you wish to stay here."

When did my life turn from inane to insane?

Annu squished the imagined eye under his foot.

The mayhem drained him. Annu yearned for the chance to absorb it all. "Wait a damned minute. Where are our rights?"

Igra retreated his hands to his lap. "You're rights are under this Order."

Shayne clutched Annu's arm, her skin cold. "This here is some bull-shit. There's no way you'll stop me seeing my Earth family any time I damn well like."

Annu clasped her hand; his mind blown. "You're not even considering other ways around this. You're as bad as Shamesh."

Igra motioned to someone outside the doorway. "That's where you're wrong. We've discussed our options at great length."

An armed man with more muscles than a Yak entered the room.

Igra's smirk exuded greed and too much power. "In regards to our former leader, we likewise have only your word regarding his demise. The lack of a body is the only thing keeping you from being tried for Regicide right now. So if I were you two, I'd keep my mouths shut. An assigned rep, Ang beside me here is accompanying you to Earth and act as our delegate."

A familiar blue band striped across the officer's gun's handle, dread overtook Annu. "You've already got tech to stop our powers. We're did you get it from?"

Igra glanced either side of him. "Not your concern." He slammed a wooden hammer onto a disk. "The board expects the requested information in the allotted time frame. Outside of this, I've made the consequences of defaulting perfectly clear. I declare the meeting convened."

Annu's guts churned, pressure compressed his chest.

How are we working with this? Hell, they aren't knowing about Zeke. Which should protects him. Nor will we tell them about the Lexicon.

Annu stepped over his chair and helped Shayne rise. "You'll get what you asked for and we'll prove how wrong you are."

You'll get some of what you asked for, and beg for forgiveness on your knees.

Shayne lead him around the table and through the open door.

Igra and his cohorts remained in the room.

Their complications turned from difficult to impossible.

Out of ear shot, Annu rested an arm around Shayne's shoulders. "As far as Ang's concerned, Zeke's my cousin we're looking after while his mother's sick. And hush-hush on most of everything else. We'll tell them about a few powers and that's it."

Shayne combed fingers through her hair. "Good idea. Thank the Gods none of the kids have any yet or they'd be more trouble. What do we do?"

Annu hugged her middle, coconut drifted from her hair. "I don't know. We'll think of something. We always do."

Eventually, maybe. Okay sometimes we have ideas.

Ang followed at a steady pace. Annu's chance of squeezing in a quickie when they got home dissolved.

I want it so bad but looking for my father's on the back burner for a while.

Chapter 3
Weddings and Weight Gain
Enki Island, Orion

Doom and despair flooded Shayne, no kitchen cupboard contained adequate food substances—only a blue tin covered in something sticky. The temperature in the kitchen rose and fell in opposition with Shayne's hormone fluctuations.

This is fucking ridiculous. I'm hot, cold, hot, cold and hungry. Arseholes. I can't fucking win.

Shayne dropped the tin on the floor; it dented. "Gross. Fucking typical. There's never anything to eat. Who's going to build a space watch thing? Or find the scientists and whatever to run it. Fuck, they better work for dented tins. Oh, and listing all our powers, I struggle remembering them myself," She kicked it across the floor.

Heat flushed Shayne. She fanned herself with a cold hand. "Why do we have to take GI Joe to Earth with us? Fucking fuckwits. Which reminds me, I found a note under my door last time I went home from another bunch of morons?"

Maybe I shouldn't swear so much? Nah. Fuck it. Sometimes gosh darn doesn't cut it.

Annu poised his foot and stopped the can's trip. "Shay, slow down. That's a lot of stuff mixed together to decipher. Who's GI Joe? And no you didn't tell me about the note or that you went back there. Again. Without me."

Jacob blew steam from his coffee, froth stuck to his beard. "I don't recall you mentioning another trip either your Graceness. I did warn you about going places alone. It never works out."

I want to strangle you. Why is he always fucking here and why is my skin prickly? My does my calf muscle ache? Are you fucking kidding me right now? I haven't been like this since I had my last treatment for the autoimmune stuff. Oh. Crap. Not dealing with you again.

Shayne stomped mid air. "Jacob, please! I don't need to hear from you right now. I can't believe I'm almost sick of being called your Graceness."

Jacob clasped his hands, his patient expression infuriated Shayne. "I'm sorry you're—I know you're busy but we must go over these sections in the Lexicon particularly future threats as Enlil and Gehenna, the Ancient Elder Gods and minor ones like The Enlian's and their leader Isaac, though their affiliation with Enlil isn't known, the natural portal locations on all planets, the divine geometry, other planets and their life forms, incantations and even what the consequences are if you travel through time or other portholes, some of your children may inherit powers, oh and a clever one is by using other demigods' powers yours amplifies, plus much more. Zeke's shown a bit of skill reading some parts."

Another mention of stupid portals. Who cares?

Hot, cold, headache, stress, stress, stress. "For fuck's sake, Jacob. The only threat around here for you to care about is the one to your personal health if you don't lay off the lectures for a while. We—" Shayne pointed between her and Annu. "Don't need this extra crap. No should Zeke be reading that book. Keep him out of this stuff. Further, I'm not time travelling or any other kind of travelling aside from Earth soon, and I fucking hate math so don't even say the word. It kills precious brain cells required for other stuff. Besides there's other things happening here in this kitchen. Like no more chocolate."

Jacob stiffened, he lifted his cup and rose. "My apologies. I'll remove myself until I hear from you."

He shuffled into the hallway and out of sight.

Guilt tickled Shayne, she slapped it into submission.

Annu stroked her calf, her ire wavered. "Flark Shay. You were really harsh with him. You crushed his little brotherly spirit. No wonder he walked out. This is what he lives for. You do remember he's the books designated protector and our teacher right? Given we don't have a whole lot of people on our side try not to piss off the ones who are. As to Zeke reading the book however, I agree. He's too young and teenage hood is hard enough without getting involved in any of our new life."

The kitchen walls closed in on Shayne, self hatred consumed her. *I'm a massive cow. I'm not handling these drastic changes well.* "Oooh. A special one-time agreement. I feel special. I didn't mean to but I can't help myself. It's all getting too much. I promise I'll make it up to him soon."

Annu's sigh warmed her leg and interrupted her anger. "I get it but you need to think before you speak. As for now, the edge in your voice is sharpening."

Fucking hell this is worse than torture. Death by own self actions shall emblazon my tombstone.

"I know okay. Please don't parent me. Just because it appears you're perfect and hundreds of years old, I'm an adult. I've even got the T-Shirt to prove it."

Annu's disappointed tone tormented Shayne further. "Fair enough and I'm not quite perfect yet but, I'm old enough not to make emotional decisions. For example, you're evading why you went to Earth without me. And who the flark is GI Joe?"

Oops. He's right again. Damn it. Real Smooth genius. Want to keep a check on the lies or what? A separate journal just for them maybe?

"Ah you were busy finding, um, Zeke or something. GI Joe is Ang, our new overseer slash baby sitter lurking outside the kitchen door."

Annu screwed his face up and talked to Shayne breasts. "Okay, but if you go again, tell me. I like to know where you are and that you are okay." Annu's stroke moved further up. "Why do you insist on giving everyone strange names?"

A hand cupped her butt; a tingle ran across Shayne's groin.

Oh my God not now. Maybe.

Shayne's pants tightened, she untied the waistband. "For fun I guess. Besides in the I.D.I.O.T.s case they made up their own stupid name, I'm just using it. I promised I'll try harder and I will. Jacob makes it extra hard sometimes. There's tonnes of pressure on us already and he dumps another ten on top. Then jumps up and down."

The further Annu's hand moved the more distracted Shayne became. "He doesn't mean to, it's not personal. Well it is but not in a bad way. This is how things are. We're the Demigod's, the responsible, focused ones."

Shayne's sex drive competed against her mood changes.

What if Wikipedia is right and I'm not just a cranky bitch? Either way there's zero point bringing it up at the moment.

The previous day's events nudged her attention.

Stop it. Enough. There's global shit going on and I'm thinking about myself.

Shayne slid Annu's hand down and returned to the fridge. "Okay. I got it. I'll lay off him. Argh. I'm pretty sure I'm going to either starve to death or burst into tears if I can't find something chocolate."

Annu's breath brushed the back of her knee. "It's always the worst-case scenario with you. I don't mean to anger you, I'm thinking eating your weight in that stuff, sitting on your butt and not training is the likely reason your pants don't fit anymore not some strange illness."

Shayne hovered mid air, open mouthed. "How—"

I cannot keep a fucking secret. I suck. But oh my fucking God. He brought up my size and lack of fitness again. Damned lucky he's so freaking hot.

"You left the page open as usual. Between communication bills and food, you and Zeke are sending me broke."

Breathe, breathe. I love him. He's actually nice—Most of the time.

Shayne floated up and re-checked the emergency stash. "Fuck it. Still empty." She lowered to the floor. "Darling, I'll ignore your misguided jabs for now. You can't blame me for eating so much. You remember I went without it the whole time I first came here. Like what the fuck? I've got to make up for it. And it's scientifically proven great stress relief."

Even if I'm a self named scientist.

"I'm spending money on stupid shit I don't want to as well. Due to lifestyles of the not yet rich and famous along with no godly pension, I'm broke and hocked a chunk of gold to pay a few bills. Those debt collector guys are relentless mother fuckers. Ah and I got some inspiration from Sam, who's being weird, which I've smoked already. Argh. I need one."

Annu bolted upright, a chill travelled across her kidneys. "You what? How could you be so careless? And you don't want me to parent you. Shayne, someone will notice it's different and where it came from. This is not how we want Earth to find out about us. Let alone there's plenty of grenberry here for free yet you buy it on Earth. I don't understand it or you sometimes."

He called me my full name. Ouch. Major ouch.

The 'you disappointed your partner' alarm screeched across Shayne's mind.

Idiot, this is why you weren't going to tell him. I suck at this. If he leaves me it's all my fault.

"Sssh. Not so loud GI Joe will hear. It's not like I had a choice about the money. What else could I do? When I get more grenberry here you a go at me for smoking too much. Which is funny because I don't see you walking around with an empty hip flask each day."

Annu's frustration added tension to the atmosphere. "And that's worth sneaking off to Earth without me and not being honest? Nice right hook on the rum too."

Shame branded her chest and enveloped her upper half.

Don't fuck this up dick face.

"Maybe. Sorry, no it's not. Okay, it's totally not worth this."

Annu's hurt sliced and diced what remained of Shayne's self confidence. "Why didn't you ask me for money? Why do you hide things from me? It hurts me."

His pained expression stabbed her heart.

Shit, shit, shit.

Shayne plastered on a smile and lowered to his level. "Please don't hate me. You don't have the currency for Earth. I really felt I didn't have a choice. I'm sorry. I still make mistakes. Who knows, you might one day, though I probably won't be there to see it."

More I didn't want arguments about my dodgy actions.

Jacob appeared in the doorway. "A dishonest demigod is not a fit spiritual guide and leader for others. This is another example of not thinking ahead. We must make time—"

Shayne grabbed the funky tin and hurled it at Jacob. "I am a good demigoddess and without your constant lectures."

Sometimes, when I don't forget.

Red faced, Jacob slipped back into the hallway.

The tin hit the wall beside the door and clunked onto the ground.

Annu rose and crossed his arms. "Enough. Calm down. That's the exact opposite of being nicer to him. Please for the sake of household peace, get in control of your emotions not the other way around."

Shayne dug herself a grave and deepened the hole. "Fuck. Shit. I'm sorry okay. I'm used to doing things myself and I thought it wouldn't hurt. Yes, you're right, I'll wrangle in my mental-ness."

Annu selected a shovel and helped dig. "We're together, as in a partnership. You should feel you can tell me anything regardless. For the sake of us all please also stop selling things that will likely come back to bite us. Shit, Shayne. To make matters worse our luck dictates the note you got is because of the gold."

I'm back to feeling like a damned kid not an adult. Why do I do these things to myself? Because I'm an asshole, assholeeoo.

Possible scenarios scrambled in Shayne's brain. "No, of course it's not. Now you're overreacting."

I hope and pray.

Annu rocked on his heels and blocked out the kitchen light. "I'd prefer to err on the side of caution if it's all the same. What did the note say?"

I'm literally in his shadow. But I know this is nothing to worry about. I haven't fucked up? Possibly. I'm going to have to make this up to him in a big, big, way. And I probably won't be able to walk properly for a few days afterwards.

Shayne slipped over and hugged Annu, he stiffened.

Fear of rejection strangled Shayne and squeezed. "It's more of a business card with 'call me A.S.A.P.' scribbled on the back. Someone from a DSI thing, or whatever. Like I said I assume debt collectors. They'll quit once the money went into their bank." Shayne pulled his arm around her waist and snuggled in. "It's nothing to worry about. Please trust me."

And I know that how?

Annu tickled her ribs and relaxed. "I'm trying really, really, hard but you truly make it impossible sometimes."

Shayne tapped his arm, her hand bounced off.

Damn you're so muscly and mmm. Wait not now. Focus on the insult.

"Fuck off. That's Jacob not me. Well, it may resemble me."

There's no may here. I let you down. Again.

"I, ah, know you're right,"

ouch, ouch, ouch.

"and the situation's complicated enough. I'm sorry. I really am; it's fine. Anyway we better get GI Joe and leave. Erin arrives at my place later and this is all new ground for us. I don't want to blow it."

The communicator on her wrist buzzed and beeped.

Shayne slid off Annu's knee away and held the device at the end of her nose:

> *'Good morning your Graceness. It's Nurse Sherryn at the Island's medical centre. This is the second reminder of your appointment for 8.45am this morning to see Doctor Ruc, for your six month check up. Which is fifteen minutes from now.'*

Shayne slapped her thigh, the coffin's walls tightened. "Shit, fuck, crap. I totally forgot I'd organised that."

Annu pushed off the stool and pinched her butt. "What's wrong?"

Not telling him isn't lying. There's no point unless there's something worth telling. I'm not suffering through two lectures in one day. Brain, make something up and make it good.

"I forgot I promised Jacob I'd help with something before we left. Given he's mad at me I better do it. You go to Earth with G.I. Joe and I'll meet you there soon."

I said good, that's not even close.

Annu held her at arm's length and squinted. "And he's sending you messages why?"

Fucking good question. I wasn't prepared for that. God have mercy on my soul.

"He didn't want to annoy me again?"

There'll be tonnes of people at my funeral purely to make sure I'm dead.

Annu cocked an eyebrow and sighed. "You're not hiding anything else from me are you?"

I'm digging another grave here and there's no more room in the cemetery.

"No. For God's sake. Can't I help someone without being questioned? There's also bugs in the pantry I want you to kill before I get there."

Maybe I could double stack the coffins and two priests.

Annu held his breath and shrugged. "What is it with you and bugs?"

"They're gross and icky. So we're all good then?"

Annu relaxed against her. "Yes. You've got a point, I'm sorry. I shouldn't second guess you as much. I'll go first but don't be long. I'm not getting stuck alone with him or Erin."

You should totally second, third, and forth guess me on a regular basis.

Shayne plastered a kiss on Annu cheek and slipped past to the door way. "All good. I'll see you soon. Love you."

Annu's voice trailed after her. "Love you too."

In the meantime I better organise some funeral wreathes. There's gravestones with my name on them.

Chapter 4
All Hail Queen
Enki Medical Centre
Enki Island, Orion

On way to the medical centre, Shayne's surroundings blurred.

I want to turn back the clock to a time of chocolate and motivation shortages. Of days fuelled by weed hazes and mixed medications; of not giving a fuck. Like last Sunday morning.

Yeah but the sucky part is I also don't get one in return. Remember when I pushed everyone away and no one gave a shit anymore? Anyway, it's stupid.

Protectors, woods and animals swished by. "Mother fuckers. I'm going to get poked and prodded not by Annu, again, only for someone with a degree to declare me full of shit."

That's probably what it is. I need a giant laxative not medical assistance.

Shayne reached the centre with her mortality in question. She poked her belly. "If he says it's time for a diet and I shouldn't smoke you're in trouble."

Double doors whooshed open, Shayne's stumbled into the entry, good tidings waited outside.

Even the highest technologically advanced hospital in existence stunk like antiseptic coated death.

Nurse Sherryn's met Shayne halfway down the hallway. "Ah there you are. Great you made it."

Breathe, don't freak out.

"Of course I did. I told you I would."

I bet the extra weight is all the shit I talk.

"Follow me, Doctor Ruc's waiting for you."

Shayne's blood cooled, memories of her near death experience months before flooded back. "He's the same doctor who—"

Sherryn patted Shayne's shoulder. "Yes. He's the one who took care of you after the attack. Which makes sense doesn't it?"

The battle images niggled Shayne, nausea bubbled in her gut. "Yeah but no. Is there anyone else I can see?"

Sherryn ushered Shayne down the hall by the forearm. "No I'm afraid not. It's okay, I promise he won't bite. You'll be fine."

I don't want to talk or think about it ever fucking again.

Shayne turned to the entry doors. "Actually. We'll do it tomorrow. I'm really late for something other than this."

Sherryn dragged Shayne around by the arm. "You booked the check up and you're not putting it off again."

Shayne plodded along like a student going to the principal's office. "Well be quick. I'm busy, busy."

What was I thinking?

Sherryn pulled harder, her forearm bulged. "Half an hour tops to do the tests and the consult. And we'll get the test results back by the end of day doing your bloods first uninterrupted."

I'd be toned like her if I exercised as much as I sat—or ate.

Shayne's skin crawled, she shrugged Sherryn off. "Fuck no. I didn't think of tests and needles. I hate needles."

Sherryn got behind Shayne and pushed. "I'm yet to meet anyone who does, trust me it's not too bad, probably better than Earth."

There's something. Not.

Shayne plodded and flopped. "Still sucks and the only way that's possible is if you do it to someone else."

You're not getting the better of me.

They weaved through a warren of vacant cubicles and into a treatment room.

Sherryn shoved Shayne inside.

Apparently you did. Damn it.

A few steps and the chair in the corner swallowed Shayne, she wriggled back and exposed her anterior elbow.

Sherryn's poised a small device above a vein and tapped.

Zap. Two vials filled and no pain.

Shayne inspected the bloodless spot. "Wow, that didn't hurt."

Sherryn patted Shayne's knee. "Told you so."

Vials in hand, Nurse Sherryn's slipped past Shayne and paused at the doorway, the doctor appeared.

Sherryn pointed at the vials. "I'll put these in to process right away."

Doctor Ruc nodded with the smile of a man ready to placate an irrational woman. "Thank you, Sherry."

He ambled over and plonked in an adjacent chair. "Shayne, it's great to see you. It's been a long time."

Shayne's chair's cushion grew nails. "Not long enough, Doc."

His smile heightened—not eased—Shayne's anxiety. "I've read over your case file, it's hard to believe it's been about six months."

Shayne mentally counted and muddled the middle. "Yeah time flies when you're having no fun."

The doctor scratched his chin with a laser pen. "I'm sure that's not completely true. Right, how have your injuries from the attack healed?"

Shayne bit her inner cheek and thrust the memories aside. "Only mental scars, a few stomach cramps lately and I pee lots."

Doctor Ruc straightened his spine. "The cramps may be internal scar tissue from the wound. How about the autoimmune issues you suffered on Earth?"

"It went away after ascension for a month or two but now if I stay there too long it niggles me in both places and,"

Shayne pointed to her pudge, "this is new and seems permanent. No amount of complaining has gotten rid of any of it."

Doctor Ruc shook his head and glanced at her belly. "Are you eating more than normal?"

Don't freeze him, don't kill him, he's asking for medical reasons.

"Maybe a little but not really."

Arsehole's suggesting I'm fat. It takes a lot of energy to be Demigodly.

"It may also be internal scarring. The other likely option is a reoccurrence of the autoimmune issues, previous damage from them or the terrible medications given to you. Again, we don't know yet."

Now to make a dick of myself.

Shayne puffed her chest and clicked her tongue. "Mmm, maybe. I'm really tired too and cranky. I'm thinking cancer or something horrible."

Doctor Ruc's eye roll deflated her hope. "Shayne, we've discussed your self-diagnosing. Last week you had a muscular disorder because you couldn't walk properly. Turned out you'd sat on your leg and in one spot too long. Funnily enough while searching for obscure diseases."

Don't freeze him, don't kill him, it's for medical reasons.

"Do you and Annu meet and discuss how to gang up on me?"

His dimples softened her defences. "Sorry, I don't meant to, you just have a slight tendency to well—exaggerate. Look, it's also probably around the time you'd enter pre-menopause on Earth too. Just to ease your mind we'll run a few tests keeping in mind we're still learning how to medically manage your human and godly selves."

Stupid half arse body. You've never been nice to me.

Shayne exhaled combined boredom and confusion. "Yes, okay. At least you're not fobbing me off this time."

Another flash of dimples and Doctor Ruc almost tickled Shayne's fancy. "Never. Besides I don't want you to freeze me or something. While I think of it are you still smoking grenberry?"

Do not make eye contact.

The muscle chart on the opposite wall captivated Shayne's attention. "Very funny and no."

Not funny and yes.

Doctor Ruc pursed his lips and dipped his chin. "Right. Anything else going on?"

The ceiling light caught the gems in her engagement ring. Doubt stabbed with each flash. "If the autoimmune's back on Earth and affecting me here too, how does it bode for my future? A Demigoddess in a wheelchair may not inspire much hope. And Annu didn't exactly sign up for a sick wife."

Doctor Ruc's eyebrows formed a caterpillar in the middle. "Let's take it as it comes, don't worry yet. There's a number of possibilities most of them linked to stress. As for Annu, if he truly loves you it won't matter and vice versa."

Shayne's self-preservation festered in the pit of her gut. "True. But to add to said stress the fucking GC forbids my kids from coming here. That's the plan soon. So, I must go there every time if the bastard disease has returned. Typical. Just typical."

Concern in Doctor Ruc's expression comforted Shayne. "I can't imagine how I or anyone would cope in your circumstances. You're an extraordinary person, a God who has a family and universal responsibilities. What you've been through and must endure each day is enormous. Give yourself a break and stop worrying so much about things which may not happen. Know we're all grateful you're here."

Reassurance disarmed Shayne, her self confidence twinkled and cramps eased. "I—ah—oh. I never thought of it that way before. Thank you."

"All true."

Shayne's blinked tears splashed her cheeks. "I feel a little better."

Doctor Ruc patted her shoulder, an apparent common trait in the hospital. "I'm glad. We'll make another appointment for a couple of days to discuss the test results. Please discuss your fears with Annu and I'd like to see you both together next time you come in."

Shayne swallowed the lump in her throat. "Crap. All right. I'll see you in a couple of days then."

"Of course."

The alarm on her wrist communicator flooded Shayne with panic, she leapt off the chair. "Shit. I'll see you when I get back. We're going to Earth for a while. Hopefully I won't get worse while there."

Doctor Ruc scribbled notes onto a tablet and waved with the pen. "Try not to worry too much. I'm sure it will all work out okay."

Shayne slipped past him and out the door. "You better be right, Doc."

Now to avoid all questions about what I did while gone.

Chapter 5
What Not in This World?
Bailor Street, Rendelshem, South Australia, Australia
Earth and Enki Island, Orion

Erin stumbled through Shane's front door, her arms laden with box decorations for the pre-wedding party and cleaning supplies into darkness.

What's the funky smell? Gross.

One foot closed the front door while a box rested on the opposite hip. "Hello? Shayne are you there? Annu?"

Dust and dirty paw prints trailed down the hallway, a dank, moldy aroma answered her but no mother of all disappointment nor her tall freak of a fiancé.

Against the wall, Erin flicked on the hall lights with her shoulder on route to the kitchen. The state of mayhem remained unaltered from Erin's last visit. "How can anyone live in this mess? Some example she is."

Which is why I refuse to call her mother until she gets her act together. If she spent more time on Earth fixing her relationships with her kids and paying money she owes, her life would be much less messy and maybe I'd want to spend more time with her.

Erin's sigh echoed; frustration dumped upon her back. "You not being here gives me time to clean before you tell me not to. And there's no way I'll let my future mother-in-law, Marg, see this mess. Cripes. I'd be divorced before I'm married. Oh why can't you be a normal parent? Especially when I really need you to."

Meters away on the other side—the pantry lurked in the far corner, a dark, mysterious and parent pinching room. Tingles trailed Erin's spine and hugged her shoulders. "What secrets do you hold connected with my family? Maybe I should find out one day. Big Maybe."

A used coffee mug toppled over, the empty chocolate wrappers on the kitchen table plus dirty plates and crap littered benches distracted Erin. Annoyance over rode curiosity and niggled Erin's good mood. "Oh for God's sake, Shayne. That's gross, totally gross. I'm so not touching that. Perfect example of bad peopling or adulting whatever. Darn it." She kicked the floor, dirt covered her leg. "I can't leave it like this. Argh."

It gives me brain pain but it's a nicer option without getting Ebola.

Shayne's ascension to Demigoddess delivered unexpected benefits for Erin. Sure of solitude, Erin cleared her mind and concentrated on one mug. It jiggled, slid an inch, hovered and shook above the table. Focus maintained its height. Erin brought the mug over to the sink and lowered it. One nasty object after the other, Erin cleared the table and benches replacing muck with cleaning implements.

Guilt removed the buzz garnered from one of Erin's two recent discovered abilities. Their arrival conflicted with Erin's human side and toppled her security wall.

I can't argue that the telepathy comes in handy, and it's easily hidden. Except that's sneaky, I don't want to start my marriage off with lies but here I am. I can't end up like Shayne. I won't allow it to happen.

Nathanial consumed her thoughts; the memory of his proposal warmed the chill.

Erin's chest tightened, fear tickled Erin's ribs and curdled her breakfast. "His parents would freak if they found out and he'll naturally side with them. He's only just gotten used to Shayne and Annu's weirdness."

Sometimes my life sucks.

"But it beats Shayne being nuts. Well, officially nuts. I can't lose him but this is a part of me too. What do I do?"

Stars twinkled, Erin's breath quickened, her chest tightened. Erin's legs wobbled, she clutched a chair.

No don't freak out. I'm meant to be in control of my emotions and not the other way around—but I'm not. I'm really, really not. Thanks to my mother for warping me—Yes, I am. I can do it. What did the therapist say to do again? Oh yeah.

Erin timed her breath with the clock's ticking, her mind cleared.

I am in control and I can get through this. I am strong enough and the master of my own mind.

Anxiety lowered, Erin carried a bucket to the sink. "Next stage of therapy is cleaning. That fixes everything." The pipes banged but filled the bucket with hot water, antiseptic smothered funky smells. The bucket overflowed, Erin dunked a sponge, cleaned the kitchen bench the normal way and eliminated time to think. Several rags, buckets of hot soapy water and calluses on her hands later, the kitchen sparkled from top to bottom. The clean room clashed against the dirty pantry door, the creeps returned.

Erin swallowed fear and puffed her chest. "No. I can't leave it like that." From the top down, she wiped the wood.

Who'd have thought a pantry contained a portal to other worlds?

A wipe over the lock and it jiggled, the door popped open. Erin jumped back, the dark room oozed freakiness. Curiosity drew Erin onto the threshold. "Ryan's seen it and he's a big chicken so it can't be that scary."

Erin stepped onto dirt and tugged on the light cord. The ground trembled, vibrations rippled across the surfaces and intensified each second. She clutched the doorway; bright light invaded the pantry and blinded her.

Bell's drilled into Erin's brain.

The former solid wall shimmied in liquid energy, a beautiful contrast to the dankness. Erin walked towards it, her movement unconscious awareness.

An inch from the portal Erin swirled a finger in the liquid wall, energy pulsed down her arm and along down her body.

Does Shayne see this from the other side? Where is she right now?

A tunnel formed in the middle and swirled; it created suction and sucked Erin in. "No, no, no. No I only wanted to watch them come. Please—"

The pantry disappeared, light exploded around her, anything tangible stretched out of reach. Erin's molecules separated, her sense of self slid along a tunnel.

Screams and other sounds warped, on Erin's right Annu and another man flew past. Erin's mind scattered, her words disjointed. "Shayne, mum, help me—"

Insanity seeped into the corners of Erin's mind, close to crazy—the tunnel narrowed in the distance. At once all parts of Erin reformed, careened towards the end and landed side first on a stone floor. The vortex retreated into a wall, the ground grumbled and stopped.

Erin clutched her chest and heaved in air; reality fractured around her. Slumped on the floor, she hugged her knees. "What the heck just happened? Oh God, am I on Orion?"

I can't be here. I have to get back home right now. Did I do this somehow?

Erin pushed off stone, the room wavered. She stumbled to the wall and probed the inert surface. "Come back. Please, I've got to go home. I can't be here. You don't understand."

A hot puddle simmered in Erin's gut, she closed her eyes.

Earth, Earth, Earth. Take me home.

"Please, please, please reopen." Sobs wracked Erin's chest, help stayed as distant as Earth. "No, no, no."

The moisture evaporated from Erin's mouth and throat, fear, actual fear, invaded her bravado.

Erin turned right into a hallway; gold edged tablets covered each side, at the end a plush green garden beckoned. She jogged though it into the sunlight and paused, two suns instead of one consumed most of the pink, not blue sky. The avoided panic attack returned in full force, a full-fledged meltdown loomed.

I can't think about how far away I am from Earth, or anywhere normal.

Erin's breath quickened; her pulse thread; her legs wobbled. Against a nearby tree she fanned air on her face. "It isn't the time to lose it. God give me strength."

Shayne—Mum, I've got to find her. She'll send me home. If she doesn't stuff up again. Only problem, where is she?

The dizziness abated, Erin turned, on her right a house's roof stood out above the trees.

That's the perfect place to start. I hope. Thank's God.

Erin wobbled along and used trees for steadiness. "I'm not staying here a second longer than necessary." A screech from an unknown creature drove Erin forwards, tears stung her eyes.

I'm so stupid. I can't do this.

Erin's own screams drowned out the creature's. "Shayne? Shayne?"

Chapter 6
Alien Environment
Bailor Street, Rendelshem, Earth

Surprised landed aside Annu onto the pantry floor.

Who the hell was that? She looked a little like Erin. I'll find out when Shayne arrives no doubt.

Ang groaned, bee-lined for the kitchen and slumped onto the tiles.

Pussy. Shayne will laugh when I tell her—Maybe.

Shayne's recent crankiness confused and terrified Annu in equal measure. Given the drastic changes in their lives he'd cut her a mountain of slack and vice versa. Despite that, the ever-wary fear of uncontrolled hormones forced Annu to live on the edge and conflicted with his adoration.

It's a long time ago but I can't remember Jade being moody like this.

Shame accompanied a side of recrimination and flushed Annu.

Oops. Not fair. Do not compare the two.

An antiquated can of bug spray in one hand and a boot raised, Annu eradicated the bug population on the pantry floor. Each time Annu approached the wall, a yet un-found alarm beeped. "What the hell is that noise?"

Ang's colour matched the tiles behind him—pallid with a hint of vomit. "Huh?"

"The damned beeping noise. It's annoying the hell out of me." Squish, squash, mush. "Flarking things. What's she breeding them?"

"I can't hear it over the sound of my impending death."

Mirth tricked across Annu and he dropped his shoulders.

Serves you right.

"You okay princess?"

Ang heaved onto the tiles. "Not at all. Is it always like that?"

A mouse poked out of a hole, Annu jumped back and hugged the wall.

I flarking hate those things. They weird me out.

"Honestly, I don't know. We've been reluctant to try it on family members because we've got no idea how a normal human might react."

"Well now you know."

Crunch, crunch. Smoosh.

Annu scraped the bottom of his boot along a shelf. "Have a cup of concrete and harden the flark up. It'll get better. Maybe."

"Great. My brain's foggy and I feel completely out of—"

Problems arose everywhere, Annu suppressed a sigh. "My heart bleeds for you. Did you tell your arsehole boss we arrived?"

Ang swayed on his back, the vomit stench freshened. "As much as I could, the signal's weak. Also, this is the first testing of the tech this far. Though, I didn't mention Shayne wasn't with us. I'm not sure why."

Hunger and disgust roiled Annu's guts, lack of breakfast complicated his stomach's distress.

Idiot should have eaten before I left. That reminds me, what could Shayne possibly be doing with Jacob that takes this long?

"Probably because she'll be here soon enough. With a way to get food if we're lucky."

A knock on the front door ignited Annu's curiosity.

Erin's got her own key so it's not her which means it's usually a debt collector. Damned Shayne and her lack of financial care.

The knocks loudened, their insistence pissed Annu off.

Annu stepped to the sink and downed a cup of water, a box of fluffy bright coloured things rested on his left. "I'm not answering it. One look at our size and we're toast." Nothing edible added frustration to boredom. "Erin's been here already and there's nothing. Damn Zeke and Shayne emptying our cupboards."

Ang rolled onto his side away from the vomit puddle. "Ohhhhh. My head's thumping."

Bang, bang, bang.

Oh do flark off.

Annu cracked his neck and rolled his shoulders. "Not this time. Someone's at the front door."

The knocking moved from the front and recommenced on the back door a few feet from the kitchen.

A male voice rumbled into the rear room. "Hello? Anyone there?"

I don't care who it is, you can flark off and if you don't shut up, I'll blast you into the atmosphere.

Slam, bang, thump.

Ang levered onto his elbows and rocked. "Whoa. What's the problem?"

Doom steeped the man's words. "Hello, Ms James?"

No one untoward can or should know we're here. "Who is this arsehole and why is he so insistent?"

Ang regained some colour and half rose. "Are you going to let them in? Who is it meant to be?"

The man's voice reverberated across the back porch and up Annu's spine. "Hello Ms James?"

Why do they want Shayne so badly? Please don't let her have stuffed up—again.

Annu tapped the box's side. "It's meant to be my future daughter in law but it looks like she's already been and gone."

Bang, bang. Clunk. "Ms. James I hear someone moving inside. You can't stay hidden forever."

The door handle shook, the lock jiggled.

The thuds and bangs escalated. "Ms. James. I urge you to comply."

Ang levered up to a half stand. "They seem quite insistent on talking with Shayne. Why don't you just tell them she'll be here later?"

How do they know someone's here?

Realisation slapped Annu. The lights on all through the house confirmed Shayne or someone hid inside.

Ah shit. I really don't need this right now.

"Because then they'll know we're here too and it's a bit hard for them not to notice two dark skinned seven foot plus tall men. Not without freaking out and that's easy to do."

The knocks boomed down the hallway and drilled into Annu's brain. His growl rippled across his belly.

A different man's voice from the front of the house intensified unease. "Ms. James. It's Mr. Smith, I'm here with Mr. Jones. We left a card for you the other day. It's imperative we speak to you."

A chill settled into his spine, Annu mumbled into his fist.

Shayne sold that gold.

"Shit, I knew it. Flarking hell."

The sharpness in the man's tone set Annu on edge. "Ms. James, we know you're in there. Please let us in or we'll be forced to take measures into our own hands."

Annu slipped off his boots, his butt hole constricted.

Always trouble. Always.

"Stay here. Don't let anyone in the back door."

Ang groped for a weapon on his knees. "Okay."

Annu slid through shadows and flicked off the lights in each room. He reached the front lounge on his hands and knees. The street light illuminated the men from behind, their silhouettes cast on the wall.

Flush against the window pane, Annu concentrated and blended into the surroundings.

In unison the men peered through either glass door panel and moved past towards the side of the house. Annu's waded knee deep in shit, the mens determination reinforced his growing fear.

Shayne's ability to flark up any given situation amazed him.

No good will come of this. Both of us—but mostly her are kind of like bad shit magnets.

Ang commando crawled along and joined Annu by the couch. "Who are these people?"

Annu nodded right and crept into the hallway. "I've got no idea, but we're getting out of here before we find out."

At the kitchen doorway, Annu crawled along the wall to the pantry, wariness cloaked his thoughts.

Bang, bang, bang.

Annu crept through the kitchen and into the back porch. He stood adjacent to the back door.

The two men made it to the back door at the same time. "Ms. James, we'll find a way in. Make it easy on yourself."

That's so not Shayne's MO.

Ang appeared, took his weapon off safety and aimed it at the back door.

Pop, boom, bang.

Annu's desire for a respite from problems burst into smithereens. "Relax, don't make trouble we don't need. They'll leave soon enough."

Oh please, please, please do.

Ang re-holstered the weapon. "I'm not so sure about that. These guys scream military to me which means they won't quit until they get what they're after. And given Shayne's not here, it's probably us."

Annu's fears realised, the situation reached another level of flarked up. "They sure aren't her usual debt collectors. Compared to them I think I'd prefer the thirty plus women coming here in the morning."

Ang's renewed colour drained. "There's thirty women coming here?"

"Apparently."

The men rustled around the back door. "Smith, contact HQ, call in the team. It's time to step things up. Move to the front of the property and cordon the whole thing off."

They moved past the back porch windows and out of sight.

Of all the times, this is the worst one for Shayne to show up.

A fixable complication lowered Annu's apprehension. "Don't worry, we're leaving. We need to find Shayne before they do. And she'll get a talking to."

Ang stumbled on his feet and straightened. "Yeah but it's a mixed blessing. I get off this planet but I'll be as sick as flark doing it."

Is it too much to ask for one day without extra problems?

"There's nothing I can do about that."

Ang followed him to the pantry. "So far, Earth's not much fun."

Annu stood before the rear wall and suppressed a sigh.

Open a worm hole to Orion, Enki island.

"I feel the same way about it—most of the time."

Beep, beep, beep.

Annu's shoulders reached his ears, tension pulled across his neck. "Will you shut up?"

Wormhole to Orion and Enki island. I repeat Enki island. Come the flark on.

The ground rippled, a point of light appeared and disappeared.

Annu's shoulders hit the top of his ears, he ground his teeth. "Huh? Why'd it do that? Work damn you."

Annu flicked his hands and relaxed his jaw.

No dicking around. Open a wormhole to Enki island.

A faint light flashed on and off. "Come on. Now really isn't the right time for this shit."

Ang slumped against the opposite wall. "It's not working?"

One more attempt garnered nothing, nada, zip. "Ah flarking hell."

Apprehension slapped Annu left cheek, despair the other.

Annu pounded the rear pantry wall, plaster crumbled under his fist. "Flark, I can't believe it won't open." Sweat poured down Annu's back, the beeps shredded his last nerve. "The noise must have something to do with the wormhole not opening."

Ang pushed off a shelf and wafted dust around. "As much as I hated getting here, I can't get stuck on Earth. How else can we get back?"

Annu's body temperature plummeted, a vein in his neck pumped in time with the wall clock. "Yeah me either. Why don't you do something constructive to help like contacting your boss again?"

Ang clicked his tongue and fiddled with the communicator. "I did. It's not working. I can't get through. And he's not really my boss; I work for the Securities Council, who—"

Did Shayne close it on purpose? Is she mad at me? Did I mess up somehow that only she knows? Focus man.

"I don't care about the logistics of your employment. I care about leaving." Thump, thump, thump. Beep, beep, beep. "Shit, flark, shit."

The only hole in the wall remained the one Annu punched into the brickwork. "What's wrong here? This hasn't happened before. What am I missing?"

Ang scratched his chin and paced. "In my opinion, the noise, the suited men, the dead communications and the no wormhole, are all connected."

Shit he's right. I didn't think of that.

"I figured as much, but why and who?" Anger cloaked his thoughts, Annu turned and faced Ang, flames tickled his arms. "This must be why Shayne hasn't turned up yet. Flark. She can't get here. Did you do this to separate her and I? What's the GC up to?"

Ang backed out the pantry door, an arm protected his face. "No, no, no. I don't know anything about it. I just got told to follow you two here, keep an eye on you and make sure you returned to the GC afterwards. That's all."

Annu's thought process muddled.

Don't hurt him. It's not entirely his fault. he's stuck too.

"Why should I trust you? Especially after what they've put us through."

Ang's Adam's apple jiggled. "Well I'd be suicidal or dumb to get myself stuck on another planet with two demigods, one weapon and no way of getting back wouldn't I? And despite what you might believe, I'm not stupid."

Annu's mind raced, adrenaline coursed through his veins. "Maybe. Hell, none of this makes any sense. This whole week, month, year's gone to shit."

Ang threw his arms in the air. "What do we do now? What are our options?"

Take control, man up. Think instead of stressing out. I've got this. I should leave several bottles of rum here for such occasions. So much for a short trip.

Annu strode to the sink and downed a glass of water. "All right. Stay calm. No need to lose it yet. I'm sure it's only a temporary thing. I'll figure this out."

And every-flarking-thing else.

"I wasn't the one freaking out."

Annu's tap on the bench tinged in the sink. "Yeah well, we've had a lot of crap thrown on us lately. It wouldn't surprise me if the Council are behind this, you just won't know about it. But I can't figure out how those insistent men fit in. No one aside from Shayne's family on Earth know about us, even considering the gold how did it get to this stage?"

It doesn't make sense.

Dread overwhelmed Annu.

With the other information aside, it left Shayne closing the doorway behind them. "She wouldn't do that."

Ang opened and closed the fridge. "Huh?"

"Never mind." Annu rifled through the box a fifth time and inspected a tub of pink goop. "I'm going to starve to death before I come up with something at this rate."

Annu swept the box onto the floor, the contents spilt across the tiles. "There's no food, no Shayne, no communication and no way home. Great, flarking great." He removed the hip flask from his jacket pocket and shook it. "And I forgot to fill this up."

"Why don't you try again? Maybe it works now."

Annu massaged his temples and bit his tongue.

Oh God's help me. This is messed up.

"Sure why not?"Annu faced his new arch nemesis—the pantry wall, rivalled only by his fiancee's mood swings. "Please, please, please, work."

He directed energy in and thrust it forwards at the wall, light flickered and disappeared.

Two more attempts ended in unspectacular fashion.

Solutions eluded Annu, he kicked until plaster and brick covered the floor. "Mother flarking, dick sucking, ball licking, twat waffle, cock sucker."

Ang's presence added to the problems. "So, ah, it's still not working then?"

Annu ignited and blasted energy at the wall;

wormhole to Orion, Shayne, wormhole to Orion.

Nothing.

"No and I don't know what else to try. And I don't have a way to contact Shayne's friends, she's got the phone thing on her."

The entire wall disintegrated, the pantry opened into the front lounge room. A small black device fell to Annu's left, a bright red light flashed from its centre.

Annu swiped debris from his eyes and picked it up. No identifiable marks, the beep increased into an ear piercing shriek.

What worries me is who put it there and why.

Annu stomped on it and plonked onto the floor amidst a sea of bricks. "That fixed you flarker and slowed down whomever it belongs too."

Ang spat out dust. "Calm down. Sit over there and think about this. We'll figure this out."

A chunk of roof dropped onto Annu's shoulder. "It isn't meant to be like this. I'm a Demigod. Someone important, going to save the galaxy and shit."

Ang plonked on the couch, it groaned. "It doesn't seem to be working out for you so far. I'm glad it's you and not me."

Annu drifted in a sea of misery in a leaky boat. "I want my woman, or mother, or a wormhole, or—"

Bang, bang, bang.

Activity around the front door eliminated a break from chaos.

Men in military garb passed the lounge room and back porch windows.

Annu sunk in a pile of shit. "Ah flark it. I forgot about them for a moment."

Chapter 7
Chicken's Home Roosting
Enki Island, Orion

Adulthood sucks and the suckage lasts a long fucking time.
Shayne smoked a joint and followed a stream from one side of the island to the other. The calm, natural environment aided by THC lowered her anxiety—a fraction.

At a fork in the river, Shayne slowed both breath and speed. "The autoimmune crap will torture me forever. I'll never get rid of it. It's so fucking unfair. Unless there's some rare mysterious disease affecting only Demigods and I've got it too? Ghost Dad are you around? Hello?"

No hazed figure of her father Ki appeared nor answered her questions; since the ascension Ki and Ann transcended to a higher heaven with terrible communication connections.

I wish you were here. I can't do this shit all on my own. I screw things up. All—the—fucking— time. I know it's selfish but come back and help me.

Her wrist communicator alarm broke Shayne's concentration, she tapped snooze. Earth and Annu waited on the other side of the galaxy for a few more moments.

I'm entitled to a stolen minute to myself aren't I? Probably not.

Despite a dawdled speed, Shayne reached the mountain side; she entered the glass lift, touched a few buttons and shot to the top. Shayne jumped out and Demigodly sped home.

The front door opened, halfway down the hallway young male stink from Zeke's bedroom whacked Shayne in the face.

Two fingers pegged Shayne's nose closed. "Oh Godth dat's poul. Theke, thwhere are thou?"

A funky haze loomed above a pile of dirty socks and underwear in the corner. "You lazy poop. I bet you haven't done half of what you're meant to. I don't need this shit right now."

Shayne mouth breathed, left the bedroom and entered the kitchen.

It likewise resembled a NATO strike zone, stacks of plates and glasses filled the sink.

The fridge door hung open; the light flickered on and off. "Oh my fucking God. That's first on your chore list."

Shayne slammed the fridge door and jotted a note onto a piece of paper:

'Dear pain in the arse. You better clean this shit up before I get back with your father soon or you won't just smell dead, you'll be dead. Love, your stepmother.'

Shayne signed off with skull and crossbones.

The shrill of Shayne's wrist comm snapped tension across her shoulders. "Really, come on."

Shayne checked the screen:

Sherryn already?

Her tongue thickened. "Oh this cannot be good."

A finger paused over the accept call, Shayne sucked on her bottom lip and answered. "Should I be shitting myself right now? Actually it's too late for you to say no."

Nurse Sherryn's expression injected fear into Shayne. "Hello. I'm sorry to bother you but there's a communication error with the system and your test results are taking longer to process. Depending on the tech people it might have to wait another day. Is that okay?"

Shayne battled relief and frustration, they drew. "Ah. I guess it won't matter."

Sherryn's smirk consumed her face. "Thank you for your, ah, patients. Get it."

Shayne plonked onto the nearest stool and ended the call. "Aha."

Great and now I'm going to Earth worrying about what the fuck is wrong with me. More so than usual. I'm not even thinking about the whole GC mess.

The front door opened, boots stomped down the hallway and into the kitchen.

Zeke strode to the fridge, removed the note, screwed it up and threw it in the bin at the other end of the room.

Good shot, boy. But beside the point.

Shayne's neurons ached, her skull tightened. "Hey, you didn't even read that."

Zeke jumped and banged into the upper shelf. "Shit. Why are you scaring me like that?"

Oh gods. How did I become the Stepmother?

"Ah, I'm not, I'm just sitting here all innocent and shit."

And stressed.

Beep, beep, beep, beep, beep.

A message alert beeped and tweaked Shayne's nerves.

Shayne cupped her hands over her ears. "Oh fuck off."

Zeke strode over and picked the communicator up off the bench. "You've got a message from someone called Nurse Sherryn."

Why is the universe torturing me? What the hell is she annoying me with now?

"Of course it is. Now put it back down."

Zeke shared Annu's twinkle in the eye, never a good sign in Shayne's opinion. "Want me to read it?"

Thud, thud, bang, bang.

Shayne banged her knee on the bench. "No. Put my communicator down."

The unintentional truth in Zeke's statement stung. "She said you cut her off and wanted to make a time for a follow up appointment. Are you finally getting some mental help? It's about time."

In Shayne's mind she strangled him with his funky socks.

Urge suppressed, she climbed up the bench and snatched the communicator from his hand. "No. Now leave it alone."

Zee's tone sharpened, he grabbed the last piece of fruit. "I don't know why I bothered. Why are you here? Aren't you both meant to be on Earth?"

Breathe, the penalties for murdering your step kid are bad everywhere.

"I got delayed but I'll leave as soon as I gather my wits."

Which could be a long fucking time.

Each bite and crunch drilled into Shayne's brain. "Good. I need some space."

Bastard child.

Shayne pushed off the bench, the stool tipped. "Zeke, you're not winning in the stepson of the year department today. Be fucking nice."

Zeke's mouth dropped. "And I care why?"

Maybe I should re-watch Mommie Dearest?

Shayne's left eye twitched. "Beloved boy, I truly treasure each moment together too. On a side note this day cannot get any more fucked up."

Zeke's eye roll solidified the shitness. "Do you always have to swear so much? What kind of mother talks like that? You know it would take a miracle for me to think nicely of you. You're a terrible influence."

Teeth gritted, Shayne deleted the message.

Drama queen.

"For fu—'s sake. This mother talks anyway she wants to. Now listen here kid, I'll be back with your father soon enough so you better clean up this shit before then. Oh and do not go anywhere."

Zeke ambled past the bench and out the kitchen door with an extended middle finger. "Yeah right."

Keep calm, he's in your life forever now and there's bigger headaches. Like staying sane.

"Grrrrr, oh my fucking Gods."

I can't wait anymore or I'll be in trouble on Earth too.

"All right already. Time to leave one shitty at me kid for another."

Shayne exited the kitchen, through the main house, out the back and stopped. "What the fuck am I doing? Idiot. I don't need to use the room anymore."

Take me to Earth aka my other home.

The ground didn't rumble, no light pierced her eyes. A big fat nothing happened.

"Are you fucking kidding me? You're going to stop working right now?" Breathe held, a wormhole eluded Shayne. "Fine, I'll use the Ascension Room like back in the stone age."

Halfway across the garden, a figure moved between the orchard trees, Shayne's heart skipped.

Is it too much to wish that it's Annu and save me a trip? Or some creepy killer? If it is Annu he can deal with Zeke and after a nice dinner I'll tell him I went to the doctors. Then comes the 'Shayne you're overreacting.' After which I'll get all huffy and he'll be puffy. I hate it when we disagree.

Shayne quickened her pace and checked behind trees. "Annu?"

No killer assaulted her on route through the orchard.

Around the last peach tree, Shayne bumped into Erin.

Huh? Have I lost my freaking mind?

Shayne rubbed her eyes, Erin stood a metre in front of her. "What—what are you doing here? How did you—"

Erin slumped, her terror stricken expression heart Shayne's heart. "Thank God it didn't take long to run into you. I don't know how I got here but I touched the stupid wall and all of a sudden bam. Which is too bad because I want to go home. I've got the party and Nathanial will miss me and—"

Shayne stepped closer and touched Erin's arm.

Thankfully the Council don't know she's here. Shit.

"Calm down. It's okay. You've got the right DNA in the right place at the wrong time. I'll bring you home before anyone knows you're gone and are here. Relax. We'll get this sorted."

Erin exhaled and adjusted her pony tail. "Good. You're still helping me set up for the party when we get back aren't you? You said you'd help me and be there the whole time. You can't change your mind now. Hell, then I'll have to organise everything myself. You always do this. I don't know why I trusted you. That whole drugging me to escape the mental hospital is your true self, not the all high and mighty god you portray yourself to be here."

Her daughter's maternal distaste opened the wound upon Shayne's soul.

Oh yeah. I'm so fucking good at the parenting thing. Another reason I'm probably going to hell when I die.

"Ah, ouch Erin. I knew you hadn't gotten over that. I admit it wasn't my best move but none of you believed me, and I had no other way. You can't deny I've really changed in the last several months. On the same token you can't keep holding past failures against me, and lastly, I never said I wasn't going to help you."

Erin's pout and crossed arms reminded Shayne of her toddler years. "I've heard that one before too."

This trip's going to be a barrel of fucking laughs.

The tunnel appeared a few metres away, a fraction of relief swept over Shayne.

******

In the doorway of the Ascension room, Erin stood akimbo. "How am I to trust you? It's a bit hard after all those years of you being a terrible parent. The last few months of trying hardly make up for that."

Shayne bit her inner lip.

Fuck me. What's with kids being arseholes today?

"This has been a lovely visit, Erin. I'm sorry you were taken to Orion this way and that I've ruined your entire existence. Listen, you'll be home in no time and none the worse for wear and can go right back to hating me."

"You better be right. I should never have gone to your place early."

On the middle floor stone, a surge of power flowed through Shayne and rippled across the ground. "Why did you go to my house early?"

Erin concentrated on the opposite wall.

Anger tickled Shayne's nape. "You cleaned it didn't you?"

Erin's nod added another level of frustration.

God dammit. That's another tick she'll put against my name.

With gritted teeth Shayne aimed her mental conniption at the wall.

Energy bounced across its surface and dissipated into a puff.

Shayne's annoyance ascended while her sanity descended. "What are you doing that for you stupid piece of shit thing?"

Erin shuffled, huffed, puffed and flung her arms. "Come on, Shayne. Why are you taking so long?"

"Stop calling me Shayne. It's mum to you." Zap, zap, zap. "Open—a—wormhole to—Earth. Now." Zap, zap, zap. "Or now?"

Unease probed Shayne's wits, no luck tore them apart. The power within her dwindled each try.

Erin's desire to ruin Shayne's day continued. "Why isn't this working? You said you could send us home. Poop, crap. Geez."

Shayne faced the wall and deep breathed.

Calm blue ocean, calm blue ocean.

"I don't understand. Why it isn't?"

Fuck it. There's a squall coming.

"Maybe I need Annu? No, because I've done it plenty of times without him."

And a tsunami rolled in. fuck calm, fuck sanity. Just work arsehole.

Breath held, Shayne focused, focused, and more focus. "No, no, no. You cock sucker, dick licking ball sack. What do try next?"

The communicator on Shayne's wrist beeped, Sherryn's latest message flashed across the screen:

"Your Goddess, I pray you are all right and the news report about you and Annu is wrong. Call me immediately."

The tsunami drowned Shayne's roller coaster world. "Fucking what for now?"

This is why I leave the news to Annu. I wish I could call him.

A horrible thought struck.

Oh God, what if I'm still the mental asylum strapped to a bed, having crazy delusions.

Shayne clung to the memories of the last several months.

No, don't be stupid. Give it time it will work. I'm panicking for nothing.

Erin tugged her sleeve. "Ah Shayne, I, I can't be stuck here. I have to go home."

Lack of control tightened Shayne's ribs, urgency jabbed at her.

Shayne fumbled with the communicator and tapped in the number. "Give me a minute. I'm sure when I try again it will work. Let me deal with one crisis at a time."

Sherryn popped onto the screen. "My Goddess. Thank the Gods you're alive."

Another waved crashed over Shayne. "Why wouldn't I be? What's going on?"

"I don't know how to tell you this. It's awful."

Shayne wanted to strangle the words from her. "Just fucking do it. I can't stand it."

Sherryn cleared her throat, her colour drained, she glanced side to side. "After my last message to you, I took a break and a news report attracted my attention."

"Right okay. And?" Bees buzzed and moths nested in her brain. Shayne hunched over. "Sherryn, what the hell did the report say?"

Sherryn swiped off sweat with a tissue and looked down. "Investigations discovered you two were linked to the production of a new psychedelic drug that's devastating Orion, and caused a group hallucinatory effect in Yebu. Apparently they'd Enki under surveillance for some months but after losing sight of you both they arrived on the island to investigate. In short fashion they found you both died in a crash nearby and are—"

The air whooshed from her lungs, Shayne's legs collapsed.

On the floor Shayne hugged her knees. "Oh my God, my God, my God. Why would they say that? They aren't even on the island. We've got to prove our innocence, show the truth."

Erin paced around Shayne. "Mum, Shayne what's wrong? Can we get to Earth or not?"

Shayne swayed and tasted metal. "I, I—"

Sherryn's grimace exuded dread. "There's more and it's much worse."

I can't believe this. How did this happen? We should be on Earth not here fake dead. Shit. They planned this.

"Please, it can't possibly be."

"It is. I'm sorry, we just received a direct communication from somewhere called I.D.I.O.T.s. They're on their way and evacuating all staff: me, the doctor from the medical centre, and the other island occupants forthwith. Please stop them?"

Shayne swallowed a 70/30 spew burp of despair. "No fucking way. That's totally fucked up."

What the fuck's going on around here? I've go no idea where Jacob is. Fuck, fuck, fuck.

"I saw Zeke before and I doubt he saw let alone believed the news. Shit, my daughter's here. I'll them both to Earth before they find us. I hope. Fuck, the Protectors aren't protected and will fear the worst."

I can't contact them without the GC knowing and no time for anything else. The kids' safety comes first.

What if I can't open a wormhole when I try again? Hiding is the only option.

Sherryn glanced behind her. "Unfortunately, they're close and I won't be able to help you. I'm sorry."

Erin bunched her top into her fist. "This is messed up. Stop talking on the phone thing and do something."

Peril overwhelmed Shayne, nausea bubbled. "Erin don't freak out yet. I'll figure this out somehow."

Liar liar pants on fire.

"Please Creator cut me some slack here."

The whir of PFD's rumbled nearby.

Sherryn's chin dropped, her breath fastened. "They're here. Go, now and don't turn back. You'll find a way to fix this, I know you will."

The call ended, the ground rumbled but not for the right reasons.

PFD's engines wound down and dumped a shit storm on Shayne.

Shayne climbed off the floor and stood in front of the wall.

Wormhole please open, Earth, Earth, Earth.

Again a wormhole eluded Shayne and cemented over hope.

Shayne's pulse raced, her head fuzzed.

Oh God, oh God, Oh God. Where can I hide them? How do I sort this out alone?

Something inside Shayne yanked panic's brakes to a halt.

Snap out of it. Fake it until I make it which won't be the first time. Besides I've got to be strong for Erin, Zeke and everyone else.

Shayne dragged Erin to the house. "Come on. I'm sorry love but going back to Earth isn't an option at the moment and there's trouble."

Erin's voice lowered; she dragged her feet. "No. I can't stay here. You said you'd send me home. It's not happening. This isn't my problem it's yours."

Shayne ducked around trees in the front orchard. "Oh believe me, my girl. It is. Now for once in your life you must listen and trust me."

And I'll pray they won't see us and kill us for real.

Chapter 8
Emasculated
Bailor Street, Rendelshem
South Australia, Australia, Earth

In the roof space, Annu scrambled across the centre beam and along the west eave, pink fluff hung from his beard, cobwebs covered his back.

Annu dug around and retrieved another device.

If we get rid of all of these, the wormhole should work again.

With the connected wires removed, the red light died. Annu tossed it at a large pile near the manhole in the middle of the roof space.

Ang popped up the hole, the black box clocked him in the nose. "Ouch. Careful."

Annu dodged a pile of rat poo. "Humph. Sorry." Along the roof's length, Annu collected three more of similar size and design. No identifiable marks, no hints, no clues. "That's twelve so far in the roof alone."

Ang blew dust from his nose. "I found four in the pantry upper beams wedged in right back. I had to climb the shelves and hoist myself up to get there. They're high tech stuff. Someone took their time setting this up and knew what they were doing."

Unease slithered up Annu's spine and encircled his throat.

Mother please make sure Shayne's alright. If the GC's got her I'll….no don't go there yet. She's fine, she's got to be.

"Here's hoping we can get the flark out of here before these bastards get in. Hey if the GC is partly behind this why would they risk your life?"

Ang scratched the bridge of his nose. "Honestly, I don't have any family and only a few friends. I'm expendable, if anything happened to me there's no one much who'd care."

"Oh, ah, that's no comfort to either of us."

Ang shrugged a massive shoulder above the man hole. "Who knows, if we live, I might meet a nice Earth woman and settle down."

Annu loosened the unease noose around his neck and searched the eaves. "It won't be necessary. This is only temporary. You're going home, I'm going home and we are not dying."

8, 9, 10, how many of these are there up here?

Ang disappeared down the man hole. "I'll keep checking the kitchen."

Annu removed the last four devices from the roof space and threw them onto the pile. "I've got no place else to go on Earth and I can't stay here. What the hell am I going to do?"

'Mother can you hear me? Hello? Are you there? I need help.'

Static faded to the buzz of his brain.

Ang returned and held up a device. "Hey, I pulled out several cameras and two sort of communication receiver units from the kitchen, all in obscure places."

Annu flinched and banged a shoulder on an upper beam. "Flarking hell. How about you announce yourself."

The smile on Ang's face conflicted with his light tone. "Sorry."

Annu crawled to the pile he'd found, dropped them all in a pre-prepared bag, climbed down the hole and stood beside Ang. "How many flarking things are there?"

Dirt covered Ang's upper half. "A lot."

Bang, bang, bang.

Doom's determination exhausted Annu.

This nightmare gets better and better. Not. At least it beats being a torture subject at that damned DSI place.

A chill wrapped around Annu's neck, he shoved the memories aside. "Please don't be a knock on the door? Already?"

Bang, bang, bang.

It swept along the hall and buried Annu's control in a pine box. "Already? Shit."

Bang, bang, bang.

Mr. Smith added another layer of despair. "Ms. James, this is your last chance to comply. It's obvious you're inside so open the door and let us in. If you don't you leave us with no choice and we'll make our way inside."

They won't just go away. What's with this flarking planet? What's another approach?

Annu's voice crackled. "There's no Ms. James here. You've got the wrong place."

A shadow shifted under the doorway.

Smith's tone turned ominous. "Are you Annu?"

Shit, shit, shit. I really didn't think that one out.

"No. Neither of them are here, you may as well leave right now."

Smith wriggled the knob and pushed the door with his shoulder. "I'm afraid we can't do that, Annu. Nor do I believe the woman isn't in there with you. Let us in before you're declared a national threat."

Annu's mouth worked before his brain. "What the hell? They stepped things up fast."

No more stuffing around. We've removed a number of devices and a wormhole better open.

Smith peeked into a side window. "Let us in and we'll discuss this."

You flarking Idiot. Protect yourself, block up the house.

Annu leaned into Ang's ear. "Stay here and don't let them in."

Ang clicked off the gun's safety and aimed. "Done."

Annu slipped through the house and with a flamed hand welded the hinges on the back door sealed.

Back at Ang's side, Annu slouched against the wall in the lounge room—the windows in sight.

The walls closed in on Annu, the tension amplified. "Back door's secure."

Ang wiped his palms on this shirt. "You're assuming they'll use standard means to enter."

Jones' sternness heightened Annu's sense of danger. "Smith, secure and arm the rear of the property. I'll alert the team. Lieutenant, dispatch the first team and install amber protocol, stage 1."

"Roger."

Annu ushered Ang into Shayne's bedroom; the blinds down it offered some protection. "You cover the back, I'll take the front. Whatever you do don't let them take us."

An explosion from the rear of the house rattled the foundations. Annu protected himself from fallen plaster. "Okay, new plan. I'm going out back, you take the front. Go."

Ang grabbed his forearm, his skin hot. "You don't have a weapon."

Annu brushed him off and ignited; only his upper half complied. "That's better than nothing."

In the back porch, the door lay on the floor, four men dressed in black aimed weapons and streamed through the opening. One stepped before the others; a plastic visor covered their faces. "Hands up and lay on the ground."

Annu projected a ball of fire at them; it threw the men backwards and out the doorway.

Gunfire erupted from the hallway; Annu picked up the door and re-sealed it. He secured the porch door, welded it closed and worked his way to the kitchen. A further explosion shook the ground and blew the front door back into the kitchen. Men's boots echoed down the hall.

Annu grabbed the door as a shield and barrelled out of the kitchen into the hall.

Whack, the door wiped out two men coming his way.

Someone jumped on Annu's back, he flung them off and incinerated the man. Bare bones and melted flesh filled his fatigues.

Zap, zap, zap.

Annu's powers diminished, hard blocks pummelled his side.

On his left, two men fired guns with blue tags, the same ones the GC had.

Annu lunged, the one on the right smashed into the shower wall. "How the flark did you get those?"

Crack, crack, crack.

Annu slammed the man's helmet against the tiles and slipped. An unseen person punched Annu in the right kidney area. Annu grabbed him and squeezed; the man's helmet and skull crunched.

The man in the shower rose and shot at Annu.

Annu ducked down, avoided the blast, grabbed the man's legs and swung him into the other guy.

Ang crashed into the wall beside the bathroom doorway with a man's neck under his arm, the room wobbled.

Annu dragged one of the unconscious men's legs and threw him into the hallway. "Where's your gun?"

Ang twisted the man's neck, crack, and dropped the body. "Some bastard side swiped me and I lost it."

Annu caught his breath, removed the nearest dead man's weapon, and gave it to Ang. He grabbed another weapon and asked, "How many you have taken down?"

"Four or five. There's a couple holed up in the lounge room and some in Shayne's room."

Annu calculated the few he'd stopped. "All right, get rid of the ones in the lounge."

Ang nodded, stepped over the bodies and stomped down the hall.

Annu held his finger on the trigger and blasted his way into the bedroom. Two men dropped, a third returned fire. Heat singed Annu's ear lobe, another belted his shoulder. Gun steady, Annu continued forward and shot the guy between the eyes.

He shoved aside pain, left the bedroom collecting the hall stand for barrier. One after the other, four bodies flew through the middle of the lounge room and collided with the opposite hallway wall.

Ang caught his breath in the doorway. "That's all of them." He picked up solid grey chunks from the floor. "They're using these instead of bullets, like they don't want to kill us."

Annu wiped blood from his cheek. "It doesn't make sense but we don't have time to think about it. Let's re-secure this place and come up with an actual plan."

One after the other Annu and Ang threw bodies outside and replaced the doors.

Annu sealed them, Ang pushed furniture against the exits.

Barricaded in the kitchen, from their position the kitchen windows offered a view out back and gave a few second advantage.

Black unmarked vehicles pulled into the driveway and drove towards the rear of the property.

Three times the men spilled from the vans into the shadows.

Screw these bastards; I'm not going down like this. Shayne, thinking you're safe is all that's keeping me sane but when we see each other next you've got a lecture coming.

Chapter 9
Hide and No Seek
Enki Island, Orion

In seconds, Shayne's peace of mind and comfort, derived from the familiar, disintegrated.

They're on our island to take it over. They've got technology blocking my powers, which is my usual go to. How do I protect us?

Erin trailed Shayne like a fly stuck to shit, and shit loved Shayne. "Shayne, where are we going now? You've thought of something haven't you?"

Shit's rancid stank trailed Shayne around bushes, shrubs, and stone structures closer to the house.

Maybe a stronger deodorant would help? Yeah right.

An image of Zeke dead flashed into her mind, her heart sunk. "Shit, fuck, shit, fuck, shit, fuck. Zeke, you better be home."

Erin's recent promotion to voice of torment intensified the situation. "Will you please stop swearing so much? Do you have any other words in your vocabulary?"

Teeth gritted, drool trickled down Shayne's chin. "Oh for fu—heaven's sake. Does it really matter now?"

Erin pursued torment's employee-of-the-month program. "It matters to me. What if this Zeke isn't there? What do we do then? Shayne what is going on around here? If I get killed, I'm ever speaking to you again."

I love you kid but I could throttle you right now. It's my turn to freak out.

"Erin, calm down. I'm the mother not you. What's going on is a minor issue with Orion's Grand Counsel—the rulers here. Actually it's meant to be us but screw it, it's a long story."

Erin clutched her sleeve and halted Shayne mid step. "What the cookies? You've angered an entire Government bad enough they want to kill you? You're infuriating and all but how did you manage it?

If Zeke's not home, what then? Where does a boy go when he may think his newly acquainted father and loathed, future stepmother are dead? A bar? A party? Did he hide when he heard the PFD's? Fuck.

Stone along the outer wall scratched Shayne's hands. "Look we didn't do anything wrong. They've never trusted us since the whole ascension and killing their former leader. Seems some people are a bit delicate about that sort of thing and are scared of us."

More PFDs soared over the mountain top. At present, no I.D.I.O.T.s aside from Shayne, roamed the gardens or house yard.

Any time now, hurry the fuck up woman.

Erin shuffled into Shayne's side and clung onto her arm. "What are those flying things? What are you going to do? Does Zeke have powers? Can he use them? Why haven't you stopped them with yours already?"

Shayne beat Erin to the front door, information overload fogged her mind. "Because, dear daughter, they aren't working and apart from the ability to stink badly and ticking me off, Zeke has no powers."

Thank Gods Annu's safe on Earth.

The front door opened, Shayne detached Erin and jogged down the hall. "Zeke, are you there? Good news. Surprise. It's me, stepmother extraordinaire and I'm not dead. And I brought your stepsister but we're all running away."

Erin ran into the back of Shayne. "Omph. It's not a well thought out idea."

A testosterone haze coveted the floor; dirty clothes covered the bed but no smelly kid.

The walls closed in on Shayne; her guts churned. "Fuck."

Room by room, Shayne checked for Zeke and sent messages to his communicator.

'Zeke, where are you? Answer me. It's important.'

Of all the times for the kid to disappear, he picked the worst. PDFs roared over the house and landed nearby.

"Fuck, fuck, fuck. All right be calm. Where does a little shit go?" Shayne turned and this time bumped into Erin. "Jesus Erin. Give me some personal space."

Erin trembled; tears welled in her eyes. "We can't wait for him to show up, they'll catch us. This is so unfair. What did I do to deserve this? I'm telling them I've nothing to do with this and I have rights you know."

This mothering thing is not easy at the best of circumstances and this is so far the wrong one. It's too late to adopt her out. Right?

Vomit burned a line up Shayne's throat. "Okay breathe. Flipping out doesn't help anything. Trust me."

Low blood pressure rattled Shayne; she hunched over and heaved in air.

Brain re-oxygenated, rationality reignited, Shayne rose. "I can do this. I defeated an ancient God and shit. This is a simple run of the mill stopping an island and personal government threat. Even with no way of fighting or removing them.

Erin promoted herself to next level tormentor. "Great, Shayne. I'm better off with Annu."

Ouch again.

"I told you, we hide somewhere until they go away."

Can't be more than a day or two tops.

Fear steeped Erin demeanour. "That's not a rational plan."

"I said I had one not that it was good. I'll grab essentials and pray Zeke comes back." Shayne propped Erin against the hallway wall. "You stay down, quiet and keep watch. If they come into the front garden whistle or something okay? They cannot find us."

Erin's bottom lip quivered, she regressed to childhood in moments."Mum, I don't want to be alone. I'm scared."

Oh God she's still my baby. I can't fail her. Keep it together. Oh and let's not fucking forget I'm sick or dying and shit.

Shayne channeled maternal care from a better parent than her. "It's not for long and I really need your help, sweetie, okay?"

Erin jutted her chin and swallowed. "Yes but be fast."

In the bedroom, Shayne tossed clothes into a bag and in the adjoining bathroom emptied the counter top. Blankets and pillows from the bed acted as a carry all on way to the kitchen. She threw identifiable food substances into the middle of the pile and dragged the haul into the hallway.

Beside Erin, Shayne pulled opposite ends together, formed a bundle and lifted. It stayed put.

The official CEO of torment Erin nodded at the pile. "You've put too much in there."

Footsteps crunched over rocks in the front garden, Shayne's peace of mind fractured.

Shayne picked through the cache and tossed out non essentials. "Shit, shit, shit. I'm such a fucking idiot sometimes." Self-disgust swallowed her whole and spat out the bones. "You're right. I don't have a good plan. I'm working on it while we're living in the woods."

Erin gasped and clutched her chest. "Wait, we're going to stay in the woods? Surrounded by trees. You better mean in a cabin or something? Right?"

Butterflies flitted around Shayne's stomach. She wiped tears and steeled herself.

I need to do not try hanging in there. Things are getting rougher. Please magically send Annu back really soon.

Shayne's fake smile hurt her jaw. "Ah no, not exactly. Think more camping without camping equipment but please, it's all I've got right now."

Erin banged against the wall. "I cannot believe I don't have a choice."

Shayne stuffed her pockets with snacks, sheets of toilet paper and carried a bottle of water, pillow, and blanket. "Sweetheart, you better start."

What am I forgetting?

At least ten kilos heavier, Shayne ushered Erin to the back door, the rear garden remained clear. "Jacob, shit. Where's he when I actually want him? Really where is he? Now I've got to worry about him too. Shit."

Erin pushed against Shayne's hand. "What? You've lost another person? Can you keep track of anyone? There's no hope for me. I'm dead."

Despair urged Shayne to fight for her house and island; desire to survive overdo and drove her into the back yard. "So far you're still here. Lucky, lucky you, hey."

Shayne hunched along the garden and into the forest edging the house property.

The suns light diminished, flocks of birds settled into tree tops, nighttime animals screeched and scattered across the forest floor.

Any second now I'll fall to pieces. Big fat chunks all over the place.

The alarm on Shayne's com reminded her to put the washing on and find something for dinner. "Normally, I'd be shutting you off and ordering take out, snuggled up on the couch with Annu, not being a criminal."

Oh woe is me.

"And not vulnerable and homeless."

Shayne paused at a patch of shrubs dense enough to snuggle into unseen and uneaten. She brushed aside sticks and smoothed out a makeshift bed.

Blanket first, pillow second; Shayne buried Erin in the underbrush. "Stay here until I come back with Zeke. I love you."

Erin wriggled and perched on her haunches. "No flipping way, Mum. Something weird and creepy will find me before you get back. I hate the outdoors. Please don't leave me."

Annu's sleeping in my bed, living it up, not a care in the world. The bastard.

"Erin, I can't worry about you while I'm looking for him. It's harder to keep two people hidden than one. Please Erin, it's for your greater good. I couldn't live with it anything happened to you."

Someone in red with dark hair ran between trees metres further into the forest.

Shit, Zeke. "Hey kid. Stop it's—"

A mouse the size of a domestic cat scampered up the tree trunk beside Shayne, screeched, and jumped on her.

In a flurry of claws, fur and flesh, the creature pried itself to Shayne's skull.

Hair and scalp on fire, Shayne grabbed either side of its body and pulled.

Both fought to remain in their assigned positions.

Tears streamed down Shayne's cheeks, amidst a stream of warm pee from the animal.

Shayne pursed her lips and tore at its fur. "Get off me, you mother fucker."

A cracked laugh burst from Erin. "See I told you it wasn't a great spot."

Chapter 10
Bamboozled
Bailor Street, Rendelshem, Earth

The intergalactic battle between Orion and Earth in Shayne's house continued. In the early morning, military troops stormed the property, blocked the perimeter off and ushered the neighbours away in black vans. Loud flying craft with search lights hovered above the house, Annu clenched his butthole.

Please Gods, keep them out for as long as possible. And while you're at it, help me the flark out.

Annu flipped the couch over, dragged it and covered most of the front lounge room windows. Shayne's bed protected the bedroom windows; her fridge covered the back door. Erin's party favours full of glitter painted the kitchen floor and added incongruence to the grave situation.

Not sure how I'm going to explain what's left of the house to Shayne later. If I can at all.

"What the hell. It needed a makeover anyway."

Annu stuck a couple of dead men's weapons in his waist band, ready for the next time his powers failed. "For all the good they'll do with no real bullets."

Artillery raised, visored men arranged themselves across the front yard and spilt into the porch, the ground rumbled under their boots.

Annu's senses heightened, adrenaline coursed, hatred and revenge fuelled him.

Boom, boom, boom.

Energy rippled across the floor and shattered Annu's core, each weakened his power. His legs wobbled, the front door flew down the hallway and imbedded into the wall by Annu. A high pitched siren screeched from the front yard.

Annu covered his ears, clutched the couch's side and grasped at lucidity.

Men invaded the house, three turned for the lounge room and Annu.

Annu ignited his upper half and blasted them into the bedroom wall.

Each hit lessened the depth and strength. "Mother flarkers."

Why the hell did I agree to go here first, let alone at all? Are Shayne, Zeke and Jacob safe on Orion? Or has it all gone pear shaped there too?

Men lined either side of the lounge room doorway, several entered via the former pantry.

Annu hovered above the ground, wavered and plummeted onto a knee. Pain ricocheted up his leg and across his groin. He raised a hand, a weak blast struck the first row of men who fell backwards and took the ones behind with them.

Boom, boom, boom.

Shock waves rippled through Annu, his ears rang, his nose bled.

Annu groped for the weapon on his waistband, his finger splayed across the trigger.

Thud, thud, thud.

The cartridges bounced off the men's body armour and around the room.

Someone grabbed him from behind; Annu tossed the empty gun and struck his elbow in a man's ribs.

Thuds hit him in the side; Annu pelted the contents of the coffee table in their direction and followed up with the table. It hit the wall and shattered, wood splinters crunched under boots.

Annu picked up the television and hurled it at men in the hall.

This isn't ending as soon as I thought.

An explosion erupted from the rear of the house, the back door hurtled into the hallway and imbedded in the wall. Another team entered the porch; Annu slammed the kitchen door and leant against it. Fear based concrete filled his mind and solidified his thoughts. "Ang, where are you?"

Six of the enemy passed the kitchen doorway carrying a bound, gagged, unresponsive Ang out the front.

Annu's throat constricted, he tossed a chair and hit a guy full force. The man dropped and took Ang's upper half with them, his skull bounced off the ground. The men at the front turned and let go of Ang.

Annu dipped his chin, ducked around Ang and rammed into the men; they tumbled out the front door. Plastic cartridges pummelled Annu, except for gas masks over their faces carbon copy men replaced the others brought down behind him.

A bright light and siren eradicated Annu's thoughts. Sense of balance and direction escaped; he sung his fists in every direction.

Bang. Crash.

Dense smoke billowed from the front, consumed the house and Annu's lungs.

Boom, boom, boom.

Energy shocks jolted Annu, pain erupted along his limbs, he swayed against the waves. Jumbled and disjointed, a weight plonked upon his back.

The gun dropped to the floor and Annu to his knees. Subsequent explosions rattled his core. Everything shimmied, stars danced behind his eyes. Clarity hovered beyond his grasp. Annu lost control and fell face first.

Men secured Annu's arms and legs and placed a bag over his head.

A male voice broke above his mind fog. "HQ, we've secured two male EBE's. The female's not at or on the premises. I repeat the female is not at or on the premises."

People shuffled around Annu; he rose from the ground. His skull went one way, his brain the other.

How did I screw this up?

"Let me go."

Radio static road the edges of his consciousness. "Roger. Our ETA for PineGap is zero two thirty hours."

The bonds tightened each time Annu struggled and bit into his flesh. "No. You can't do this…Let me…go. I've got to…"

A sharp hot pain shot across Annu's arm, a blurry face injected liquid through a small needle. It burnt in his veins, his eyes closed, a copper taste filled his mouth.

Lucid enough, Annu spat in the doctor's face and clawed at her arm. "No, no, no."

She removed another syringe from her lab coat and jabbed his other arm. Annu welcomed oblivion and drifted away.

Chapter 11
Camping Outdoors is Fucking Intense
Enki Island, Orion

Shayne's former non-drug dealer and acclaimed godly status soared beyond the horizon. Hunched from a sleepless night of near misses with Zeke on the upper mountain, around each corner lurked new worries.

On the forest's edge several metres from Shayne's position I.D.I.O.T.s swarmed the Protectors Compound.

Desperation clung a sweaty shirt on Shayne's back. "There's like a never ending supply of these fuckers. They must come off a conveyer belt or something."

Shayne crept around a tree trunk, a group of men crossed the forest meters away. She returned to her original spot. "I'm so fucking tired, hungry and over it."

Erin's insistence on accompanying Shayne added layers of concern and responsibility to 'this is too fucking much' zone.

Erin shuffled in dead leaves and appeared unable to stay still. "Where is this damned kid now? Why does he keep running away from us? Are you sure we need to find him?"

20 questions is a fun travelling game not a way of life.

Shayne pulled the communicator from her pocket. She turned on the news notifications on her communicator.

It's a good time to pay more attention.

No messages from Zeke and no salvation from anyone else.

And I've still got no fucking idea what to do. Come on neurones work.

Shayne grasped at straws scattered across her mind and pulled a short one. "Ah yes, Erin. He's my fiancee's son. I'm guessing the relationship will be over if I lose his only child." The straw snapped.

For fuck's sake, if I'm trying, I'm dying.

Shayne selected Jacob's number. "While we wait, onto plan D or J. Whatever's next in line." Shayne's intestines knitted a jacket.

Please answer and please don't hate me. I can live with either one.

Jacob filled the screen, his expression dower. "Who is this? Why do you have Shayne's communicator?" He blinked and rubbed his eyes. "Your Goddess, is it really you? You're not dead. How is it possible?"

I wonder that myself every flipping day. So far so good.

Shayne brushed dirt from her pants. "Yes I'm still around. It's a long story. Actually it's a short story but anyway. Hey, sorry I've been such a bitch to you lately but on another note, obviously, I need you."

Shayne slowed her breath, Erin hovered beside her.

You're invading my personal space kid. But if I tell you that it will only start you off again.

Jacob placed a hand on his chest, his eye twinkled. "I'm so relieved. See you do need me sometimes? Is this the result of those forgotten messages?" He searched around Shayne. "Why isn't His Godness beside you? Is he all right?"

Oh fucking hell.

Lack of moisture in Shayne's mouth cemented her tongue to the roof. "No and no."

Don't cry and don't be a stubborn jack arse.

"Yeah all right I do need your help. Annu's stuck on Earth. I never made it there in the first place because I can't open a wormhole and none of my powers are working. Plus I'm in the woods with my daughter from Earth who's got sucked up here by accident, when I see Zeke he runs away and I.D.I.O.T.s are everywhere."

Don't freak out. Be cool calm and collected. This is my fucking job and all.

Erin peeked over Shayne's shoulder. "Can he help us?"

Shayne moved out of Erin's way and bit her inner cheek. "Give me a minute here please."

Jacob smoothed his robes and walked around a dark room, the screen moved with him. "Oh no. That's not good. Not at all. I knew they were up to something. I'm sure they've had this planned for a long time. I've hidden the book for safety."

Stupid thing. Like I care about that.

Nausea consumed her, Shayne hunched and clutched her stomach.

Of all the times to get sick. Bastard thing. I bet it's hunger related.

It slowed, Shayne lifted her chin. "That's kind of irrelevant because it's happened."

Jacob appeared and disappeared into shadows. Light, dark, light, dark, light, dark. "Yes you're right." Dark, dark, light, spin. "You must stop the counsel's men somehow, get Annu back plus Zeke, your daughter home and everything will be back to normal."

Is that all? Sounds dead easy. Not.

Shayne swallowed panic and farted fear. "Jacob, stop walking in circles. You're making me dizzy."

Jacob plonked onto a chunk of stone, it wobbled. "Sorry. I do that when I think."

Erin tugged on Shayne's sleeve. "Come on. What's happening?"

Shayne brushed her off and frowned.

For the love of all things fucking holy.

"Have you seen the Protectors? Is there anyone left who'll help us?"

A problem shared is a problem halved and all.

Jacob steadied his seat, his belly jiggled. "The protectors were removed first. Before the men reached the temple, I escaped through a back passage and hid. I lost contact with anyone else shortly thereafter. Until now, I thought I was alone and you were both dead."

Shayne heart gained twenty pounds and weighted her chest. "Have you possibly seen Zeke? If taken by I.D.I.O.T.s, he hates me so much he'd give me up. Crap what a mess."

"I'm sorry; I haven't seen him for days."

Dread clouded Shayne's mind. "Crap, shit, fuck."

Worse case scenario it works in my favour if he doesn't know I'm here and alive. The suckage increases.

Jacob's tone darkened. "Again, I must say that with proper attention and time, perhaps this could have been prevented."

Why did I call you? Pompous bastard.

Let it go for now.

Shayne devoured the last muesli bar and staved off the next round of nausea. "Yeah no probably not. Where are you? Do you have any food?" She licked both sides of the wrapper. "And a pillow?"

Erin pushed off the trunk, threw her arms in the air and paced. "For God's sake. It's not the time for a long conversation. Hurry up."

I'm trying to be nice and in control. Start as a kinder mother and all but I'm going to blow a gasket in a minute.

"Erin relax. It's fine for now. So far they haven't come into the woods because they've got no reason to. Jacob, where are you?"

He raised some unreadable packets and pointed to bottles of water. "I'm in Ki's tomb and I have some food supplies but no bedding."

Oh fuck no, not my dad's burial place. Not that it matters whose it is, no-one's coffin makes a great hiding spot. Creepy weirdo.

Shayne shoved the empty wrappers under a rock. "Well, I'm in the east woods about 3 kilometres from the garden up top of the mountain. Meet me us here, there's less dead stuff."

Jacob patted his left breast and puffed out his chest. "I can't climb or walk any further, it will kill me. I've got a bad ticker on its last replacement and I'm out of medication."

How did I fucking not know that? Oh, because I don't care. Bitch.

Before guilt attacked her, Shayne pushed it under her arse and squished. "Oh, ah, right. I guess I'm coming to you then."

Jacob's kind expression ejected the guilt an inch out from its prison. "Please be careful Shayne. There's no telling what these people will do if they find you. Message me when you're on your way. I'll meet you outside the tomb if I can. "

Shit, shit, shit. The lift's in the middle of the mountain top through the ascension room, which is of course, through the God's Garden.

"Okay. Can do. I'll leave soon. Pray, lots. I'll start."

Oh God, oh God, oh fucking fucking God. Please help me get to Jacob without being killed or capture. Amen. Fucking, shit, fuck.

Jacob gripped his jacket's lapels. "Are you sure you can handle this? You've not managed well on your own lately and aren't using a lot of fore—"

Swipe, call ended. Shayne shoved the communicator back in her pocket. "I don't need that kind of negativity right now."

Erin crossed her arms and oozed more school principal than loving daughter. "More walking and climbing down a mountain as well? Are you kidding me? This place is awful."

Shayne gathered her meagre essentials and rose. "Ah no. We're on a highway to hell. Yeah, yeah. I'm on a highway to hell."

What's the next part?

"That's all the word's I know. We're on a highway to hell."

Erin grimaced and covered her ears. "Please stop. Do not sing. My ears can't take it."

A high pitched squeal erupted behind them, Shayne jumped and jogged in the other direction.

Shayne lowered her voice. "Too late, kiddo. We're in hell I tell you. Fucking hell."

They passed a ripe Grenberry bush; sweet smoke followed by a sweeter relief stood so close yet so far.

I don't have time to get fucked up and Erin's lecture isn't worth it.

An edge to Erin's tone flooded Shayne with guilt. "Do not even think about it, Shayne."

She's right it's a shitty thing to do in front of the daughter whom already hates me. Shit, I'm making mature decisions and crap.

Shayne crept past it, the communicator buzzed, an inch from her nose she squinted:

> 'Unidentified Flying Objects have placed themselves over several large and small Orion cities. Strange messages have been reported coming from the objects, which are not yet translated. Frightened local inhabitants evacuated to city centres. The Grand Council have been moved to secure, yet unnamed island. Tap here to read full story.'

The first and only news report Shayne received shattered her.

Shayne covered her mouth with her hands, life's fragile balance faltered. "Oh no fucking way."

For the second time Shayne's legs folded, she hit the ground.

Erin appeared beside her and patted Shayne's back. "Are you okay? I'm too scared to ask what's wrong."

Shayne blinked repeatedly, her mind frozen. "Fucking aliens, aliens have invaded. And it's not me this time."

Erin paled and joined Shayne on the ground. "Mummy, I want to go home."

The trees blurred, the air thickened. "Me fucking too."

Chapter 12
Stoned Cold
Pine Gap, New South Wales
Australia, Earth

Awareness blurred, lost definition and drifted out of reach. Annu swayed, a bump lifted him an inch in the air, his leaden eyes refused to keep open.

Why am I moving? What, what happened?

Annu's thoughts turned into dead grass snatched away by the wind. He licked his lips, a next generation hang-over simmered behind his eyes.

What the hell did I do last night? Did a bird shit in my mouth?

The cold, hard surface beneath and Shayne's absence at his side confused Annu further. "Shayne?"

Annu attempted standing but restraints held him in place. "What the flark is going on? Where am I?"

A muffled reply from a distance preceded a whack on his shoulder. "Stay down."

Annu's obscured view returned memories amidst horror, the bag sucked into his mouth each breath; any movement disturbed his equilibrium. The bitterness of fear tainted his tongue.

I've got to get out of here.

Annu twisted his wrists, metal bit into his flesh and likewise his ankles.

And how am I going to do that?

He inhaled, held his breath and grasped at calm.

Ignite and burn the restraints off.

Heat trickled under the surface and disappeared. Lack of control and hopelessness created a pit in the bottom of Annu's gut.

Ang mumbled from a million miles away. "Annu? Is that you moving? Are you conscious?"

Who'd have thought I'd be relieved at him being alive.

Annu shuffled back against a wall, pain ricocheted across his skull. "Yeah for all the good it does. Where are we?"

"Don't know. Can't see."

The floor clinked under a tap of Annu's boot.

They bounced over bumps similar to when he'd travelled in what they call a car last with Shayne. "We're in some kind of vehicle. Shit."

Ang clicked his tongue, his tone indicated no fear. "You know, this part wasn't mentioned in my orders. I anticipated at least getting to know a few people before getting captured by an extra-terrestrial government. But, I guess you can't always plan for these things."

Tell me about it.

Someone on the left prodded Annu's shoulder with a hard object. "Less chit chat you two or the doc gives you another shot."

Flark. I'd forgotten about those men. How many are in here with us?

The fuzz on Annu's tongue thickened. "Why are you doing this? Who the hell are you? What right do you have? We've done nothing to you."

A man grunted in front of him, his words bounced with bumps on the road. "I don't answer questions I ask them and I said shut up."

Nothing around Annu offered help freeing him. "Well start now. Who the flark are you and why the hell are you doing this to us?"

Arrogance tainted the man's tone. "For the last fucking time shut up or get another three shots of the shut up drugs. Personally, I prefer the shots. It's quieter."

How far away from Shayne's have we gone?

"Where are you taking us? Take this thing off me."

Whack. He jabbed Annu in the ribs. "Not until we arrive."

Annu twisted in his direction, pain tore across his wrists. "Answer me flarker. Where are you taking us? You're going to pay for this."

The man's groan escalated Annu's frustration. "Jesus Christ. Triple the dose from last time doc. Hell give it to me, I'll do it."

Annu tipped his chin, a crack of light under the hood showed his boots on a metal floor. "Fuck you."

Crack. "No, fuck you."

Pain erupted down Annu's shoulder, he lurched sideways. "Mother fla- fucker."

A woman sounded close. "That's enough. Don't damage the subjects and further don't tell me how and when to do my job. I don't answer to you Lieutenant Dingle."

A chill settled in Annu's kidneys, bad scenarios invaded his mind.

She disassociates us from them, which makes her equally as dangerous.

Annu flung his shoulder to move the sack and failed. "We're not subjects, we're people. Ah, I'm half God, but the rest is human and all of me deserves some basic rights."

Dingle's arrogance lightened, fear fractured the man's bravado. "You're not normal human being from Earth, you get no rights."

Say what?

Annu dipped his ear, his thoughts disjointed. "What do you mean?"

The woman doctor's shrill drilled through Annu. "Dingle, do you're damned job and stick to your own closed mouth policy or I'll report you."

Dingle droned in the enclosed space. "Yes ma'am. Don't come crying to me when they rip your face off and wear it like skin."

The woman's tone sharpened, each word sliced off her tongue. "One species and one instance, you're out ranked. I'd stop now."

Do they collect people from other planets here? What kind of place do they work for?

The vehicle slowed and turned a sharp right, Annu slammed sideways into a hard surface.

Like I need more pain.

Annu stomped on the floor. "Flarking hell. You'll pay for this."

If only what they say were useful.

The brakes squealed, the vehicle stopped. Annu swallowed his Adam's apple and stretched an inch; the wrist bonds pinched and tightened.

A voice came from outside the vehicle.

Dingle groaned and slapped metal. "God damned check points, waste of time. They know who we are."

The vehicle shuddered forwards, Annu's mind churned in a fight against the drugs. *Shit, shit, shit. 1100, 2200, 3300.* They stopped again, *1100, 2200* and shunted. Two more check points, 1100, 2200, 3300, 4400, 5500, 6100, 7100 and the journey ended.

Boots clinked across the floor in front of him, metal scraped across metal.

Dingle kicked Annu's ankle. "We're here, fuckers. Good old Pine Gap, freezing one day, windy the next. You're out first doc."

Annu scooted to the end of the seat and clung to awareness.

The first chance I get, I've got to take it. Where is Pine Gap? Hell it makes no difference. I still don't know where it is or how to get back to Shayne's.

The bag lifted, artificial light stung Annu's eyes; he blinked until they adjusted.

Ang waited at the edge of the steel bench. "So what is this Pine Gap place?"

A uniformed guard from the back of the van aimed a weapon at Ang and nodded at Dingle. "Get up, arsehole."

Ang smiled at the guard and clambered to his feet. "I guess that's a no to answering my question then?"

Dingle motioned upwards with his gun on Annu. "All right, this is how it's going to go. I'm going to unlock your legs so you two can walk into the building and we don't have to carry you again. You're big bastards. But, when I do that, if you run, fight or even blink, I'm authorised to use any force I deem necessary, as long as I don't kill you and that includes at lot of shit." He poked Annu in the knee using the butt. "Are we clear?"

100 metres from the open van, large secured doors hid Annu's immediate future. "Yes."

I can't let them take us in there, we'll never get out.

Dingle used a gadget to remove laser-like ties around his ankles; his blood recirculated.

Annu rubbed the sore spot and readied to pounce.

The man beside Ang repeated Dingle's moves, and once done, cracked his knuckles.

Dingle continued going up notches on Annu's 'to-kill once free' list. "Stand up slow, follow me through the door and wait." He faced a younger man. "Wilburs, you follow right after the other guy got it."

Wilburs disappeared behind him. "Yes, sir."

Dingle turned towards the door, Annu rose, his muscles screamed.

Annu reached the roof and blocked off Wilbur's view of Dingle.

Annu caught Ang's eye and sneeze-nodded. "Ahchew, run."

Dingle jabbed the gun in Annu's back. "What'd you say?"

Annu gritted his teeth. "Achoo. I sneezed."

Dingle grabbed a handful of Annu's jacket and pushed him out the door. "Move it."

Feet on solid ground, Annu's legs wobbled, he leant against the back door and steadied. Woods and forest surrounded either side of a facility, fenced off by razor wire and several laser beams. An array of large bubble things projected from the ground.

What concerns me most is what lies unseen beyond the doors over there.

Dingle dug the gun in Annu's ribs. "Move. I warned you."

On the precipice of the building, Ang looked over his shoulder, winked at Annu and fell onto the ground.

Wilburs lost his feet, summersaulted and stopped metres away.

Annu threw his weight into Dingle's side. The gun flew out of Dingle's hand.

Dingle thudded onto the dirt.

Annu landed on top of him. Annu punched Dingle in the jaw and pushed him off.

On his feet and hands behind him Annu grabbed Ang. "Now, let's go."

Annu stumbled around the vehicle down a road, Ang beside him.

Sirens deafened any of Dingle and Wilburs yells, Annu half jogged half stumbled towards the woods.

Chapter 13
Confronted
Enki Island, Orion

Surrounded by forest light years away from home Erin's chest ached, her legs wobbled. Shayne slowed, the trees thinned, daylight remained a few hours away. A couple of kilometres forward and the edge of the mountain appeared.

Nathanial must be going crazy looking for me. He'll think I've disappeared into thin air unless he realises what happened. And then he can't really tell anyone or come get me. What's going to happen to me? What if I am stuck here forever? With m— Shayne. Oh God, oh God, oh God.

Erin's emotions consumed her, the urge to cry and scream collided.

No, no, no. I've got to keep my senses at all times. I can't react like Shayne expects me to. I have to be better, smarter, in charge. Which reminds me of another thing bugging me.

"Shayne, Sam, and I have concerns about your and Annu's lightning fast relationship. You've been single for some time but after mere months of meeting you're madly in love with Annu, living together on another planet and planning a wedding. I'm getting married to a man I've been with for years and actually know him inside out. What kind of toothpaste does he use Shayne? What's he really like deep down inside when things get tough? Have you considered any of this?"

Shayne stiffened, her shoulders raised ear height. "Are you serious? You two have been talking about us? It's none of either of your fucking businesses."

Typical response from her. Getting stuck with Annu would have been better.

Erin poked her tongue into her inner cheek. "We're both concerned and rightly so. Let's face it, you don't make great decisions and you act on impulse. Along with running purely on emotion not rationality."

Shayne's shoulders shifted up to her temples. "Ah thank's for your personality critique, Erin and thank you for the relationship advice coming from your worldly experience. Shocking as it is I've got my life figured out. Sam can get over it. All Annu's hiding from me is a pile of dirty socks under the bed. Look, we've been through some pretty big stuff together, I'm not young and he's well, fucking old in comparison. Can you walk faster, please?"

I'm not giving up on this. We will resolve it one way or there other.

Erin's lungs burned, she gulped air and caught up with Shayne. "Yeah we'll see. Isn't there another way down this mountain other than climbing? I'm not trained in this stuff or anything like it."

Shayne's sharp tone heightened the tension between them. "Yes, if you want a two day trip on foot or you try using the lift in plain sight of the people who will kill us."

This is so weird. The whole situation is out of a science fiction book.

"Like in the movies? They'd actually kill us? And there's no other way?"

Shayne squinted, her eye twitched. "Yes kill dead. Not a little bit, a big bit dead. Like I've said a million times, there's no there's no other way. We're climbing. Deal with it."

Oh yeah your sarcasm fixes everything. How'd I get stuck with you as a parent?

Over exertion lumbered Erin's body, she maintained a slim figure through good genes not exercise. "What is the likelihood you'll get your powers back in time? There's two separate groups of beings creating mayhem now. I still can't figure out how you managed to get in this situation. Nor can I figure out how you're capable of doing it, even with me and this Jacob person. I can't be stuck with only you to help me. I just can't."

Shayne stopped and faced Erin. "That's a lot of cants. You might want to work on that. I get you're stressed out and all but calm the fuck down and quit it with the million questions. I'm doing everything I can albeit not much right now. Give me a break, please."

She never understands me, she just doesn't get it. She's not in a relationship like mine and Nathanial's. She knows nothing.

Pent up frustration washed over Erin, disappointment its wake. "How can I? You've never been big on organisation let alone having any sort of plan for what you're doing like ever. You couldn't look after me when I was young on Earth let alone millions of light years away from it. This situation is well beyond your capabilities. This is way bigger than money troubles and bad parenting. Admit it, it's past you. Maybe if you surrender they'll consider not killing you and send me home."

Shayne spoke through clenched teeth, her cheeks flushed. "You know what Erin—"

A couple of alien ships flew overhead; Shayne ducked and dragged Erin down with her.

Shayne let go of Erin and crept along the ground face up. "This may not be the time but I'm sick of this poor me, my mum is a crazy demigoddess and she's never taken good care of me bit. No I wasn't always perfect—" A handful of Orion ships followed the other craft, "but I was the best one I could be. And part of being a good parent means recognising when you aren't one and doing what is actually best for your kids. Even when I had an emotional fucking breakdown I made sure you two were taken care of, which meant allowing someone else to do that until I got myself sorted. And those people never liked me, but it didn't matter because they'd love and care for you anyway."

Indignation raised Erin's chin and filled her with self righteousness. "You mean Nanna and Pa? We spent almost a year living between them and Dad. How could you leave us so long?" The mention of her father automatically induced tears, Erin sucked on her bottom lip. "Thank God, Dad was always there for us until—"

Don't think about it now. Push it aside.

Shayne faced trees in the other direction. "You'll never know how much I hated doing that. It's the hardest thing I've ever done and I still punish myself every single day for it. If I didn't you'd be much angrier at me than you are." Shayne swiped at her cheek. "I'm sorry I wasn't strong enough, I'm sorry, I fell apart in other ways after I got you back. I'm sorry I still disappoint you. I'm sorry for so many things Erin. You'll find out one day that being a parent isn't easy. Hell adulating isn't easy, though you seem to have managed it quite well despite me and my dumb arse behaviour."

That's a lot of sorry's too you know.

In a small way, Erin understood, but not enough to accept it.

I can't let it all go yet, I can't forgive you. It's too raw.

"I just, I just, I needed you and you weren't there. It's like you're never there when I need you. When I got older I thought maybe you'd have more time to spend with me but you filled it with wallowing in self pity and running up bad debts. Now in addition to that there's a whole other planet you're involved with and a new boyfriend and new life. All vying for the time that should be mine."

Boom, boom, bang. One of the ships exploded over the lower island, debris rained, gun fire erupted below.

Shayne rose and ran hunched over. "I hate cutting this short but we've got to keep moving, Jacob's not well and waiting. I don't want to disappoint him either."

Erin followed and removed a rock from under her foot. "Oh, nice one Shayne, turn this all into feeling sorry for yourself and it's all about you."

A growl from her mother shot up Erin's spine, all at once the years drifted away.

Shayne's subsequent sigh rippled across the ground. "All right. I'm sorry. It was a cheap shot but you get my point."

This is will be a terrible few hours until this ends. She does not understand where I'm coming from at all and she doesn't want to either. We're back were we started except on another planet.

"Not really no."

They reached the lowest cliff face. Shayne leant over the edge and retrieved old looking climbing equipment.

Shayne slid one of two harnesses to Erin. "Sorry kid. That's tough at the moment. At some point, however, you and I are going to put this shit to bed once and for all but not right now. Okay?"

Not on your life.

Erin wriggled in one leg at a time. "Not likely. It's going to take something pretty catastrophic for that to happen."

Chapter 14
She'll Be Comin' Down the Mountain…Somehow
Enki Island, Orion

The I.D.I.O.T.s and aliens covered most of the island and left almost nowhere safe. Annu stuck on Earth, a step son in places unknown, a daughter in a pissy mood and mass invasions added to Shayne's misery. Worse still it all hovered out of Shayne's control.

In the woods at the base of the mountain, the conversation with Erin lingered and tore the bandaid off Shayne's parental confidence.

How long will Erin hate me for? What if she knew how her father really treated me? Would she love me or hate me? All the unreported beatings, the verbal abuse, the…I can't think about that time again. Dead or not, I can never tell her, she loves him. This is so fucked up and neither of us have any way to get away from each other or personal space at all.

Shayne trudged amidst thick bushland and Erin dragged along beside her. "I love you but you're hurting my head."

Crap. That's how Annu feels with me most of the time. Another issue to work on.

Erin's anger fuelled silence matched the sky, thunder grumbled, lightning cracked. "Right back at you."

A sense of failure shadowed Shayne's existence.

No matter what she did or how she did it, Shayne failed at life.

Military PFDs did regular passes, Shayne's anxiety level rose each time.

Keep it together. There's too much at stake.

Shayne's lungs burned, she hunched behind a stone monument and shallow breathed. Her pocket hummed, newfound hatred for the communicator brewed. "Fuck off you stupid portent of terrible news."

Erin lunged at Shayne and shook her arm. "Is that someone who can help? Please, please be help?"

Hot, cold, gassy, hot, cold and hot again. I'm not coping well.

Shayne fanned her face and retrieved the communicator. "It's probably Jacob wondering where the hell I am. Ha. Which makes two of us."

Shayne swiped the screen, an Orion News notification appeared on screen:

> *'We've been updated—the other worldly visitors are from the planet Mars 54.6 million light years away from Orion. Their means of space travel is not yet determined. However, two minutes ago, one of the larger craft—a mother ship over Orion, has destroyed Leba, a small town outside Yebu with a population of one thousand. Further details will be provided when they are received. For now, the Grand Council and Peace Office are urging all citizens to remain inside unless they've been advised to evacuate. Do not interact with the craft under any circumstances. Previous efforts to do so have resulted in immediate death.'*

And the rain from hell continues.

The communicator dangled in Shayne's hand. "Unholy fucking shit. They're Martians, really? What did we do to them? This is really, really bad."

Jacob's from Leba. Fuck.

Shayne's liver lodged in her throat, she slipped the comm into her pocket. "Oh Gods those poor people. Jacob's people. I've got to do something. Fuck it and the Grand Council will be here any minute. The whole planet's gone to hell in a paper basket." Her voice crackled. "We're on a highway to hell, on a highway to hell and—"

Erin placed a hand on Shayne's back. "Again, who doesn't sing badly at a time like this? What's happened now? Don't lose it, I need you."

This is too much, I can't deal with it alone. I need help. And lots of it.

Zoom. Another group of PFDs flew up the mountain side.

1, 2, 3, 4, 5, breathe.

"The aliens blew up Jacob's home town. He'll be crushed. If he doesn't know already."

Without powers, how can I fix this before anyone else is hurt or killed? It's all fucked up.

Erin slumped to the ground beside her and trembled. "That's awful. They'll do that —"

Yells and nearby laser fire dulled Erin's words.

Shayne placed a finger on her lips, "Shh," pushed Erin into some bushes and crawled in beside her. "Shit, shit, shit."

Erin clutched Shayne's arm. "Mummy, they're going to find us. I'm, I'm scared."

Shayne's blood rushed, her ears buzzed, her whisper hid disconcertment. "Not if I can help it. Just stay still and keep quiet."

Inhale, 1, 2, 3, 4, 5. Exhale, 1, 2, 3, oh fuck, fuck, fuck, maybe even the 'c' word. Actually no. Not unless the world ends or something. Maybe. Oh God, Oh God, Oh God. I can't do this. I'm going to lose everything I love and then—

A Martian craft zipped past and dropped a bomb a few metres from their position, everything happened in slow motion. Shayne grabbed Erin and held her tight.

Boom, boom, boom.

The ground around them exploded, Erin ripped out of Shayne's grasp and flew sideways; Shayne thrust in the other direction and landed on her back in a pile of shrubs.

Shayne's ears rang, maternal instinct dragged her up.

Dirt and debris obscured Shayne's vision, dust filled her lungs, grit sandblasted her face. A dislocated shoulder screamed, cuts and abrasions covered available flesh and seeped her clothes.

Shayne rubbed her eyes and stumbled through grey smoke. "Erin, Erin."

Thud, she hit a knee high rock protruded from the ground. Pain rippled down her shin, blood trickled into her boot.

Shayne stepped around the rock and pulled her finger back into place. "Erin, Erin?"

Fear burnt the back of Shayne's throat, scenario after horrific scenario played through her mind. "Please let her be okay. I beg you. Erin?"

I can't lose her, I can't bare it. I've failed her like I always have.

Shayne shook herself, determination probed her thoughts.

No, I can't give up on her. No matter what I will get her back. Oh crap and Zeke too.

Shayne limped and searched. "Erin, baby, it's mum. Answer me. Please."

Tears mixed with dirt and muddied her cheeks.

The smoke cleared, a massive crater now replaced the dense forest Shayne and Erin had hidden in.

The moisture in her mouth gummed in a ball. "Erin, please be okay. Please."

Around the crater uprooted and destroyed trees covered everything. No legs, or daughter stuck out to alert Shayne as to Erin's presence, bile burnt the back of Shayne's throat.

Through debris Shayne followed the edge of the crater and lifted tree trunks, throwing them out of the way. "Erin, Erin, Erin, Erin."

A few metres away a troupe of I.D.I.O.T.s stormed out of a mass of trees and in Shayne's direction.

Shayne dropped and wriggled under an upturned log.

This is just getting fucking ridiculous. Please don't let those fuckers find her before I do. Please Creator, dad, someone, anyone?

A woman soldier leaned over and inspected something under a mass of broken metal. "Hey over here. I see a leg moving."

No, no, no, no, no.

The woman slung her weapon over her shoulder, bent down and lifted chunks of metal. "Holy shit."

Two men joined her, the first looked over her shoulder. "It looks like one of the demigods? She's been here all along? Hell she and the other one probably organised the invasion. Igra was right."

The woman tipped her chin. "I'm not sure it's her, this one looks younger. Radio HQ and see what their orders are."

I've got to get her away from them. But how?

Chapter 15
Man On the Run
Pine Gap, New South Wales
Australia, Earth

Cold wind belted between vehicles in the transport depot, Annu crouched behind a truck and shivered. Ang stretched his calves and stumbled over his feet.

Annu slipped his legs under his butt and brought his wrists in front. "This is never happening again. I hate this flarking place."

When Ann moved the restraints beeped and a light flashed in the band.

Sirens bored into Annu's brain, search lights searched the complex, save and except where they hid—for now. Streams of boots passed, tension and precision underlined their military movements.

What did I ever do to deserve all this? I mean really?

Anticipation cramped Annu's intestines, and calculated the possible schuss of their two options; flark all or none and none left town. "This trip gets better and better. Any worse and I'll consider surrender."

Fatigue weighted Annu's muscles, cortisol replaced his blood.

I bet they're using real bullets now.

Ang examined his restraints an inch from his face. "Whatever these things are made of they're hard to break."

Annu placed a section of the band in his mouth and chewed. "Dammit. We need a tool or something. Until we get them off they hold us back and this spot won't stay undiscovered much longer."

Ang dragged the band back and forth along the bottom of the truck bed before him. "Agreed. What's the plan boss?"

Boss? That's a change up.

Annu chewed the other side, a minuscule amount of black substance came off.

Annu spat it onto the ground and worked around the spot. "Now everything's gone to shit I'm in charge?"

Ang placed a boot against the wheel, held a piece of metal between the bond and yanked. "Pretty much."

The bond stayed, Ang head butted metal on the truck's rear. "Shit."

Boots crunched on gravel at the depot's opening, Annu dropped and rolled under the truck bed.

With only a millimetre between his gut and the bottom, Ang wriggled beside him. "Much longer went quick. What'd you come up with?"

Annu shallow breathed.

Focus, stay in control.

"Steal this vehicle, get some weapons and my powers back, kill all these fuckers and we're out of here."

Lights flooded the transport depot, men loaded into the vehicles first in line and drove out of the bay.

Another group surveyed the large hanger on foot.

Shit, shit, shit, shit, shit. Think. Come on.

The truck above them roared to life, Annu crawled backwards, dust billowed in his mouth. "Well we're not stealing that one then."

Ang's feet shuffled next to Annu, engine noise dulled Ang's voice. "It's not like you could drive it anyway."

Annu grumbled to Ang's leg. "I'd have figured it out but it's a moot point."

Ang's boot scraped along the next truck bed. "I do agree with the blowing the living shit out of this, whatever it is, before we leave."

Annu wriggled under the next vehicle, it drove over him. "Oh I promise you, I flarking will."

Into a space between parked trucks Annu rolled to the rear of the building, Ang close behind him.

Annu scuttled out the opening and outside, meters ahead they hit a chain fence topped by barb wire and lasers.

This is way too much exercise for one day.

Annu caught his breath and rested on his haunches. "It looks like this covers the entire perimeter."

A couple of steps forwards Annu brushed against the fence, electricity shocked up his arms and into the restraints.

Annu's upper half seized, his mind and words rattled. "Holy flarking shit balls—"

Ang yanked Annu away and broke the connection.

The current ceased, the restraint's light went out; the clasp popped open.

Annu flicked it off and massaged his wrists. "Flarking hell yes."

Ang raised an eyebrow and cracked his neck. "I'm not looking forward to my turn."

Ang pursed his lips and touched the fence, his jaw rattled.

Annu grabbed Ang's shoulders and pulled.

Ang's restraints fell to the ground. "About time." He pointed to some woods. "We came in maybe two clicks in this direction and past four check points. If we follow the dirt road and stay hidden, we'll hit a main road or similar out of here."

Unease swallowed despair and Annu scratched his cheek. "How can you be sure? We we're blindfold."

Ang's shrug blocked out the light. "Ah because that's what I do. I'm military."

Ah duh. Idiot. I blame stress.

"Yeah all right. You're temporarily promoted to boss. Get us out of here."

Ang motioned forwards and crept adjacent to the perimeter. "First and foremost weapons and lots of them."

The wet grass tickled Annu's belly.

This is bat shit, crazy as flark.

"That's another problem to get around. Where is the armoury?"

Ang raised a finger, a smirk softened his harsh features. "Doesn't matter if we get some off those mother flankers."

Lights illuminated in and around their direction.

Ang paused and dropped. "Hit the ground and stay there."

The light swung back and forth close to Annu's feet, he sucked in his breath and turned his feet sideways, the light passed.

Annu mumbled into the grass. "My heart can't take much more of this."

Side to side, up and down, around and around, light brushed Ang's side and ran down the fence line, another circled back the other way.

Voice's cleared, the ground rumbled, boom, boom.

Shock waves rocked Annu's core and disrupted his equilibrium. "No, no, no, no."

Unsteady, Ang rose and dragged Annu off the ground around the building. "Stay with me. You're too big to carry far."

Annu swayed and grabbed Ang's shirt. "Whatever that is, is messing with everything."

Boom, boom, boom.

Annu struggled to stay upright, his leg's buckled.

Gods get us out of here, keep us safe. Give us something to fight with. I beg of you.

A troop of armed men barrelled around the same corner they'd turned.

Ang slammed Annu back against the wall.

Annu edged along its length attached to Ang.

This is humiliating.

At the end of the building Ang veered left, the fast move disorientated Annu, he held Ang tighter.

Ang boomed over the sirens. "Those shock things are proximity based. They don't affect me like you. That's one blessing."

Halfway along, they hit a doorway secured by a protection system, Ang jiggled the handle.

Annu rested against the door frame, a surplus of lactic acid surged. "We need to kill it stat. Whatever it does to me isn't good."

A light from above illuminated Annu, someone close yelled. "They're here."

Men in black invaded the area, dummy bullets thunked against the building and around them.

Plumes of thick white smoke blinded Annu, he lost contact with Ang.

A foreign emotion, vulnerability ruined Annu's courage and offer a different kind of torture. "Hey, where'd you go?"

Ang pushed him from the side and into a clear spot. "Run."

Annu tugged Ang by the sleeve. "Not without you."

Ang removed Annu's hold. "No you're more important, I'll hold them off. I should have realised that sooner."

Thunk, thunk, Annu ducked and missed a mass of shots desperate to call his chest home. "No, don't be stupid."

Ang collected a piece of debris from the ground and charged at a group coming straight for them. "Go."

Gunfire erupted, cordite sullied the air.

Ang froze, red patches flooded his chest; he fell forward and hit the dirt.

Annu fought between killing and saving energy for escape. "You bastards."

Go, don't make his death for no reason.

Annu stumbled sideways, tears streamed his face, his eyes burned. Breath held, he squinted against the smoke, and ran blind.

If this is what feeling helpless is like, it can go screw itself.

A metre ahead, arms grabbed Annu from behind.

Annu flipped around and brushed them off, another replaced the first.

Annu punched in each direction, his blows missed more than hit armour.

A dirt tornado formed from a craft above and replaced the smoke.

Boom, boom, boom.

Pain exploded and ricocheted across Annu's skull.

Boom, boom, boom.

Annu dropped, his chance at freedom ended before it began. Annu's being discombobulated, someone stretched his arms behind his back and secured two sets of restraints.

Chapter 16
Oh Begotten Child
Enki Island, Orion

A combination of grief, several hard metres, a shit tonne of Martians plus a set of bad shin splints later and Shayne lost sight of the I.D.I.O.T.s whom carried an unconscious Erin.

Shayne clutched herself and buried self-hatred. "Oh Gods, Oh Gods, oh Gods, oh Gods."

I can't get dressed these days without using powers. What I really need is an army. And not one made up of a sick middle aged demigod and an about-to-be shattered brother of the gods.

Shayne did a three sixty on the spot: trees, bigger trees, shrubs and even more trees, her chest heaved. "Which way do I go?" Desperation soaked her shirt. "What am I actually doing when I find them?"

Let's not forget I've got no freaking weapons. I might have come a long way since from when making toast seemed a difficult task, but Erin's right, this is well beyond my means.

High pitched voices broke Shayne's concentration, she froze.

Shit, shit, shit, fuck.

Boots crunched on sticks and marched in her way.

Shayne dove into ferns, crawled into a ball and dragged branches over. "If I can't see you, you can't see me."

What can I use to fight with?

No useful weapons revealed themselves out of thin air or any assistance scrambled out from leaves.

Fuck it. Story of my life.

A dozen odd Martians ran past her hiding place, their former undecipherable language became clearer the more Shayne heard it.

A deep voice broke above the roar of flying craft. "They went this way. Lieutenant Jakjak, you take two men and go after them. I'll lead the rest of the team back to the main compound. Intel tells us there's a strong room the leaders are in and where they'll bring the girl."

The only strong room on the island is in the Protectors Compound. We never considered needing it for its actual purpose. Hang in the baby, I'll come get you if it kills me.

The Martians separated into two groups and went in opposite directions.

Shayne's stomach fluttered, a tiny ripple followed. "Don't you start complaining. I don't have time for you."

Oh chocolate, where for out thou chocolate. I'll deny my father and refuse my name for your sweet, sweet goodness.

The coast cleared, Shayne wriggled out of the bushes and gained her bearings.

What's the quickest way there? Which way would the I.D.I.O.T.s go?

Oh yeah, I have no fucking idea exactly—let alone reach Erin before they get to the safe room.

The dense forest offered no suggestions, Shayne's thoughts muddled. "And I am where exactly? Where the fuck is north? Is it even called north here? What looks familiar?"

Shit, stop wasting time.

The possible direction of the I.D.I.O.T.s and half a group of Martians waited for Shayne's arrival.

Lack of food, sleep and sanity fuzzed Shayne's mind, fatigue shackled her legs. "I can't give up. I won't give up."

I.D.I.O.T.s and Martians yelled amongst laser blasts, burnt wood invaded the air.

Shayne wove around trees and stopped short of an open area. Where once native flora and fauna beautified the dark surrounds now an array of bodies covered everything.

Under shrubbery Shayne followed its perimeter, half her mind focused on now; the other half took a holiday.

One of the men who'd Shayne knew last carried Erin, covered a wound on his side with a hand and fired his weapon in the other in a circle.

A dozen Martians laser blasted the man, the shots dismembered an arm; he fell forward, blood covered his uniform.

Fuck. Now I can't ask him where Erin is. And it's not like I can go and interrupt or interrogate people. Fuck. Fuck. They're not stupid, Erin's obviously my kid.

Shots skimmed trees and thrust pity for dead I.D.I.O.T.s into the back of her mind. "No fucking way. If they hadn't taken over the island they wouldn't be in this position. Where is she? Why can't I see her or anyone else?"

Shayne's attention flipped between forwards and beside her.

At the last section of clearing evidence of the fray trailed deeper into the forest.

The other two I.D.I.O.T.s bodies laid battered, dead and bloody atop a pile of rocks sans Erin.

No body means hope.

Shayne vomited in her mouth, the three shabby wounded Martians who'd earlier followed said I.D.I.O.T.s argued between themselves metres away.

With them in her periphery, Shayne crept another pile of bodies.

One after the other she turned their faces to her—no dead Erin.

Keep it together. Do what I have to.

Shayne threw anything capable of hiding Erin out of the way. "Erin? Erin? Please Creator help me?"

Distracted by her plight, Shayne missed the arguing Martians arrival.

They blocked out the suns.

Shayne grabbed a large rock and climbed up her knees.

Low blood sugar reeled Shayne's brain, her knees wobbled. The hold on the rock loosened.

Passing out is not an option, so get over yourself. I can live without food a little longer.

Shayne clutched tighter, raised it and shallow breathed. "Back up, mother fuckers."

The taller Martian kept his weapons on Shayne.

The one on the left followed suit, the third appeared weapon free.

If I'm going to die like this I'm taking those purple grape looking mother fuckers with me.

"I fucking dare you to move closer." Shayne gritted her teeth and snarled. "Back the fuck up. I'm not afraid to throw this. Who's got my daughter?"

Shayne's arm trembled, the rock weighed more each second.

Show no fear.

A taller, Barney-coloured version of the 'My Favourite Martian' showed no emotion. "You don't look like the others."

A sour taste filled Shayne's mouth. "Well, duh dickhead. Who's got my daughter and why are you doing this to us?"

MFM sneered and spat the words. "You're one of the Demigods everyone's looking for aren't you? You're certainly not the godly adversary we'd expected."

Everywhere I fucking go people give me shit.

"Mmm. I guess we're all disappointed today. If you're going to shoot me then do it, I'm too fucking tired for chit chat."

He waved the weapon side to side. "Shut up. Put down the rock and come with us."

Once surrender offered release, now it promised regret and failure.

Fuck this, fuck you and fuck them too. And the horses they rode in on. Or ships.

"No. You'll have to shoot me first."

The MFM wannabes expression darkened, his eyes slits. "As you—"

The smaller Martian to MFMWB's right launched at MFMWB and tackled him to the ground.

The other Martians watched open mouthed, their weapons dangled.

Shayne hurled the rock at one in front of her. "Take that arsehole."

Crack, it hit him between the eyes.

Gob smacked, Shayne blinked. "Goddamn. If I'd have tried doing that it wouldn't have happened."

The wounded Martian dropped the weapon; a hand covered and stemmed the blood flow.

Behind him, two Martians fought, the others switched their attention.

They apparently hate each other too. What's with these guys? Are they constipated or hangry?

Shayne collected a gun and hobbled into the forest with no clear plan of action.

Muscles ached in places Shayne forgot existed. "Erin? Erin it's mum, answer me."

Shayne stumbled over upturned tree roots and face planted the ground.

A fresh level of agony consumed her; Shayne inhaled dirt, gravel stuck into her chin.

All the suppressed emotion and lack of assistance pummelled her.

Shayne rolled onto her side and allowed sorrow its pleasure. Sobs wracked her chest and intensified the pain in each sore spot. Snot covered the places tears missed.

A tap on her shoulder flipped Shayne from depressed to terrified. She grabbed the gun and whirled around, her head spun. "Shit."

Shayne regained equilibrium, one of the Martian from the fight stood over her, a weapon stuck onto his hip. He offered his hand.

Shayne mustered courage and aimed at his head. "What the fuck do you want?"

Chapter 17
Incarcerated Hell
Pine Gap, New South Wales, Australia

Restrained and immobile, military men carried an Annu kebab into a hanger-sized warehouse. Annu wriggled and struggled to no avail, he'd lost all control.

Motors whirred, alarms beeped and a female voice crackled out of speakers.

Passed small transport vehicles and scientific equipment stations, they carried Annu onto an elevator, his brain swam, his equilibrium shook.

The men placed Annu on the floor, the carriage dropped, his guts went with it.

They descended lower and lower, Annu's mind raced.

This is not good. How far down are we going? What is this thing?

The box shuddered and stopped, doors clambered opened.

Annu's breath shallowed, the air thinned, the temperature cooled. "Where are we?"

Is there any point in praying anymore? No one listens or cares unless they get something out of it too.

The men walked silent into an entryway, unadorned except for a solid, steel door at the end.

Annu kicked and yanked. "Let me go, flark you."

A man in front waved at a black object hanging from the ceiling; a light flashed, a beep rang in Annu's ears, the door opened.

Am I invisible?

"Hey. Stop this before it goes too far."

The men paused, electric shocks rocked his body, Annu seized and jolted.

This cannot get worse. Even my brain hurts.

The current ceased, they carried him through the doors and entered an underground complex, sectioned by make-shift walls and filled with armed staff. Every hundred metres the group stopped at a checkpoint.

I'm all alone here with nothing on my side. What if this is the end for me? If this underground hell is the place of my death, do I not deserve a happy life with Shayne? What did I do wrong?

At the last checkpoint, they travelled down a hall and passed room after sealed room. Annu's piece of mind wobbled with each step forwards.

No. Get a grip. Think logically. If there's a way in, there's a way out too. I can't give up yet.

Sterile and nondescript, the building and people left no impression and suggested no escape route other than the carriage.

Antiseptic tainted the air; the fluorescent lights burned Annu's eyes. The noise in his head muffled external sound.

They entered a section devised of clear prison cells a short distance up.

Screw this.

Annu struggled against the bonds.

Zap. Another jolt of electricity tightened his balls and puckered his butthole.

Dingle's gravelled tone reminded Annu of his presence. "Keep still or I turn it all the way up."

I'd rather you didn't. I may never get them back down again.

Annu's tongue thick and numb, he slurred. "When I get out of here, you're the first I kill."

Amusement coveted Dingle's tone. "Is that right?"

A sharp jab to the left arm and warm liquid spread across Annu's chest, whatever they'd injected into him altered his senses and ruptured the fabric around his world.

Coherence blurred and at least removed Annu's care factor. "This is some good shit."

Annu stopped going forwards and swung sideways, a solid surface underneath him replaced the air, the men blurred.

A room rotated around him, four men blended into one, Annu waded amongst fog.

Pressure released from wrists and ankles, Annu slumped onto his side, what he laid on shook. "Help...I'm lost. Shayne, Ang."

People shifted, their faces mashed together, their movements staggered.

Someone prodded Annu's forearm and clicked fingers, the same woman from the truck spoke. "Doctor, please record, pupils reactive and dilated. There's bruising and abrasions from prior altercations which didn't occur in Section 7G. Nothing new there but also nothing broken. Visually the skin appears of human elasticity and make up. Naturally we'll require scientific testing and documented results."

Warm fingers pressed against Annu's neck and cheek.

"Pulse fast and consistent. Have someone check it every couple of hours. I don't want to lose one of the best specimens we've had with such similarity to us. Amazing."

Worms crawled under Annu's flesh and wriggled into his brain. Lights danced behind his eyes, he tasted rotten strawberries and defeat.

A male leaned over Annu. "You'll be all right. Don't try and fight, it's useless. You'll only get hurt. I promise it will be over soon. Rest now and this will pass."

Where am I? How, how did I get here? "Over? Please, let me go."

The woman sounded near, yet distant. "For God's sake. Must you always placate them? It's unnecessary and creates extra problems."

The man scoffed and shuffled around the bed. "You don't have to treat them like animals, Janet."

Their words dismembered, bounced around the room and tumbled along the edges of Annu's brain. "Help…me…Janet."

The woman growled, her tone sharpened. "Now see what you've done. It knows my name. Thanks, Tony."

Annu grabbed at the woman's coat. "Janet, Tony, please get me out of here."

Her, he and the others disappeared in a blur of colours.

Annu's tongue stuck to the roof of his mouth, he clutched the side of the bed and rode the next ebb of drugs effects.

I've got to…do something…

Time became intangible, transient, impossible to pin down. Seconds, minutes and hours blended together in an incompressible mess. Objects on the opposite side of the room appeared kilometres away; an identical bed, a metal toilet and sink shielded by a waist height metal protrusion and a drain hole in the floor.

Annu focused on details, they drifted further away. "Let me out."

Sweat teamed down Annu's back and chest. He swallowed bile, his mouth filled with saliva.

Annu slipped off the bed onto the floor and lay on tiles. The cold allowed some clarity.

What do they want with me? How will I get out of here? I need help.

Shivers racked his body, eyes closed; Annu placed his mouth on the edge of the drain.

Armed and helmeted men, the occasional lab coated or full suited person occupied the hall outside the room at irregular intervals.

When it allowed, Annu rolled in the other directions; on the right, colours flashed, on occasion a figure hovered as if it watched him.

There're others, not just me. How long have they been here?

A pair of legs stopped outside the door, a hatch dropped open.

Annu licked his lips and cleared his throat. "Where am I? Who are you people? You can't keep me here."

They pushed a tray into the hatch, closed it on their side and walked off.

The thought of food sickened Annu. If he didn't move, his mind cleared in increments yet his body lingered.

Each physical action created a ripple effect and exploded along the rest of him.

Annu ignored bodily mayhem and slithered to the door. Perched on his elbows, he banged on the glass.

Electricity ripped through his arm and down his body. Annu seized on the floor, his brain vibrated. Annu relived his fourth birthday and the time Irica brought him his horse Johnny.

Chapter 18
Mother Ship Star Fuckers
Enki Island, Orion

Shayne waved the gun side to side and rose. "Get the fuck away from me you purple weirdo."

The being thrust his hands in the air. "I don't want to hurt you. I want to help you or you help me more so."

Another pile of shit I find myself in.

"Why the fuck would you help me or I help you?"

Why would anyone help me?

His calm demeanour eased Shayne's tension—a fraction. "My name's Jakjak. Please don't be scared. I'm not like the others same as you. I never wanted to come here and fight. I couldn't take anymore and told my superior officer what I thought. It didn't go well. They're after me."

"I don't care. Fuck off. I've got my daughter to find." Shayne's soul tore, her maternal confidence plummeted.

Get it together, this is my new motto.

"I don't care about your name or anything else right now. Where's my daughter or stepson? Did you see them? Do you have them?" Shayne lifted the gun and walked around him. "Answer me, Jackie."

He turned around with his hands raised. "After the ambush I saw a girl who looks like you run into the woods. I lost sight of her, and I didn't see her on the way to you."

Erin's recent alive status delivered a modicum of relief. "Oh fuck, shit, fuck.This is a huge forest. As long as she hasn't been caught again she could be anywhere."

Mum's coming kiddo.

Shayne lowered the weapon and her shoulders. "Thanks for ah, not being a dick and trying to kill me. Good luck to you I'm out of here."

Shayne strode off in the opposite direction, her mind a flurry.

I've lost two kids and a fucking fiancee but I'll get one kid back. How does one exactly achieve these things? I'm a god damned professional screw up. Literally.

Her finger remained close to the gun's trigger in her pocket. "I might take up Ninja training after all this. Being sneaky will come in handy."

Jackie jogged up beside her and tugged her sleeve. "Wait, you can't leave me here alone."

Shayne shrugged and brushed him off. "Ah, yes I can. Go away. I'm not a fucking refugee camp and I've managed alone so far and if I can do that you'll be fine."

Jackie continued shadowing her. "I've got no where to go. Now I've deserted my own people want me dead. I don't know this planet. By the look of it you need all the help you can get."

Shayne kicked a tuft of grass and chewed her lower lip.

I can't in good conscious leave him alone but for fuck's sake. Conscious I fucking hate you.

"Oh fuck, shit, fine, whatever. But you take care of yourself. I've got other things to worry about."

Jackie took one step to Shayne's six. "This fuck shit you say a lot, is he your god?"

A combination of admonishment and amusement tickled Shayne.

Well I might start now. He might actually answer me.

"Yes it is. But he's only mine and fickle as all fuck."

Lightning crackled across the sky, clouds rumbled.

Okay, okay. I'm just kidding. Relax.

Jackie's nod filled Shayne with shame. "Oh, okay."

A sense of doom preceded the buzz of Shayne's pocket; the communicator trembled in her hand.

Jacob appeared disheveled on screen. "Your Goddessness. You've taken so long. What's happened? I see the Counsel's men in the distance and I'm almost out of medication."

Shayne's chest tightened, her heart skipped. "Jesus Jacob. I, ah,"

I'd kind of forgotten about you. Fuck. And your home town.

"I got waylaid. I've lost my daughter Erin, and Zeke. I don't know where they are and I'm not going or doing anything else until I've got them back. I'm sorry. I just can't get there yet."

Jacob's expression dropped, his chest heaved. "I'm sorry for being selfish. Don't worry about coming to get me. I'll take care of myself, you have more important things to worry about, like saving Orion, and I'll make my way to you somehow."

Why me? This is unfair. Why do I get stuck with all the hard stuff? Annu's revelling in my house while I'm suffering. "Fuck, fuck, fucking fuck. Jacob I don't need this guilt trip right now. I have to make sure the kids are okay and I've got no idea where they are. If I make it there I'll try and get your medication. I'm sorry, I can't waste time."

"If only you listened to me more." Jacob looked around Shayne and frowned. "Who's besides you? It looks like one of those alien things. Oh Gods, are you alright?"

The forest thickened the nearer the compound's direction, Shayne's calves burned. "Apparently he's not like the others and another short story I don't want to go into at the moment. Either way I'll be around somewhere finding my kids. You'll have to tough it out alone unless by someone chance you find me."

Military PFDs chased and fired upon two Martian ships. One of the Martian ships exploded and scattered the woods. Burnt metal sullied the air.

Jacob ducked at the subsequent noise above him. "I understand your desire to find your children but in the meantime what about this war? The entire island is consumed by enemy. I can only imagine what the rest of the planet is like. There's potential for thousands to be killed while you're out looking for two people. It's precious time you don't have."

Guilt sliced Shayne across the chest and flushed her cheeks.

Okay ouch. I know he's right but I can't do the whole greater good for the greater number thing. I've let my kids down too many times. And Okay now how can I not tell him and or how can I tell him without looking like a huge bitch?

Shayne's shirt hem caught in a mass of thorns, she tugged it free, the communicator wobbled.

It's never a good time but first he needs to remember who's the boss here.

"Jacob, there's something I need to tell you in a moment. However, first of all I'm not discussing my anti-end of war time schedule with you. This is my call not yours."

Jacob placed a hand on his chest and exuded disappointment. "I beg you to reconsider your priorities. Only you can save the people, if you wish. Time is of the essence. It's your duty to the planet and the galaxies to stop this and bring peace between planets."

What the fuck do I do? Screw this shit.

"Look, give me a minute here. You want me to forget about my kids until later on, during which time they could get killed, maimed or worse, get my powers back without getting caught or dead and save people who don't know about me yet from a government who tried to get rid of me or us in the first place?"

Jacob licked his lips and jabbed a finger. "Well, yes, that's about it. You have it within you to succeed; this is your destiny and all. You'd be better prepared if you practised some organisation."

Fuck you Jacob, fuck you. Why are you always right? I wish you weren't even here sometimes. Now if I'm going to suffer so are you.

Venom tainted Shayne's tongue "You're home—"

Shayne's pesky conscious interjected and slapped her in the face.

Not the time nor for the right reason.

"You're right. I'm sorry. I'll be in touch."

Call ended Shayne and returned the comm to her pocket.

Jackie cleared his throat and straightened. "We aren't going to find your children yet?"

Shayne jumped.

Fuck I forget you were here. I've really got to focus.

"As much as I hate myself no. He's right. I'll just magically save all those innocent people and pray it works out in the end."

The most terrible-worst-sucky-parent of the century award goes to drum roll please...me, fucking me again. Dear FuckShit who art in heaven allowed by thy name.

The clouds grumbled, the ground shook. Shayne curled into herself. "All right, all right. Sorry."

One of these days my mouth or brain will be the death of me. *She faced Jackie.*

"So tell me exactly what you're people want and I'll work on it."

Chapter 19
Foiled Again
DSI Facility, Pine Gap
New South Wales, Australia, Earth

Three failed escape attempts, several shocks and a migraine later Annu inspected the almost invisible plastic-type seal between the walls and the floor. He probed the edges, zap, zap, zap.

Annu trembled, the hair singed off his fingers. "For flark's sake."

The plastic fork Annu saved from breakfast broke a tine. He used the other three to stab at the slight rubber seal in the corner.

The blue bird being next door rested against the glass and watched Annu and often chirped.

A minute piece of the seal broke off and left an equal sized hole behind. "Yes albeit a small success I'll take it."

Back hunched, Annu manoeuvred into a better position and dug at the hole; the middle tine snapped off and stuck into the seal. "This here is some bull—shit. I'm the great demigod Annu and I'm on the flarking floor scraping off crap with crap."

The bird-being tapped the glass.

A voice tickled the back of Annu's mind.

'You are Annu, son of En ah—'

The being paused.

'Ann?'

It's female. Why did she pause before my mother's name and how does she know us?

Annu's interest piqued, he tapped the fork on the floor.

"How do you know who I am and who my mother is? Do you know my father? Who are you?'

'I'm Ankor of the Blue Sphere Beings and the head of The Universal Peace Alliance. We are among the oldest in the galaxy and protect precious or dangerous artefacts among other things. Your appearance here must mean you're aware of our plight. Rejoice you'll save us all and join our group."

No pressure or anything but can you save all of us? Oh and by the way it's impossible to get out of here but I'm sure you'll figure that out too.

Annu rested against the wall, his brain ached.

And another problem. For flark's sake.

"Ah no I wasn't aware of this place until now and I'm here because of a bad sales decision my fiancé made. My presence here is a complete accident or a coincidence."

Ankor flapped wings on her back and hovered above the floor, excitement showed in her movements.

'There's no such thing as accidents or coincidence. You of all beings should understand that. Our blessed Enki, the Creator would have sent you here for mission or lesson. Often both. Where's Shayne's cell?"

Tight muscles grabbed across his shoulders, Annu rolled them. "Too bad if that's the case. Shayne's stuck on Orion. Safe I hope."

"Oh dear. You're stronger together. Perhaps this is the lesson to go along with the mission. Enki never fails."

Other people maybe. I'm too old to learn.

"I've never heard of the Creator referred to as Enki. I guess it explains my home's name." Annu stretched his legs in front. For the first time since his arrival a moment of companionship equalled sanity. "It doesn't explain how you know about me though."

Ankor nodded and returned to the ground.

'Yes Enki is the creator God. The older inhabited planets in the galaxy all know of your mother, you and the Annunaki all along. After ascension and the gateways re-opened all know about you. My kind are linked the same way I'm communicating with

you. Distance and time is no barrier. I then prayed to Enki for your help and here you are.'

And there you go. The bastards can't win every round. They shouldn't underestimate the power of good.

For everyone else but me of course.

Annu's brain ached, he switched forms of communication. "Irica told us a few things about the Annunaki, my mother and Shamesh but not much else. Now Ann's in a spiritual retreat of sorts after the success. It's difficult to communicate with her there unless it's urgent. Nor for general conversation."

Ankor shuffled between her feet.

'There's much more to the story than Irica knew. And one day it will affect you.'

Hasn't it already?

Annu held his breath and leaned closer. "Do tell."

A tentative expression crossed her face. *'Perhaps in—'*

The clunk of boots down the hallway cut her off and raised Annu's blood pressure. "Oh for flark's sake. We'll finish our chat later."

I need a drink, or six. No, bottles and bottles.

Annu slipped the fork into his pocket and lunged onto the bed.

Don't come in here, please don't come in here.

Annu's neighbour flitted, her demeanour changed from peaceful to agitated.

Guards strode passed Annu's cell and stopped at Ankor's door, it slid open, four guards and two doctors entered. Two guards remained outside the doorway, the other guards and the doctors went for Ankor.

Annu pounced off the bed and strode to the adjoined wall. 'Hell I didn't meant to take her."

Two male guards grabbed Ankor and held her down, one of the doctors, a female, removed a syringe from her lab coat.

Annu's knocks on the glass rippled along the wall. "Hey, you fuckers. Leave her alone."

Funny how the only Earth word I use on a regular basis is a curse.

Ankor flailed, the female doctor jabbed the syringe into Ankor's shoulder.

Annu kicked the glass, a small fracture appeared; the guards at the doorway turned to Annu's cell.

Ankor went limp; one of the guards scooped her off the bed, her arm dangled down his thigh.

Bang, bang, bang, kick after kick, the crack grew.

A growl erupted from deep within Annu. "I said let her go or I slaughter every one of you."

An alarm shrilled, beings in other cells roused. Screeches and wails instead of the normal quiet urged Annu on.

Despite Annu's ardour, the guard holding Ankor carried her out of the room.

"Shit." Bang, bang, bang. "I'm flarking coming for every one of you. I'm going to rip you to pieces."

The hallway guards with raised their weapons and burst into Annu's cell.

Sharp pain exploded along Annu's spine, volts of electricity coursed, Annu dropped, fell face first and flopped around. Teeth gritted, his jaw rattled. Annu dragged himself towards the open door.

Boom, boom, boom, a suppression weapon activated down the hallway reverberated his entire being.

Annu's thoughts scattered, his mind wobbled, he collapsed. *I, I, I.*

Someone shuffled around him, a jab to the arm and ambient noise dulled. Annu's will deteriorated; oblivion welcomed him.

Chapter 20
In the Woods Today is a Huge Surprise and It's Not Teddy Bears
Enki Island, Orion

An explosion separated Erin from Shayne, an ambush gave Erin her freedom and separated her from sanity. Deep in woods her visit to Orion lacked the freedom and fun she preferred on holidays or being away from home.

"I can't believe I got away. It's not as hard as I thought."
Erin rubbed her arms and shivered; night fell over the forest and transformed it from slightly creepy to downright terrifying. "Maybe."

Unusual animal sounds combined with the dark scared Erin and worse still the dappled moonlight intensified the scariness.

At some point, Erin had gotten turned around and headed in a different direction.

Oh God, oh God, Oh God. What am I going to do?

"I wonder if it's too late to join the Girl Guides?"

Erin's chest heaved, her breath quickened, tears filled her eyes.

I'm alone, scared, want to go home and I want my mum. Maybe I shouldn't have escaped those huge men. Where's the Jacob man hiding? Is it nearby?

An animal shrieked from the trees, leaves and branches fell to the ground.

Erin gulped in air, her mind fogged, fear lumped onto her back.

What the h is that?

In dense bush, the bottoms of Erin's pants soaked up evening dew, a chill settled into her bones. Erin paused and rolled the hem up, something flashed between trees on her left.

Where's Shayne when I need her? As usual not here.

Anger replaced fear. Erin rubbed her hands behind a tree trunk. "Okay, okay, okay. Calm down. It's my imagination and so far I'm not dying out here. God damned Shayne. This is all her fault. Why does she have to make everyone so mad? Is she looking for me? Ha. As if. Like she could save me."

Which leaves no-one who'll help.

Memories of Erin's teenage years returned. Shayne's explanations hadn't satisfied Erin's maternal standards.

Why doesn't she act like it? Am I such a terrible child? I swear I am not going to be like her when I'm older. I'm never leaving my kids and most of all I'm not nuts. Crazy better not be hereditary.

A peek around the trunk revealed no creature about to pounce. Leaves and sticks crunched, movement between trees soared Erin's anxiety into the stratosphere. Lack of light ruined a definitive cause.

Footsteps a metre behind peeled Erin off the trunk and into a run. Over rocks and around trees, Erin avoided unknown nature.

A male's voice trailed behind her. "Hey, you. Stop. I'm—"

Erin swallowed vomit and groped her way into denser forest.

Clunk, Erin connected with a tree branch protruding from a fallen tree, she hurtled forwards, her left side banged into the ground, and pain erupted along her body. Each breath scratched across her ribs and dragged out her oesophagus.

Tears trickled down Erin's face, blood from her knee seeped soaked her pants. "Oh God, oh God, oh God."

Erin slowed her breath and bit her bottom lip.

I'm okay, I'm okay, I'm okay.

Rolled onto her back, pain stopped her halfway. "Maybe not yet."

A young male waved over the fallen log. "Hello there. Are you all right?"

Erin's scream deafened her thoughts, despite pain she scrambled away on her hands and butt. "Get away from me."

He stepped over the log with room to spare and raised a palm. "It's alright. Shhh, they'll hear you. Listen I'm not one of those government people. I'm Zeke, Annu's my ah—biological father."

The similarities apparent, Erin regained composure and smoothed down her shit. "You're Zeke? Then why are you following and scaring the heck out of me?"

Zeke squatted and still towered over her. "I noticed you weren't with Shayne anymore. She's a self-imposed bad luck beacon and a massive pain in my arse. You're Erin right? You look like her and she's talked about you a lot. I'm okay on my own but by the look of it you aren't. Company sounds good to me."

Zeke's insults raised Erin's hackles, hidden parental indignation burst forth. "Yes, I'm Erin but how dare you speak about Sh, mu, ma, whatever like that? You clearly don't really know her or what she's experienced. Like right now she's been kicked out of her home with people wanting to kill her but still searched for you."

Where did that come from? I can say what I like about her but no one else can? Perhaps I should be more mature about all this. Is this what crazy feels like?

Zeke straightened his back, admonishment in his tone. "Fair enough. It wasn't the best way to start. I'm sorry. I guess we have different relationships with her. Maybe you're the miracle, and I should give her a break. You are almost an exact younger version anyway, and you act just like her."

Oh he didn't say that.

Erin rolled on her butt, the ache travelled down her legs. "And you look like your father. Anyway, are you going to help me up or keep insulting me?"

"Yeah, sorry. I guess you get that." Zeke reached down, slipped an arm under Erin and lifted her off the ground. "Are you hungry?"

Erin's energy plummeted, fatigue thickened her thoughts.

Bent over, Erin sucked in air. "I think, I think so."

Erin's leg gave way; Zeke grabbed her under the shoulders and held her weight.

No, no, no. Stop. Come on now.

Homeostasis waited disjointed, Erin licked her lips. "Food may upgrade you from annoyance to friend. Got any?"

Zeke pulled a couple of silver packets from his pocket and handed one over. "Here, it will help a bit."

Two bites and the whooziness abated. "Thank you. That's better. So Zeke, what now?"

Wait, what if he doesn't want me to go with him?

"You are staying with me right? Please don't leave me out here all alone?"

Zeke's frown lined a smooth forehead. "No, of course not. I'd never do that. It's definitely an extreme way of getting to know each other before we're legal siblings."

Holy cookies. I didn't think of that.

"I guess you're right. I've, we've got an older brother and there's room for one more."

Zeke slipped his arm around her waist and helped her walk. "Sounds good. I hope he feels the same. I'm an only child and my mother's sick."

I can't imagine not having Ryan.

"I'm sorry. I hope she'll be all right."

"Me too but doctors aren't sure if she'll make it."

As much as Shayne drives me nuts I wouldn't ever want her to die.

"I don't know what else to say except, I'm sorry."

Zeke's presence brightened the forest and lessened loneliness. "It's okay. I could do worse than Annu and Shayne. Do you have any powers?"

Relief from solitude comforted Erin, she released a deep breath. "Sort of but they're not working at the moment.

"Oh. Lucky you. I can read the thick book of their's and understand it but I hardly think that will help. Shayne hasn't mentioned any of your abilities."

"She doesn't know yet. How come they haven't found you? It's a bit unfair, I've been kidnapped and the rest of the night's not looking good."

Zeke took one step to Erin's five. "I've discovered when I concentrate on not being seen, they go past me. So far, anyway."

"That sounds very much like a power to me."

"Any chance you got the luck Shayne missed?"

Erin caught up with Zeke. "I don't think so."

Zeke shrugged and smiled, the resemblance to Annu grew. "Never mind. Let's find someplace to lay low for a while. It's only a matter of time before—"

A bright light illuminated the forest, Erin squinted, her eyes slowly adjusted.

Zeke leaned to Erin's ear level and guided them in the opposite direction. "Flarking hell. I've been talking to you and not paying attention."

Please don't see us. Please, please, please.

Erin's left leg dragged, over work added twenty pounds per step.

Indecipherable yells came from the light's direction, followed by movement headed in their direction.

Erin massaged her thigh, Zeke directed from tree to tree. The noise and light came closer.

Zeke pushed Erin away and into some ferns. He reached for her arm too late—armed purple beings surrounded Erin and Zeke.

Zeke shoved her behind him. "Please, don't shoot."

Erin's blood cooled, fear gripped her chest. "This is not a good way to get to know each other."

Chapter 21
Karma's a Nasty Bitch
Enki Island, Orion

No time to figure something about before these bastards find me and I've got no collateral. Jackie said they want proof of Shamman's death and what else?

Whizz, boom, boom, boom.

A barrage of explosions disintegrated Shayne's peace of mind and concentration.

Shayne dove into shrubbery. "For fuck's sake. This shit is ridiculous."

A paste formed on her tongue, her belly growled. "What else does Her Royal Fuckness want?"

Jackie brushed leaves off and wriggled a finger in his ear. "What?"

Why do I have him with me again? Oh yeah, I didn't want to be alone.

"What—else—does—your—Queenie—fucking—want?"

Jackie's sigh scraped along Shayne's nerves. "Shamesh damaged Mars' atmosphere some time ago and we've lived underground. When the gateways reopened the Queen heard of his death and with it a way to return us to our former glory. She declared we'd gather Orion's resources which includes the Demigods and anything else she desires. She wants Mars fixed and doesn't care how that happens or who dies for it."

Shayne's blood pressure soared, her skull tightened and squeezed her brain.

I hate my life. I really do. Erin is never going to forgive me. It's going to be all my fault. Isn't it?

"Well for fuck's sake I'm giving myself or Orion up to her. The past is the past. And I can't make up a cardboard cutout of Annu anyway. Geez."

Jackie raised his monobrow and stood. "I'm a little confused as to what response you expect from me?"

Shayne suppressed a scream and clenched her fist, a craft above exploded, debris showered the forest. "Help me out here." She passed trees, trees and fucking more trees.

Would Queenie really tell if Annu wasn't real? No guaranteeing she'd leave anyway.

"How good's her eye sight?"

Jackie jogged, long feet slapped the ground. "Help in what way? Her eyesight's impeccable of course."

Fuck it. Won't someone cut me some slack? Think, think. I'm trying but it's not really my strong suit. I should really work on that.

"Alright plan, come at me. Anytime now."

Or now. Hello?

Jackie escalated to the highest level of dickheadedness. "Do you have any idea where your children are?"

He's still talking? For God's sake.

"Shh, I'm thinking."

How can I get the resources she needs without giving myself up? With no powers I'm a sitting duck and so's the rest of Orion.

A brilliant idea rattled her brain jar.

Hey wait a minute.

They left the shelter of the last forest and delved into the open area kilometres from the last scroll mound.

Shayne jumped and clapped. "Ah ha. I've got it."

Jackie paused mid stride and clutched his chest. "I'm positive you didn't get it from me."

Is it possible he's more annoying than I am?

Keep it in, there's enough other people to kill, legitimately.

Shayne's eye twitched. 'Grrrr. Listen. After I've got the kids, she's got no idea what Annu looks like, so we'll take an I.D.I.O.T. hostage, steal a ship, go to Yebu, and get fucking Queenie to see sense. I'm totally likeable. Won over by my charm she brings us back to the island and the I.D.I.O.T.s are at my mercy. I get my powers back and add creating resources to our list. Actually my powers are most important but I can't get them first. Fuck shit yeah this can work."

Jackie stepped out of the way of a massive dragonfly and almost hit Shayne's side. "Who's the 'we and us' here?"

Shayne moved out of his way, stumbled over a rock and bit her tongue.

Mother fucker.

"Ouch. That's your fault jackarse. The 'we' is you and me dickhead. You said you wanted to help or at least pay your way."

Jackie stayed an inch from Shayne. "I don't recall saying anything like that and I'm still a little confused about my role in all this."

I know how to get you to move.

Shayne mustered a fart and failed.

Instead, Shayne burped and a trickle of pee ran down her leg.

Great, just great. Never mind. I've got a solid plan now. It's doable. Hell, I've done worse stuff and made it out alive and better for it.

Shayne turned and patted herself dry. "Actually you know what, I can't take your negativity anymore. Either support me or you're alone again, okay? Actually forget it, I'll steal the damned ship myself and actually why did I ever let you tag along with me?"

I'm not sure he deserves company anyway.

Jackie slouched and dropped a few steps behind. "I'm sorry. I should be more help. I'm just useless. No good for anything. They're justified in killing me."

Who's a drama fucking queen today? Geez.

Shayne straightened her pants and jabbed at him. "Oh, for God's sake. Do you need a tampon for your mangina? If anyone's going to feel sorry for themselves it's me. Get over yourself."

A pre-warn to pee alerted Shayne, she clenched her inner thighs.

Of all the freaking times. Think of something else, like chocolate or puppy dogs. Now that makes me miss Bear. Rosie will take good care of him until I can bring him here.

In dried grass Shayne snaked the long way around close to the ground.

Rocks and sticks dug into her knees, fatigue lusted for Shayne.

Shayne clung by a thread and dragged herself along it. "I do kind of feel a little better now I've worked something out without my powers. First plane we see, we're stealing it. It makes searching much easier too. How awesome am I?"

Jackie swatted bugs from his face. "Ah very?"

Shayne ate them.

No point wasting nutrients.

"Damned straight."

Shayne selected a grasshopper, chewed it in half, peeked above the top of the grass and scooted for a group of rocks metres away.

Her bladder tingled harder; Shayne squeezed and quickened her crawl." As a demigoddess surely menial bodily functions disappeared but no."

At the first rock, Shayne scrambled behind it and made room for Jackie.

Breath caught, Shayne gained her bearings. "If I'm right and it does happen occasionally, just over that hill there is where we're some craft landed earlier."

Jackie's two Adam's apples jiggled. "It may as well be a million miles away with so many enemies on the island."

Shayne clicked her tongue and perched onto her knees. "There's that negativity again." She tugged his sleeve and pointed. "Let's go."

With Jackie a bee's dick away, Shayne crept around a corner and into the front of the Martian she'd hit with the rock, like forever ago.

His shock at seeing Shayne equalled hers.

Oh fuck me sideways and call me Sally.

Shayne walked backwards into Jackie and tumbled over his legs. She landed on the ground with a thud, three weapons aimed at her.

I shouldn't joke, it will probably happen.

A check for the weapon in Shayne's pocket emphasised her lack of attention.

It must have fallen out.

"Oh shit."

Jackie cowered into her back. "We might need God fuckshit for this one."

Shayne's maniacal laugh billowed around the area, her bladder relieved itself and she didn't care.

At least I don't need to pee anymore.

Chapter 22
Mixed Messages
Pine Gap, New South Wales, Australia, Earth

On the bed in a different iron cladded cell, Annu lost count of how long he'd spent on Earth. Hours and days mere concepts woven together by a drug induced hangover.

The light dulled vision, a plastic aroma tainted Annu's taste buds.

Mother flarkers are going to pay when I find a way out of here. Where is Ankor? I want to know about my mother and anything else she knows about my family.

Annu kicked dints into the rear wall, a second later the metal popped and un-dented.

Irritation crawled under his skin. "Flarking hell. Nothing works."

Annu rose and shoved the bed across the room; it hit the opposite side and bounced back a metre.

Flutter, flutter, flutter.

Ankor's presence tickled his mind and abated loneliness. *'I'm sorry they moved you because of me. Thank you greatly for trying. No one's done that before.'*

In the middle of the room Annu rested against the steel bed frame.

'I accomplished nothing. They still hurt you and removed me. The only thing I've done is increased the complications to my escape.'

Like a humming bird, Ankor buzzed along his brain. *'Do not doubt yourself. This is only the beginning. You've brought me*

and all the others a chance to get out for the first time. I know
you can do this.'

Responsibility lumped more weight onto Annu.

*Everywhere I go beings need me and they're increasing in
numbers. I must stay focused on the bigger picture. Like not
dying here.*

'I pray you're right.'

*Should I push my luck a little? Why not? I've got nothing to
lose. Start small and work up.*

*'You mentioned there's more to the Annunaki story than Irica
knew. Why is that? How is it relevant?'*

Hesitation flashed through Annu's thoughts. *'It will distract
you.'*

The bed rail bit into his lower back, he repositioned. *'Please.
I'm tired of people—or whoever thinking they know what's right
for me and you're the closest I've come to finding out something.
Is it my father? Do you know him?'* A moment passed, Annu rose
and paced around the bed. *'You do don't you? Ankor? Please?'*

Hesitation accompanied her words. *'Yes but I, I know. It, it
isn't relevant to your current mission and may detract you.
There's also larger reasons you don't know about some things.'*

Anger broke the mental connection, Annu grabbed the bed
rung into a ball. "Please stop hedging. I don't mean to be rude, but
either tell me or don't. But stop dragging it out."

*'I apologise and I understand your yearning and wanting to
know. I've seen you're a good man Annu but I can't detract you
from your current mission and believe me such information will
do just that. I'm a foolish woman who shouldn't have said
anything at all.'*

*It's like talking to Irica back when she refused to tell me
anything. What's going on?*

"That's even more frustrating than telling me nothing. How
else am I meant to know if no one tells me?"

'I'm sorry. When right I or someone will.'

I'm so close to the truth and I deserve to know.

Annu's conscience intervened.

No, she's right. That's all I'm focusing on. Damn it.

"What can you tell me then?"

'Shamesh and the Annunaki didn't act under the Creator, Enki's instruction as believed. In fact Enki charged his brother, Enlil, with taking care of his creations including human beings. Enlil already grew tired of Enki's creations and denied they should have souls or a place in the heavens. Optimistic and hopeful Enki assumed once Enlil spent time with the creations he'd see their potential and the wonderful things they're capable of. However Enlil never intended interacting with other beings or leaving the heavens. Instead he created a group of minor Gods, the Annunaki, in his stead. Initially, the Annunaki did what Enki wanted Enlil to do. This frustrated Enlil, he'd wanted the opposite and started manipulating Shamesh. Others followed and created a war. That's when all the troubles began.'

Annu slumped onto the head bed, his mind blown.

The creator has a name and an evil brother? Another piece of the puzzle.

'What happened to Enlil and why have I never heard of him? Why don't many people know this story?'

'The answer is one of the part's which will shock you. After the downfall Enlil's punishment was the most severe. The Creator feared the spread of his evil and all but removed him from the minds of his creations. He gave Enlil a human form and in-prisoned him in an alternate dimension called Gehema or hell beneath Enki Island. It also contains the Ancient Elder God. He now not only runs the underworld but his evil seeps into the worlds regardless. It's only physically bound him.'

Holy flarking shit. Hell's below Enki island?

"This evil god Enlil is under the island I live on? How? Can he get out?"

Ankor's sigh warmed his mind. *'Not easily. It takes the blood of a direct relative of Enlil's and reciting an incarnation within the divine Lexicon at a specific time and place. Similar process to the ascension. He's tried and failed before but there're rumours his last chance is coming. If he doesn't make it this time, he becomes human permanently with no powers and no chance at freedom. It also means he can be usurped and tortured with the others.'*

Unease tickled Annu's nape and realisation broadened his horizons. "The being who created Shayne and I's parents is evil. We're all born of evil."

'In effect yes, but this neither defines nor changes you.'

I've got evil in my core. Is that what makes me dark? Will it ever take over?

*'*How could you possibly know that? Does he know my—"

The metal flap in the middle of the door flung open.

Dingle yelled into the hatch. "Move away from the bed and put your wrists through the slot."

I'm going to spin your head on a spike with a finger.

"Flark off Dingle. I warned you. You'll flarking regret this."

The man's scoff had no fear. Dingle hit the hatch with a black plastic stick. "Yeah, right. Even when you're out of that cell you can't do anything about it. You're fucked mate, and I'm making sure of it."

Dingle's voice reminded Annu of an untuned guitar.

Annu growled, rose and kicked the bed back to its position.

Dingle's tapping increased. "Put your wrists through now or 1000 volts is coming your way."

Doom rippled down Annu's back, he swallowed bitterness. "No. Fuck you."

'Are you all right? What's going on?'

'I can't talk right now. I'll get back to you later. Perhaps.'

'Annu—?'

Dingle peeked into the hatch, his features grotesque under artificial light. "If I come get you, you'll regret it."

Annu's shoulder muscles twitched, his shirt collar tightened against his throat. "What the hell, I live for regrets."

I've got to get out of here and kill them all.

Chapter 23
Oh Crap On a Cracker
Enki Island, Orion

Jackie paused, shrieked and ran into the forest like his life depended on it; one of the Martians chased him.

You're fucking kidding me.

Shayne's mouth agape, she gave him Jackie's absence the finger. "You mother fucking traitor, double traitor. Go trip and fall, may God Shit Fuck smite you."

A little thunder and lightning chastised Shayne.

Will I ever learn?

Four Martian weapons focused on Shayne, she dropped the gun, her heart fluttered.

Fuck, shit, fuck, shit, fuck, shit. Fuck. This gets better and fucking better. If worse now means better.

Shayne backed up against the rock and lowered her hands. "Relax take it easy. I won't hurt you if you don't hurt me."

I'm talking utter bullshit. But you don't need to know that.

With her foot Shayne dragged the gun through the dirt closer to her.

The four Martians moved aside, their apparent boss walked over with a self satisfied smirk. "Finally. You're coming with us to the mother ship. It would be better if we had both Demigods, but nonetheless you'll suffice. The Queen will be pleased." He motioned at the men either side of him. "Officer's Raphie and Seanen, restrain the woman. As for the traitor, upon his retrieval the Queen shall deal with him."

Raphie hesitated and faced the leader. "General Flet do I order the others to cancel the search for others?"

General McFucker more likely.

General McFucker puffed out his chest, hands behind his back. "To err on the side of caution and due diligence, I suggest troops continue looking but the main focus remains the same. There's a planet to control."

Raphie and another man moved for Shayne, she lurched sideways to avoid them and missed.

One grabbed her arm and dragged her in front of General McFucker.

Shayne wriggled against the ties, they cut into her skin. "Hey, stop grabbing me. I said I'd go with you. Lay off me and stop killing people."

A restrained Jackie preceded Captain Frost into the area metres behind the General. "I have him, sir."

Sucked in dipshit. Shayne mouthed and glared at Jackie. Oh oh, oh, oh, I think I'm in trouble. Oh, oh, oh, oh, oh oh. I think you're in trouble.

The General raised a finger and didn't turn around. "Excellent. One moment and we'll take them back to the ship for securing."

Fucking waste of time and lives.

Shayne rolled her neck, the muscles tightened. "Thanks for listening to me ARSEHOLE."

General McFucker stood an inch from Shayne, his musky breath wafted. "Do not call me that. If you're compliant the Queen may allow you to live once she's done. A long time away."

A killer migraine brewed, Shayne pushed it aside and crossed her arms. "Well so she fucking should. She's getting what she wants and I expect the war to end right after."

Which never, fucking ever, happens to me.

General McFucker's sigh sickened Shayne. "That's not happening. We didn't initially intend taking over, but this planet is perfect for colonisation. We no longer want to fix our planet when this one's better. With your help we'll travel to all galaxies, those who don't surrender will be executed."

The whole ascension thing has been bad as much as good.

Shock bent Shayne over and branded her stupid. "Fucking what? Queenie's got delusions of grandeur or she's been licking those red toads in the woods. Last time I did that I ended up naked chased by a block of chocolate riding a seven foot rabbit."

Thinking about it they never gave my lollypop back.

General McFucker wriggled his ear. "My translator must be broken. I can't understand a word you said."

Focus. Except I don't know what to do now. The rules have changed and I suck at that. Along with just about everything else.

"Understand this fuck arse, the second I get a chance you're fucked. Proper fucked too. And if my kids aren't safe I'll come back and do it again."

The kids flashed into Shayne's mind, her soul ached, her chest tightened.

General McFucker walked a step ahead of her. "You use that word fuck a lot. What does it mean?"

Shayne's mouth opened and closed. "All sorts of things. It's not a one meaning type of word.

Don't say it again or the next bolt of lightning is directed at me.

"Right."

Once, the only thing in Shayne's hands contained chocolate or weed. Now, people's lives lay in her hands and no amount of licking the packet fixed it.

Grief tore Shayne to shreds, emotion lodged in her throat. "You've got to stop this war. I beg you. No more deaths."

General McFucker's shoulders stiffened. "Do shut up."

I'll attract attention to us, hope the I.D.I.O.T.s notice and shoot the Martians. Downside is I'll probably get shot too. Or in the ship I'll create a huge scene and, and, and, um. Take out anyone in the flight deck and take control. Find the kids and blast the crap out of the compound. But for that to work I'd have to turn on the ship and figure out weaponry etc. Fuck it. Next idea, anyone I know who'd help me would be in Annu's communicator directory.

Out of options and in crisis Shayne mind turned to a default setting—annoyance. "You guys are evil, murderous mother fuckers. We could work together and all be happy. There's no need for this. Please stop."

The sour breath returned millimetres from Shayne. "If you don't shut up, I'll kill you right now and tell the Queen you escaped."

Shayne waved away the smell. "Whatever. That's not even the best death threat I've ever had. In fact it's not in the top five." Shayne thrust her wrists at him. "Take these off."

General McFuck clasped his hands in front. "No. Absolutely not."

I.D.I.O.T. PFD craft zoomed over them and disappeared in the distance.

I could surrender to the I.D.I.O.T.s but it might be worse.

Shayne steeled herself and sucked it up. "You're an arsehole."

General McFucker steered Shayne in the other direction. "Our ship this way, not far away from the edge of the forest."

Awesome. I'll rest for a few minutes while I figure shit out. I might see Erin or Zeke. Maybe see if there's in food while I'm in there. "Righteo then."

Two Martians walked beside Jackie, the other two beside Shayne, she dragged her feet.

Shayne's appetite growled louder than her heartbeat. "Have you got anything to eat?"

General McFucker spoke over his shoulder. "No."

Shayne imagined daggers stuck in his back. "Fuck it. Of course not."

General McFucker faced Shayne. "You'll survive or not. You're choice."

Why does so much crappy stuff happen around us? We're like the black cat of families. Being a demigoddess isn't really working for me. It might be time to consider a new career. Like a landscape gardener or maybe a lion tamer. Both have to be easier than this shit.

General McFucker pinched Shayne's upper arm. "Are you in there?"

Pain rippled under Shayne's flesh. "Ouch. Yes. A tap would have sufficed you arsehole."

Shayne brushed him off and fought kicking him in the shins.

A male voice erupted out of an unseen communication source: 'Ship four this is ship five. We confirm we have two young human beings in captivity. One white, short and irritable. The other brown and tall. We advise we're leaving the island and returning with them to Yebu.'

Maternal fear diminished, Shayne relaxed, tension released from her shoulders. "Oh thank God they're alright and I know where they are."

Well stupidly I'm in the right place. This is going to work out perfectly after all.

General McFucker tapped a device on his collar. "Good work, Four. We now have the female demigod and shall meet you there within the hour."

Yay. I'm going to see Erin and Zeke soon. No matter what happens now, they're okay. I will totally win Queenie over. I'm likeable aren't I? Wait, don't answer that.

Ship Four's captain boomed. "This will ensure good favour with the Queen. Perhaps she'll give us our own province here for our good work?"

Those purple mother, goat, horse fuckers are not having this annoying, death defying fucking planet.

General McFucker glanced at Shayne and smiled. "Yes I believe you're right. Over and out."

When this is all over I'm going to eat until I vomit and lapse into a six month coma. I'm won't lie down and cry.

"This shit cannot get anymore fucked up."

A clearing and craft appeared ahead, death mixed with success chilled Shayne.

Shayne held her breath and prepared herself. "I better get a window seat."

A ramp emerged from the side of the craft and lowered to the ground.

No food, no kids, no fucking idea.

Zing, zing, zing.

The guards beside Shayne heads exploded, green blood covered Shayne. Their bodies dropped, General McFucker turned to the noise, zing.

A laser shot him between the eyes, he slumped over.

Vomit trickled between Shayne's fingers, she trembled. "Fuck. Fuck."

Something hard pressed against Shayne's skull, a female voice sent shivers down her spine. "Finally got you. Now turn around with your hands in the air."

Hands raised Shayne moved a step at a time.

Martians gone, good, Jackie held at gunpoint by I.D.I.O.T.s, I'm about to die, really fucking bad, bad, bad. "Well colour me surprised. Today did get more fucked up."

Chapter 24
Dissected and Dejected
DSI, Pine Gap, New South Wales, Australia Earth

Steel cuffs clasped Annu's wrists and ankles to a metal stretcher. Annu bucked and struggled, volts of electricity surged from Annu's balls to his skull.

With my luck this will affect my sperm count when I actually need those guys.

The will to fight dwindled per amp pumped into Annu, fear embraced him with cold arms.

From the other side of a laboratory, men in full protective suits and clear visors aimed weapons at Annu. White suited doctors busied around tables filled with surgical equipment you'd find in a torturer's den.

The clanks and clinks of steel against steel chilled Annu's marrow.

What the hell are they going to do? I've got to get out of here.

Annu stretched an arm, zap, zap, the current ran down his side and across his kidneys. "Who are you people? What do you want with me?"

A woman by the bed side spoke into a small black object. "Subject appears to be in good health, seven feet eight inches tall, middle aged or thereabouts. A few scars noted prior to capture but no major former injuries or illnesses. Reacts similar to electricity to Earthlings."

Who is she speaking to and why is she describing me?

"Hey woman I'm talking to you. What are you doing?"

She put the device in a pocket and poised a syringe inches from his face. "I'm giving you a shot in your leg. It only stings for a few seconds."

Reflex jerked Annu, zap, zap, his left side paralysed.

This is a living hell. I'm going to die here if I don't do something.

A strap across Annu's forehead tightened. "No, wait, stop. Back up. What's in that?"

She sighed and the jiggled blue liquid inside the syringe. "Truth serum. Try to relax it makes things easier for everyone. It doesn't have any lasting effects on humans. However we aren't sure what it will do to you, yet."

A rub of his arm produced further jolts. Annu jerked and seized, his teeth rattled.

The voltage diminished, Annu blinked and cleared his vision.

I think my brain's bruised. Who am I again?

The jab stung, thick fluid burned under Annu's skin and ambled along his veins.

The woman spoke over Annu to someone out of sight. "Because of his size I doubled the dose. It should take effect soon."

The room wavered and the roof tiles formed animals. "I feel funny. Am I meant to see weird things?"

A man's voice erupted on his left. "Thank you, Doctor Beale. Please step aside."

A metallic taste invaded Annu's tongue. "Blah. A cat shit in my mouth."

A man bent over Annu. "Answer our questions and this ends quicker. Where's the woman demigod?"

I remember who I am now.

Warm fuzzies wriggled along Annu's spine and tickled his ears. "I told you Shayne's on Orion and didn't come with us. Duh."

The man smelt of garlic and off milk. "Why didn't she come with you?"

The doors of Annu's mind unlocked one by one. "It doesn't matter why now. Even if she'd tried after I got here, I'm guessing it wouldn't open for her either."

The man shuffled closer to the bed. "What plans did you have for Earth?"

Annu struggled focusing, everything blurred. "I don't know what flarking plan you're talking about but you need a breath mint or six."

The man breathed into his hand and sniffed it. "I, ah, had curry for lunch." His lack of confidence disappeared and he dropped the hand. "Dammit, what are your plans for Earth?"

Annu pushed his upper lip out with his tongue, sucked in his cheeks.

His tongue numbed. "Bell, thirst thyme doing, do duild Blay, a blew blouse bleeeing dou duys bestroyed blit."

Annoyance tainted the man's tone. "What? Hello. Earth, any plans?"

Annu's tongue unnumbed. "Huh?" His first girlfriend Emi popped into his mind.

Damn what a summer we had.

"Does anyone else crave cherries right now?"

The man jabbed Annu with a pen. "Answer my questions."

"I forgot she had red hair and that arse. Impeccable."

Her father nearly caught us a couple of times.

"Shit, I was like twenty-five so it must be over five hundred plus years ago. What she's doing now?"

She'd be dead silly man.

"Oh yeah."

Annu's laugh filled the room, tension released from his shoulders.

This isn't so bad after all.

The woman Doctor stood on the bed's other side. "Wow, twenty-five. A late bloomer. Out of interest, do you have sexual organs and procreate like us?"

Annu licked his lips, they buzzed. "Of course I do and better than you Earthlings if I do say so. As for sex, well Shayne and I do it all the time."

Damn, I'm good.

He wriggled his eyebrows. "Do you wanna see my sexual organs for yourself? But no touching, I'm a committed man these days."

A smirk conflicted with her serious demeanour. "Ah, I'll say no—for now."

The male agent grunted and jutted his chin. "That's quite enough, Doctor. I'll ask you if I need your help." He refocused on Annu. "What are the full extent of your powers?"

Words trickled from Annu's tongue like a waterfall. "Mmm, great question. I'm charming, whitty, make an excellent Yak curry, and like I mentioned, I'm awesome in bed." People out of sight chuckled and egged Annu on. "Hey don't tell Shayne but it was really me who ate her chocolate and not Zeke. She'll pitch a huge fit. I don't know what's going on with her lately. Do you?"

To Annu, the man stretched to the roof and pinged back down again. "When and how did this relationship begin? Did the woman go to Orion voluntarily or did you take her by force?"

Boing, boing, boing.

"You mean Shayne? If she heard you call her 'the woman' she'd rip you a new one. As if I could make her do anything. No one can unless she wants to and that's rare. Technically I guess she didn't voluntary to come to Orion at first but when she got a look at me it all changed. Now she doesn't want to leave—much."

The man's mouth wobbled. "Ah, you admit forcing her onto on Orion? Had you planned on kidnapping other Earthlings and taking them to Orion?"

The fog in Annu's mind spread into the outer regions. "Are you mental or slow? Why are you talking in past tense? I didn't kidnap anyone."

"Then how did she get there? Flew?"

Crickets buzzed around Annu's skull. "Ah, tell them to shut up and don't be an I.D.I.O.T. The whole thing is divine intervention. Or so they say. What we went through wasn't easy you know. We had to get the scrolls, defeat Shamesh, ascend and shit like that. All right we didn't exactly have a choice but still it's a godly thing. You wouldn't understand."

The man's monotonous tone droned. "This Shamesh, can you confirm he's no longer a threat to Earth?"

Annu's energy fluctuated, fatigue weighed him down. "Hell yeah. We didn't technically kill him, he died when Shayne leapt into a hole with him; we ascended and obtained the god's powers. Now we're meant to bring the planets in the galaxy back together and spread the Creator's word, but it, ah, as you can see, it hasn't worked out so well for us."

The man killed Annu's drug buzz. "And it won't work out well on Earth either."

"What do you want from me?"

"More than you imagine and suffer for. We've waited for a God for a long time. I wish we'd gotten the woman too and knew your parentage before hand. If you're like this, at least one of your parents will be something else all together."

If you only knew what I didn't know.

What?

The man's face split in two and each side bobbed. Annu squinted, the man rejoined into a six foot arsehole.

"Well thank the Gods or whoever you only got me. Listen. What's with you fella? You're such a mood killer. I bet you don't get invited out to parties much do you?"

"Alright I'm done with nice. We won't get straight answers out of him easily. Let's step this up to the next level." He gestured over Annu's torso. "Doctor, start with full DNA samples plus biopsies and go from there."

The opened doors in his mind closed in succession.

Annu's brain jiggled the handles and kicked the doors. "Wait, what? Hang on a damned minute."

******

Annu clenched his jaw and gritted his teeth, helplessness his only companion.

What the hell are they going to do to me next? Come on man stop this. When I get out of these restraints I'm going to strangle the bitch first and kill the others using her as a weapon. When, if, maybe. Flark. Gods' help me.

The woman doctor pried a finger between his lips. "You're making this harder than it should be. I must scrape inside your mouth. Open it or I'll shock you again."

Annu clenched and stretched in the other direction. "No. No more tests. What's with you people and electricity?"

Her sigh fogged her visor, the blue eyes beneath emitted no emotion. "I can't understand a word you're saying. Open your damned mouth."

The air vent above caught the wet patch on Annu's crotch and sent shivers across his lower half.

Humiliation remained the least of his current problems. "Archaic, cruel bitch. Let me go."

She wedged a tool between his teeth and forced them open.

Determination conflicted with the lack of control, Annu's current and biggest problem. "Mmnmmndhg."

Apt hands removed small amounts of flesh from Annu's inner cheek and under his tongue.

Blood dripped in Annu's mouth, his inner cheek stung.

A successful fight against the restraints mirrored Annu's chance of escape. "You flarking cow."

The jolt began at his feet and shuddered its way up. Annu flopped as the restraints allowed, the charge stopped. A dull thud pounded between his ears, his surroundings wavered.

The tips of Annu's fingers tingled.

The woman moved from Annu's top half and pried a finger free from under the restraint.

She scraped a sharp metal device under his nail and clipped off the ends into an open vial.

The man who'd questioned Annu earlier re-appeared over him. "How many issue have you created?"

Annu blinked to clear his vision, his ears rung. "What?"

The man grated against Annu's nerves. "How many children do you have?"

Pain exploded across the top of Annu's skull. The woman dropped a clump of his hair into a clear bag and sealed it.

Sweat poured down Annu's back, his hands clammy. "Ouch. Flarking hell."

The man poked him in the upper arm. "Children, how many do you have?"

A fleck of rationality interrupted.

Hell, Zeke. Please be safe.

"None, I don't have any." Annu's tongue thickened. "What does it matter?"

"How old are you?"

"Flark off."

"Doctor. Next sample."

The woman flashed a torch before both eyes, followed by drops into Annu's left one. Numbness seeped into his cheeks and mouth. Annu stopped blinking, a light hurt his retinas.

A metal clamp appeared in the doctor's hand, she brought it to Annu's eye in laboured movements.

Flarking hell no. No. No. No. The bitch enjoys this.

Annu pushed himself back into the slab. She slipped it under his eye lids and clicked the clamp open. The needle from the syringe in her other hand caught the light. Terror clutched Annu's chest. "What are you...no, no, no."

It pierced his eyeball, fluid filled the syringe, terror gripped his soul and twisted. Once full, she removed the needle and the clamp. Annu's sense of realism fractured.

Sans instruments, his left eyelid drooped full of lead.

This can't be real. It's too horrific. Any second now I'll wake up from this nightmare in our bed at home, with Shayne beside me. No evil government doctors taking pieces of me, not held prisoner without escape and other beings relying on me. This can't go on.

The woman doctor unbuckled Annu's belt and opened his pants. Annu clenched his inner thighs and pushed back. "Get the flark away from there." The buttons popped open in a line and revealed the favourite underpants he'd prevented Shayne throwing out a number of times and some of Annu's family jewels.

The woman doctor froze an inch from his bits. "Holy shit. I, I, I."

The man grunted and raised a finger. "Doctor."

She blinked in succession and shook herself. "His underwear. I see men are attached to crappy underwear all over the galaxy."

The Doctor removed another long syringe from the table beside him and moved towards Annu's balls.

Annu's sack constricted, his arsehole tightened. "No flarking way in this universe or any other you are coming near me with that thing." Annu bucked, kicked, flicked, wobbled, and jiggled. Despite a mental fight against the electricity zaps Annu's crotch betrayed him, happy for contact and desperate for freedom.

No, no, no, no. It's inhumane, cruel and unjust. What have I done to deserve this torture?

The needle pierced the delicate skin and delved into his testicle.

She drew on the syringe and removed Annu's his life essence via force—not Annu's preferred choice.

Helplessness and hopelessness run down Annu's cheeks and salted his lips. "You flarking cock suckers. Leave me alone."

The doctor removed the needle and reinserted his goods where they belonged.

Despair combined with hatred in Annu's gut, it churned and gurgled.

She placed a blanket over his lower half and shifted aside.

The male agent persisted like a migraine. "Exactly how old are you?"

Annu's care factor dwindled. "For the love of the Gods, five hundred and forty eight give or take a couple of years. Now will you leave me alone? Surely you've got all you need?"

"Do others on Orion have powers or is it only Gods who've got access to those powers? Do you have contact with any?"

Apparently flarking not. I look forward to tearing your head off your shoulders and shoving it up her arse.

"I'm not telling you anything. Go screw yourself."

Volts flooded Annu's system, he peed himself for the second time in three hours.

"You'll talk or I'll make you talk." Zap, zap, zap. "Do you maintain contact with any of the Elder Gods, your father and those known as the Annunaki?"

Clarity tickled Annu's brain—two people beings of late mentioned the Annunaki. "Those guys show up everywhere."

Duh, I am one.

The man gave nothing away. "Answer the question."

Annu fought consciousness.

I'm so flarking tired.

"What do you know about them?"

Zap, zap, zap.

The man tapped a pen on the bed. "Are you or are you not in contact with them?"

Annu's tongue stuck to the roof of his mouth. "Go fuck yourself."

The next shock rattled Annu's brain against his skull and brought back memories of his first pet. "Rex, a two-foot hamster."

The man's pursed his lips made him fishy looking. "What?"

I haven't been fishing for such a long time. I need to take Shayne.

Annu's eyes burned, tears welled. "Irica gave him to me for my sixth birthday. I miss her." Another zap clanged his teeth together and reset his focus. "Damn."

"When did you first become aware of who you truly were?"

Annu sucked on his bottom lip, his intestines churned. "I, I, I."

The woman doctor grabbed the man's hand above the button. "That's enough. Anymore and you'll fry his brain and I want that later."

Peril enveloped Annu; he clawed at the man and concentrated on his name tag. *'Agent Shooks.'*

Chapter 25
A Double Hostage
Enki Island, Orion

I'm frankenfucked. Why does shit always go wrong for me?

The I.D.I.O.T.s Shayne evaded the days before filled the space around her.

This is just typical for me. What the hell did I think would happen? That I'd come in here and it would be easy? Stupid, stupid woman.

A female bulkier than a rugby fullback clutched Shayne. "Holy flark. There you go. It is her."

Fuck, fuck.

"Fuck, fuck, fuck. What happened to Jackie? Did you kill him? I got used to the purple fuck.

A man half the woman's size shrugged. "I told you it wasn't a waste of time following her."

Shayne gave them a two handed bird. "Great. I've been found by the I.D.I.O.T.s nasty version of Abbott and Costello."

Costello lowered her gun against Shayne's temple. "Raise your hands and get up slowly." She looked around Shayne. "You smell funky."

Shayne's entire plan flew away with the wind.

Now I won't see the kids soon unless I get myself there. Crap, fuck I've screwed up again.

"No worse than your armpits bitch."

I must stop watching talk show repeats.

A group of Martian's emerged from behind a bunch of rocks and ambushed the I.D.I.O.T.s. Abbott and Costello scattered.

Amidst a parade of laser fire, a blur of bodies passed by.

Shayne dropped, ducked, rolled and hit something solid—Costello.

She dragged Shayne behind a fray-free mound.

Smash.

Costello slammed Shayne against rock.

Pain erupted from Shayne's spine, she kicked body armour. "You mother fucking dickwad. You're so dead when I get the chance."

Costello cuffed Shayne's wrists and ignored the blows. "You've got five seconds to order them to call this off before I blow your stupid, smart arse face off."

I'm so sick of looking at gun barrels. They all look the damned same.

Shayne vomited in her mouth, sweat poured down her back. "No. I can't because you're wrong. I've got nothing to do with this whole mess. I swear to the Gods. They came of their own accord."

After we reopened the way here and all.

Wind belted passed, Costello yanked a chunk of Shayne's hair. "Bullshit. We've seen you with one of them and I know he's the one you've asked about. All in all it looks pretty friendly to me."

Shayne's skull burned, her eyes watered. "He's different and has no author-i-tay with the others. In fact, they want him dead too. Shayne swallowed courage and burped failure. "What did you do to him?"

Costello twisted Shayne's hair around her palm. "Something tells me you talk shit most of the time."

"Ouch. Bitch. Did we go to the same high school?" Shayne rose with her hair. "For the hundredth time this situation isn't my fault. I fucking said that. I was going there to calm her down. She wants the whole planet now."

I realise it's totally my fault for ignoring things but I'll never admit it.

Costello's screwed up her face improved her features. "Duh. We know."

Act tough not stupid all right?

"Fine. We can work this out another way."

Costello stepped around bodies. "Put it away and keep it there."

Shayne's feet dangled centimetres above dead people. "Gross. Are you going to listen to me?"

Costello regained composure and dragged Shayne by the hair forward. "Ah, no. I don't care what you've got to say. You're not meant to be here in the first place. The only reason you are is because you want to see the destruction you orchestrated."

Anger pushed Shayne ahead, determination drove her muscles. "I fucking knew it. I am right; you did set us up to stay on Earth? You mother fuckers."

The gun barrel pressed into Shayne's temple. "How long have you planned this? Is destroying an entire planet fun where you come from? Where's the other one of you?"

I don't want to die. But at least I'd sleep.

"Oh my fucking God. I'm too tired to explain it in stupid to you. And, it's Annu, not the other one," Shayne suppressed a sob, "he's on Earth. We don't want to kill anyone."

"You lie remember." Costello held Shayne off the ground one handed and spoke into her lapel with the other. "Lieutenant Doyle reporting in. I've got the female Demigod. She says the other one's not here, if he was he'd be be her side. Might be just three of them stayed behind."

A bigger voice of torture crackled from Costello's collar:

Igra shot fear up Shayne's butt. "Excellent. Bring her to me immediately. I'm informed her children are in one of the Martian craft on way to Yebu. We'll retain them on Yebu. If the Martian is still with her, bring him too. NimNim can interrogate. You've done well. Over."

Costello lowered Shayne a fraction. "Thank you, sir. The Martian evaded us but, his own people are after him. He won't last long. Over."

Malice dripped from Igra's words. "Ensure you don't lose her along the way and don't trust her at all. She's a pathological liar. Over."

Even a traitor doesn't deserve to die by unfriendly fire.

Costello scoffed and glanced down. "I know. Over."

Shayne kicked, clawed, and missed. "Please get my kids before then, anything might happen to them."

Creator I sacrifice myself to keep them from harm. I beg you.

Costello carried Shayne all the way to the Protector's compound.

Toes pointed Shayne missed the ground by millimetres.

Fuck which reminds me. No one's mentioned Jacob.

He's a victim of his own decree.

"I might occasionally tell a lie but I'm all of out of luck, I'm so lost without you. I cannot explain I've needed you so long. I'm all out of luck—"

I'm losing my mind.

Costello raised Shayne back to shoulder height. "Do shut up or I'll forget my orders and shoot you."

Be strong. Have faith.

Shayne flapped her arms and pretended to swim. "Yeah, yeah, yeah. You know that's the second time I've heard that today, and I evaded the first attempt. I'll do it again. You fucking watch me."

Hatred oozed from Costello, her lip twitched. "I'm not here to talk or make damned friends. I'm here to do a job. No shut the flark up before I knock you out."

In her mind, Shayne grabbed a hammer and chipped at the crack in Costello's serious facade. "Well that's good then because I don't want to be your friend either. If I was though, I'd have told you, you look shit house in beige or whatever that colour you're wearing is."

Costello's cheeks flushed, she glanced at her pants and at Shayne. "What? What?" Clink, clink, a fracture trickled down the facade's middle. Costello shook herself, the fracture repaired. "Has anyone ever told you they wanted to kill you?"

They reached the clearing before the compound gates, Shayne's chest tightened.

Here comes the next fucking mess to save us from.

"Mah. Once, twice, fifty times. Who knows I don't pay much attention anymore. They also say I'm a bad singer but whatever. Want to hear some?"

Costello stayed close to the compounds permitter. "Flark no."

Shayne swam in the air and puckered her lips. "Something smells fishy around here." She sniffed Costello. "Yep, it's you."

They reached the secure room's doorway.

Shayne slumped and hung limp. "Ah fuck it."

Costello lowered Shayne onto her feet and maintained contact. "Please, please, please let me win the chance to kill you in the office raffle."

Shayne likened her situation to the prisoner on death row. "If this day continues like this I'll surrender voluntarily."

The door opened and revealed Shayne's next fate. A strong push ushered Shayne into the lit room, the door closed alongside a chance for escape. I.D.I.O.T.s parted, Costello dropped Shayne in the middle of them.

Fake it until I make it baby. Right? Right? Hello? Ah whatever.

Shayne sucked in her chest and straightened her shoulders. "Hello fuckers. Let's get this shit over with. By the way I'm not helping unless my kids are safe."

Chapter 26
The End's in Sight, Right?
Pine Gap DSI Facility
New South Wales, Australia, Earth

Between Dingle on Annu's left, another two guards beside and behind, Annu's confidence drained. Lesions and open biopsy wounds on his back inhibited non-painful movement. Remnants from the last spinal tap set off muscles spasms down his spine.

Instead of fighting, Annu embraced the different levels of agony; it allowed him to focus on something other than dissection and death.

How long will this go on? Why aren't I being saved?

The group hit steel doors at the end of a hall way. Dingle placed his finger over a display and swiped a plastic card down a slot.

Dingle returned the card to his pocket. "What a pain in the arse."

How far have we gone?

"Where are you taking me?"

Dingle dug the gun's butt his into Annu's thigh. "Shut up."

Opened doors lead into a laboratory section off into work stations. Minor pain fought major pain, Annu swooned. "Keep it up flarker, you're just adding levels of torture I'll inflict upon you."

Dingle rolled his eyes. "Humph. Yeah right. Now shut up."

Zap. Volts amplified Annu's body crisis and dulled his mind. At another check point a different guard copied Dingle's security procedures.

It's impossible to get through any section with a finger and a key card. This gets more complicated by the minute.

At the end of another hallway they entered a tin box and filled it like sardines, Sweat and body odour amplified in the enclosed space. They lowered Annu onto a cold floor and stood around him. "Let me go damned you."

Between the drugs and electric shocks I'm not sure I can move.

Problems against Annu tripled, a happy ending seemed an intangible concept like time.

Dingle dug his boot into Annu's rips. "For Christ's sake shut the fuck up."

It shuddered and descended, Annu's heart dropped, his ears popped. They stopped, doors opened, guards at either end lifted Annu. His back bowed, abdomen contracted. Artificial air burned his lungs, the light dulled. "Am I underground?"

Everything looks the flarking same.

At the end of a row of offices, Annu swayed at another secured doorway, the sign's warning bold and clear:

'Sector 7G, restricted to Gold Status Personnel only. Trespassers shot without question.'

I've been forsaken, forgotten. Nothing but refuse. No worth of my own.

Father, whoever you are, if you hear me, help me.

I hope I don't regret asking.

Dingle poised before a display pad in the wall, a pink laser scanned an eye and a series of locks clicked.

What day is it? Where the literal flark am I? If you won't let me out, let me die fast.

A metal door opened into another laboratory section except for a wall of sealed cubicles a fraction larger than the cells running on sides.

The goop breakfast curdled in Annu's gut. "What the hell is this place?"

A stone faced guard on the other side shoved a rag into Annu's mouth.

Dingle's sigh infuriated Annu. "Thank fuck for that."

In three separate cells beings banged on the door, screeched and shrieked.

Their cries tormented Annu, the loss of personal control never more evident. "Mpmphbhbhd."

You're all going to die.

Beside an unoccupied cubicle a full suited doctor placed coloured vials into a machine.

Annu kicked, flopped and flung like a puppeteer-less puppet. "Mphodjdde."

This is some bullshit.

Two guards slid metal bars across and opened the door.

The doctor shifted aside and stood above Annu, he removed the gag.

Annu bucked, the guards dropped onto the ground. "Flark. No, no. You're not putting me in there."

The doctor placed a black device on Annu's gut and pressed a button.

Annu vibrated, his brain rattled, his skull tightened, every muscle contracted, spasmed and relaxed. After shocks rippled Annu, the restraints opened and fell off. "I, please."

Hoisted off the ground and escorted into the cubicle, the door sealed Annu's fate.

Annu slammed on the walls, the air evaporated, he rammed his shoulder at the wall, it reverberated. White gas emitted from slits and filled the room. Annu held his breath, his lungs burned. "You won't get the better of me. I don't give up easily."

Annu gasped and inhaled thick muck. The room blurred, he slumped against a wall. The fog intensified and infiltrated every gap.

Annu slipped onto the floor. "Someone help me."

Dread ruined his thoughts and invaded his body.

Please, please help me. I can't...go on. Please end this now. I beg you.

The white light of Heaven evaded Annu, while the dark embraced him and offered release from suffering. A pit of despair formed, self pity lapped Annu's feet.

I want to die, just let them kill me and take what they want. I'm done.

Tears streamed Annu's cheeks, saliva evaporated, each breath inflicted fresh hell upon his lungs. Gas sucked back into the vents it came from, the room cleared. Fresh air filled Annu's chest and woke his brain. "Stop torturing me and kill me if you must."

The door creaked, Dingle entered the room. "No. Not yet."

Arms slipped under Annu and lifted him. "There's plenty more fun to come first."

Annu failed to support himself.

No. No more. Please.

"Why do you hate me so much? Why do you take part in this?"

Dingle's sneer intensified the dread. "Personally because when I was a kid one of you fuckers abducted me and did shit to me before dumping me in the woods. No one believed me; it ruined my fucking teenage life. Ever since, I've wanted to return the favour."

Annu searched for humanity in the man and found none. "There's good and bad in every creation. You can't throw us in the same pile. This is cruel."

Dingle carried him under the shoulder and resisted eye contact. "No it's my orders."

Annu wriggled, the men tightened their grip. "Not...like...this. Please—"

The beings in the other cells quieted, Annu under the guards assistance exited via the rear door into a dark hallway.

Annu faced the man on his other side. "Please, let me go. You can't think this is right." He yelled down his torso. "Someone, stop this madness. I'm not a test subject, I'm a person."

None of the men acknowledged Annu's presence aside from the odd sigh and readjustment of position.

The only way is if I embrace the darkness in me all of them will die even if I don't like how it feels after.

Given the chance, I'm not sure I care if Enki banish's me for going too far.

They entered a room with a large metal cubicle in the middle. Fire-fighting equipment surrounded it. An unsuited male Doctor waited next to it, gauges and other computerised equipment adorned its front. As before, Annu ended up in the cubicle.

The Doctor typed on a keyboard and focused on the display. "Lieutenant Dingle. What's the requested strength on this one?"

The darkness edged deeper into Annu's psyche, the light drifted further away. "I'll burn you all to dust."

The doctor's name tag blurred.

How far between the last section and the next? Flark. I can't, can't tell.

Dingle tapped a foot and tutted. "Captain Shooks said a quarter only. You should extrapolate from that strength without risking our lives."

They're giving me some powers back. Finally, a break. Hang on a little longer. Shayne, Zeke.

The Doctor's whine annoyed Annu. "I don't think that's a good idea. Just put him against the back wall."

Stop talking and just do it already.

The guard opposite Dingle nudged the Doctor. "If you've got objections Doc, take it up with management."

"Thank you for your advice, Major Burrows. Please move out of the way."

Hurry up. Come on.

The metal wall cooled the burns on Annu's back, he struggled on his feet.

Hold on just a little longer. Something will work out, it has to.

The door sealed, the air buzzed, goosebumps covered Annu.

A loud click preceded a short, sharp burst of energy.

It rippled along the floor and into Annu. Fatigue lifted, wounds healed and pain diminished.

Annu relished a deep breath and absorbed the respite.

With power came lucidity. "Now that's what I'm talking about."

Slots opened in the walls and released a barrage of ammunition.

Annu encapsulated himself into a fiery aura, the rounds bounced off, lava trickled from his fingers. "I told you I'm coming for all of you."

The floor melted, the walls crackled and dinted. Annu thrust fire at the door way, it buckled inward, the hinges twisted, rivets popped.

Dingle and the other guards leaned against the door; the intensified heat forced them to move.

Annu aimed at Dingle.

Crack. Crack. Snap.

The doctor slammed his palm at the keyboard.

Annu's powers flickered and dwindled into nothing.

Remnants of the energy burst and healed wounds remained.

I'm not giving up.

"You bastards want me, come get me."

******

Inside another room in the same section, the energy Annu retained hummed under his skin. He calculated the distance between the table and the guards.

Five metres in either direction. The table will wipe out a few of them in one swing. I've still got this room and the next several to get out. I'll need one or two of the guards to get through them.

Another check of Annu's, restraints and Smith, languished in a chair opposite.

Agent Shooks, on Smith's, right drummed his fingers, both men exuded a dangerous combination of arrogance and power.

I'll tear you apart with my bare hands and smack him around with your limbs.

Smith slipped his glasses up his nose. "I assume by now you accept lack of cooperation got you nowhere but pain?"

Ire filled Annu's veins and heated his skin.

Calm down, not yet.

"Ah no. The exact opposite in fact. I'm going down kicking and screaming. There's no way in this hell or any other you're chopping me up like a flarking science lesson."

Please Gods keep Shayne safe at our place, still pissed at me, worried about the Council and feeling hormonal. On second thought torture fare better than the hormones. A distinction without a difference these days.

Shooks's shrug jiggled his fat neck. "We get the information like this or more tests."

Annu imagined ways to kill both men in one move.

They'd clean blood from what's left off the walls for months.

"Fine. I guess you may as well reveal why you are doing this to me and the others you've got trapped here? And how did you know about Shayne and me? Why do you want us so badly?"

Smith leaned back, the chair squeaked. "For underground global and one day universal control of the masses. Earthlings are happy and content living as consumers, not questioning anything they're told. There's other benefits of physical alien being retrieval; we managed stay afloat by bleeding aspects of stolen technology into the public, we harness their world changing technology, and abilities for ourselves. You and the woman are pinnacles of universal godly power for Earth via us achieve its rightful place in the Galaxy. I only imagine if the public knew of your Godliness world religions would fall and long held governmental social structures. Panicked people don't buy things or follow instructions. Furthermore from a strategic point of view we can't risk any beings taking over or starting war before we're truly ready. Thus we closed the wormholes."

"You arrogant bastards. You won't get away with this. Do you know my father?"

Smith swished his hand around, stale tobacco wafted in Annu's direction. "Unfortunately not. It's somewhat protected information. Clearly neither do you."

I'll never know at this rate.

Annu's mind twisted in knots, his brain slotted puzzle pieces in place. "You won't get away with this."

"If that were true, we'd have been stopped long ago. Funny thing, we didn't even have to try hard to make this happen. It fell into our lap. The Grand Council contacted us first which lead us to discuss our mutual interest—you two. In no time we came up with solutions: they take over Enki Island while you were both on Earth and do whatever upon your return, in the meantime we temporarily close the wormhole while we ran our experiments on you and reopen it to return you both to Orion. Thereafter we agreed to share information only no physical contact until agreed. We never had any intention on returning either of you. Instead we'd extract everything we could and finally have the capabilities to travel to planets further away and taken them over. It almost derailed things when you arrived alone and the woman remained on Orion. Both of you are incredibly powerful together. By now she's suffered their predestined fate for both of you. A shame really. Stupid creatures. But, lucky for us you're far more powerful than we expected and don't need her."

Shock and despair cold cocked Annu, his breath heaved, the air thickened.

No, it can't be. No way. They couldn't have. He's lying. Is Shayne safe? She'd have hidden surely?

Vomit trickled into Annu's mouth, fear pounded his thoughts. "No, I don't believe you. It's a ploy. It's not possible. How could they contact you? As far as I knew you weren't technically capable of that degree of interplanetary communications."

The walls closed in, Annu's sanity dangled by a thread.

He hasn't mentioned Zeke yet. I hope they're together. Small favours and all.

Smith leant on the table, his smirk grotesque. "It's more than possible, it's real. Some of the projects we're able to do since we captured the blue being you befriended is contacting other planets once we've established their location and visa versa."

Annu's blood pressure plummeted, his vision blurred.

The torture they've inflicted upon me they've done to her, they'll do anything to get what they want. They'll pay extra for this.

Gritted teeth pained Annu's jaw. "That explains the contact how did you find out about Shayne and I to begin with?"

The answer struck Annu, frustration compounded grief.

It's not me that's signed our death warrant, it's the woman I love. I can't lose another one.

Smith's glasses tilted to the left. "You worked it out didn't you? Yes, she attracted our attention after a great deal of unusual seismic, magnetic and energy readings were recorded on her premises. They stopped a long time ago and coincidently reoccurring after she moved in. When she sold the gold she filled out her information for the receipt. The highly unusual and otherworldly geological make up sealed the deal. It's all worked out quite well."

I told her, I warned her. Why didn't I stop her or do something about it? Shay gets lead astray so easily. We should never have separated even for a moment. I swore I'd always protect her.

The temperature in the room dropped.

It all makes sense now. No wonder Igra had been smug; he'd planned our demise ahead of time. Out of our way they'd find everything we'd hidden, kid included, when they got to the island.

Annu's faith dwindled further, bad people existed everywhere. "You're more evil than Enlil."

Shooks scraped his chair across the floor. "Oh please. Together you've killed dozens of people over the last several months many consider that evil. It's strangely fitting you die on each others planets."

I can't believe this. Is this the universe we really live in? What the hell can two demigods achieve when we're up against this? Not that it matters anymore. Nothing matters anymore.

"This can't go on. God help you all when I'm free."

A guard behind Annu scoffed. "If there is a God he sure isn't here."

Shooks banged the table top and scowled at the guard. "This isn't time for a theological discussion."

Smith flicked a hand. "I think we've indulged you more than enough. You'll be returned to your cell for a last meal and collected again at twenty hundred hours this evening. Guards, take the subject."

Think man, think…

This is more complicated than I realised. We're flarked, fucked, rooted and screwed. If I don't make it home, I'm sorry I've been such an arsehole lately Shay. I love you and I don't blame you for this.

Chapter 27
A Flock of I.D.I.O.T.s
Enki Island, Orion

Shayne's one hundredth close call played out around her. "While I'm rethinking careers I may as well throw midwife in there. I spend most of my time with 'c' words a.k.a. vaginas and arseholes anyway. I may as well get paid for it. Except I couldn't deal with the mushy, yucky stuff."

I wonder what a flock of I.D.I.O.T.s is called? A fucktard sounds about right to me.

Igra's gut preceded the rest of him emerging between two guards. "This is an unwelcome but fortuitous timing nonetheless. You've got one minute to explain how you'll end this war and live young woman. The technology, weaponry and protection you've got on this island alone far exceeds our expectations and I'd rather be alive to use it."

Shayne collapsed against a nearby counter top.

Shit, shit, shit. How can I get out of this? My usual half arsed way? Nope. I better use my whole arse again.

"It's pretty fucking obvious we had nothing to do with the stupid Martian invasion. They've got their own agenda. It's you with explaining to do. Why all the fanfare and demands at the meeting when you'd planned your own invasion and effectively kill us when we got back anyway?"

Igra regained composure. "We weren't in a position to oppose you when you're on Orion. You would have stopped us easily. Gone and it worked perfectly. That is until your Martian behind you and his friends attacked."

Jackie, where?

Shayne spun, two I.D.I.O.T.s held him in the corner.

Thank Gods. Even though he is a traitorous, purple bastard.

Anger launched Shayne at Igra, she scratched his cheek. "You're a mother fucking piece of shit. I'm going to gouge your eyes out and rearrange your face. You better not lay a finger on my kids."

I.D.I.O.T.s swathed Shayne and restrained her by the shoulders.

Jackie disappeared in a sea of beige.

Shayne's blood boiled, self-righteousness egged her on. "I'm fucking warning you."

No emotion from Igra infuriated Shayne further.

Igra removed grapes from his pocket and popped them into his mouth. "I'm not scared. I've got all the collateral. You've got nothing but a collaborator on your side at the moment."

Starvation betrayed Shayne, her stomach grumbled; she flipped between rage and hunger.

Oh yum. The sweet, sweet juice. I fucking hate you but I want your food. You sure don't need it.

Shayne followed the grape from his fingers to his mouth. "Fuck this. I'm not doing what you say."

The grape squished between Igra's teeth, juice splashed her cheek.

Frustration at critical levels, Shayne kicked at Igra. "Argh. If I had my powers you'd be fucking French toast and you'd want to eat yourself."

Huh? Great starvation made me delusional

Igra stuffed a handful of grapes into his gob. Squish, squish, splash. "That's the biggest injustice in this situation. What kind of God gives imbeciles such as you powers? It's a travesty."

Mental exhaustion dumped a wet blanket on Shayne's back, she rested against an I.D.I.O.T.s side.

Fuck it. If they insist on keeping grip on me, they can hold me up too.

"Bring it up at your next general meeting with him if you want. I only imagine the pain and suffering if someone like you had them."

A smile lined Igra's plump face. "Opposed to yourself and Annu? My haven't you two done a marvellous job. Even your own planet rebukes your assistance."

Shame burnt Shayne's face, hatred opened her mouth. "Fuck you. We've never knowingly or willingly killed an innocent person. Probably. Like you can talk; what kind of leader ditches his people and hides while the planet is destroyed?"

Igra spat a seed onto the ground. "A better one than you. The people need a leader alive. You're so self important and arrogant. Not to mention a waste of time, energy and gullible."

Shayne wanted to rip the smug expression off Igra's face and wear it as a hat. "Wait, how'd you find about Earth?"

The smirk grew. "Ah Space Watch and the other tech from Shamesh. A group called DSI or something happily reached an agreement, which I'm about to breach to obtain Annu back early and bring this debacle to an end."

Oh fucking shit balls. If we both live through this I'm never going to hear the end of this. On the upside my man's probably alive and he's coming home.

Shayne struggled, fingers dug into her flesh. "Whatever. Hurry up and give me my powers back. I'll open the wormhole and when Annu gets here he'll kick your fat arse until gravy comes out."

Igra's shrug removed a layer of disbelief. "That's all you've got? Be nice and I'll consider allowing you to live as my, shall we say—demigodly slave once it's all over."

I hate you so much I hope you choke.

"I don't fucking think so. I'm slave to no one except a few debt collectors and once a fortnight for Annu. This is harder than the whole Sham-man debacle."

Once again rainbows and unicorns remain a fantasy.

Igra waddled to a bank of computer equipment and tapped the middle box. "Sham who?"

Please Gods, please let Annu be okay. I'm sure he will; he's stronger than four men.

"Fucking Shamesh or whatever the fuck you want to call him."

Anger tainted his tone. "You mean Shamesh my mentor. The one you killed?"

Huh? You're fucking kidding me.

"You're what?"

Sour grapes wafted in Shayne's direction. "My teacher you imbecile."

I must work on being so oblivious and dumb.

Shayne shrugged stupidity to the side. "Of course. Why didn't we realise there's an evil old fuck's disaster club. Do you all get matching pens and a secret hand shake? Actually I don't fucking care. It makes no difference."

"You are so annoying. Not a word out of your mouth makes sense or reason."

How does one go about getting smarter one wonders?

"You can go fuck yourself and hurry up."

Igra's smile returned in full force. "Without powers that I control, what makes you think you've got any say? You might prove useful but don't overestimate your importance in the food chain or my caring."

An epiphany surprised Shayne for the first time.

Is that what getting an actual idea is like?

"Ha. Fuck you fat boy. You can't win the war without us or I'd already be fucking dead."

As quick as fear in Igra arrived, it disappeared. "How about I order a strike on the craft carrying your kids."

Fuck he called my hand.

Shayne's bluff against a pair of threes failed. "No, please don't. I'm sorry."

Igra crossed his arms, his belly wobbled. "Comply and I'll ensure they are enslaved not killed."

Igra jiggled a packet of biscuits, Shayne followed their movement. "Am I getting through?"

I'm at his mercy. Fuck I hate it when that happens, and it's a lot.

Resignation slumped Shayne's shoulders. "Give me the fucking biscuits and turn that shit on."

Poor bastards being related to me. DNA disaster, a bad luck version of a sexually transmitted disease

Shayne caught the packet Igra threw. On automatic, fingers tore it open and filled her mouth. Crumbs dropped onto her chest, she licked the tip of her finger and collected them.

Fuck you, you fat fucking son of a bitch.

The black box beside Igra captured his attention. "It's in a limited capacity in order for you to open the wormhole. Once Annu's returned I'll turn it on fully but you're both completely under our control. At any moment I can switch it all off and let you die like the rest."

The biscuits soured in Shayne's belly. "Yeah I know. Just do it."

Igra glanced at the display and tapped an icon.

Energy tickled Shayne, her true self so close yet so far. "Some's better than none."

Shayne held her breath and swirled. Nothing happened.

You're fucking kidding me right?

Igra rolled big fat sausages at the end of his palm. "Is this a trick? Open it."

Swish, swish, swirl, swirl. Nada.

Hope of Annu's return dissolved. "I'm trying, fuck stick. It's not working."

Igra stomped his foot, the ground trembled. "Earth must have still have us closed off those duplicitous bastards. How rude. We had bigger plans for them. How rude. Never mind. You'll fix it once this is over. Now the planet's fate is all on you."

Fabulous. Just what I need.

Annu is probably not safe at all. None of us are and we've got to fix it.

Despair washed over Shayne, she swayed with the current. "You're a freaking monster. Who does this shit? Seriously?"

Please be a bad dream, or a bad trip. Did I eat any mushrooms from the forest I shouldn't? Yeah I'm sure that's it. Not.

Igra's clap rang in her ears. "Enough. Before I release you and your strange friend, you are clear on our arrangement?"

Shayne counted cracks in the concrete. "Yes, you fat fuck."

Igra cupped his hand around his ear and tipped forward. "Sorry? I can't hear you."

Shayne grasped at wandering dignity. "I said yes. You fucking heard me the first time Iggy about to pop."

Levity accompanied Igra's movements. "Wonderful. In that case, let's get this underway."

Creator, God, Dad, Ann, whoever the heck is around and can hear me, please, I beg of you help me stop this mad man. Even God FuckShit.

Anyone will do.

No?

Chapter 28
The End is Nigh but Not Nigh Enough
Pine Gap, DSI Facility
New South Wales, Australia, Earth

The room shrank, Annu paced away cabin fever. His thoughts festered, his mind brewed and churned. When he reached the door and kicked the metal, it reverberated up his leg. "How is it that doing things the right way is harder, painful, and strips you bare. At the end there's no apparent pay off. Conversely the wrong way is quick, efficient and the pay off fast."

The creature on the other side raced around its cell, banged on surfaces and gestured. Its shrieks interrupted his funk.

The pit of Annu's gut gurgled, lava trickled down his arm. "Someone would have alerted Shayne. She'd escape with Zeke. Hell, what if that was Erin I saw going to Orion."

Ankor filled his mind, a link between them remained. With practice the headache receded. *'I'm sure they're safe.'*

'I pray you're right but perhaps you are yet to realise the depths of evil some are capable of. If she's dead my world's ended, it's all over.' Annu dipped and slowed his breathing. *'Do you have a way to find out? Psychically I mean?'*

'No, I'm sorry. Not with diminished powers. It limits me greatly.'

Annu combed fingers through knots, oil slicked over his skin. *'I can't think of a way out of here yet, but damned if I'll let them kill me and anyone else. This crazy nightmare will end.'*

Calm from Ankor warmed Annu's mind. *'Which is why you are here to save us. It's part of your greater plan. Although, I admit the odds are against you. Only two beings have ever* escaped, but were found not long after, and killed. The facility is a labyrinth, and the security thus far is impenetrable.'

With that encouragement I'll probably join them. 'How did they get out of the cell?'

Hesitation tainted Ankor's words. 'One, a biologically a jelly fluid substance squeezed under the door, the other's blew it up.'

Defeat niggled at Annu. *'I can't do either of those things.'*

'We'll find a way; I have faith in you and the Creator.'

Desperate for it to rub off, Annu grasped onto Ankor's belief; it trickled through his fingers into a puddle on the floor. 'You might want to keep a lid on that for now. I'm starting to think the Creator likes tormenting me.'

Ankor's tone darkened. *'You are a gift from the Creator to return peace and spirituality to the Universes. Enki instilled you and Shayne with the power to do so. Being human and God means you've got a greater understanding of humanity's flaws and can work with, instead of against them. At times it's more challenging than others and it's not helpful to think this way. It's in the darkest times we must seek the light. It's easy to lose faith when things are going well. It's harder keeping it while things are difficult such as now.'*

Difficult is a push, horrific is closer. Admonishment accompanied contrition. 'Yes, though waiting for last minute arrivals of a solution to happen are wearing on me. If it keeps up I'll have some kind of attack.'

'Stay focused. Think of your family, and pray. The answer will arrive.'

Despite no access to a clock, the time spent in the cell acted like a bomb timer; Annu's nerves the wick, his life the deadline.

I'll try the high road again. Mother, Creator, Enki, help me please. Show me a way out of here. I beg of you before the dark answers and consumes me instead.

Annu paced and waited for an answer.

Tic, sizzle, tic, sizzle, tic, sizzle, tic.

The glass door rattled, the volcano erupted.

The doctor who'd shown Annu some sympathy, Tony, checked either side of the hallway, scanned a keycard and dropped into a pocket.

Flark. No, not yet. I need more time. Shit, shit, shit.

Annu backed up against the bed and clenched his fists.

The lock released, the glass slid open.

Tony entered with an arm across his middle and a palm raised. "It's all right. I'm not here to hurt you." Tony looked behind him every few seconds, sweat beaded across his face. "In fact, I'm trying to help you."

Anticipation pushed Annu off the bed; he bunched the man's lap coat in his fist and lifted.

Heat oozed along Annu, he singed the coat. "How? You going to end it quicker?"

A large piece of paper fell out of Tony's pocket.

The doctor trembled and licked his lips. "No. I swear; I'm on your side."

Annu deposited him on the ground and crossed his arms. "How can you get me out?"

The doctor smoothed down his coat and collected the piece of paper. "There's not much I can do but this is the layout of the facility." He handed it to Annu, the paper shook. "You see, it details all the security checkpoints and exits. Also, I've marked the room with an 'x' where the machines are that inhibit your powers."

Here's the eleventh hour reprieve with Budda's second arrow.

"Aha. Right. Thanks it's something. Why are you doing this?"

The doctor wrung his hands, sweat dropped onto his lapels. "When I started working here over two decades ago, it was in the belief we'd learn from life on other planets and positively interact with them. For some time I believe they placated me, louring me in until they tricked me into doing things I, I, that aren't right. I signed a confidentiality agreement and if I talk to anyone or even try, they'll kill me. I can't live like this anymore. Someone must bring this place down from the inside out. Not me, I can't do it but you. I know you're the right one."

Thump. Another pound of responsibility weighted Annu's shoulders. "Okay great, but I still can't leave this room."

The doctor removed the key card out of his pocket and handed it over. "This is a duplicate of mine. Obviously they'll find it missing soon enough. You'll still need another to get through the doors. Unfortunately I can't help there. Unless you use the time between them when they're getting you and taking you for tests. I don't know. You'll have to figure it out."

Annu tumbled over logistical possibilities. "Even if I make it out, whatever tech they use on me with drains my energy. They're resonance weapons all but destroy me and there's the drugs."

The doctor's eyebrows formed a worm. "I've marked the sector those machines are in. Obviously they've ensured security by separating their suppression technology. It's on the other side of the facility. Getting there is your first priority."

This is getting complicated.

"How does this stuff work?"

"Basically it blocks all extraterrestrial beings powers via a microwave energy system. Once you turn it off or destroy it they're at your mercy. Like I said go there first."

The weight on Annu's back lightened an iota. "Thank you. I never expected this and it helps a lot. Anything else I should know?"

The doctor shuffled and exuded fear. "It's the least I can do. The only other thing is there's a lapse in security between three a.m. and three-fifteen. If perhaps you could keep me alive when this goes down I'd appreciate it."

We'll see you might get lucky. Shit.

"Flark. I hadn't noticed. If you don't get in my way and turn on me you'll live."

"Good. It's a deal." The doctor shrugged and swiped sweat from the end of his nose. "Drugs are released through each cell's air vents to subdue the beings, more so at night time. It makes it easier to manage. I'll shut off the air vents to your cell this evening during the guard change. I can't do more than one without getting caught. The security office is at the end of the cells. Here," He pointed to a small room. "And the lifts are here. Always guarded, I'm not sure how you'll get by them."

Me either. Flark. It's getting harder every second.

Annu punched the wall, the glass wobbled. "It doesn't leave me with much time before they get me. I have no way of knowing when that is and it doesn't get me through the doors. Shit, I'm halfway to nowhere."

The doctor turned and waddled towards the door, his's nervousness rubbed off on Annu. "I can't help, or stay anymore. I blocked the camera in here for a few minutes. Good luck."

Annu swallowed the lump in his throat. "Thank you."

The door slid shut, Annu's limited options provided a small chance at escape.

Chapter 29
Fripples
Martian Mother Ship
Enki Island, Orion

Can I scam more food before I go? The I.D.I.O.T.s released their hold on Shayne, she rubbed her shoulders. "Finally. I'll have dents in my skin for a week now. I'm not twenty one anymore you know."

A woman, in the loosest sense of the term, pushed Shayne towards Iggy, she dug in heels.

Out of sight, Jackie yelled. "Let me go. Stop hurting me. I'm on your side."

Shayne lunged at Iggy. "You mother fucker. You said you'd let him go when I agreed to help you."

Two I.D.I.O.T.s grabbed Shayne, her feet dangled above the ground.

Iggy hovered over the black box; a finger waved the display screen. "Let me get one thing clear right now Earthling, you—"

A shuffle and whine from the other side of the room broke Shayne's concentration.

Six out of the twelve original Council members who'd attended the meeting days ago stumbled, dishevelled and bound between guards.

Surprise branded Shayne's chest and crept up her neck. "Oh-my-God. You're holding members of your own Council against their will?"

Iggy slammed the top of the console and stomped his foot. "They found out about my intentions with you and didn't agree."

The rush of emotion plummeted Shayne's blood sugar levels, she bent over. "Fine, whatever, just hurry this up. Oh and give me some more biscuits."

Iggy tapped an icon on the screen; a tingle ran from Shayne's feet to the top of her.

Each tap of his finger surged energy through Shayne, fatigue lifted, hunger diminished, her sense of self returned.

Icicles formed along Shayne's arms and spread across her skin, the guards stepped away.

Iggy's mouth agape, his cheeks wobbled. "Oh my, oh, oh."

He reversed the order of process on screen.

The energy abated, Shayne sagged. She clawed at him, guards re-grabbed her. "Why did you turn it off again?"

Iggy flushed, the fear in his eyes dwindled. "I, ah didn't expect, I." He jabbed a finger at her. "I have your word you'll behave or you know the consequences?"

Stay calm, don't lose your shit now. Yeah right.

"Oh, my fucking God, you fat fucking stupid moron. YES."

Smack, Iggy's hand connected with her cheek; Shayne's face whipped in the opposite direction. Shayne's ears rang, her eyes watered. She blinked and cleared her vision. Iggy lifted Shayne's chin with two fingers. "As I said, don't forget who you are working for."

Shayne spat blood at Iggy and bared her teeth. "Get on with it or I'll strange you with your own testicles."

A sneer melted, Iggy returned to the console and turned the systems off.

Energy raced up Shayne's spine and spread into the rest of her. "Oh fuck yeah. Hello." Shayne's powers returned in waves, her brain cleared, icicles replaced her blood.

Shayne erupted in a blue aura, and rolled her shoulders.

I'd forgotten how good this feels, how did I manage to get by before without powers?

Everyone around her jumped back several metres.

Shayne pointed at Igra. "Now radio the other I.D.I.O.T.s and tell them to help us not kill us, release Jackie and give me more food for the road."

The I.D.I.O.T.s will make great bait.

Unable to hide the fear in his eyes, Iggy motioned to guards behind Shayne.

A guard shoved food at Shayne; others untied Jackie and pushed him towards her.

I need to get this shit sorted out ASAP.

With a belly full and Shayne's brain at working capacity, a brilliant idea struck.

Crap? Are you sure? Yes. Pretty sure. Okay. Don't think, do. And quick.

Iggy pursed his lips, his chest puffed. "Sergeant Lyn under Lieutenant NimNim, you and your team keep a close eye on her and give military assistance. Those who disagree with the change in direction execute."

'Oh you're so being called Nimrod. Nimrod.'

Sergeant Lyn hesitated, his teeth gritted, his face expressionless. "Yes your Grace."

Lieutenant NimNim stepped forward, anger steeped in each movement. "Sir, I cannot in good conscious work with that Earthling or the other alien."

Iggy cocked an eyebrow. "Unless you want to be added to the list of defectors you'll follow those orders."

Nimrod straightened his back and thrust out his chest. "Yes, sir."

With a few hand gestures from Nimrod, I.D.I.O.T.s filed past Shayne out the door. It closed behind them.

Jackie stood at Shayne's side, shaken and stirred but no olive.

Shayne touched his shoulder, he retracted. "I'm still pissy at you but we'll get to that later. Are you okay?"

He shrugged and wrapped his arms around himself. "I don't want to go back out there."

Shayne's thoughts tangled into knots. "Me either but we've got no choice. But listen here buddy if you don't fuck me over again I'll keep you safe. If you do you're dead too."

Do it now before it's too late.

She widened her eyes and spoke between her teeth. "Stay right beside me, okay?"

A confused expression befell Jackie. "Trust me, I will."

Iggie's squint gave him swine-like features. "Ah, you speak their language. Is this a power or because you know them?"

You stupid fat fuck, I want to tear your face off.

"Oh for fuck's sake. A power okay."

Iggy relaxed his stance. "Fine. I guess it will speed things up."

Shayne clutched Jackie's arm, power focused into her hands. "Yep."

Shayne aimed and froze Iggy with the mike in place. "Oh fucking finally. I've been hanging to do that. Fuck you so much."

His mouth remained open, Iggy's frown a permanent accessory albeit a moment too late.

Shayne whipped around, I.D.I.O.T.s charged, she blasted them. The first dozen froze complete.

The others stumbled on leaden legs. Success strengthened Shayne's flow until nothing but I.D.I.O.T. popsicles remained. "Ha-de-fucking-ha. I don't fucking think so arseholes."

Jackie huddled on the ground; his arms over his guts, icicles brushed his hair. "Oh, oh, oh."

The ambient temperature dropped, Shayne shivered and clicked her fingers in Iggy's face. "I can't believe I actually did it but I did. Shit. I should have used one of their communicators first and find out where that craft is."

Jackie rose from his knees and waved in Iggy's face. "You froze them. You froze them all."

Shayne nodded towards the captured Council members. "Except for those guys. Give me a hand to untie her; she can do the rest."

An older woman, her robes tattered, swiped a tear. "Thank you, Shayne. You might not remember me from the meeting the other day but I'm Counsellor Marguerite. We were wrong all along, I'm so sorry. He's the problem, not you and your partner. We had no idea until this all happened. How foolish."

She spoke up at the stupid meeting. She's on our side.

Shayne patted the woman's hand and helped her stand. "It's okay, maybe it's better you found out this way. Then there's no confusion or no one believing me. Do you have a way to contact Iggy's men?"

"No I'm sorry." Margarite pointed at Iggy. "What will you do now?"

Anxiety replaced adrenaline, Shayne faked confidence. "Not much, try and call off a few wars and find missing loved ones. You know the usual. You?"

Marguerite crossed her arms. "What are the chances you can manage so much on your own?"

Shayne shoulders tensed, time wasted away. "Mmm, a little more than the chances Iggy-about-to-pop will be all warm and fuzzy when he's defrosted—if he is. Wait here until I come back and get you. It's obviously the safest place on the island."

The other woman massaged her knees. "I assure you, we won't be rushing to do that."

Shayne met Jackie in the middle, shoved packets of food into her jacket pocket and a water bottle into her pants.

Why didn't I? Look at that son of a bitch over there, freezing isn't enough. When I come back, I'm making ice cubes out of you.

An iced Iggy-about-to-pop gawked, everything he'd done and said to this point came forefront of Shayne thoughts.

You fucking bastard, you deserve to die but I can't kill you in cold blood.

Shayne re-blasted Iggy and the I.D.I.O.T.s to ensure a deep freeze. "That should do it. Now let's fuck this shit up."

Chapter 30
Miss Robinson Crusoe
The Arctic Ocean
Between Yebu and Enki, Orion

The craft hovered for a moment and shot off at high speed. Erin clutched the arm rests, her fingers imbedded into the cushion, her heart fluttered.

Oh God, oh God, oh God, oh God. Please don't let us crash and die. This isn't a normal way to travel.

Zeke stretched his legs and filled the seat. "Relax. It's perfectly safe. If it wasn't, these guys wouldn't have made it here."

Ocean in each direction stressed not comforted Erin. "What part of this is okay? I'm not eating cup cakes and getting doilies off my grandmother while she complains about my mother who's sitting inches away. An exciting event in my life. Instead, I'm on an alien planet, in an alien space ship, with aliens and they're taking us to who knows where to do who knows what to us."

Zeke threw up his hands, concern marked his face. "You're an alien on this planet. It's okay, really. I swear I won't let anything happen to you. Not while I'm here anyway. Once we land I've got it worked out. I'm the king of sneaking out unseen."

If I'd told anyone else what happened they'd commit me to a nut house. Maybe I'd get Shayne's old—oh.

Shame swept over Erin and flushed her cheeks. "I never thought I'd say this but I owe my mother an apology."

Great self confidence and encouragement help's one's mental health, but Zeke's a child. He can't protect us both. Mum won't know we're together let alone with the aliens? I'm sorry for being such a bitch sometimes and not telling mum how much I loved her. I just hung onto a grudge so long for what reason? Nothing worth it.

Tears welled, Erin choked on a sob. "Great, I think crashing and dying is preferable to what may come. We might have a better chance at survival. This is a nightmare. I want my cupcakes. I bet your dad ate them."

Zeke's hand squeeze calmed her nerves a fraction. "I'm sorry this happened, but I mean it, I'll take care of you. That's what brothers are for."

"Sure, as a big sister my first advice is don't lend my mother money and—"

A volt of electricity flowed from Zeke's hand to Erin's and covered their hands in a blue film.

Erin tightened the hold, her mind raced, her blood pulsed. "That's so weird and awesome."

Martians moved around the flight deck and into a hallway paying little attention to the pair.

Erin slipped her hand out from under Zeke's and wiggled it.

The film and electricity dissipated. "It must mean something."

Zeke examined his palm. "Ah yeah, for sure. It happened the first time we touched hands."

A tingle ran across Erin's shoulders, up her neck, and filled her with energy.

Erin's skin buzzed; identical to on Earth when her power first arrived. "Oh wow. It's back. We'll escape and help Mum. Thank—"

Thoughts from others invaded Erin's mind:

'Focus this way, focus that way. How can I see everywhere at once when the radar's over there?'

'Did I lock the front door before I went to the base? I don't think I did. Millard will be angry when she gets home.'

'Where are we to keep those humans until the Queen comes? I'm not going to occupy them. Their eyes are too close together and their wide.'

Zeke shook her shoulder. "Are you all right?"

Erin brushed the errant thoughts aside. "Apparently I hear and understand others' thoughts now too. I wonder if I not only hear, but also influence them. I'll convince the pilot to fly back to the island and send mum a message."

Zeke's eyes widened, he nodded. "Hell yes. Do both."

A semblance of control diminished Erin's fear. "You keep watch and let me concentrate."

Eyes closed, Erin sorted amongst mind mess and honed in on the pilot:

'I'm exhausted. We've been going for days without rest. Perhaps once the Queen sees we've got the DemiGods. Or allow us leave and another troop stays to oversee the takeover.'

Erin injected her thought like a syringe and pictured moving his hands on the controls: *'We need to go back to the island before the Queen gets here. Must ensure we've got control there.'*

Zeke whispered in Erin's ear. "He's saying nothing but his hands are on the steering controls. It's working."

'What? Where did that come from? That's not our orders. I'm a stupid man. I must be losing my mind.'

Zeke's sigh warmed Erin's neck. "And their off again," he poised his hand above Erins, "I'll help."

Erin held a deep breath and refused giving up. "No. Give me a minute I can do it myself."

Alright woman, make being stubborn worth it. Try something he's more likely to do and not fight against:

'I return and gain control over the island and I may get my own squad. We're not far away; it won't take long to go back there.'

Zeke bounced on the seat. "It's working again. He's changing coordinates. Come on."

'Wait, we'll still have to fight for it. That wastes even more time. What's going on?'

'Nothing, it's a good idea. I'm just over—'

Zeke slapped his leg. "Flark it. He's changing them back. We can't stuff around."

The connection with the pilot dwindled like the thrill of having another brother. "No pressure or anything. Now please shut up and let me focus."

Not a good time for pig headedness.

Erin clasped Zeke's hand, everything amplified within her.

She manipulated the steering column beneath his fingers. *'We have to go back there now.'*

The craft veered sharp left and dipped.

Erin smashed into Zeke's side, the air forced from her lungs.

Martians stumbled into equipment and each other into a pile on the floor.

'Quick. Straighten the ship up.'

An angered voice broke Erin's mental connection.

A taller Martian strode over to the controls and gripped the pilot by the shoulders. "Melani. What the hell are you doing?"

Erin pushed off Zeke and shook herself. "Shit. This is harder than it looks."

Oops. I swore. Sorry. I'm a bad teacher. But, well the occasion called for it.

The pilot paled to teal and rubbed his wrist. "Sir, I, I, I'm not sure. My head isn't right."

The taller Martian released the pilot. "Distraction's cost lives. Get it together."

Zeke stroked Erin's arm, his tone softened. "Minor slip up. Don't give up."

Another touch of their hands and vitality surged through Erin. "I got this."

'Turn the ship—'

Boom, boom, boom.

An explosion ripped through the ship, screams, torn metal and alarms deafened all other noise.

The ship lurched upwards not forwards, Erin tumbled onto the floor and stopped against a cupboard.

Zeke grabbed for her hand. "Erin, hold on."

Erin reached towards him and fought gravity. "I'm trying."

Boom, boom, boom.

Smoke filled the cabin, they tipped to the left, a large section of wall sucked outside and took Zeke with it.

God help us.

Erin slammed against the roof, bounced off and fell down a hole in the floor. Each obstacle banged into her; she summersaulted and landed atop a pile of seats shoved into the middle of the cabin below by the impact. Pain scored Erin's ribs, her breath sharpened, black smoke stung her eyes. She removed a chair leg from her back and levered onto her elbows. Blood trailed down her cheek and arm. Aside from bangs on the rest of Erin, a lump formed on her forehead. A crack underneath sickened her, and she clutched a chair beside her. At the top, the pile shifted and dropped inches.

Erin's intestines cramped, the fragile structure faltered. "No. No. No."

A couple more chairs fell, the crack widened, the floor collapsed. She dropped another two sections, out the craft's bottom, and into the open ocean. Iced water fought Erin's warm body, breathing hurt. She flailed, splashed and tried to stay afloat. "Someone help me. Help. Hello? Someone?"

A chunk of debris hurtled towards her from above, Erin paddled with one arm in the other direction; it continued its descent with her head as the target.

Please be safe Zeke. I'm sorry.

The debris landed right beside Erin, the impact's wake plunged Erin into the darkness, light from the sky faded. Water filled her mouth and her throat, she choked for air. Exhaustion added cement and pushed Erin further down. At the brink of death calm arrived.

It all makes sense now.

Erin stopped and relinquished to a liquid grave. An intense light illuminated the surface, grew tendrils and trailed towards Erin. Warmth, peace, love and compassion removed remnants of fear and desperation.

The light snake wrapped itself around Erin, the urge to breath ceased, Erin's body drifted down, her soul lifted up and to the main light.

Chapter 31
Ironic Despair
Pine Gap, DSI Facility
New South Wales, Australia, Earth

Silence while the other occupants slept enveloped Annu. Rather than comfort, it emphasised his perilous position and solitude in a huge task. On the bed Annu patted the map and keycard in his pant's pocket.

Despite two missed, required components—finger print and the other card—their presence eased Annu's mind. "One minute we're fighting with the GC, I go to Earth to kill bugs in Shayne's pantry and I end up a prisoner in a flarked up military facility planning a solo coup."

Albeit flarked up, but the one place I've found someone with answers about my father and I still can't get it. Jacob mentioned that Enlil in the Lexicon days, weeks, whatever ago. Given he's so close to where we live, knowing about him is proactive but on the other hand screw it, he and Enki can fight their own battles from hereon.

Unlike trouble, brilliance evaded him. No ideas or fortuitous answers arrived as to how or where he'd obtain the rest. The calm divinity once provided for Annu dwindled. Instead, resentment and bitterness grew.

"Anything I do in the future will be well thought out and rational." Annu's heart ached, loneliness weakened his reserve. "Oh Shay. What a mess. I wouldn't swap your hormones, blanket stealing, farting, food ruining arse for anything. I hope you're home worried about me with Zeke and Jacob driving you nuts."

Flark, I love that woman. In a zillion years I'd never believe I'd find someone like her. They deserve more than me. All things considered I make a terrible husband and an equally shitty father. Am I worthy of all I've been given?

The glass door rattled; Annu rolled onto his side and rose. "What do you want?"

Dingle stood on the other side holding a tray of food. A swipe of his card and the door opened.

Of all the people to come, it's you.

Annu slid onto the mattress's edge and perched forward. "I said what do you want?"

Dingle entered, readjusted the tray and slipped the card into his shirt pocket. "Your time's up mate." He poked at things on the plate. "Since you didn't tell them what you wanted it's rib-eye steak and some flashed up veggies."

Since the Ascension Annu's powers negated requiring a physical fight; lack of practice aside and even with them, he'd still drain Dingle's life like a bottle of rum.

Pent up frustration simmered, hatred and disgust drove Annu. "You picked the wrong God to mess with."

Fear wavered Dingle's levity, the sneer returned. "That's what they all say. I don't care whether you eat it or not, you're time's up."

Vengeance waited on the precipice, Annu slow breathed, his skin tingled.

If I get the zapper thing off him, he loses an advantage. More so when shoved up his arse.

"You're dying today not me."

Dingle's demeanour changed, he tossed the tray at the opposite wall. Crockery and cutlery clanged; food ran down the wall and onto the floor.

Dingle cracked his knuckles and clenched his fists. "You arrogant piece of shit, mother fucker. I've waited for this moment."

Annu launched, grabbed Dingle around the middle and dropped his weight forward. "Back at you."

Dingle slipped further in unidentifiable food and slammed onto the ground. "Fuccckk."

Annu landed on top of Dingle, the walls shook; he brushed the stun-gun with his fingers. "Humph."

Dingle's head reverberated off the tiles and projected forwards.

Annu's nose connected with Dingle's skull, agony and blood splattered. *Or not.* "Flark me."

I'd forgotten what true pain felt like until this place. Remembering might do me good.

Mid Annu's nose reconstruction, Dingle wriggled his upper half from under Annu and pole-drove his elbow into Annu's temple and shoved him.

Annu slumped against the wall and smacked his cheeks. Six months of cobwebs cleared out in one go. "Damned. Flarking little bastard. You got a few good ones in I'll give you that."

On his feet in the middle of the room, Dingle raised fists and bounced between feet. "For all your piss, vinegar, and size I thought you'd put up more of a fight. I'm disappointed."

Annu aligned his jaw and rubbed the bridge of his nose. "I haven't started yet, boy. You'll know when I do."

Dingle lifted his chin and smirked. "Please. You're old and powerless. You've been subjected to torture for a period of time and drained of your power. You can't win. I'll allow you to give up and I won't tell a soul."

There's a saying about old bulls and young steers but it escapes me right now. Be smarter not faster.

Annu rolled his neck and stood, a shadow fell over Dingle. "Neither of us is going anywhere until this is finished."

"I'll make it easier for you and fight one handed." Dingle removed the stun-gun from his belt and thew it across the room. "And I'll fight fair."

The stupid bastard actually thinks he'll win. And live. Oh the ignorance of youth.

Annu served up a grin. "Aside from experience I've got advantages you don't. And, your confidence exceeds your abilities."

Dingle cocked an eyebrow and puffed his chest. "Powers you don't currently have aren't included."

"Is that right?" Annu's nose and other wounds healed. He swiped blood from his cheek. "I bet if I remove one of your body parts unlike me it won't grow back again."

Dingle's Adam's apple jiggled; he moved for the stun-gun, realisation drained his colour. "That's not fair. I got rid of my weapon."

Annu's stepped closer, his finger tips ignited. "Was it fair when you kidnapped, tortured, tormented me and the others in this gods forsaken place?"

Dingle eyed the exit and backed towards it. "I followed orders. It's nothing personal; I hate all of you equally."

Annu's growl rattled the walls; power's aphrodisiac surged within him. "Well I assure you, I took it very personally."

The first hint of mortal peril appeared in Dingle; he spun and reached for the door. "I'm out of here."

I don't flarking think so.

Annu grabbed Dingle's other arm and pulled. "You're not going anywhere."

Dingle shrugged away from Annu and held the card near the display, his hands shook. "Let me go."

Annu held tighter, one big yank and the shoulder joint dislocated. "Not on your life—literally."

The card flew out of Dingle's hand, he screeched.

Annu balanced his weight, tightened his grip and pulled. "Not so flarking tough now are you?"

Muscles tore from the shoulder joint, a series of cracks followed.

Dingle banged on the glass using his knee. "Help. Someone help me."

The man's visible agony faltered Annu's vigour. '*Have I gone too far?*'

Dingle's head lolled, his body twisted.

A detached arm flopped into Annu's palm. "Nah. A not so lucky break for you, but I get the irony."

Dingle lay against the door, blood pooled, alarms and sirens wailed.

Panic pierced Annu's daze. "Shit."

Annu separated the hand, tossed it adjoined to the card under the bed, and the arm back at Dingle.

One step from the bed electricity flowed through Annu's cell and dropped him to his knees.

Armed security guards filled the hall outside, another surge of amps immobilised Annu.

A fresh torture tormented Annu, helpless and unable to move, the door opened a few steps away.

That's just flarking cruel. You're screwing with me again.

Dingle slipped into a medic's open arms. "He, he, I."

The electricity intensified, Annu gritted his teeth. The brief glimpse of control allowed hope a fresh chance.

Please don't look for the missing limb or card yet. Please, please, please, I don't care which one of you does it, but give me another chance.

A guard collected Dingle's dismembered arm and put into a bag. "What the fuck happened in here?"

Lasers scanned Annu's cell, staff and guards carried Dingle down the hallway.

As soon as the coast clears a little I'm out of here.

Chapter 32
The Worm Turned
Enki Island, Orion

Outside again, reality slapped Shayne. The temporary respite and returned powers didn't change the war on the island. In the short time gone, the battle progressed down the compound towards the entry gates. Assorted bodies scattered the ground among building debris and amplified a grave atmosphere.

Shayne guided Jackie past the main wreckage, out the gates and to outer woods. "Now the morons are working for me the kids should be safe until we arrive on Yebu."

When this is all over I hope everything goes back to normal. Firstly my sanity.

Whiz, whiz, boom.

A projectile from a flying craft hit the ground and exploded.

The team of I.D.I.O.T.s around Shayne retaliated and blew the ship from the sky.

Covered in dust Shayne dragged Jackie behind half a tree. "Every fucking minute. How are there any of those fuckers left?"

A ball of fire crashed into the forest nearby.

I won't be finding out anything if I fucking die here. At least the fucking I.D.I.O.T.s are working for me, kind of. Argh.

Jackie hugged a tree trunk. "What are you going to do? Can you freeze the craft they're in from here?"

Shayne raised an eyebrow and jutted her chin. "Dude, I'm not a long range missile."

Jackie pitched a hissy fit and flung his arms. "Well what can you do then? I thought with these powers of yours, you'd fix everything but it turns out they won't. I should have kept running, hidden better. Anything but here with you."

For fuck's sake. He's sooo dramatic. Will someone give me a break here and be on my side.

"Um arsehole. Let me clarify a few things. I've got powers but I'm not a fucking magician. I levitate but not fly, freeze, project and blast energy, see the future, sort of, open wormholes and a couple of other things I didn't tell the Council about, which turned out a good—"

Shayne's thoughts swam laps around her brain.

Oh shit. Maybe Earth's re-opened their side of the wormhole in the last five minutes?

Jackie clicked in her face. "Hello? Are you all right?"

Shayne swatted the interruption away.

I'm exhausted, hungry, sore and over it. If it doesn't work again there's a chance I'll flip out for—

Click, click.

Two hands waved in Shayne's face. "Hello in there?"

Oh he's talking to me. "Huh?"

Jackie's frown shortened his face. "You stopped talking half way through a sentence. Are you all right?"

Oh shit, yeah, you.

"Not even fucking close but I'm trying a wormhole again."

Shayne swished, a pinpoint of light appeared.

Fuck yeah.

It increased to coin size and disappeared. "Argh. Come on."

Jackie probed the space the light appeared in. "It's still not working."

Shayne held insanity at bay. "It might. Maybe. Give me a second."

Okay, mind clear, no pressure, open wormhole now.

Shayne squeezed an eye open, nothing happened. "Fuck, shit, fuck, shit."

There really is no easy answer or quick fix to this shit. Actual thinking and work are required. Does my brain even remember how?

Jackie frown deepened, the tension in the air crackled. "Have you been praying to fuck shit?"

His innocence flushed Shayne with embarrassment. "Um, yeah sure. The almighty God Fuckshit."

What does it matter if I fib a little? Who am I to say it won't ever be a religion?

"And so far that hasn't worked out either."

Thunder grumbled, lightning cracked.

Okay all ready. Cut me some slack.

Jackie let go of the tree and sighed. "No other solution but you?"

Shayne kicked said tree, the grass and anything close. "Ah duh."

Jackie's squeal relieved Shayne's frustration a fraction. "Ouch. Why'd you do that?"

Boom, boom, boom.

Explosions rocked the grounds. Shayne wobbled, she leaned against Jackie. "It made me feel better."

Martians marched out the gates towards the I.D.I.O.T.s.

A handful of Shayne's I.D.I.O.T.s, shot their way to her.

Shayne's sigh warmed her face. "Thank Gods."

Jackie worked on elevating his useless status. "Perhaps you should beg rather than pray to FuckShit."

God FuckShit showed the same amount of compassion and attention for Shayne as her mother. Since this whole mess began, he'd answered exactly none of her prayers and requests.

And threatened me with smiting via storm several times.

Though I can't blame him for that. I'd do the same to me.

NimNim aka Nimrod stopped a metre short of Shayne.

He cracked his knuckles and clenched his teeth. "What's your plan and make it fast?"

Why do people keep asking me this?

Shayne's mouth worked before her brain. "To punch you in the face right after I use you all to end this and eat my weight in chocolate."

Nimrod wrapped his hands around Shayne's neck. "Aggghhh. You worthless creature."

The woman, Lim, grappled and pried Nimrod off. "Keep your cool. As much as it sucks we need her."

Nimrod flushed from chest to cheeks. "Fine. Get out there and sort this out. Now."

Shayne straightened her back. "I am fuckarse. Get whoever you can together on the island and—"

Awareness exploded in Shayne's mind. Ambient noise disappeared, the world around her altered, replaced by a blurred image of water, a human descended deeper. Large objects floated above and around the person. A weak kick and the person floated inert. Shayne bit her lip, the person turned around.

Erin.

Shayne's soul bifurcated and left a permanent division with no chance of repair. "I'm too late. It's all my fault."

The scene faded and reality returned.

Grief dropped to Shayne knees. "Oh Gods. Erin. I must save her."

Jackie leaned over and stroked her back. "What happened? Where did you go?"

No. Don't give up.

Shayne levered off the ground and paced. "My daughter Erin is drowning and I don't know where."

Which Martian ship is she in? Where were they now?

Nimrod stopped her mid rotation. "What's wrong with you? Get your shit together or so help me I'll shoot you anyway."

Shayne erupted in icicles, put up her aura and froze the gun. "Do you know if an I.D.I.O.T. ship shot down a Martian craft on the way to Yebu?"

Red tinged Nimrod's coco skin, his arm trembled. "Even if I knew I wouldn't tell you shit. You've got five seconds." The weapon moved to her temple. "Three."

Nimrod tapped a button; nothing changed aside an iota of fear.

Shayne wore her own self satisfaction well. "Ha fucker. Iggy turned that shit off. Now the worm has turned. Well, it burrowed first but anyway. Find out where that crashed or you're fucked."

Nimrod maintained the gun Shayne's head and his waist height. "There's no time for anything else. More people will die."

Shayne lowered it with a finger. "Either you help me out or you die in a shitty way."

Where are you baby? Help me find you.

A touch on his forearm and it froze beneath Shayne's fingers.

Nimrod recoiled and spoke into his lapel. "Headquarters, what's the location of the Martian ship that went down in the ocean? STAT. Over."

A crackled, disjointed and indecipherable screech responded.

Mmm. Maybe it's because I froze Igra next to the communication machine. Fuck. I screwed myself over there. Gods come on help me out. She'll die without my help.

Nimrod wriggled the button on his lapel. "I can't hear you. Over?"

The image of Erin under water repeated through Shayne's brain, a vice plonked on her chest.

Shayne sucked on her lip and concentrated. '*Erin, it's mum. Hang in there, I'm coming for you but I need your help. Where are you?*'

Hang on, if Erin's under water, where's Zeke? Why didn't I see him too? Shit, fuck. I'm not failing them not matter what it takes.

'*Erin, where are you?*'

A tingle sensation tickled Shayne's mind. '*Mum. Mum? Help me.*'

'Hold on. I'll find you.'

Shayne jabbed Nimrod's frozen limb, chunks of ice attached to skin fell off. "Well?"

Nimrod withdrew his arm and tried sticking bits back on. "I, I, I'm sorry the communications have fried. Don't freeze me anymore."

I'll be too late to save her. Do harder. "Fuck it. Get me in a ship in that direction right fucking now."

Teeth gritted Nimrod puffed his cheeks. "No. I—"

Shayne snap froze him and stepped around him. "Okay then. Who's getting me a ship ASAP?"

All the other I.D.I.O.T.s raised their hands and disappeared into the forest amidst pleas of assurance.

In their stead Jacob arrived, pallid and bright red. "Shayne. Thank the Gods. I found you. I couldn't wait any longer."

Shayne's chest tightened, guilt served a plate of humility. "Jesus, Jacob. I forgot about—never mind."

I'm so not winning the Demigoddess of the century award today. Well probably no time soon that's for sure.

An I.D.I.O.T. Craft landed in the next clearing, the ramp dropped.

A woman stood at the doorway. "Ready to leave when you are ma'am."

"Good. About fucking time." Shayne helped Jacob walk. "After I save Erin and Zeke, I'll drop you both at the hospital. You just take it easy and rest okay?"

And I'll try not to forget about you again.

Jacob half turned to Shayne. "Erin? What happened to her?"

Oh baby, please be okay. Please, please, please.

"Basically in a round about way, me happened, but I'm working on it. A lot's changed since we last spoke."

Creator if you only listen to me once, please make it this time.

Chapter 33
Escape or Die
DSI, Pine Gap
New South Wales, Australia, Earth

No time wasted, Annu bolted down the corridor past two dozen quiet cells and reigned in responsibility.

I'll be back to save you all. Hurry up man, don't waste time.

Muscles ached from lack of movement, each step towards the guard's room yanked Annu's hamstrings but returned circulation. Voices erupted from the room, Annu wiped his hands, desperation drove him forward. He stuck close to the wall and hid next to the entry.

Two guards lingered outside the office, the tall one held the door open with a foot; the shorter one sipped a drink. Stale tobacco and coffee wafted into the surroundings.

On the door's precipice the tall guard adjusted his waistband. "Did you see what happened to Dingle? That guy's a fucking douche bag. He never learns."

Annu's heart thumped, anger for vengeance re-awakened.

He didn't get half of what he deserved and I'd do it all over again.

The shorter one smoothed his hair and used the window for a mirror. "Didn't see it, but heard about it from some guy from Sector 7G while out having a smoke. Nasty business. It serves him right going in there with those fucks, the cocky bugger."

The tall one stepped away from the door, it clicked closed. "It's not the first time and I doubt it's the last. Plus he picked the worst cell to go into, dipshit."

The short one's chuckle irritated Annu. "Does he ever think? Come on, we better do the physical security checks. Not the best time to slack off."

They ambled away from the room and turned left away.

Annu removed the keycard and opened the door. Inside the room consoles, monitors, devices and machines covered every wall.

What the hell are all those? What am I meant to do with them?

The map shook, Annu turned it three sixty degrees and breathed. "All good. Stay calm or I'll screw up." He flipped it the other way, it made sense. "Oh hello. Right, here I am."

The first set of equipment matched the doctor's first red mark on Annu's left.

All the lights, buttons and bits confused Annu, the walls closed in.

I forgot to ask how to turn the machine's off.

"Shit flark."

A search around the desk revealed no obvious off/on switch. "Improvisation time."

Annu delved behind the boxes and pulled the cords out, one by one the displays flicked off.

Come on, hurry up. Fighting them off will waste more time.

A succession of clicks followed Annu; he completed circuit and ended at the entrance. On bad luck's cue, a series of alarms wailed and increased in volume.

A red light flashed above the door, with the keycard in hand, Annu's butthole puckered. "Aw crap. That's a hurry up I didn't want."

Part way into the next section admonishment wrapped around Annu's throat.

Now to get Ankor and the others out without getting caught. Flarking hell.

Footsteps boomed along the concrete in Annu's direction.

Map in his pocket, Annu did a three sixty and bolted for the cells. "Argh."

Beings roused, some stumbled into the hallway, one or two perished upon contact with the environment.

Annu weaved around creatures and past his cell. "All of you, come on. Follow me."

Half asleep Ankor huddled in the corner, and flinched at the light.

Annu shook her leg, it fell limp. "Hey. It's okay, it's me. I'm getting you out of here but we must be quick."

Ankor probed his features, her feathers tickled. *'It's really you? I'm not dreaming?'*

Two arms under her, Annu lifted and rose. "Yes it's real. It's not a dream."

'Oh thank the Gods.'

Ladened down, Annu climbed over the ledge and into the corridor, again. "Not this time. It's all me."

Guards stormed the sector's entry, large blue hog-like creatures bounced out of the first few cell's and attacked the guards nearest.

Limbs hurtled past Annu, blood and guts rained like gory confetti.

Annu's appetite for the next few days nose dived.

Disgusting.

"We might avoid those guys."

Ankor wriggled and adjusted her position. *'They're Elarian's, violent and dangerous but can be reasoned with if it's before they get angry.'*

Annu diverted attention between the entry and mushed things on the ground. "It might not be the right time for a discussion. Perhaps later. Can you walk or better yet run?"

'I'll try.'

Ankor wavered on her feet, her fragility evident. *'Maybe not.'*

Annu guided her to open doors, hope inflated. "I'm not doing this for nothing. Don't give up on me. I can't put my protection up or it would fry you. I'm sorry."

'It's not your fault.'

That's where you're wrong lady but I'm making it right. I got this.

Metres into the adjacent section hope deflated. Armed and serious guards destroyed Annu's escape buzz.

Men, beings, and sundry yelled, sirens roared.

Each wail lessened Annu's heart's life span. "I swear this place will kill me."

A fresh wave of creatures emerged behind Annu. They swarmed the area and swept the guards back.

Ankor clutched his sleeve, her fear palpable. *So much anger and hatred. It's not right.'*

Annu moved her behind him and shuffled along. "Don't focus on it. Sometimes pain and death pave the way to peace."

Sometimes, not very often.

Huge eye and headed small grey beings garbled and nodded at Annu on route past.

There are some strange arse creations here.

Ankor swayed and knocked into a falling guard. *'Oh. I'm so—'*

Annu scooped her up and shouldered him the other way. "Stay with me."

The taller guard from before spotted Annu and raised his rifle. "Fuck no."

Bullets skimmed Annu's head; Annu propped Ankor against a counter.

Annu barged the guard and toppled him. The guard slammed into the ground. "Flark, yes."

The crowd consumed the guard.

I'd have been out of here by now if I'd kept going. Don't think like that.

Annu collected Ankor and headed for the exit. A whack against his back deterred but didn't stop him.

Why not?

Ankor wriggled, Annu collected a guard in the chin with his elbow.

Behind several rows of assorted intergalactic war the first exit shone in all its glory.

Projectiles and bullets flew in each direction; cordite and burnt plastic sullied the air.

Annu slipped into the dark spot beside an office. "I've got de ja vu."

Skirmish erupted swept past and further along.

Ankor's chest heaved, her eyes dulled. *'Where do we go now?'*

Annu followed the walls around and ended at the other side. "Patience, I'm working on it, woman."

A fraction of light illuminated the map; Annu traced their past route and the next sector to get through.

With uncertain faith and Ankor, Annu raced fifty meters and ducked into a dark corner.

The first checkpoint appeared several meters away. "Now the next, tiny, little thing to fix is getting all the way out of here."

Chapter 34
Matriacial Mayhem
Between Enki Island and Yebu, Orion

The I.D.I.O.T. craft flew in another loop over the ocean, no sign of a crash site devastated Shayne.

It should be me, not you. Fuck it.

Jacob and Jackie sat along the back wall of the flight deck, their presence both comfort and concern for Shayne.

Keep it together. There's too much at stake to fall apart.

Shayne paced and massaged her temples. "You two aren't helping at all and are stressing me out. It's all fucked up. This god stuff sucks. It's worse than being an adult. And that's a big call."

Jacob's shrug and Jackie's silence dumped a pile of poo on sanity's scent.

Whatever.

Devoid of Erin's location or sense of it, Shayne tossed bad scenarios aside confidence.

Brain, this is one of those times you need to work. Do your thing. Help a brother out here.

'Erin, Erin Erin?'

Nothing. Still nothing.

Anticipation clawed for release like a caged cat, in particular the one Shayne locked in a cupboard at nine.

Shayne brushed over the scars from said encounter on her forearm. *'Please, please, please answer me. Erin?'*

'Zeke, Zeke, Zeke, are you okay?'

Come on. One of you give me something to work with.

Distress circled Shayne's runway and descended for landing. "Fuck, shit, fuck, shit, fuck, shit."

Calm down and concentrate instead of going around like a lunatic. This is too much at once. I'm going to, no. No. No. I can do this damn it.

Shayne plonked onto an empty seat near the doorway and closed her eyes.

Five deep breaths and ambient noise faded.

"Erin, Erin, Erin, where are you Erin?"

The craft's floor trembled, light opened Shayne's eyes. *"Erin, Erin, Erin, Erin, Erin."*

The pilot and co-pilot pivoted in their seats, mouths agape, eyes wide.

A wormhole formed large enough for Shayne to jump into, relief flooded her. "Oh thank fuck, you finally worked. Look what happens when I actually try. I'm an arsehole."

A mix of voices erupted from the adjacent cabin: "What the hell is that?"

"I'm not getting sucked into there."

Shayne put one leg in and spoke over her shoulder. "Keep going to Yebu. I'll, ah, probably be back."

Enveloped by light, Shayne's particles slid along a tunnel until it narrowed at the end. Instead of the usual ground to land on, a dark liquid beckoned.

Reformed, Shayne enveloped herself in an aura and dove feet first into the water. Despite protection, Shayne held her breath and feet up. Fear of failure fought Shayne's bravado.

Calm down, I'm okay and the kids need me. Get over myself.

Shayne illuminated the bubble and thrust debris out of the way.

Nothing yet. Please, kiddo, be here.

Under a cabin seat a body dangled, the moisture in Shayne's mouth evaporated.

Between beats Shayne reached Erin and dragged her into the aura.

A blue hue replaced Erin's usual pallor, a cut across her cheek seeped. Shayne pushed hair off Erin's face and felt for a pulse.

Creator if you save my baby I'll be the best, damned demigoddess you've ever seen. Erin doesn't deserve to die. If need be take me instead.

A faint bump restarted Shayne's heart. "Thank fu—, never mind." Shayne laid Erin on her side and patted her back. "Erin, baby. Wake up. It's mum."

Water trickled from Erin's lips, her arms flopped.

Fuck, I haven't done first aid for a long long time. What do I do again? Oh yeah.

Shayne stuck a finger in Erin's mouth and cleared out gunk. "This is so disgusting. You better not die."

Two bangs on the back, Erin vomited water and gulped air. "Mum?"

Shayne rubbed Erin's forearm. "Yes baby. It's mum. Thank you, Creator."

Erin groaned and lapsed into unconscious—but breathed.

Okay wormhole, no dicking around, to the hospital please.

Shayne clutched Erin, the wormhole formed amongst the sea, sucking up their bubble and volumes of water.

At its end Shayne tumbled onto a tiled floor and collapsed holding Erin. Water washed them along the floor and into Orion Emergency ward's reception desk. Shayne bounced off and away from Erin.

People screams and yells faded, Shayne scrambled after Erin and held her close. "Hey, I need a doctor now."

The woman behind the reception desk froze; a communicator dangled an inch from her ear. "What? Who, who, what are you?"

Shayne channelled a possessed person and growled. "Get me a fucking doctor or you'll find out the wrong way. My daughter drowned. Help me."

A hospital bed rattled down a hall towards them, people in white coats pried Erin from Shayne's arms, placed her on the bed and hurried to elevators further down.

Shayne jogged to keep up and held Erin's hand. "It's all right. They'll make you better. Mum's here. I won't let anything happen to you."

Mmm. Right, dickhead.

The truth dragged down Shayne's throat and choked her. "Anymore."

I shouldn't be a parent. I suck. I'm barely able to take care of myself.

A nurse stuck patches on Erin and attached cords to machines; another placed an oxygen mask over Erin's mouth.

The elevators drifted further away each step further.

Please Creator, please please make Erin okay. I know I've already asked for a lot but I need this. If she dies my life is over and it's all my fault.

A middle aged doctor opposite Shayne examined Erin. "How long was she under?"

Shayne cut off a sob, tears escaped down her cheek. "I don't know I can't be sure. At least a few minutes. Look—you have to save her. Please let her be okay."

The doctor's calm tone didn't alleviate Shayne's anxiety. "She's breathing with assistance for now. We'll do our best."

Guilt homed in on Shayne, she travelled down a dark road, alone, desperate and useless. "Okay. Please whatever you can."

I hate myself. This is my fault no matter what anyone says.

They reached the elevators, Shayne stepped over the ledge.

The doctor's back stopped her. "I'm sorry. You can't come, there's not enough room and we can't keep an eye on you too. Someone will let you know when you can see her."

Maternal responsibly collided with duty and tore Shayne in pieces. "But I should be with her."

Even though I'm to find Zeke and stop more people dying.

Shayne kissed Erin's cold cheek. "I'll be back soon. You're getting better. You hear me?"

Erin squeezed Shayne's hand. "Mum."

Shayne returned the squeeze and shoved her hand between the closing doors. "You better not let her die or you're dead too."

He nodded, the elevator left with half of Shayne's soul.

Fucking hell. Why is everything always so hard and traumatic for us?

Shayne leant between elevator doors and re-focused.

The logical place to look is the area I found Erin.

Not strong enough for actual participation, Shayne's astral self searched. *'Zeke, my pain in the arse stepson. Where are you?'*

An image of Zeke lay atop a piece of craft alive and dishevelled rewarded Shayne's efforts.

Loud voices came from the emergency department Shayne had entered.

What are the chances this is a good thing?

Security officers stormed entered the hallway and aimed guns at Shayne. "Stay there whoever you are. You're wanted for questioning."

Shayne froze the guns and opened a wormhole. "I don't have time for this shit. You should be outside protecting the hospital while I work on getting rid of the Martians all together."

The officers lowered their weapons and their mouths.

Shayne stepped inside and fixed on Zeke's location.

You know this is becoming a rather handy form of travel.

Outside the tunnel, Shayne hovered above the crash site.

A left turn showed Zeke metres away, another layer of stress alleviated.

At sight of Shayne, Zeke waved. "Hey, I'm over here."

Shayne zoomed to him, at least half her world made sense again. "Another heart attack followed by another kid rescued. Off to the hospital with you too my boy."

Zeke rested against the aura's border and examined himself. "Aside from a few scrapes and scratches I'm okay. No medical intervention required."

Frustration scraped along Shayne's newly installed self confidence. "My Gods you're as stubborn as your father."

Why not push my luck? Sometimes works.

"Can I assume this is the miracle you'd need to accept me?"

Zeke hugged himself. "Yeah maybe, we'll see. I'm leaving my options open."

Shayne reopened a wormhole.

Hey hang on

She paused mid swirl. "You are just like your father." She delved into her pocket and touched funk. "I've got something else to try before killing her. Fuck yeah. "

Could one of my plans work when I really need it to? Is it too much to ask for?

Zeke tugged her pant leg and shivered. "Great and all but let's get back into the real world, please?"

Ah duh. Wake up genius. I'm fucking it up already.

Shayne completed the circuit and tugged Zeke. They landed inside the ship among a silent crew, the tension intensified. Shayne gathered courage from deep, deep, deep, inside her. So deep it hit the Earth's outer mantle. "Not far from Yebu, I see."

Zeke sat beside Jacob and crossed his arms. "I hope you've got shit worked out, Shayne."

Unease crept up Shayne's legs and wrapped around her kidneys. "Of course I do. Oh ye of little faith."

Screw you, fuckers. I've got this shit. Erin will be fine, Zeke will be fine, Jacob and Annu will be fine. We'll all be fan-fucking-fine.

Chapter 35
A Mother Fucker of An Angel
Yebu Medical Centre, Yebu, Orion

Where am I? Why does everything hurt so much?

Awareness blew in fragments and scattered across Erin's mind on a gentle breeze. Rolled onto her side and rested on an elbow, Erin's brain wobbled, the room spun.

Erin lowered back onto the bed, her breath quickened. "I feel terrible. What's happening to me?"

The water, I drowned. Am I dead?

Fear gripped Erin between cold strong fingers and squeezed. One eye open and memories returned, Erin's surroundings cleared. In a too large hospital gown, Erin lay on an equal sized hospital bed in a single patient room hooked up to machines.

I remember, the bright light and a beautiful Angel saved me.

The machines constant beeps rang in Erin's ears.

I'm alive in a hospital.

Cords attached to machines restricted Erin's movement, each try and they pulled tight, the machines beeped quicker. An attempt to undo the strap tightened it, Erin smacked the bed. "Who brought me here? Where is everyone? Why am I alone?"

The sense of solitude and an unfamiliar place regressed Erin into a child. "Is anyone out there? Please? Hello?"

Nothing resembled an Earth version of a nurse's call button in a line of buttons up both guard rails.

I'm all alone, I've been left here.

Erin's blood pressure escalated in competition with her heart rate. "Oh God, oh God, oh God."

From the top down Erin pushed each button, at the last one in line, the door wooshed open.

An Idris Elba look alike in white uniform lurked in the doorway. "Can I, ah, help you?"

Why isn't he coming into the room? What the hell's going on?

Erin tugged the sheet over her chest and lifted her arm. "Where am I and how did I get here?"

Idris looked either side of him. "I believe your mother dropped you off here with instructions she'd return if possible."

Mum brought me here. Did mum save me? Is she the angel too?

An alarm shrilled, Idris grabbed the door frame. "Heck. If you're able to get dressed, find a safe place to hide. Sorry."

He disappeared amidst medical staff and hospital beds rattling past her room.

Erin lurched forwards, the cord attached to her chest detached. "Wait. What's going on?"

Erin slipped off the bed to a bevy of unhooked tubes and onto the floor. Her legs wobbled, the guard rail aided her walk around the bed.

More alarms dulled noise and drilled into Erin's ears.

On the bedside cupboard, an unusual fabric bag stored her wet dirty clothes. "Poo."

Erin reached towards a locker on the opposite wall, the door opened.

My power things still work. Not that they helped me at all last time.

The door opened further, Erin retrieved a top, pants and sock-type shoes. "Not flash but I can't be fussy."

Erin changed slow, muscles she didn't know existed complained.

Outside the doorway staff pushed hospital beds in all directions.

Injured people aged from the elderly to children lined either side of the hallway on seats or against the wall.

Erin's stomach leapt into her throat.

I didn't realise how much me or the universe needs my mum. All these people who've lost everything haven't given up. I must do what I can too.

A small child in tattered clothes a fraction older than the kids in Erin's class stumbled around alone. He approached passing people whom ignored him, a cut above his eye wept down his face and snot covered his chin.

Ah great. My favourite kind of kid.

Another bed barrelled for the kid from the other end of down the hall. Erin's maternal instinct drove her to gather him in her arms and get him out of the way. "Jesus. Watch out."

The fast action dizzied Erin, she grasped at clarity.

Get it together. Breath. I'm okay.

Erin's equilibrium steadied, she carried the boy into a room. "It's okay. I've got you. What's your name?"

The boy's tears amplified Erin's compassion and blocked out everything else. "Eli."

Keep calm and he won't freak out. The poor kid.

"Eli. Where's your parents?"

Eli sucked on his bottom lip and swiped snot with his sleeve. "I'm not sure where my daddy is and I can't find my momma. She'll be worried about me."

Erin blinked away empathy and stroked his cheek. "It's okay, sweetie. I'll help you. Where was the last place you saw Momma or Daddy?"

The boy's words tumbled from his mouth. "We haven't seen Daddy since the town blew up. Momma carried me all the way here, we got attacked out front and she felled down. Lot's of red stuff covered her. Last I saw a doctor covered with a sheet. He said so she didn't get cold. Momma hates the cold. Then lots of other people got in the way and I lost her."

A maternal yearn pitched a tent in Erin's front yard, her ovaries glamped in style.

Feeling sorry for myself about ridiculous things is over. Jesus. The poor kids an orphan and everyone else here is homeless, injured or dead because of this invasion.

Erin swept empathy and pity into the camp fire.

He doesn't need to hear the harsh truth right now.

"Well Eli, I promise I'll stick with you until we find your parents, okay?"

Eli nodded; he gripped the bottom of her shirt. "Okay."

Erin bent down and opened her arms. "I'll carry you again and that way no one can hurt you."

Eli stepped into her embrace and held on while she stood. "Okay."

His weight strained Erin's tired muscles, instead of complaints Erin pushed onwards and reentered the hallway.

Erin shielded Eli's eyes, the rows of dead and injured increased the further they went down. Every room occupied by doctors and near-death patients gave no indication as to what Erin must do or go next.

Maybe if I walk around the whole place some other family will notice him. If they don't, then well, I'm not so sure.

Erin turned at a corner, the ceiling lights went off and emergency lighting on. Beds from one side of the room crashed into the people in the hallway, cries of pain and cursing forced Erin to cover Eli's ears.

Erin stuck to the wall or edged around beds and people.

Hands reached towards her, voices pleaded:

"Help me. Please. I need a doctor."

"Where are my legs? I've lost my legs."

"They're all gone, all of them. Gone. They'll kill us all unless someone stops them. Will you stop them?"

Erin shifted out of their grasp, hugged Eli and pushed. "It's okay. Ignore them. I've got you."

At the end of the hallway, open doors paraded a mass of bodies in black bags on top of each other.

Erin's bowel churned, a shiver tickled her nape. "Oh geez. That's, that's messed up."

Eli turned towards it and reached out. "I saw Momma in there."

Erin swallowed bile, her soul tore.

I am not going in there and neither is he. I can't tell him his parents are dead.

"It's pretty full in there. We might go around another—"

A loud boom preceded an explosion down the end of the room in front.

The ground shook, the walls trembled. Debris blasted through the door way and into the hall; Erin and Eli flew back the way they came and into a mass of people.

Eli thumped into Erin's chest and winded her; dust and detritus clouded the area.

Chapter 36
Elevate Me
DSI Facility, Pine Gap
New South Wales, Australia, Earth

Annu carried Ankor over his shoulder to the check point behind his new friends—five reptile-like creatures lead by his former cell neighbour. Flicks of thick tails swept aside most obstacles with no effort from Annu.

If these guys are like this without their powers, I'm glad I didn't piss them off.

Someone grabbed Annu's shoulder and yanked him back.

Annu stumbled and lowered his arms. "Shit, shit, shit."

Ankor hit the ground and tumbled, absorbed by the mob. "Annu—"

The atmosphere thickened, Annu jumped up and down. "Ankor?"

A guard blocked the view; Annu grabbed him by the bullet proof vest and hurled him at oncoming guards.

Arrays of creatures swamped the area; random cries of pain alleviated some of Annu's stress.

Annu climbed on the back of a guard for extra height. "Ankor?"

'*Where are you? I can't see you.*'

The guard bucked Annu off and turned, he punched at Annu.

'*I hear you. Go a little further down. You're close.*'

Annu ducked and elbowed the man in the throat. "Hit something. Make a noise."

Knock, knock.

Ankor rested against a wall hidden behind a cupboard. '*Here I am.*'

Relief struck, Annu lifted Ankor by the shoulders. "Are you okay?"

She'd aged since they'd left the cells. '*Not really, but I'll keep going.*'

Weighted again by Ankor, Annu's pace slowed. "You hang in there. There's only two check points and then we're at the lift."

Ankor lagged, Annu's arms swallowed her. '*I'm weak, it's the atmosphere. I'm not sure I'll make it out or get home. You go on without me.*'

The extra care, not her weight, took time. "Like hell. You're going back to your family and so am I. Enough of talking like that."

Please let my family be alive. I'm not thinking otherwise right now.

Whoomp.

A rush of electricity ejected air from Annu and threw him sideways. "Shit."

Ankor fell onto her hip and winced in pain. "Annu."

Me having an easy life is obviously not in someone's plan.

Annu reached for Ankor and missed. "Damn it."

Another strike to his lower back thrust Annu onto his knees and into convulsions.

Ankor and his surroundings blurred.

Annu gritted his teeth, wobbled a finger at her and turned. "I'll be right back to get you."

A lopsided Dingle held a long taser stick, blue energy bolts shot towards Annu.

One armed or not that mother flarker's dying this time.

Annu dodged another charge and tripped over his feet. "Umph."

Dingle jabbed the stick, glanced at his stump and trembled. "You aren't getting out of here this time. I owe you."

Annu rolled in the opposite direction.

Dingle zapped concrete and yelled. "Fuck."

Annu kicked the stick out of Dingle's hand and shoved him. "You've got no idea."

Dingle flew into a blue blob thing and bounced forwards into Annu.

They hit a wall, Annu's spine crunched, fresh pain re-woke him.

The taser remained in Dingle's hand; hatred burned the back of Annu's throat. "Wrong again, arse wipe."

With little room between them, Annu jabbed Dingle's thorax and rabbit punched him in the guts.

Dingle dropped onto his knees and vomited. "I wish you'd never come here."

Annu delivered an upper cut to Dingle's chin. "Me too, but someone else's pain never felt so good."

Dingle's eyes rolled, he passed out.

Kill him or leave him?

Annu shoved Dingle aside. "I'm not wasting anymore energy on you. You'll die with the rest of—"

Hands grabbed Annu's middle and unsteadied him. "For flark's sake."

Annu jutted his elbow and landed on top of them. "You prick."

The guard beneath huffed and puffed.

Zap, zap, zap.

Volts of electricity surged from Annu's butt cheek up and down him.

Annu dropped and seized; his arms and legs flailed. Mid-spasm, Annu groped at the black device in the guard's hand against his hip, Annu's teeth rattled.

Blue feathers glimmered a few metres away. Ankor dragged herself to Annu's attacker.

Ankor placed a hand on the guard's ankle. Ankor held the guards ankle. Her colour faded the longer the physical contact.

He shifted the device from Annu onto himself. "What the fuck?"

The return of equilibrium cleared Annu's mind, the guard's own fits to ease Annu's anger.

The occasional muscle twitch and leg tic slowed Annu's rise from the ground. Each movement confused messages between brain and body.

Upright, Annu slid to Ankor curled up next to the guard and pried her off. "Thank you but no more. I'm okay and you don't have anything left to give."

'All right.'

Ankor back in his arms, Annu limped around dismembered guards or beings joined together by trails of blood.

A number of reptoids joined Annu.

The largest one and supposed leader clicked his tongue, amber liquid wept from wounds on his chest.

Mental and physical fatigue weighed Annu down, the desire to crawl up and die struggled with duty.

This is getting too much.

A larger reptoid stood before Annu and offered his arms. "Click, click, click."

Annu paused mid-pass and raised an eyebrow. "Are you sure?"

It nodded and jutted its arms. "Click, click."

The second Annu released her, regret paused him. "Please, be careful with her. She's like an older sister to me. Stay close."

The reptoid's stern expression comforted Annu. "Click, click, click."

Let it go and get them all out of here.

Limp, slide, and walk, Annu reached the first check point now absent of guards.

Annu poised the keycard and digit at the display near to the door. "Flark, yeah."

The lead Reptoid slid past Annu, kicked the door off its hinges, and burst into the next section.

Annu stepped over leftover chunks at the bottom. "Well, that works too." He jogged and reached the leader. "Hey, thanks, clear the way to the lift and I'll get us out of here."

Blood dripped from the leader's claws, goop dribbled from it nose. "Click, click, click."

Annu retrieved the map and touched something mushy, brain matter. He flicked it off. "Okay then. It's, ah, a deal."

Down a dark corridor littered with a variety of human and non human body parts, they approached another check point.

Half of Annu wanted it unmanned, the other half wanted to rip the bastards to pieces.

The reptile leader tore the door from the guards' office and charged into the room.

Blood splashed and a foot rolled out the door way.

Annu faced the reptoid beside him. "Remind me never to piss you guys off."

"Click."

Screams from the office followed by three detached arms and four legs.

Inside the room, no human remained whole, only segments scattered every surface; a reptoid sucked on a torso.

I won't be hungry for a while.

"Righto then."

The lead reptoid licked his fingers. "Click, click?"

Annu massaged his nape and pointed to the map. "Do you mean where next?"

A blob of yellow goop escaped its mouth and hit its chest. "Click."

Ankor's closed eyes and shallow breath suggested sleep.

Please just be asleep rather than dying.

Time constraints niggled, Annu lead past rooms and into another hall.

'*Where now?*'

Annu flipped the map around and pointed to a corridor to their left. "Down there is one more checkpoint before the lift. You'll get us through right?"

It blinked two sets of eyes and bounced away. "Click, click."

Bang, bang.

The door at the end hurtled it into the next sector.

Zing, zing, zing, boom.

Gunfire exploded around them, the lifts metres away pushed Annu on leaden legs.

Annu picked up the door and wiped out guards behind him.

Sober beat down upon Annu. "Mental note, never go anywhere without alcohol again. I'm now on Shayne's side there."

No one ever tell her though. There'd be no living with her after.

Chapter 37
The Worm Un-Turned
Enki Island, Orion

The peace of mind Shayne obtained from the protective aura she'd installed around the ship and Erin in hospital remained the lone consolations. War, death, and pain clung like the clothes on Orion's skin.

Not even these arseholes deserve any of this. I'd kill for any illicit, mind altering substance. A toad or mushroom, anything really.

An added worry, body odour prevented Shayne near anyone with sense of smell.

Another day without a shower and even my arm pits right suffice.

Although safe for the moment Jacob's health worsened and risked wormhole travel for him.

Shayne wriggled into the chair and secured her pony tail.

I can't believe I'm still doing this shit alone. I hate my life.

Shayne massaged her temples and vetted emotions. "All by myself. Don't want to be all by myself," She raised the pitch, "anymoreeee. Don't want to be—"

Jackie cleared his throat and raised a finger. "Ah—"

Jacob clutched his chest. "Oh the pain and torture."

Zeke on her other side rolled his eyes. "Here we go. Will you stop tormenting us all?"

For fuck's sake. There's no pleasing some people.

Shayne's mind calmed, her shoulders relaxed. "Don't want to be all by myself. Anymoreeee. All by myselffff. Don't want to be all by my selfffff anymoreeeeeee."

Zeke rose from his seat and threw up his arms. "Shayne, I speak for us all, I wish you were, but you aren't by yourself. Please stop? I beg you, it's already tense in here and you're hurting everyone's ears. Hell, I'll even keep my room clean for a month if you stop."

Maybe I should consider his offer. Nah, fuck it. It makes me feel better. Bless you, Eric Carmen. Your words set me free.

Shayne embraced her not so inner diva. "All by myself anymoreeeeee. All by myself and shit, don't want to be fucking by myself—anymore."

Jackie pounced off the seat. "I, ah, please I agree with the boy. I'll keep his room clean too."

"La, la, lah, not listening. Fuck you all and the horses you rode in on." Shayne stood and opened her lungs. "Anymoreeeeee. I want to be all by myself, I want to be all by myself once before I mean again."

The co-pilot turned in his seat and roared. "You might freeze me for this but for the love of Orion shut that infernal noise up and put your arms down, I'll crash on purpose."

I'm sick and tired of people complaining about my singing. There are bigger problems here.

Shayne sniffed under her arm and fell onto her seat.

Like me.

 "Fuck you're right. Okay."

I'm probably, possibly, maybe a bit selfish.

Shayne gave everyone the bird. "Fine. All right. Whatever. Kill my only means of stress relief."

Fingers pegged Zeke's nose closed, he stepped back. "Great. Thank you. We'll work on the smell later shall we? For now, what's this other plan you came up with?"

Jacob's chest heaved, he flushed. "I wondered that myself."

Don't fucking die on me.

Shayne's sigh warmed her chest in lieu of breasts. "Yep. You Jacob, getting medical attention, everyone helps and loves every, fucking, minute of it. Not."

At seven plus feet, Shayne often forgot Zeke's youth until he spoke. "I can't see how they'd mistake me for Da—Annu. Plus, I don't look old enough to be your fiancee. Your grand child maybe."

Jackie leaned forward and nodded. "Once again. I agree with the boy. There's a distinctive difference in generations between you. It's a big stretch in truth and that smell is awful."

Ah ouch. I'll ignore them given the circumstances.

Shayne's cheeks burned, she plastered her arms to her sides. "Right. Thanks for the self esteem boost. Is Queeie short sighted, because I'd rather not blow her up if I can help it?"

The copilot spun on his seat. "Ma'am. Yebu's outskirts are only a few k's away. Where do you want us to land?"

What does K's mean again? Is it like clicks?

Shayne rolled her neck side to side and willed enthusiasm.

Any second now…Waiting…still waiting. Aw fuck it.

"Not too close to the hospital they see us, and not too far that we've got to walk a long way. I don't want shin splints as well."

The co-pilot's frown marked a young face. "That's not helpful at—"

A female voice erupted from the communication system:

"This is an emergency broadcast. Since the arrival of more alien ships, the east side of Yebu has been hit including the medical centre with many already injured people. All citizens are urged to evacuate the city safely via the Social Centre in each city section immediately. They've warned further attacks will occur. At present, the Grand Counsel has not been located for advice or comment. The Peace Office urges evacuees to use extreme caution."

Beep, beep, beep. "Breaking news: a much larger ship, known as a mother ship contains the Queen and has breached Orion's outer atmosphere. Get out now before no where—"

The voice of doom ended, communications gone, no static, no crackle, dead like the chance of Shayne's success.

Erin. The one place I thought would fix her killed her. All those security guards after me are dead too and the patients. I've wasted too much time. Where's my baby? She never should have been here to begin with. I'm going to slaughter all of them for this. No fucking mercy. Unholy revenge.

Shayne's blood cooled; her back spasmed. "Oh Gods no. Get there quick."

Clouds of black smoke streamed from Yebu's docking lanes.

The pilot yelled over his shoulder. "That whole area just got blown up. It's not a safe place to land."

I'd rather worry about Erin and boys, unplanned pregnancy and PMS. Not this. Never this.

"No where's fucking safe. Land near there I'll walk."

Sergeant Lim strode into the flight cabin and loomed over Shayne, her breasts heaved.

Zeke skidded along the floor and landed in his seat. "Look out. Block of angry flats coming."

Lim's acrid breath assaulted Shayne. "You froze the Grand Counsellor didn't you? That's why we haven't heard from him."

The pilot and copilot glanced at each other and spoke in unison. "Fuck."

Lots of fucking going on today and no orgasms or chocolate involved. Sad, sad, times.

Jackie and Jacob leaned back against the wall.

Rage flowed through Shayne's veins. The perfect patsy for an emotional spaz presented itself.

Shayne pushed off the seat and lifted her chin. "Bitch, back the fuck up before," Shayne pointed at the cargo hold, "you end up like Nimrod dripping on the floor in there. Oh and get a fucking TicTac or something. You're breath smells like cat shit."

If her and I stood next to each other we'd wipe out a whole row of enemy by odour alone.

Lim recoiled for a second and regained her composure. "Admit what you did."

A number of I.D.I.O.T.s from the adjoining cabin created a beige wall between her, the next cabin and the escape hatch.

Shayne's neck ached, she lowered and hit boobs. "Don't be ridiculous. You're stupid leader is fine. He's just super busy."

Super busy at being frozen. It's a lot to deal with. Shayne stifled a laugh and bit her tongue. *I think I've gone mad with grief.*

Lim grabbed at Shayne. "You're a complete maniac. If you didn't have powers I'd—"

Icicles formed on Shayne's arms and dripped onto the floor. *Go with it.* Shayne shoved Lim into the beige wall. "You'd fucking what? If you feel that passionate about Nimrod feel free to defrost him once this is all over. Until then get a grip."

Lim stumbled and regained her footing. "When it is, you'll answer for your crimes against Orion."

Shayne's frustration overtook her give-a-fuck level. She stroked a line down the woman's arm and faced the crowd. "All of you listen and listen good. You'll see your precious leader again—"

In the frozen food isle of Cosco.

"But in the meantime, I'm the best and only chance, so either fight by my side or off you fuck. This isn't about you, me, or him; it's about the innocent people being slaughtered out there."

Lim's sneer scraped the last layer off Shayne's nerves. "Then why are we landing outside the hospital where your daughter is instead of hitting the enemy straight on ASAP?"

This has been such a trying day. I need a sit down, have a Bex or a fucking packet of valium.

"Fuck you and your valid point."

The pilot cleared his throat. "You better decide quick. We're here."

The engine wound down, they approached the west outskirts of Yebu.

I'm the worst parent and person in the entire universe but I can still do the right thing now.

The disarray, ruin and despair embodied Shayne and silenced everyone in the flight deck. "New plan. Land near the I.D.I.O.T.s' Peace Office compound. With luck there's some of them left. We'll use safe rooms there for the survivors and raid the armoury. Lim you find out wherever the protectors got evacuated too and get them together. We need everyone available."

A bald middle aged man beside Lim/Costello nudged her.

Lim slumped, her dour demeanour echoed the group. "Yes Ma'am."

Why do I smell sulpher and see hell on the horizon?

Shayne stretched and shook out stiff legs. "Jacob, there's no going to the hospital for you at the moment. You'll have to tough it out beside me or find somewhere to hide."

Please God, it might be too late but save Erin. Again. Please. If you only listen to me once, let it be this time. As well as the times before. Can I get a few more IOU's?

Chapter 38
Shafted
DSI Facility, Pine Gap
New South Wales, Australia, Earth

Three floors up and in between the next level; the stalled elevators forced Annu and co on top of the carriage roof. On either side of the shaft, air vents appeared each 4 metres or so.

Ankor slumped against a steel cable and struggled to breath. *'Exhausted. Not any help. Sorry.'*

She embodies my own desires. I've created a huge mess and I'm not sure I'll get out the other side of it.

"Stop it. It's fine. The only way out is up the wall and into the first of those vents. Where it takes us from there is a surprise."

Ankor's presence in Annu's mind weakened. *'I'm sorry, I'm nothing but a burden.'*

"For the last time, you're not." Annu knelt and offered his hand. "From my knee get onto my back and hold on tight."

Ankor clutched his arm and fell onto his knee. *'Thank you.'*

She caught her breath and allowed him to lift her onto his back. She wrapped her arms around his neck and legs; her feathered feet tickled his arms.

Two steps to the wall on the roof wobbled the carriage and Annu's confidence. On the precipice of the roof a gap of centimetres remained between it and the wall.

Give me the strength to do this and not kill both of us. Someone, please.

Annu dug his toes into a low notch, stretched and wedged his fingers into a higher notch. "Climbing time. Hang on."

One foot released, Annu raised his knee and pushed to the next one. Annu repositioned and climbed another two notches, the vent's entry in sight three levels away encouraged him up the last parts.

At the edge Annu released his hands and lunged at the vent.

The first quarter of he and Ankor made it, Annu wriggled the rest of the way in and collapsed. "This has been a hell of a day."

Ankor slid in and rested against a wall. '*Are you all right?*'

Annu's arms burned, his legs tensed. "Not at flarking all. But it doesn't usually matter."

On hands and knees, Annu brushed the vent's roof.

Shuffle, shuffle, shuffle.

Annu dragged along the floor and banged into Ankor's back. "Shit. Sorry."

Ankor slipped between his legs and grabbed his heels. '*Does this work better?*'

Annu scooted on his palms and made more distance. "Yes. Thank you."

Amidst half light Annu reached a T-junction, guards mumbled outside the vent.

Zing, zing, zing.

Bullets sliced the bottom of the steel, Annu grasped Ankor's hands, slid her between him and into the left side vent.

Annu collected Ankor and positioned her underneath him. "Flarking hell. Move with me."

Ankor clung to Annu's sleeve. '*I prayed for more time.*'

Heat from a round skimmed Annu's heel and sliced the sole of his boot. "Clearly no one heard you."

Further into the ventilation system, the pressure in Annu's ears decreased, he wriggled his jaw.

I'm going down instead of up again and I can't turn around.

A metre from Annu's feet, an explosion decimated a section of the vent blowing Annu and Ankor further down. Noise roared; sulphur, cordite, and burnt hair invaded the enclosed space.

Metal debris imbedded into Annu's side and sliced his arm, his abdomen spasmed.

A black hose slipped into an opening before the impact site.

Annu propelled faster on his haunches. "Shit, shit, shit, shit."

Ankor dragged along the ground. '*What is it?*'

Water streamed into and along the vent.

Annu gained traction and speed, along with cuts and abrasions. "Nothing good."

Ankor slipped, banged into the walls and disappeared around a corner.

Annu dove for and missed Ankor. "I'm coming."

Water lapped his feet and seeped into his boots. The crack and tear of metal behind him elevated Annu's blood pressure but lowered his hope. The floor wobbled, Annu lost purchase on the sides; ice water billowed under him and swept him forward.

The waters moving too fast, I can't get a grip to turn around. Try something dickhead.

Annu spread his arms and legs in an attempt at traction. The water gushed and pushed him sideways. Annu's injured shoulder smashed into the wall.

Numbness transformed to fresh agony, surrender occurred to Annu. "For the love of the gods."

Jaw clenched and swept sideways, Annu smacked into a wall, water rushed up his nose and down his throat. Annu's breath caught, he spewed snot and vomit.

Annu's ankle caught on a corner and twisted in the opposite direction to his torso; pain rippled up his leg and into his groin. Wits scattered, Annu's mind froze.

Two hands on the floor, Annu flipped himself over and pulled his other leg back to the other. Pain spared no part of him with its oblivious and uncaring view of his survival desires. Water pushed Annu down and invaded every open orifice. He gagged, his lungs burned. Annu's hands slipped, another wave threw him sideways.

It's now or never.

The vent beneath collapsed, Annu's guts dropped, he grasped at air. "Oh shit, oh shit, oh shit. This isn't my decade."

Annu and his surrounds fell, smashed their way several floors and ended via the ceiling of an unoccupied office.

Stopped by a wooden desk, the impact forced the air from Annu. "You're flarking kidding me? Really?"

Water from the open roof showered Annu; he rolled off and onto a carpeted floor.

The pain from various injuries cleared Annu's brain.

Shit, Ankor.

Annu held a breath, his main wounds healed each second, the others lingered.

When I get my powers back I'm having a party.

"Ankor. Are you in here? Are you okay?" A clock on the wall ticked, the roof groaned. "Ankor? Can you hear me? If you're in here make a noise so I know where you are." Silence amplified fear, Annu kicked aside roof debris. "Ankor?"

A broken name plaque on the desk with Smith's name on it re-ignited Annu's rage. Annu stepped onto instead of over computer equipment. "Please be in here somewhere."

'An—'

Where are you?

'Over here.'

Tap, tap, tap.

Annu threw obstacles aside, relief offered hope. "Again."

Tap, tap.

Crumpled against a wall and covered in dirt, Ankor waved. "Thank the Gods."

From the time of their escape until now, she'd faded and lost most of her shoulder feathers.

Annu cupped her face and bit back tears. "Not for the second time. All me, again. We've made it this far."

Aside from the mess in the middle of the room, the rest of it appeared in tact.

Annu lay Ankor on the floor and put a cushion under her. "Hang in there for a little longer. I'll try and find something helpful."

The nearest desk drawer contained stationary items, the one above it held a gun and bullets.

Annu retrieved the weapon and stuck it in the one in tact pocket on his pants beside his groin. "Don't go off in there. I might need you again one day."

Behind the desk a bookshelf had a first aid kid stuck to the side of it. Annu selected bandages, gauze and pain killers. The dripping roof provided water for Annu to swallow them.

Arms laden, Annu hobbled to Ankor, bent down and placed a hand on her cut shoulder.

A speck of pink light emitted from his hand, not enough to heal a pimple. "Flark it. Stuck with the old fashioned way."

Ankor's eyes closed, her breath shallow. *'Are you sure you want to take me?'*

Annu poured a brown antiseptic liquid onto her shoulder and placed gauze over it. "For the millionth time, yes. What's with you women and assurance. When this is over we're having a talk about believing in what I say."

Ankor gritted her teeth and winced. *'You're amusing.'*

Medical tape stuck to Annu's hand, he flicked it off and taped up the last visible injury. "Yeah that's me, the comedian. Maybe that's where I'm going wrong thinking this is all serious business."

A map on the opposite wall attracted Annu's attention; he shuffled over to it and rubbed his eyes. "Holy shit. This shows exactly where we are and where the emergency exits are. Flark yeah. About time."Annu skidded over and collected Ankor, boot laden footsteps boomed outside. "Of flarking course."

Ankor lost consciousness and slumped in his arms. Time to gather his thoughts evaporated. Annu wove around the desk and debris, one handed he opened the door.

The corridor filled with DSI guards and staff not yet aware of Annu's presence. Head dipped, Annu turned left and power walked down a twisted hallway, Ankor bounced in his arms.

You'd be much quicker without her. Shut up. Left, left, right, left, right. Flark.

Annu hit an unexpected wall, the air thickened.

Calm down and think. Okay, which way do I turn now?

"Flark it."

People spoke in the corridors behind him; Annu scooted into another section filled with offices. "Shit. Shit. Shit. Wrong way."

Annu backtracked and continued down the corridor past the junction on his left.

DSI Agents marched down an adjacent hall, Annu's heart stopped. "You know what, this is ridiculous."

Annu entered a section with a large red cross above the main door.

It's a medical centre. Maybe someone can help Ankor?

Staff busied in cubicles and readied equipment for a sudden onslaught of injured agents.

Annu slipped by turned backs and bee lined for an open cubicle near an emergency exit sign.

Two metres from the next step in the way out, someone tapped his shoulder.

The gun rested on Annu's waist band out of reach, he flipped around, Ankor wobbled, limp.

Tony, the doctor who'd given him the map, raised his arms. "Don't shoot. It's me. It's okay."

Annu relaxed and adjusted Ankor. "Help me out here."

Tony glanced at Ankor and nodded at a nearby cubicle. "In there, quick."

Annu slipped in behind Tony and lowered Ankor on a bed. "Two problems, can you fix her and which way is out?"

Tony's examined Ankor in a practiced routine. "The first one perhaps but not fast. She's quite delicate, not adapted to our air and has a few major injuries. Not a bad job on the makeshift first aid though. I'll have to sneak her into the recovery machine somehow."

Fatigue weighted Annu's shoulders. "And if you don't?"

Tony's head shake sickened Annu. "Sorry. She won't make it."

Annu held an eye twitch and leaned on the bed. "Where is it?"

Tony pointed to the other side. "It's past the nurses' station and around the corner."

Annu moved towards Ankor, pain shot down his side.

Flarking don't have time to hurt.

"I'll get you there. You fix her and we're out of here."

Tony opened a drawer and removed surgical paraphernalia. "By the looks of it, you need help too or you're good for no one. won't make it far."

Annu's patience diminished, he bent the bed rail. "I can't waste any more time, they'll find us any second. Plus I'll heal when my powers return."

Ankor groaned and curled into the foetal position.

The sense of responsibility attached to Ankor created anguish. "You swear you'll fix her?"

Tony nodded, the gravity of his expression confirmation. "I'll do whatever I can."

Gun in hand, Annu waited beside the door. "You better."

Tony opened it, checked outside and closed it. "They're still busy up the front of the hospital; we've got a few minutes at best."

Gun at his chest, Annu clasped the door handle. "Stick right behind me."

Tony picked up Ankor and swallowed. "Don't worry, I will."

A major drinking bender hovered on Annu's horizon and damned the consequences. "One way or another, when this day is over, everyone will know not to mess with me again."

The click of the door handle acted like a bomb timber about to detonate. Annu shivered and slipped out the doorway into the hall, Tony nipped his heels.

Annu's chest tightened, his hands shook passed the Nurse's station and two vacant offices. Every sound threatened quickened the timer and set Annu further on edge.

******

Sometime soon my luck, such that it is, will run out.

A couple of near misses later and Annu squeezed into a small space occupied by a high-tech chamber with enough buttons to occupy Shayne for a week.

I miss you so much. If it wasn't for you, I'd be dead.

Tony tapped a display screen on the side of the device, a glass lid opened. He placed Ankor into the chamber and closed it.

The machine beeped, lights and lasers scanned Ankor, lighting up the room; she relaxed into the mattress.

Seconds passed as minutes, and minutes as hours.

Annu's patience reached its limit.

This is taking forever.

"For Gods sake. How much longer?"

Tony swiped a finger across the machine's display. "After it finishes assessing her injuries, it says how long the cycle takes."

Tick, tick, tick, tick, boom. "Well make it flarking quick. Listen, when we're out of the building, find somewhere safe. I'm bringing this place down."

"It's about time someone did." Three beeps from the machine interrupted, Tony raised a finger. "It's going to take three to five minutes."

Annu stepped the short space around the room. "Shit. She might end up half baked."

236

Sweat beaded across Tony's forehead. "Ah that's not possible once it's started. I'm sorry I should have mentioned that but with all the commotion I got distracted."

Panic formed a film on Annu's tongue and dried his mouth. "Flark. I could throttle you."

Tony trembled, he plastered on a smile. "Please don't. I'm sorry."

Keep it in check and save it for those who really deserve it.

Annu reigned in his temper and refocused. "Where do I go from here?

Tony's shoulders dropped a fraction, the sweat continued. "Did you notice the painted lines on the concrete ground?"

Flark. "What lines?"

Tony stroked his beard and pointed. "There's a series of coloured lines—wayfinders, through the facility. Each colour relates to a security clearance level, but also to the emergency exits. Follow the blue lines painted on the concrete ground; they'll take you to the exits, which comes out on the east side of the building. From there you'll have to make your way around to Building A, where the tech you want is."

"That's—"

Footsteps approached outside the room, men grumbled.

Annu held a finger to his lips. "Ssssh."

*Fi*ght or flight instincts mashed together.

How can they not hear my heart beating against my chest?

The handle jiggled. "Anyone in there?" Agent Shooks spoke through the door. "Nurse, what's in this room?"

She squeaked rather than spoke. "The healing capsule. As far as I'm aware there's no patient in there."

Jiggle, jiggle, bang, bang. "Open it."

Annu leaned beside the doorway and aimed the gun at the door.

"I can't. Only doctors have access and they're all occupied. Oh except for one, Doctor Curtis. He's static and on back up."

Annu raised his eyebrow, Tony nodded.

"Well go get him."

The voices drifted away from the room.

Annu lowered the gun and sighed. "Fun's over. Get her out."

Tony avoided eye contact. "I can't. Remember the capsule's sealed until it finishes. It's still got three minutes."

Annu's confidence smashed like atoms. "Flarking hell. Well try anyway."

This shit goes from bad to worse. I've little choices here.

Tony tapped at the machine. "I'm sorry. I thought we'd have more time. It's okay to leave her here with me."

Annu's head spun, common sense contradicted duty. "Flark. All right." He pressed a palm on the capsule. "I'll see you both soon. Take care of her."

Tony nodded and shifted against the wall. "Of course."

Bang, bang, bang on the door.

Jiggle, jiggle of the handle. "Wait a second, I've got to swipe the card first."

"Hurry up. He's nowhere else and it's no coincidence."

Annu's, his body temperature dropped, he gripped the gun.

Shit, flark, hell, crap.

The lock clicked, the door opened a fraction.

Annu pushed it closed.

I'm buying a few seconds and nothing more.

Shooks grave tone lightened. "Got you. You're fucked. Smith, get more men here now."

He banged on the door; Annu shoved harder and splintered the wood in the middle.

Another push from Annu, half fell into the room, the other onto the men outside.

Use Tony, it's all I've got.

Annu clutched Tony and dug the gun into the doctor's ribs.

Forgive me and go with me here.

"One step further and he gets it."

Tony flinched and raised his hands in the air. "No, don't shoot."

Annu ushered Tony to the door. "Back up."

Shooks in front, all weapons stayed aimed on him, fingers rested on triggers.

Annu jabbed Tony in the side. "I said back up. Now. If he dies, he stays dead. Me on the other hand."

Red dots appeared on Annu's chest, a guard in the middle spoke under a visor. "Step away from the doctor."

Annu shot a round at the ceiling; plaster showered him and the floor. "For the last time get out of my way or the next one's in him and the second in yours."

From being tortured to having hostages all in twenty-four hours is a little disconcerting.

A sneer twisted the Shooks' features. "No matter what you do you'll never survive. In a matter of time we'll have you again. And I assure you next time will be worse than before."

"For once I'd love someone to tell me it'll be better than before. Apparently not today." Annu thrust Tony at the men. "Get the first row of guns and bring them to me."

Annu dug the gun into Tony's back.

Tony collected a pile of guns in his arms and carried them over to Annu.

The extra guns provided the confidence Annu lacked. "Put your hands in the air, turn around and walk out away, nice and slow."

The men followed directions save except turning, and watched Annu's every move. Devoid of other sounds, tension in the hallway escalated.

Annu walked backwards with Tony towards the exit. "I haven't had this much attention since, ah hell, I'm not sure. Ever."

A door handle dug into Annu's hip, he dipped beside Tony's ear. "I'm sorry for the ploy. I had no choice." He jiggled the handle and opened the door. "Everybody stay put and no one gets hurt."

That's bull shit. Most of you will get hurt the second I get the chance.

Tony's lips stayed sealed. "I know."

"Keep that in mind for the next minute or so." One handed Annu lifted Tony by the shoulders, threw him at oncoming guards. "Sorry."

Several agents and guards tumbled into each other. Smith one sideswiped Annu.

Annu grabbed Smith, threw him into the next section and blocked the door behind him.

Chapter 39
Paused Advantage
What's left of Yebu Hospital
Yebu City, Yebu, Orion

Erin's stomach slammed into her ribs, air burned her lungs, her arms flailed.

I must save the kid, the others and the others. Please everything stop for a minute.

Everything even the stench of death and antiseptic stayed in place. Erin lowered onto the ground, the mayhem mid air remained. "Holy crap."

I did that? Another new surprise. Hopefully easier to control than the last. Please be okay Zeke.

"Well that's, ah, new and kind of freaky. What now?"

Solitude amongst a silent magnitude allowed a flood of emotions, anxiety arrived a fraction before a total melt down. Erin patted her cheek and slowed her breath.

Remember what my therapist said. Focus. Calm down and assess the situation before I panic. All right. I'll assess away but if she's wrong I'm un-inviting her to the wedding.

Eli hovered an inch above the ground, his terrified expression tore shreds off her resolve. Erin guided Eli beside her and into a corner, protected from further harm. She returned to the upheaval. Other arms, legs and body parts in a variety of states likewise demanded immediate attention. Truth shattered Erin's self worth, the emotional meltdown still loomed. "I can't do this by myself."

This is too much. I'm not going to be able to help these people. What a fool to think I could? Stupid therapist. Stupid. If there's ever a time to panic, now is a great time. Is saving some is better than none, or is it worse?

A bunch of chairs metres from the top of the room shifted, Erin's blood cooled.

No. Get it together. No emotional bull crap. This isn't about me. This time my emotions can kill people. Please God help me out here. I—I can't do this alone.

Warmth swept across Erin's nape, a beam of pink light pierced through the roof, swirled around Erin, settled at her shoulders and wormed in. Peace, calm and a serenity she'd long sought filled her.

No, all lives count for something including mine. This is real, important, urgent, what really matters. These people have lost so much, and I can help some of them. If I die in the process, I've finally done something worthy in my life other than getting married. I have so much more in me than I ever imagined and I've set it free.

Tension ebbed from Erin's shoulders. "Can I bottle this clarity? It's gold."

Erin focused on the objects in the way and shifted them into an open hallway on her left. Once the space revealed a person, Erin dragged them like a balloon to the floor and laid them down beside each other, each tied together with an invisible blend of stubbornness and sense of purpose. One swipe moved a bed leg about to impale a young patient, Erin added her to the others. If she considered the work and concentration to come, the borrowed courage dwindled. Relief accompanied a successful save, pain and a torn soul for those already dead.

She mentally shifted two doctors and a nurse; her brain ached. "Keep going, one step, or person in front of the other. Soon enough I'll be done and find mum again."

Oh mum. I wish I could thank you. Maybe I can?

'Mum, it's Erin. I'm okay, pretty much. I'm going to save whoever I can here at the hospital then come find you. Don't

come to me. You've already got enough to do. But it's okay because I have a couple of powers to help. I'm sorry I didn't tell you before. I love you. Mum. I'm sorry for everything. This is not as easy as it looks. Accept God answered me straight away. Me. I can't—'

A table and two chairs plummeted from the roof to the ground. The thud woke Erin and a number of midway frozen people roused.

One thought consumed Erin, stop, the errant furniture and people re-froze, piece of mind returned.

Planes roared over the hospital, Erin's calm fluttered. "Oh God, please no more bombs. Please, please, please."

They passed; no other artillery hit the hospital.

Erin held sanity tight to her chest. "All right. Either way I'm running out of time."

Chapter 40
The Bad, The Sad and The Fucking Ugly
Enki Island, Orion

A quick food refuel and Shayne quivered before the assembled group of I.D.I.O.T.s, Peace Officers, plus rescued Protectors under a thus far impenetrable vehicle depot.

Even with the solitude power delivered, Shayne's mood darkened. One goddess against a vast enemy and not all evident.

When much is given, much is expected. Well, then I need to go on a responsibility diet and drop like two hundred kilos.

Erin's mental conversation dangled in Shayne's mind. When combined with Jacob receiving treatment in the Peace Office, a minutiae of relief arrived.

Thank you Big G for keeping her safe but I've got some questions later. Oh and please get me through the rest of this.

Tears welled in her eyes. Shayne chewed her finger nails and spat the remnants.

Gross. I can't believe I'm so stressed I'm back to nail destruction. Come on I.D.I.O.T., talk. They're waiting for you.

"Thank you all for coming. As confirmed, our air force numbers are the lowest but even a dozen makes a difference. Shared intel confirms if you manoeuvre under the martian craft, a missile aimed in the middle of the energy beam brings it down. However, try and keep ariel fire away from safe zones. We don't need to add friendly fire to our list of sins. In terms of their ground forces do not wait for them to shoot first or you're dead. They have no compunction about killing anyone and have made it clear they want our planet. We and I mean all of us will not let that happen."

Lim stood with several others, a mixture of I.D.I.O.T.s, Peace Officers lingered in their own group at the back not merged with the others. Their mumbles, sideways glances, and expressions of destain niggled at Shayne's patience.

I feel like I'm back in fucking high school and am the unpopular girl.

Doom erected a mental prison around Shayne which incarcerated her thoughts and common sense.

I'm going to completely screw this up and I won't even have to try. No don't. Just keep moving forward.

Shayne straightened and yelled above PFD engines meters away. "You've got your teams and orders. Stick to them and remember getting citizens to safety is number one priority. As for me, I'm going to the mother ship before the Queen gets here. On route I'll get rid of as many of these purple, pumpkin looking fuckers as I can. This lessens their numbers for overall attacks and therefore other people who'd be killed otherwise. No more innocent people are dying."

A horrified look on Jackie's face delivered a swarm of regret. "Ah what?"

Great, just what I need. A sensitive alien.

Shayne patted his shoulder. "Oh not you. I mean the others. You're much better looking than the rest of them."

If you're into purple pumpkin looking beings.

The distant yet close mother ship added cells to Shayne's stress prison. "So in short when I'm close to the craft thing I'll pretend give myself up to get on the ship with Jackie and Zeke's help. If she won't compromise she's dead and so's the rest of them. I'm not fucking around with negotiations. They surrender or die."

Where the fuck did I get all that from?

One of the male elder protectors, Davi, stepped forward from the second row.

Davi's deep voice reminded her of Annu. "Forgive me for speaking out of turn but we should protect you, your Goddess not the other Orionian's nor these people behind us. What trust should be place in those who tried to get rid of you and everyone else? The way they treated us while in captivity is subhuman."

A scoff from the back of the group raised Shayne's hackles.

Those mother fucking pieces of shit. No wait, I can't kill them yet Grrr. This is too much stress for one little person.

Shayne swallowed a vomit burp. "Right now and quite hopefully from hereon this isn't an 'us versus them' situation. This is for the greater good of an entire planet and possibly galaxy. I can't protect more people and not worry about losing any of you if you're all with me. Please trust me despite not having any choice. Those are your orders. Am I clear?"

Davi puffed outhouse chest and nodded. "Yes, my Goddess. I apologise."

Shayne spoke out the side of her mouth. "Don't worry about it. I'm feeling you believe me."

What will it take for everyone to believe in me? Nothing short of a damned miracle.

Davi returned to his place in line.

Zeke cleared his throat; Jackie shuffled his feet and nudged her side.

Oh shit. It's worse than forgetting to thank people at the oscars.

"Of course huge thanks to Zeke and Jackie for helping too. Anyway, everyone, comms must stay on and keep in touch."

An explosion from the other side of the city rocked the ground, buildings shook, smoke clouds filled the sky.

Fuck how many dead now? So many, too many. No more, please.

Shayne groped at determination. "Get the fuck out of here, be safe and maybe we'll hate each other alive again."

Shayne stood between Zeke and Jacob, enveloping them all in her protective aura. Close to buildings and solid structures, Shayne followed a trail of rubble and ruin into a less damaged section of the commerce areas. A block into the next and six Martians rounded the corner, a fart bubbled in Shayne's butt. Weapons raised and cocked, they formed a line and fired at Shayne. The shots bounced off the aura and ricocheted off the ground, hitting nearby buildings.

Shayne raised her arms and waved. "Shit, there could be people in there, you fuckers," and blast froze them mid-rage.

Hands akimbo Zeke tapped his foot. "Ah, that's great and all but there's going to be a lot of frozen aliens to get rid of later and if they die in between, they'll stink too."

Don't get cranky at him. He's only trying to help.

"Well my genius stepson, what do you suggest instead?"

Zeke maintained an even crackle. "Hey, why not send them back to Mars through a wormhole?"

Holy fucking shit. The little bugger's right. Damn. Why didn't I think of that?

Shayne walked around the frozen Martians and into the former market area. "Well you got me there kid. I've got no come back other than, wait for it, I want to break knee. I want to break knees. I want to break knees for the first time and this time I know it's for real."

Zeke slapped his hands over his ears. "This is true torture. Stop, please."

Show no mercy.

"I'm falling in love. God knows, I want to break knees."

Goosebumps covered Shayne's arms, spit evaporated.

Oh oh. Something wicked this way comes?

Her aura around them faltered.

Zeke looked side to side. "What's happened?"

Jackie rubbed his arms and moved closer. "Why did it go away?"

"I don't know. I'm working on it. "Shayne's energy dwindled, she closed her eyes and concentrated, nothing happened. "What the fuck? Of all the times to be screwy, this is a shitty one. Come on."

Shayne's body temp lowered, boots crunched on stone behind her.

Don't turn around yet, get rid of these two first.

"Both of you run and hide. Don't come after me, I'll find you later."

Zeke attempted turning around. "Not without you. You need—"

Shayne stopped him and shoved him forward. "Run fuck you."

Zeke grabbed Jackie's jacket, ran down the street and disappeared into an alley way.

The moisture in Shayne's mouth and throat disappeared, she faced the new foe.

A damp, stiff Nimrod patted himself with a towel and a thunderous expression. "Now it's on. You're going to pay."

Shayne's butthole puckered, she tip toed backwards.

Oh fuck, oh fuck, oh fuck, oh fuck.

"Oh look at you all defrosted and shit. You know, this is not the best time for interruptions."

Nimrod held a black device aimed at Shayne. He and bitch faced Lim stood in front of a team of their cohorts.

Shayne shuffled quicker and scouted for an escape route. "Are you shitting me? Where did you get that from? That all got turned off and shit."

Nimrod motioned behind him. "That's an interesting story but not nearly as interesting as your death will be."

Two men strode over, grabbed Shayne and restrained her with a strange metal cuff.

Chapter 41
The Alien Coup
DSI Facility, Pine Gap
New South Wales, Australia, Earth

Smith the hostage locked the hospital doors, opened the next and gave Annu the second keycard. Down a short hallway, Annu entered a hanger full of strange craft, high tech equipment and people who worked on them. Despite the intrusion the staff worked undisturbed and absorbed in their tasks.

Any second now one of them will clue on. I must be calm and not attract any more attention to us.

Annu moved the gun to the Smith's back and wrapped an arm around his shoulder. "Nice and easy, fella. Pretend we're work mates or something. Once I make it out of here, I might let you live."

Smith stiffened; his tone hateful. "It's not hard for them to get out that exit. If you surrender, we won't kill your friends."

Annu's cool, calm, plan crumbled like week-old bread. "How kind. Why aren't the alarms going off yet?"

Smith shrugged Annu's hand away. "It's a separate section than the others. Kind of a safe room and fittingly the place you'll die."

Fear is not going to stop me this time.

They passed a disc shaped object, lights flashed on the top and sides. "What are those things?

"Crafts from other planets."

Annu's blood heated, he twisted the gun barrel. "These are the ships from all the beings you've got prisoner here. You mother flarkers."

Smith winced but didn't break away. "It's a matter of national security. If they come here, they take their chances. If they crash, it's our right and duty to protect Earth and utilise technology available."

A worker repaired a hole in the side of the ship filled Annu with hatred.

Annu pinched the Smith's shoulder. "You're the ones who bring them down and make them crash. You've got no right keeping beings hostage or doing the horrific things you do. I'm going to—"

Agents broke into the hanger; they alerted workers who searched for the disturbance's source.

Annu dragged Smith behind a ship and along the wall. "Stay flarking quiet or you'll get a bullet to the back of the head. Trust me, it would be an improvement."

Smith twisted his torso and fumbled for the gun. "Hey, over here."

He groped at the handle and flipped it out of Annu's grasp, it bounced on the floor.

Annu reached for another in his waistband. "You bastard."

Smith escaped Annu's reach, dived for the weapon, missed and hit the concrete.

The agent landed on his back, Annu grabbed the Smith's side and smashed him at the ship. His skull bounced off metal, bone crunched and brain smooshed, the man's body dropped to the ground in a splatter of blood.

Annu kicked the man in the ribs twice and bolted to the exit. "That'll learn you."

Gun fire echoed in the hanger and sirens wailed.

Annu ducked and weaved around machinery. "Any miracles for sale or offer? I'm ready for a couple."

Two agents caught up to Annu; he picked up a black box between ships and hurled it at them.

The toss collected one agent and careened him into the second. No sooner they fell and another half dozen agents locked him in their sights.

Zip, zing, zip.

Two bullets skimmed Annu's ear, the other sliced his shoulder. Annu leapt over equipment, caught the edge and tripped.

Boom, boom.

A section of ship exploded above him, Annu brushed himself off and ran. "Flarking hell."

A bullet seared Annu's shin and imbedded into the wall. "Shit, shit, shit."

Annu sucked in his gut, squeezed between two ships and into a bunch of workers. He ducked down and barrelled his way forward. Someone or something sideswiped Annu onto equipment. He pushed up with his legs and limped to the exit a hundred metres away Annu. Pain erupted across his upper thigh, Annu dropped onto his knee, blood dribbled down his leg. "So it's a no to the miracles?"

What's the evil version of a miracle? One of those would do.

Annu shoved aside agony and rose from the ground.

Don't give in, keep going, you're close. Find something to block them with.

A bank of electrical equipment next to an open fuel tank provided the perfect diversion. Annu ripped out cords, rubbed them together, created a spark and tossed them at the fuel tank. A spark entered the tank, fire trickled around the lip. Annu leapt out of the way, the ship exploded.

The upside, it blocked the agents access to Annu, the down side, metal debris dug into his back and legs. Part of Annu wanted to give up and end the inevitable sooner rather than later.

The other part pushed, urged, and cajoled, not willing to die.

Flark, I can't keep doing this.

The outer exit provided one war over and another beginning.

So help me if I ever make it home, I'm not going to another planet ever again.

Into the night, the cool air fought the warmth in Annu's lungs and sharpened his clarity. A vice crushed his chest and slowed Annu. The pain killers from before dwindled; receptors in his brain woke.

If I can live after being killed by Shamesh, I can make it through this. Maybe. Perhaps. Ah screw it. Move, now.

At the rear of the building, moonlight illuminated the crumpled, blood spotted map and revealed the location of the weapon and ammunition centre close.

Annu chose left and replaced the map.

How I'm getting in there alive and destroy it.

Around a corner Annu hid behind trash bins on route and refuse. "Did anyone else make it out?" At the edge of an open area spot lights from ships above showed other beings and agents in various stages of battle. A light flicked by, Annu ducked down. "That's a yes. Time to rally the troops."

Annu smacked, face first, into a bin and bounced back. "What the—"

A disheveled Shooks grappled Annu's legs. "You're not getting out of here."

Annu kicked him in the gut. "Are you kidding me? I've got enough problems."

All the frustration, pain, torture, and woe expended itself onto the main torturer before him.

Ambient noise faded; sirens and lights drifted into the background. Nothing existed except Annu and another arch enemy.

Shooks heaved and unholstered his weapon. "It's just you and me. I told you we'd kill you."

Hatred overrode frustration—adrenaline compensated for pain. "And I told you, I'd kill you." He dug a shoulder in Shooks' torso and hammered him at the wall. "You've missed first place on my to-die list, but you're about to make up for it."

Shooks lurched forward on impact; his teeth clanged together, bad breath wafted. "Humph."

Shooks fist dodged Annu's cheek.

Annu grabbed the man's arm and yanked. "You flarking piece of shit."

Bone crunched and muscle tore, Shooks wail tickled Annu's spine and across his ball sack. Vengeance garnered satisfaction. "Effective new move."

Another, darker part of Annu, crawled out from under a rock and craved the agonising justified death of another. It consumed, demanding recompense and due attention.

Annu allowed it to flow and embraced a distant friend. "Now I'm getting somewhere."

They all must die and this place wiped from this planet.

Shooks dropped, Annu punched him in the head, his face crumbled. The agent slumped onto the ground, blood poured from his mouth. Annu pointed the gun between Shooks' eyes. "When you get to hell say hi to everyone there for me."

Reason and light attempted its own invasion.

Stop. Don't do this. He's already done for, I don't need to kill him.

Hatred's strength knew no bounds.

Yes, he deserves to die. They all do.

Annu squeezed the trigger; the contents of Shooks' pea brain minus the peas showered the area. The dark inside calmed—sated for now.

Chapter 42
Close Encounters of The Fucked-Up Kind
Enki Island, Orion

Powerless and no-one who cares, knows where I am. I've got nothing to work with. Totally screwed.

Held by Nimrod's men Shayne swallowed self defeat and denial. "Is it too late to discuss this? I'm sure there's an agreement to reach."

Lim stomped by Nimrod's side around corners and down dark alleys back in the direction Shayne came from before.

Nimrod strode a metre ahead. "Yes, it's way too late."

Solutions to Shayne's problems played out one after the other.

Okay so the 'I need fucking help, these bastards all need to die and I know how I'll do it' plan will kick in any minute now.

Any second...All right. Why does this keep happening to me? The me part I guess.

Shayne kicked at Nimrod's legs and missed by several centimetres. "Hey, Nimrod. Where'd you get that device from? I won't tell anyone you told me."

The I.D.I.O.T. to her left yanked Shayne back. "Shut up."

Shayne's arm muscles ripped, she twisted and eased the pain. "Ouch. Jesus, take it easy. Hey Nimrod answer me."

Nimrod looked over his shoulder. "Stop calling me that. We've had the tech all along. We gave you the illusion of control which served a purpose—it got you with us. Not to mention we discovered exactly what your powers are and you're followers. Which are being herded up as we speak."

Oh God, the kids and Jackie. The protectors, they were right and still ended up back in the I.D.I.O.T.'s custody.

Anger smothered fear, Shayne struggled against her bonds—they pulled tighter. "You're a bunch of goat fucking, genocidal maniacs. While you're doing this more of your planet's people die. What the hell's wrong with you?"

Lim stopped, turned and stood centimetres from Shayne. "It's time you did what you're told."

The I.D.I.O.T.s on either side of Shayne paused mid-stride.

Whack.

Lim backhanded Shayne across the cheek. "Ah that's much better. Since I can't kill you yet, I've wanted to do that for so long."

Shayne's brain wobbled, her teeth rattled. Everything around her hazed, Shayne massaged her jaw.

Restrained by the shoulders, Shayne lunged for Lim and spat blood on her pants. "You fucking ugly bitch."

Lim raised her other hand and sneered. "I'm going to smack that look right off your pale face."

Nimrod's clap broke the daze of the coming bitch fest. "Lim, enough. Leave it, her, be."

Like a trained dog, Lim returned to Nimrod and stood closer than friendship dictated, he stroked her arm.

Oh great. They're lovers. Argh, I don't want that visual image in my brain.

In two steps, Nimrod loomed over Shayne, his smile terrified her. "I'd been keeping the good news to myself but the time is fitting. With your assistance, once we've restored order, you'll be publicly vilified as the instigator of the invasion. You and your children will be sentenced to death. The opposing counsellors will be revealed as co-conspirators and likewise punished. Igra, if he survives as I did, myself, and our group, will install a new government as heroes. So yes, you'll be responsible for ending this just not in the way you wanted."

A chill entered Shayne's toes and crept up her legs, a horrific thought followed. "Oh, my God. This all works in your favour.

You come out looking like the best Counsel ever and saviour of Orion, not the giant douche bag you are."

It's actually not my fault this happened. For once. Mostly anyway.

Nimrod rocked on his heels. "True. My, you look smarter than you are." A Martian ship zipped by, Nimrod turned around. "Keep moving."

Shayne relied on the guards hold, swung a leg to gain momentum and kicked.

Nimrod remained so close yet so far.

I need to grow another few inches. Fuck it. You get my best death stare.

"That's going to come and bite you on that cold arse of yours. One way or another I'll stop you. I'll make you beg me for mercy then slaughter you like you've done to others."

If I can.

Nimrod's laugh chilled Shayne. "Stupid Earthling. I'm going to make your death nice and slow."

Psycho mother fucker. There's still time to get away. The first chance I get I run.

"Are you taking me to your secret squirrel head quarters? The place you get together with your I.D.I.O.T. friends and jerk each other off? Or is it a sex den and you're the gimp? I can see you in a rubber mask. It's something you should consider adding to your wardrobe."

Nimrod paused, his shoulders raised to his ears and continued forward.

Shayne dug in her heels and dropped her weight. "Hello? Are you listening?"

The I.D.I.O.T.s raised Shayne a few centimeters; her toes dug a path in the dirt.

Okay next bright idea?

Shayne sang louder than impending death. "Hello, it it me you're looking for? I can see it in your pies; I can see it in your news. Tell me is there someone loving you. Tell me how to spin your heart 'cause I haven't got a poo—"

A boot to the back of the shin cut her off.

Shayne swung in the guards hold. "I'm never going to give you up, never gonna say goodbye, never gonna run around and dessert you. Never gonna give you up, never gonna say good pie. I won't run around and pervert you."

The guard on her left struck Shayne's back, crack. "Shut the flark up. Boss can we kill her right now? I beg you."

Another person who wants to kill me. He's so not on my Christmas card list this year. I could actually make lists of people who want to kill me.

Nimrod's groaned over his shoulder. "I wish but no."

Never give in, never surrender and all that kind of shit.

Shayne's vision blurred, she tipped her chin. "You could have just asked me to stop arsehole."

The guard grumbled and stared ahead.

The I.D.I.O.T. and Peace Officer compound appeared only three blocks away and muddled Shayne's thoughts.

Okay not as much time as I thought. Fuck, Shit, shit, shit, shit.

The group approached a thick metal door on the ground opposite the compound.

Shayne wriggled, the men tightened their grip and pinched skin.

Nimrod leant over an electronic keypad. "Lim make sure alpha team has maintained contact with her children."

Lim smiled, not a pretty sight. "Roger."

A fat arse wobbled behind the others and turned behind a building.

Despair weaved a jacket upon Shayne's back.

Shayne smacked the men's hands. "No, leave them out of it. Please. I beg you."

Nimrod placed his thumb on the keypad; it emitted a series of beeps, a door clicked. Nimrod opened it and revealed an escalator leading into darkness.

He pointed to the guards beside Shayne. "Take her down there and be quick about it."

Shayne struggled, kicked wriggled and screamed. Undeterred the men picked her up by the shoulders and onto the escalator.

"Ah creator. Since you seem to answer Erin's prayers quickly can you do mine?"

A warm fuzziness calmed Shayne. *'I do answer you straight away as well but it get's a little messy in there and you're easily distracted.'*

Admonishment flushed her cheeks. *'Oh shit. So you're the rational, logical voice in there louder than all the others?'*

'Yes my child. It is I.'

Geez I'm such an arsehole. I need to tidy up my brain. Why can't I concentrate on one thing at—

'Ah, Ashera? This is a perfect example.'

'Shit. Sorry. Pardon the pun but maybe give me a heads up next time.'

'I do. Listen more and talk—'

I hate myself sometimes. I'm a bad creation.

'Shayne?'

I just can't seem to help myself. *'Okay well sorry again. Could you possibly help me out here too?'*

'The answer is already before you, it's now up to ah never mind—'

I should totally ask for bigger boobs while I'm here.

The fuzziness abated but left behind a resolute confidence.

I can't lose hope and faith because I am hope and faith. I am what makes the difference, I am the saviour, I have within me to solve this problem and quickly. I shall be a fool no longer.

At the very least I'll work really hard at it.

Chapter 43
What the Living Flark?
DSI Facility, Pine Gap
New South Wales, Australia, Earth

Annu wiped brain mush from his cheeks, kicked Shooks in the nuts and shot him in the chest.

No way I'm risking you coming back again.

A different form of power seeped into Annu's deepest regions and filled an empty void.

DSI agents invaded the strip of land between the buildings and an outer forest. Annu aimed the gun and emptied the clip into the first row.

A drove of reptoid beings on the roof, pounced off and onto agents.

Annu dismissed watching them suffer and entered the open area. "Not far to go."

The woman doctor who'd defiled and tortured Annu fought with a humanoid alien. The blue skinned being clawed the doctor, whom stabbed needles at it and rolled towards Annu.

Excellent it's the next one on my to-kill list.

Jab, jab, jab. The reptile slowed and fell on the doctor.

She dragged herself from under it unaware of Annu's presence.

Annu aimed head height and squeezed the trigger. "Die bitch."

She hit the ground; her obliterated skull delivered no regret, empathy, or a punishment from above.

Shit. Killing people doesn't feel as bad as I thought it would or should.

Annu stepped around the doctor's body. "I can live with it."

A force smashed into Annu's ribs and winded him.

They hit the ground together, pain roared along Annu's back. He clutched the front of a vest and flipped the female agent over.

Annu landed with his knee in her guts. She grunted and grabbed at his shirt. Annu dragged her upright, swung her and released.

She hit another agent, the two mashed bounded off each other.

In the moment it took to pry themselves off, dog-like beings came around the corner and tore chunks out of both agents.

Move idiot, move.

Annu checked the map, did a one eighty, headed forward, passed the tech building and reached the ammunitions depot.

Splat, splat, splat.

Creatures swooped from the sky, collected agents and dropped them.

A body flew into a DSI craft, cracked the windshield and landed inside. The craft spun and crashed into the tech building on Annu's left.

Spinning rotors detached from the plane and careened for him, Annu scrambled to his fee and ducked for cover.

The rear of the tech building blasted into and across the open space. The ground vibrated, percussion deafened Annu, burnt flesh infiltrated the air.

Annu's parade of vengeance stalled. "I, ah, well that saves me some effort."

People on fire fled out the opening and rolled on the ground, the flames aided by cold air increased.

Tall orange humanoids spilled out after them, some blackened by fire or not harmed at all.

Annu struggled with lack of control. "I need a handle on this shit."

A second explosion rocked foundations and destroyed the entire building. Metal sheets, machinery parts and all manner of refuse covered everything.

Energy surged and revived Annu. Fatigue and pain disappeared. Power built from a spark into an inferno, a red aura encapsulated Annu. He rose and hovered meters above. All Annu's injuries healed, godliness poured over him. "Now I can flarking end this nightmare."

In the other direction an agent carried Ankor in his arms. She wriggled, clawed and scratched at his face. He gripped her tighter, and carried her from a building to the rear of the compound.

Annu's anger roared unbridled. "Where the flark is Tony?"

The doctor's body lay bloodied around the corner.

Damn. Sorry Doc.

On way to Ankor, an electronic whip wrapped around Annu's legs.

A series of high pitched beeps intermarried with vibrations rocked Annu.

Annu lowered against his will, a small group of military men held the cable's other end and obscured Ankor's location.

No, no, no, no, no.

Fists clenched, Annu grabbed the cord and dragged the men several feet.

They secured the cable to a winch on the front of a truck, one push of a button and the cable reeled, Annu descended centimetres at a time. Fresh shock waves rocked Annu; he dug his fingers under the cable and pried. Agony ripped down his hands and up his arms. The ground approached fast, unprepared Annu yanked up and raised the lost distance. The truck's tyres left the ground.

The men yelled; each of them grabbed a section of cable.

Annu stayed in place and concentrated all his power into arms.

The outside layer melted, the next two peeled away, its blue light diminished, the shock and agony stopped. Instant relief refuelled Annu.

An ignited Annu blasted fire balls at the men. "You mother flarkers. I'm done playing with you."

Consumed by fire, those not already dead rolled around and stopped. Burnt flesh and black smoke stung Annu's nostrils.

Annu flew to the compound's rear. "Please be okay, Ankor. Please."

A Black triangle craft whooshed by, Annu spun on an invisible axis and ended in the direction he'd come from.

The craft dropped bombs. Percussion waves rippled from the ground into the sky and annihilated dozens of beings.

The choice between helping others or Ankor tormented Annu.

Am I saving Ankor for the right reasons or only to find out more about my father? In the meantime the rest are on their own? Flark it. I've gotten all messed up. It's not right.

Annu flew after the craft. At the ruined area's edge, white light enveloped him, the current reality altered. Flash, he landed knee first onto a brown floor, dazed and confused aside a stark non-decorated room cleared.

Annu rubbed his eyes and shook his head. "What the flark? Where am I? Did my father answer me?"

A group of uniformed, bald, four feet grey skinned beings streamed out of a doorway. One of them adorned with the most medals on his jacket approached.

Not unless they work for him, if so what's the big secret?

The closer he got, familiarity niggled Annu and paternal excitement abated.

Damn it.

"You're a better dressed version of the people who attacked us on Jupiter what seems forever ago. Listen, I'm sorry about what happened there, total misunderstanding but you better let me go or it will be much worse than before."

The being crossed hands in front of him. "I'm afraid I can't do that."

Oh joy. Another level of hell to endure alone.

Chapter 44
Mother Fucker Ship
Enki Island, Orion

The metal door slammed closed on Shayne along with any shred of luck. Only determination remained in tact. The restraints on her wrists unlocked and fell off.

Shayne massaged her arms and kicked the metal door. "You bunch of mother fucking, cock sucking, dick licking, bad breath spraying, beige wearing c, c, I'm going to say it. Cun—"

Something moved behind her, Shayne turned, the once Enki imprisoned counsellors now sat on a bench running down a concrete wall. Their collective expressions dragged Shayne down further.

One of the females sparked Shayne's recognition.

One of the Counsellors I helped at the safe room. Marge something maybe?

"Ah shit. They got you guys again?"

Maybe-Marge nodded, curls bounced. "Yes. I'm afraid so."

Resignation lay upon Shayne and dug in its elbows. "We're all in some crap then. What about the frozen fat fuck? "Please tell me he's not around somewhere?"

Maybe-Marge rested against the wall. "The I.D.I.O.T.s took him with them. Although he wasn't in good shape. I'll be surprised if they can resurrect him and pray they can't."

Ah yeah. He can stay that way forever. I don't want to deal with him ever again.

"Yeah me too. That's all I need."

How the fuck am I getting out of here? Where's Houdini when I need him?

Dead like I'm gonna be.

A check of the room revealed concrete air vents. A welded seal prevented taking the lid off to wriggle out. Artificial lights hung from the ceiling on cords likewise with no way elsewhere and apart from a possible ramp, the long bench bolted to the wall offered nothing.

All in all they'd done a fabulous job of incarceration.

Had I have known this was here a couple of days ago, I'd be here on purpose.

Maybe-Marge followed Shayne's movements. "I guess this changes things for you too."

Mmm. Remember the whole I am hope thing.

Shayne rolled her neck and shoulders.

Sometimes I really hate you brain.

"That depends, do you know a way out of here?"

Maybe-Marge pointed to the sole metal entry and exit in the bunker.

Frustration clipped Shayne's words. "Okay, duh. I meant a way out that doesn't include the door?"

One of the roof lights flickered and backlit Maybe-Marge. "Sorry. No. This was built as an impenetrable bunker for keeping counsellors, delegates. Grand counsellor Igra has the only key useable on this side should an event such as this occur. Not quite this way of course."

Shayne's temples ached, her flank muscles tightened. "Why does it always rain on me? Is it because I got fried when I was seventeen? Why when the sun is shining I can't escape the lightning, oh where did the blue sky go-ooo. Why is it raining so old?"

Maybe-Marge raised her hands. "Ah, I, ah, can you please not do that?"

Seriously it might be time to consider that I suck. But not today. Fuck it. "Sure, fine—"

A white light appeared before Shayne. It aimed and swallowed her whole. The bunker and counsellors disappeared, flash, she landed feet first onto a different floor. Her mind lagged a minute behind.

In the middle of a sterile, strange round room Annu talked to a four foot tall humanoid.

"Holy shit. Finally." Shayne launched at him and wrapped her legs around his middle. "Oh my God. I can't believe it's you. You're here. Thank you, Fuckshit and God."

Annu kissed Shayne across the face and pulled back. "I'm ah, excited to see you too." At arm's length Annu inspected her ratted, torn, dirty clothes, disheveled hair. "What the hell happened to you, woman? Are you all right?"

Shayne choked on her own body odour.

I look like fucking crap and he still loves me. I want to snuggle so far into him I hit organs.

"No. I'm not and it's a long story but it's so much better now we're here together. Actually, where the fuck is here?"

The green being tapped Annu's shoulder. "If I may interrupt for a moment, I'll answer that."

The here and now slapped Shayne on the arse.

The kids, the Martians, fucking Nimrod, and what the fuck?

Shayne wriggled out of Annu's arms and faced the being akimbo. "Who the fuck are you? Do you have idea the shit storm you've interrupted? Send me back to Orion. Like fucking now."

The being straightened, his medals shimmered. "I'm afraid that's not possible. Allow me to introduce myself, I'm Captain Lauch of the Jupiter Space Federation. I believe you met some Juplings by accident some days ago. Fortuitous really. "

Annu slowed beside her. "Listen Captain, I'm needed on Earth ASAP too. There's a huge situation to deal with, beings to save and people to kill."

Disappointment and surprise dampened Shayne's semi-good will. "Hey wait. Honey, I need your help first. I can't do this anymore with out you. And now Nimrod is after the kids."

Annu's shrugged, his shadow enveloped her. "Who's Nimrod? Which kids? Erin and Ryan?"

Shayne ejected frustration with a sigh. "The big I.D.I.O.T., never mind. And Erin and Zeke those kids."

Annu's stunned expression obliterated what remained of Shayne's joy seeing him. "Something huge must have happened for you to consider him your kid too."

This is all taking too fucking long.

"Ha flipping ha. You're right though. This is why you've got to come with me to Orion."

Captain-being retained his composed demeanour and swept an arm before him. "Once again, sorry to interrupt. After trying to get hold of you for several months with no success, we'd left countless messages. In your absence our problem escalated to this point. I must insist on you joining me in my quarters. There's much to discuss and time is of the essence in this matter."

Shit, fuck, shit. That's why the name's familiar. But it's the fat fuck's fault too. Great. Fucking fantastic.

Shayne erupted in blue and stepped closer to the captain. She jabbed at him. "Listen, buddy, I don't want to hear what you've got to say, what your matter is, or even why you've got three eyes. I only care about my kids and stopping more people from dying, which, while I'm here, is happening anyway."

Captain-being tapped a device on his wrist, Shayne's powers wavered.

Shayne's anger shot through the roof. "What? Are you people getting this shit off Ebay or what? Did someone have a sale on these things? Every man and their dog seems to have one. For fuck's sake. I really need to work on being stronger or something taking over the damned company."

Annu wrapped his arm around Shayne's shoulders, his forearm muscles bulged. "I agree one hundred percent with my fiancee except for where I want to go back to is Earth. You seem well mannered and all but if you keep pushing us you'll find out the hard way why you shouldn't."

Damned you're so hot. Look at you all muscly and shit.

Captain-being's sigh frayed Shayne's one surviving nerve. "It appears we'll have to do this the hard way. Such a shame."

Half a dozen green beings streamed into the room.

Three stood beside and restrained Shayne, another six surrounded Annu.

Seriously?

Shayne wriggled and squirmed. "You're a polite James Bond on the outside and a Ted Bundy mother fucker on the inside."

Undeterred, the guards dragged Shayne's arms behind her back.

A growl erupted from deep within Shayne. "Get the fuck off me."

One click secured Shayne's wrists in high tech restraints, on her right Annu suffered the same fate.

Captain-being swept an arm across himself. "After me, please."

Shayne death stared like never before. "Only if you take this shit off and make my kids safe. If not, hell is raining on all of you."

He retracted the arm and arched an eyebrow. "I'm not sure it's a good idea."

"Well, I fucking do." Shayne held out her wrists and raised her voice. "Why does it always rain on me? Is it because I lied when I was seventeen? Why does it always fucking rain on me?"

The guards squealed and covered their ears, Annu cringed.

Don't take it personally at the moment.

Captain-being's mouth dropped open. "All right. Stop. Take off the restraints from both of them now. Someone get a DNA linked location on the children?"

Shayne crossed her arms. "I fucking thought so. Now we're getting somewhere."

Chapter 45

SSDP - Same Shit Different Planet
Jupiter's Outer Atmosphere
Jupiter Space Federation Crew Ship

Annu ambled down a tight hallway, flipping between ecstatic to see Shayne and despair. The last days before events streamed into his mind: captured on more than one occasion, tortured, suffered physical and metal anguish at the hands of maniacal Earthlings yet killed plenty in return.

I'd only started. I went through all of that only to end up in another messy situation with desperate people. What the flark is going on? This is mental. I need a flarking drink. Or ten. And some time out. Like far far out. Maybe try a new aftershave too.

Annu stopped mid step and clutched Shayne's arm. "Before we go any further I'm catching up with my fiancee and a stiff drink."

Though I'd prefer my fiancé with my stiffie.

The captain frowned and opened his mouth.

Annu cocked his eyebrow, his shadow filled the hall. "It's not negotiable."

The captain trembled for a moment and straightened his back. "All right. My office is the third door on the right. I'll meet you there in five minutes."

Annu shuffled Shayne closer. "Done."

The captain turned a corner; other Juplings went up and down the hall into different rooms with electronic pads or other equipment, glancing at Shayne and him as they passed.

Shayne wrapped her arms around his waist and snuggled in. A wet patch formed on his shirt. "Everything is a total mess and I can't fix it myself. I thought I could but I can't. Or sort of thought but a big fat no. Thousands of people have been killed or hurt in a between Mars and Orion. Totally separate shit. Even the GC didn't expect it. More every second we're here."

Annu stroked her hair and swallowed a lump in his throat.

I'm sorry, I should be thinking and worrying about you and the kids. No one else.

"What's happened? Where are the kids?"

Shayne pushed off him and held her breath, her lip quivered. "Well after you went to Earth I couldn't open a wormhole there or anywhere else because the GC shut off everything power wise. They'd planned on 'investigating' Enki and using what they found against us when we got back. Remember the whole if you contravene this act we're arrested and put to death? They had that all sorted. Starting off by a news report telling everyone on Orion we were drug runners who died in an accident. But, things even got fucked up for them because right after you left, they took over Enki. They had it for all of five minutes and fucking Martians from fucking Mars invaded. They wanted to drain the planet of its resources first but then decided they'd just have the planet for themselves, without Orionions. Long story short, I froze Igra and freed myself only to get captured again. Erin nearly drowned, was in hospital but that got blown up, I lost Zeke for a while too but got them back until I got captured again right before this and put in a bunker with the other counsellors. I'm not sure they're safe or where they are. Or Jacob for that matter. They're smart but both these enemies are smarter. Fuck. I'm so sorry. Don't hate me."

Erin? So she ended up on Orion. I did briefly saw her on the way to Earth.

Annu processed the information influx. "This is a lot to take in all at once. Of course I don't blame you or hate you. I thank Gods you're currently okay. Hell, these Juplings better find the kids. I'm sorry you went through all that alone."

Shayne twirled the end of his shirt in her fingers. "I hear you there my love. I'm stressed the fuck out. I don't know what to do anymore. What happened on Earth?"

I missed you so much. I didn't even realise how much until right now. You referred to Zeke as one of the kids. Wow.

Annu massaged her shoulders and her nape. "Nothing as global in one way but, genocide on other beings for their powers and technology by those DSI people you received that card from. The GC had an agreement with them too. DSI abducted Ang and I from your house. Unfortunately Ang got killed in the process. After arrival at their underground facility I've been tortured and experimented on, managed to escape and get my powers back and finally able to give the bastards what they deserved only to end up here. I must return and free the others as soon as I know the kids are okay."

Dark rings below Shayne's eyes showed exhaustion. "Yeah I heard about the DSI thing. I'm so sorry again. I'm working on not screwing up anymore, believe me. Fuck. What a mess. They weren't fucking around. It's like most of the universe fucking hates us and really, really, want us dead. We pose a bigger threat than we thought, particularly together. Let's just go, I'll open a wormhole. We'll sort out Orion, Earth and come back here after."

Could we? Should we? Or are we dooming ourselves and Jupiter now and in the future?

From experience yes.

"As much as I want to, we can't. It will come back and bite us on the arse later. If there's one thing I've learnt so far it's we need more control over our emotions and being proactive of things. Not pushing them aside and waiting until they come to us, or getting blinded by personal agenda."

I came close to making a huge mistake. I have a family who loves me and problems to eradicate. That's who I am.

Shayne's cheeks flushed. "Yeah you're probably right. For the hundredth time. Doesn't change our current being in three places at once problem though."

Annu tickled her ribs and accompanied her down the hallway towards the captain's office. "Ha. I may be wrong sometimes and you right, but not necessarily at the same time."

Shayne poked his belly. "Whatevers."

At the doorway, Annu bent down and kissed Shayne. "We're stronger together, we'll get through this. Hang in there."

Shayne tapped the door, it wooshed open. "Now I've seen you, everything's almost normal."

She shuffled in and sat on a chair opposite a desk.

Annu leaned over the Captain's desk and slammed his hands down. "What's this damned problem you require us for?"

Shayne swung her legs over the chair next to him and grabbed some sort of fruit of the desk. "Yeah, hurry up. It can't be that hard. Let's get this over with. Have you found the kids yet?" She placed the core on the desk and pulled another piece from her pocket and chomped. "Oh food, how I've missed you."

I want to grab Shayne, go home, look after her, tell everyone else to flark off and sort out their own issues. Except for the children of course.

Annu massaged the base of Shayne's neck, she slumped into his hands.

The Captain's demeanour darkened. "I understand your positions so I won't delay this any further. Firstly, I apologise for the way you were treated initially, that was a misunderstanding. Had we have been notified at that time, we'd have made contact with you and we wouldn't be here now. We're at this juncture because we'd attempted several times and recently tried new software. We almost gave up trying when we got a result and aren't about to let you go now."

Annu's care factor frayed around the edges. "Unfortunately we had no control over that but it all changes soon. Thanks for the apology and in other circumstances I'd be all over making friends but at this moment it's redundant so please get to the point."

The Captain nodded; his mouth a thin line. "Millenia ago when Shamesh, made his way around the universe he used the multi-universal and inter-dimensional portal on Jupiter. After the rebellion and his capture, the portal became inactive and the cave around it sealed off. However, approximately six months ago, the portal reopened and grew each day. And not only has it been sucking things in, it's spat out all sorts of creatures which reek havoc, it's mass doubled and it effects time around it. Soon enough it will consume Jupiter and its remaining people. We've evacuated as many as we could, but we've reached a crisis point and that's where you two come in."

The fruit dropped from Shayne's mouth onto her lap. "Oh fuck me. Those messages I forgot about. I'm so fucking sorry for like the twentieth time today. It's on me."

Annu sagged, godly duty lumped onto his back. "Again? That's twice you've had a part in what's gone wrong, Shay. This can't keep happening."

But it's weird they wanted us for the portal and it related to Shamesh. There's something to the tip that brought me here. Something I'll work with after this.

Shayne collected the fruit, blew off dirt and ate it. "Well, seems I'm no where near God like yet and fuck up. Darling, we can't all be as perfect as you. All right. Just because you don't make mistakes, some of us do."

I nearly did but I didn't. I learnt from it. This is when the age difference becomes apparent.

Chapter 46
The Replacements
Yebu City, Yebu, Orion

With the boy safe amongst relatives, Erin weaved around hospital bed for the exit. Despite the chaos, people paused and stared until pain or injury diverted their attention.

These huge people are scared of me, a little, white Earthling in comparison.

Most people avoided the open wall of the emergency room and stumbled through the hospital's remaining door like the familiar action saved their sanity.

The urge to stem the flow and join Shayne overwhelmed Erin, lack of a subsequent reply from Shayne amplified Erin's struggle.

'*Mum, where are you? I'm coming to you. Please answer me.*'

Erin waited for a break in foot traffic. Behind scattered adults a group of children broken, battered, and adult-less filed into the hospital. Compassion wrenched and lurched inside Erin.

I can't stop to help them. They'll be okay. I want this finished not just so I can go home but so these people stop suffering. I never knew what suffering and pain really meant until I came here. I've underestimated Mum, Annu, and myself. I haven't truly lived before.

The last one passed, Erin exited into the late afternoon; two suns set on the horizon and backlit the largest Martian craft.

Building debris from the last bomb blocked a chunk of road and forced Erin to deviate around it. Erin climbed the edges, a thought struck.

I could move this crap out of everyone's way.

Erin rose and waved her arms. "Everyone move out of the way and I'll get rid of this stuff."

People ignored, stared, or hurried away in the other direction.

Erin shook off the creeps and shrank against a wall. "Wow, I'm the different one here. Out of place, strange and it doesn't feel good."

An arm swipe cleared the road and revealed a mass of closed businesses.

Horror rippled down Erin's back and pooled on her shirt. "Where am I, and where do I go now?"

Don't lose it. Breathe, just breathe.

'Mum, where are you? I need your help.'

Erin slow breathed and attempted to gain bearings. "Ah, duh. I can't get figure out where I am when I've never been anywhere but here or the island."

The odd person or small group shifted between buildings, while the mother ship filled most of the sky.

I'm sure I'll run into Mum or Zeke along the way.

Erin rounded a corner, a familiar voice preceded terror. "Oh no."

The officer, NimNim, appeared a block from Erin. "Make sure the woman is brought up in half an hour. The Queen arrives not long after that and we need the woman to take control."

A large woman kept pace with NimNim. "Yes, sir. I'll see to that myself. Will Igra be ready?"

Erin slipped around the building's side and leaned in.

Where is she? What are they going to do to my mum?

Noise from above muffled NimNim. "No. And I'm not sure he ever will. He's been moved to a chro-chamber. I can't believe how much trouble one little earthling caused. It feels so good putting an end to her and the male."

Stay put, don't give myself away or I can't help.

Erin's blood cooled, she gripped a misplaced brick.

They haven't killed her yet. I must find her.

Lim loudened, they walked passed Erin's hiding place. "It's kind of interesting that she's willing to sacrifice herself for Orion."

Ah Mum, what the heck? Now isn't the time for heroics. From you, anyway.

NimNim cleared his throat. "You're not gaining sympathy for the woman, Lim."

Erin lost them behind rows of stone.

Lim's voice crackled. "No, not at all. I just…never mind."

Their boot steps paused; a metaphorical hand of terror stole Erin's courage and ran away.

NimNim's voice carried. "Good. Go with a few men to pick her up, and we may as well include the other Counsellors too. It solidifies our position."

"Yes, sir."

Gravel crunched, Lim reappeared a few meters in front, Erin snuck around the building and followed her.

Two abandoned streets down, Lim met with two other soldiers.

Erin hugged the wall and considered a life of subterfuge.

This spying stuff is harder than the movies make out.

Lim's demeanour screamed 'I'm superior to you.' "Take me to the bunker. NimNim wants her and the counsellors—"

A rustle behind shocked Erin, her legs wobbled.

A touch on the shoulder and Erin melted in fear. "Eek."

Zeke put a finger on his lip and clutched her shoulder. "Shh. It's okay. It's me. Thank God's I've found you."

A Martian stood beside him, his arms across his waist. "Finally. Everyone's been worried about you. Well, three people at least."

Erin shrieked and dragged Zeke away from it. "What are you doing with one of them?"

Zeke unclenched her hand and held her in place. "He's not a bad one and he's kind of your mum's friend. Mine too now, I suppose."

Why doesn't that surprise me?

Erin gritted her teeth and slowed her breath. "You almost gave me a flipping heart attack."

Zeke emitted the worry Erin hid. "Those arseholes over there took Shayne…your mother. They're using her to stop the queen and then killing her. We've got to stop them."

Erin peeked around a wall, the coast clear. "I know. I heard them talking. They're getting her from some bunker thing. I figure I, we, follow them, let them to unlock the door, pounce, freeze whatever, get Mum and go from there."

Zeke nodded and combed fingers through his hair. "Good plan. I know where that is. We'll beat them there and wait."

Everything will be okay once I've got Mum back. She'll take charge of it all. I pray.

One last look confirmed the trio of guards had left and their time shortened.

Erin pushed off the wall. "Bugger. Come on, or we won't make it."

A Martian craft blew currents of air between the businesses.

Erin covered her ears.

'*Mum, we'll be there soon. Your daughter will rescue you.*'

Zeke clutched her sleeve and walked behind the building into an alleyway.

It darkened the more alleyways they turned down, Erin's legs ached, missed months at the gym came back to bite her.

Back in the direction Erin came from, they passed a massive complex: 'I.D.I.O.T. G.C and P.O. department. What are those things?'

Sounds official like.

Erin tugged Zeke's jacket. "Hey maybe some of those guys in there can help us."

Zeke's growl unsettled the atmosphere. "Most of those are the ones in on all the usurping your mother and my father."

I'm in a nightmare or a bad horror movie.

Disappointment slid down Erin's back and off her butt. "Oh, oh crap. Trust mum."

Zeke's lightened demeanour offered little hope. "Actually, if it weren't for her we'd all be slaves for an evil God now, and everyone here would be dead."

Shame flushed Erin's cheeks, she turned away. "Oh. I, ah, didn't think of it like that."

The guards stopped before a huge metal door on the ground and checked the area.

Zeke, Erin and the Martian hid behind a military vehicle.

Lim inserted a key into a lock and turned the handles. "Why do I always get the menial jobs?"

Both sides of the door clanged onto the ground, Lim entered the bunker.

Give her enough time to enter. 1, 2, 4, 5, 6, 7 and so on.

Erin concentrated, wriggled her fingers. She faced Zeke and the Martian. "Let's go."

At the door first, Erin clambered onto the escalator and down a tunnel stacked with military boxes before another door.

Lim wriggled a key into a lock, pushed a series of buttons and waved her hand over a display.

A few clicks and the door opened towards her.

The woman stepped over the precipice, her jaw dropped. "What the flark? Where the hell did the woman go? There's no way out."

Huh? Oh Great. Where is she now?

Erin jogged, climbed over the metal lip and paused time. Lim and a bunch of other people froze mid word.

******

279

Erin carried the shoulder end of a paralysed Lim and Zeke carried the bottom half into the entry chamber. They laid her on the ground against a wall and in quick order Zeke restrained her with a nearby plastic cord.

Everything around stayed paused in time, the air stagnant from lack of movement.

I cannot wait for this to be over one way or another. I'm exhausted. I can't take much more.

Zeke patted Lim down, removed the weapon and communicator from her waist and shoved both into his jacket. "They'll come in handy for sure."

Fear for what came next weighed on Erin's conscious.

We're going to get killed. I'm a primary school teacher and Zeke still goes to school. We've got little or no chance. What am I doing? What if I never get home or get married? He'll never know what happened. Stop or I'll freak out and if I've learnt anything it's that doesn't help. Besides, mum's managed her way through worse situations and I'm even more capable.

Erin pushed the negative aside and returned on the present. "Good thinking."

The Counsellors Erin released, filed out of the unlocked bunker and into the entry way.

Mum's Martian huddled in a corner. Only Erin and Zeke appeared to understand him. "Oh dear. Oh no. This isn't good. Not at all."

Erin's arms hurt from the load, she massaged her biceps.

God he's weird. Trust Mum to make an alien friend. My time here gets weirder and weirder.

A woman several centimetres taller than the others approached Erin.

Be brave. Fake it until I make it as Mum says. I see I'm not calling her Shayne anymore.

Her tattered robes resembled Erin's nerves. "I'm Marguerite, the second in charge, was the second in charge. You look like Shayne but younger. If you're looking for her I'm afraid she disappeared, literally."

This can't be happening.

'Mum where the heck are you?'

Erin blocked out negative reasons for the lack of maternal replies. "I hope so but neither you, nor us, have any idea where mum went or how to get hold of her and Annu."

The concern in Marguerite's tone irritated not comforted Erin. "I mean no offence but unless you've got powers and an army, we must come up with something else."

Darned woman. How rude. There's no pleasing some people. I'll show her.

"We do have some powers but apparently we'll be doing whatever it is without your support and encouragement. Geez. Give us a break."

Zeke stuck his hands in his pockets. "Shayne came up with an idea we'll make work. We look enough like our respective parents to at least pass as them and get onto the ship. If we can't change the Queen's mind, together we can stop her in another way."

Marguerite's eyebrows formed a caterpillar in the middle of her face. "I'm sorry, Son. That's rather a simplistic and unrealistic outlook, but I can't expect anything else given your age. NimNim and his team are looking for the three of you and while they've made some leeway, there's still a lot of Martians. And given how NimNim and Igra albeit frozen have gotten, they're executing their clandestine plan with horrific precision. We can't let our fate rest in your hands."

Lucky the therapist has been working on my self confidence or I'd cry right now.

Erin replaced tears with ire.

Why can't things be easy? If Mum has to deal with this all the time it's no wonder she's scattered sometimes.

Erin's stood akimbo, her thermostat rose. "For goodness sake. Whatever."

Zeke puffed his chest and blocked out half the light. "Let's go Erin. It's a long walk to the mother ship."

The woman's sigh blew stale breath into Erin's face. "Perhaps I've judged you too harshly. I apologise. I speak on behalf of all of us you shall have our help as well."

The upper hand presented itself to Erin. "No offence,"

Actually lots of offence and you can suck it up

"but you have no powers at all and there's only twelve of you. What help could you possibly provide?"

A smile softened the Marguerite's features. "Clever girl. I see you've inherited your mother's sense of humour, determination and sarcasm."

I'm realising I'm more like Mum than I thought. And I don't mind. But I'm never telling her that.

Lim roused, her groans bounced off the wall. Everything frozen in place dropped a few centimetres.

Erin's eyes widened, her heart skipped. "Oops. The guards up top will wake up soon too."

A shuffle to the corner and Erin re-froze time around Lim.

I'm going to practice this power after this. I'm not taking them for granted anymore.

Back at Zeke's side Erin nudged him. "No time like the present. I'll go up first and fix the guards. You follow with the counsellors."

Zeke wore his new purpose like a cloak. "Done sis."

Hands poised, Erin entered the escalator, at the top, a guard popped up; she paused him. Erin shoved the guard; he landed on the back with a thud.

Zeke exited the escalator and ushered the counsellors from the shaft one by one into late dusk. "Come on. This way."

The fallen guard's radio crackled. "Team one, here. Willi, what's your location over?"

Erin flinched and clutched her chest.

Surely I'm too young for a heart attack?

"Crap. Get out of here and find somewhere safe."

Mum if you don't hurry up I might have to say the 'f' word.'

The blast roared, frustration raised Erin's hackles. "Even though the I.D.I.O.T.s have gained advantage, I'm over this."

Zeke tripped over building debris and banged his hip.

A gash on his brow trickled down his cheek. "Flarking hell. These near misses are getting more near and less misses."

JakJak swayed, his purple paled. "We can't give up. Your mother would never give up."

Erin's anger burned her tongue. "Stop talking like she's dead. She's not. I know it and we didn't say we'd give up."

JakJak recoiled and dipped his chin. "I'm sorry. I didn't mean that."

Erin brushed herself off and helped Zeke to his feet. "It's alright. I'm sorry I snapped. It's hard on all of us."

When she comes back mum will see we fixed things. All this will be worth it. We've just got to hang in there.

Zeke hooked his arm in Erin's and used her as support. "Come on. We've got a ways to go."

They passed ruined shops and turned down alleyways.

The creeps burrowed under Erin's skin and infested the rest of her. "I don't like this."

Jackie turned his upper half in her direction. "Why?"

Zeke caught up and grabbed Erin's arm. "This is the quickest way."

Doom circled around the alleyway and ambushed Erin. "Sometimes quick isn't good. It doesn't feel right."

Zeke dragged her towards the alley. "If anything happens you can blame me, ah, us."

Erin released her jaw. "All right, I'm going to."

Movement behind them turned Erin and Zeke in unison.

Jackie leapt into Zeke's side and clutched his shirt.

A group of armed I.D.I.O.T. soldiers lead by a lean woman stormed their way.

Erin swallowed, tugged Zeke's arm and waved at Jackie. "Run."

Two steps and a laser rope wrapped around Erin's feet; she jolted and landed face first on the ground. Her nose mashed, gravel and rock grazed her face. "Oooh."

Zeke moaned to her right, Jackie yelled to her left.

Erin struggled against the restraint, electric shocks rippled through her body, her teeth rattled. Someone grabbed her by the shoulders and flipped her onto her back.

A woman and a gun appeared in Erin's face. "By order of the Grand Counsel you are arrested on charges of treason and terrorism. In lieu of your parents, you'll be tried accordingly back at head quarters and the punishment carried out. In this case when found guilty—which you will be—it's the death penalty," she nudged Erin with the gun butt, "Do you understand what I've said to you, earthling?"

Erin blinked, her body racked with pain. "No. I don't. You've got the wrong people. Please let us go."

The woman kicked Erin's knee and raised her voice. "I repeat do you understand what I've said to you?"

This can't happen. How can we get out of here?

"Yes but no. Please listen to me. This isn't necessary."

The woman's expression shut Erin's mouth. "Raphe, Adamski get her up."

One each side, they hoisted Erin like she weighed no more than a loaf of bread. Back on her feet the restraint limited movement.

Zeke punched, kicked and clawed at the officers beside him. "You flarking bastards. When I get out of here and my father comes back you're all dead."

An officer held a small black device next to Zeke's neck, his body seized, his eyes rolled into his head.

Erin lunged at the officer. "Stop, leave him alone."

The Officer stepped back and smirked. "For now."

The woman spoke into her lapel. "HQ this is Lieutenant Cris. We've got the fugitives and we're going back now." She turned and stuck a finger in her ear. "Affirmative. ETA half hour."

I have to do something. What can I do?

Erin trembled, reality kicked her survival instincts into gear. "Let us at least try a peaceful way?"

"Unless they suddenly appear, you'll replace your parents and you better have something to work with."

I'm dying and I'm only starting to live.

The woman turned away from them and spoke to another officer.

Mental manipulation isn't going to work, we don't have a way to fight them.

I know what we should try.

Erin clutched Zeke's hand and helped him from the ground. "We're out of here."

The blue film enveloped them.

Zeke cocked his head and tightened his grasp. "Doing that didn't turn out well last time. You sure?"

"We've got to try or we die, but I've a different idea. Pray with me."

"Our Father who art in Heaven, hallow be thy name and the rest of that. You've helped before, this time please release us from our captors and reunite us with parents, Shayne and Annu."

Chapter 47
Holy Portal of Hell
Jupiter Outer Atmosphere and Jupiter

Shayne paced in front of Captain Being in the room she'd arrived in. "Have you found them yet?"

I've got my man back in a physical sense. We're no where close to done and I've disappointed him big time.

Captain Being's frown eliminated hope. "My men did twice and they've disappeared again."

How many times can one lose their kids? I'm up to four or something.

Annu wrung his hands on an identical spot. His attention wavered and lasted no longer than five seconds. Annu's mental absence allowed another kind of fear—abandonment.

What if he's quiet because he doesn't want to be with me anymore? Maybe all the time by himself changed his mind? Like an epiphany and shit. Or the whole DSI fuck up, the kids, the messages, and so on.

I'm fucked, but let's face it. It was only a matter of time.

Shayne hugged herself, her blood cooled. "How'd they just vanish? Unless, unless—they're dead. No. No. No."

Annu straightened, flames trickled across his hands. "Let's not think the worst case scenario. It'll make me angry and no one likes it when I'm angry."

Captain Being paled to lilac, his obvious concern softened Shayne's anger. "I don't know. I'm sorry. They'll keep searching but you must shut the portal before it's too late. There's less than an hour and half."

Shayne's heart fluttered, despair nipped at her heels. "Not good enough. I can't keep doing this. I'm losing my mind. Screw your portal and your planet. I'm done."

The safest place for them is probably far away from me anyway. I don't deserve to ask for your help but Please Creator keep them safe.

Jupling's behind tech equipment tapped at screens.

Annu's flames calmed, he leaned against Shayne and hugged her waist. "It will be okay. I know it. I hate it but we must compromise. It won't take long and we'll search for them together."

Captain Being's clap scraped Shayne's nerves. "A sound idea. Thank you."

Shayne suppressed the urge to rip the skin from Captain Being's face. Her part in their present situations stopped her.

I pushed aside those messages, I failed to pay attention to anything or think further than the next five minutes. This is all on—

The floor rumbled, a buzz came from the middle of the room, a blue light appeared and increased in size.

Shayne slapped her thigh and jabbed at the Captain. "Now who the hell is this?"

Annu crossed his arms and faced Captain Being. "Are you expecting someone else?"

Captain Being shook his head. "No. I've got no idea what or who it is."

The blue extended upwards and sideways, two human shapes appeared inside it, after a flash the light faded.

A dazed Zeke hugged himself. "Something worked."

Erin rubbed their eyes. "But— " Erin's squeal sent tingles up Shayne's spine. "Mum. You're okay. We heard you'd disappeared."

Shayne's pulse raced, she ran over and hugged both. "Ah ditto. Thank the Gods. How did you get here? I thought the worst. By the way you're wearing GPS tracker things from hereon."

Annu encircled them all; his heart thudded above Shayne's head. "What a relief. I second the above."

Erin exited the embrace and sighed. "It's been— horrific. I don't want to go over it all again but we escaped certain peril by praying pretty hard while holding hands and bam."

Zeke faced Annu and hugged his middle. "I'm sorry I've been such an arsehole. I didn't realise how hard this all is."

Shayne's heart melted, she hugged Erin again. "You two have some sort of power together. You're here and safe, nothing else matters."

Annu blinked a few times and embraced Zeke. "I never thought I'd hear that from you son. It's all part of the learning process. As much as I want to stay with you two, you must stay here while Shayne and I endure another task. It won't take long."

I forgot for a moment.

Shayne's elation nose dived. "Argh. This is fucked up too. I promise when this is all over we're taking a family holiday somewhere arsehole free."

Captain Being strode to Annu's side. "Regardless of the delivery means, you have what you wanted. Will you please close the portal?"

Annu cleared his throat and rolled his eyes. "Yes."

Shayne nodded and released Erin. "Captain, you look after these guys while we're—"

Erin crossed her arms and raised an eyebrow. "There's no way in anywhere I'm being away from either of you."

Zeke tipped his head at Erin. "I second that. Besides we might be helpful in ways you don't know of yet."

It's worth considering and I don't want to let them away from me either.

An unexpected source returned Shayne's hope. "We appreciate everything you've done immensely, but Annu and I are doing this alone. Apparently Mum isn't yet done paying for their screw ups. You're coming for peace of mind alone. You're fighting days are over."

******

Holy shit. They're learning and training before they use their powers again.

It's definitely less stressful seeing they're safe. Except for the damage being done to Orion and crap on Earth. Each minute things escalate once again in our absence.

Erin stood beside Shayne, and Zeke beside Annu.

Shayne clasped Erin's hand, a light from the roof highlighted Shayne and Erin, the room disappeared, a mix of sensations discombobulated her.

Hold on, hold on. It will stop in a second or two. 1, 2, 3.

The surface softened, sand and wind blasted from all sides.

I can't see a fucking thing properly. Hey and on the upside this is totally unexpected family time. There's a bonus. Again, sort of. Even though Annu probably hates me.

Shayne covered her eyes with an arm and turned in a circle. "This is fucked."

Erin clutched Shayne's sleeve, and shielded her eyes with a hand. "Where's Zeke and Annu?"

Grit sullied clear vision aside from the huge black void.

Shayne wrapped her arm through Erin's. "They're close and we can't miss the huge portal thing. Thank fuck I'm not dealing with the mayhem alone anymore."

Just do it and get it over with. After all this is done, I'm going to eat so much chocolate I'll get shares in Cadbury's and smoke so much weed Snoop Dog gives me a medal. And maybe Parent of the Year.

The moisture in her mouth evaporated, Shayne held her breath. "Erin, I'm truly sorry for being a shitty mother. I'll always regret it but I'll make up for it if you let me."

Erin encircled Shayne and pulled her close. "I forgive you Mum. I didn't want to see things from your perspective before landing on Orion and caught in a war. It's taught me a lot, things I never wanted to know yet needed to. Thank you for doing what you had to. I hope when I have children I'm half the mother you are."

Shayne's parental and personal confidence rose from zero to possible hero. "Thank you so much. I love you."

A gust of air smacked Shayne in the knees and reminded her of their present location. "Oops. I'm surprise those two haven't come collected us."

Erin in tow, Shayne pushed against the wind to where Annu and Zeke landed two obscured metres away.

In the now vacant spot, Shayne hunched and pursed her lips. "Honey? Zeke? Hello?"

Why'd they walk off without us? He's so pissed at me he left without me?

Erin tied her sleeve to Shayne's. "I'm making sure we can't get separated."

Calm derived from the return of Shayne's family lowered a level. "Good idea. Surely they can't be far? Of all the times to walk off."

"Honey? Hello?"

Sand, wind, sand and the big black fucking thing in the sky with weird shit coming out of it.

Erin cupped her hands in front of her mouth. "Annu? Zeke? Come on."

A dark shape emerged from the dirt fog and ambled in Shayne and Erin's direction.

Finally. Thank the Gods.

Relief lessened the creep factor, Shayne spat dirt and waved. "Hey. There you are. Where'd you go? Never mind, let's do this."

The figure quickened, the closer it got the less it resembled her chocolate hulk and the more it appeared monsterish.

Shayne's aura erupted icicles over her and covered Erin.

At a metre away it cleared, a demonic dog-pig-horse-kangaroo thing ran for Shayne. "Oh, fuck no. What the mother fucking hell is that? Definitely not Annu. Shit." Marrow chilled, Shayne clutched Erin and jumped out of the way, it ran passed. "Annu, Annu, Annu where are you. We've got some fucking work to do now. Where is my damned man and his son?"

Seriously. Where the living fuck are you?

"There better not be more of those things." Erin pointed at the portal. "Hey, it's smaller than when we arrived not long ago."

Anticipation gripped Shayne's chest. "Fuck. Captain Being said it grew not shrank. Great, more time constraints."

An image of Annu and Shayne with their powers merged and the portal closed flashed across her thoughts. *Okay, so I find him eventually, but not showing me anything helpful for now.*

Screams came from the portal.

Erin clutched her chest and paled. "What the hell is that? I'm not going in there."

Frustration reached critical mass in Shayne, no chocolate hulk and no end to their millionth plight. "Wait outside it with Zeke. We won't be long—maybe."

Erin's shiver chilled Shayne. "I'm not sure that's a great idea either."

Shayne shook of the heebie jeebies, urgency beat sanity. "In the meantime while looking for them the other two situations are worse without us. I'm going to lose my fucking shit in a minute."

Zeke emerged from a wall of sand, his hair a mess.

He wavered a few centimetres from Shayne and Erin. "It's taken ages to find you again."

Shayne wiped her eyes and released a breath. "Ah ditto. Where's your father?"

Relief arrived and held panic at bay.

Zeke's concerned expression re-opened the gates. "He walked into the flarking portal in a daze. I tried stopping him the entire way there, it's like I wasn't there. I'm sorry, I'm not going in after him alone."

Say what now?

The reformed shreds of sanity tangled, Shayne's chest tightened. "You're kidding me? Were meant to close it from out here not go into it."

Zeke's terseness smacked irritation on the arse and sent it running. "I realise that, clearly he doesn't. Unless you're leaving him in there, are you helping me get him out or not?"

Disappointment and disbelief emblazoned medals to Shayne's chest.

We had a happy family for what forty five minutes maybe? All it takes is a stupid portal and we're separated or ready to kill each other again. I'll be the bigger person.

Shayne's gritted teeth ached her jaw. "Sorry Zeke. I didn't mean to patronise you, I'm just shocked too."

What the fuck is up with Annu? Me. It's always me.

Zeke relaxed his shoulders and moved closer. "Yeah. Me too. This global catastrophe stuff's pretty stressful."

Erin nodded, she tugged her from her mouth. "I agree."

Shayne held out her hand. "You're spectators now remember. No more worrying or danger. Zeke, hook your arm in mine and we'll trudge towards it."

Zeke stood in front of Shayne. "The wind's stronger closer. Hold onto me and I'll walk in front to block off some of it. It'll make it easier."

Tears stung Shayne's eyes, dirt stuck to her cheeks. "I underestimated you kids. Thank you."

At her side Shayne linked with Erin and clutched Zeke's jacket.

A black mass stumbled past them, Erin flinched and buried into Zeke's back.

Zeke stuck his arms behind him to protect Shayne and Erin. "You're all right."

My nerves are shattered, my mind's fried. Emotional rollercoasters are no fun.

Shayne covered the other two in a protective bubble. "I'll make sure of it."

Each glance the portal closed another couple of metres.

At its edge, Zeke stopped before he released Erin and Shayne. "Here we go."

Apprehension formed a lump in Shayne's throat. "You sure you want to come? I understand if you want to stay outside."

I'm wavering between being alone and their safety. I'm losing votes for that parenting award.

Zeke and Erin nodded in unison. "Yes but no."

Shayne wriggled her fingers in liquid space. "No matter what stay with me."

All the way inside and an acrid aroma stung Shayne's nostrils, old style flame torches light stone hallways. Death and pain emanated, the creeps slipped up Shayne's spine and tickled her ribs.

Erin and Zeke emerged from a stone wall to Shayne's left.

Left, right, before and front, all directions lead into other hallways. Behind, a stone wall now replaced the portal.

Shayne hugged herself. "This is just fucking lovely. Someone needs to redecorate or get a cleaner in."

Erin stuck to Shayne's heels. "It's won't be by us. Let's not spend too much time here."

Zeke took lead along a hallway, his voice echoed. "Da? Annu?"

Shayne's butthole crawled up and settled in her throat; a trickle of pee ran down her leg.

There better be a fucking toilet in here soon. I am not squatting in a corner.

They reached a junction; Shayne clenched her inner thighs and flipped her finger in each direction. "Eeny meenie, mini mo. Catch a big I.D.I.O.T. by the toe."

Please make this easy. For once.

Shayne re-connected her aura and gathered her wits from the ground. "Alright. Left it is."

Part the way down a furry thing scooted from one side to the other, Shayne's brain froze; another trickle joined a small puddle in her underwear.

A growl came from further down the hallway. A pair of red eyes broke the dark.

The moisture in Shayne's mouth evaporated. "Oh fucking crap. Shit. Fuck."

Erin leapt onto Zeke's back and wrapped her arms around his neck. "No. Just no."

The creature's growl deepened, claws scraped across stone, hot stinky breath blasted their way.

Shayne's aura jiggled, she clenched her inner thighs. "Ah. Nice demon dog. Stay there."

Erin climbed Zeke's shoulders. "Keep it away from me."

Zeke struggled to steady himself and Erin. "Calm down or we're in its way."

The scrapes came closer, the creatures drooling muzzle poked into the torch light.

All Shayne's nightmares paled in comparison.

It crept along, another head on either side of the beast turned Shayne's way. She blasted it—heat steamed and defrosted the ice.

Zeke's jaw and shoulders slumped. "That's fucked."

The creature shook off the remnants and quickened its pace.

Shayne backed up and hit stone.

Zeke wrangled with Erin sliding down and turned in circles. "Will you stay still?"

The creature growled at Zeke, and bared its teeth.

Zeke paused mid-turn and came centimetres from its nose. "See. Oh shit."

Oh no, no, no, no, no. No. Think brain. Do something.

Shayne balled her wits and juggled. "Let's do the mash. Let's do the monster mash. Let's do the mash."

Not that something. Another thing. That never—

The creature stopped moving and shuffled on the spot.

Hang on a minute. Hah. It's coming in handy. Fuck all you naysayers.

The creature's howl refocused Shayne.

This probably isn't the time though.

"Let's do the mash, it's a three day bash. Let's do the mash."

Three snouts wailed and drilled into Shayne's brain, it shook its body.

Mmm. It's working don't overanalyse.

Shayne did a mental run through her playlist. "I stay up too fate, got nothing in my brain. That's what people say, mmm. That's what people say. Mmm. But I keep screwing, this up, then I have to, fix it all. That's what people say. Mmm."

The creature's wails increased in pitch, it trembled swapping expressions between confused and scared.

Let it out, don't hold back.

"Cause payers gonna pay, pay, pay, pay pay. Haters gonna hate, hate, hate, hate. I'm just gonna bake, bake, bake, bake, bake. Just bake it off. Bake it off. Bake it. Bake it off, baby."

The creature turned a three-sixty and bolted into the darkness.

Shayne strode and released pent up talent. "But I keep losing, can't stop, won't stop grooving. It's like this music in my mind and it's gonna be all right."

Erin climbed down Zeke's back and rubbed her arms. "It's gone now, Mum. You can stop. Plus side, we've finally got a use for your, ah, singing."

Shayne pressed pause and left good grace behind. "Yes. Exactly. So there."

Zeke patted his sides. "Do I want to know why my back's warm?"

Erin turned towards the wall. "Ah, ah, it's water leaking from the roof. I got a little on me too."

Shayne stepped forward and into Erin. "It's safe to have a little space between us all."

Erin's tone lacked her usual indignation, she shuffled behind Shayne. "Yes. You're right. I'm an adult. After all."

But you're still hiding behind Mummy. It's the first time. There's no way I'll refuse it.

Zeke stayed beside Erin, a metre behind Shayne. "Just in case."

Part way down the tunnel they hit a dead end.

Shayne veered left into an identical tunnel, and swallowed ready for the next song.

Don't cack out now, throat.

She gestured over her shoulder. "Hurry up. I said not so close not lag behind."

A few steps ahead and lack of response turned Shayne around.

Instead of Erin and Zeke, stood a stone wall.

The earlier juggled wit balls landed on Shayne's head one at a time. "No fucking way. Someone is so, so fucking with us."

Nothing but stone, stone, dirt, goop, stone, or stone. No kids. Again, again, again.

People are gonna stop trusting me with children including my own soon. Or now.

Chapter 48
Self Imposed Damnation
East side of Jupiter

An unseen force controlled Annu's movements into the portal and along a series of hallways.

Calm fell over Annu yet confusion landed on his shoulders. "Why am I here? Who are you?"

There's somewhere else I'm meant to be. Where?

The man's voice captivated Annu and blocked out other stimuli. "I'll get to that in a moment. First, please forgive me for not being in your life earlier. It wasn't my choice. In fact until you asked for my help I didn't know you existed. I'm stunned and ecstatic to hear from you. You've been kept secret."

Annu moved unconsciously, slow and steady forwards. "Forgive you for what? I didn't ask for your help whoever you are. I asked for—"

Holy shit. Can it be?

"Yes, it is I, your father who calls to you."

Truth formed glue between the puzzle pieces. "Really? Why not come to me? You haven't told me your name."

"The only name that's relevant is your father. I can't leave the place I am because of a disagreement long ago I'm somewhat restricted in those terms. Enki can be hateful as you've experienced. It's something you may assist me with.

Annu's heart fluttered, his mind fumbled. "Did you fall with Shamesh or take allegiance with Enlil and punished? Why the big secret?"

I need, no, I must know. I spend all my time thinking about other people. It's time for me now. All else waits until I'm ready. We'll fix the rest later.

Niggle, niggle, stroke, stroke. "Please, after so long I'd rather speak to you face to face. There's not much further."

Annu entered a room walled by mirrors, all with different images on their sides. "What is this place?"

"It's a gateway to other dimensions, the one over there is to space and time, next to it the heavens, hells, many places. I'm at the end."

A chill tickled Annu's kidneys and slowed his pace. "This isn't, I shouldn't be here."

The unseen force yanked Annu by invisible rope to the end of the room.

In the middle of the wall rested a gold framed mirror, on the other side stood a man older, otherwise identical to Annu surrounded by a red skyline.

Tears ran down the man's cheeks, he clenched his hands. "Annu. You feel the power within you, does it all make sense? Together we're unstoppable."

The truth slapped Annu across the face and wrapped around his throat. "Almost. You're Enlil aren't you?"

Flark it. It had to be didn't it?

My mother and Enlil. No wonder she didn't want to tell me. Flark. I had to know at all costs and I got what I asked for. So much for not making emotional decisions.

His father's eyes and tone darkened. "Yes, but do not believe what they've told you. The victors write history and it's usually a false, inflated account. Let me and I will give your old life back. Jaid, Junior, the simple days. Before all this responsibility and stress. Or if you still wish I'll tell you how to undo all the damage. My way. Not the other way."

Annu's heart relived the losses over and over.

I'd hold them and never let go.

"What other way?"

Enlil's eyes lightened, the sky behind him flicked between blue and red. "My brother with the great press agent, Enki. You've experienced it; there's never any thanks for the sacrifice and near death several times. No glory or an easier life. It's always pain and suffering for what? Faith and hope are ways of him making his creations feel cared about."

"How would you give them back?"

"Give yourself up to me, join me and we'll take over."

Shayne and Zeke flashed into his mind, Annu tore the invisible rope in half. "Seven or so months ago had you come to me with this offer I'd take you up on it. Not anymore."

Enlil erupted into flames, his anger lit Annu's. "You're making a mistake. Don't go. If you join me we'll rule together—side by side."

Annu erupted, the power surged within him. "Not this time. I'll burn—"

The similarities between Annu and his father—the embodiment of evil—destroyed Annu's ire.

What does this mean for me? Am I doomed to repeat history? Only if I allow it to.

Annu diminish the flames and relaxed his stance. "No thanks. Pain and suffering seems to suit me. Besides, you can't get out of there without me. I've heard all about that too. Don't contact me or my family ever again."

Enlil's confidence faltered. "You wanted to know who I was. This is all your doing."

"Yeah and I regret it. Looks like you're never too old to make mistakes but also goes for fixing them.

"I have your family trapped. Without me they'll stay stuck."

They came after me despite the danger. They risked their lives and others for mine.

Annu pulled the mirror off the wall and held it over his knee. "I've heard that before. Now let them go or you're in pieces."

"You'll regret this, my boy. This isn't the only portal."

Annu's growl came from his toes. "Let—them—go."

The sound of stone scraping across stone came from outside the room.

One hand each side, Annu cracked the mirror over his knee and tossed each piece in the opposite direction.

Enlil's face filled both sections. "I'm your father Annu. There's much more to learn. You're wrong about me."

Annu turned and walked away. "I don't care anymore. You no longer exist to me."

His footsteps again his own, he jogged past the other mirrors and out the doorway.

Every direction appeared the same, no markings or identification anywhere.

"I'm such an idiot. This never happened."

An off tone, high pitched screech filled Annu with joy.

Shayne's singing usually sent shivers up his spine for all the wrong reasons. This time a huge pile of relief accompanied it. "I need a hero. I'm holding on for a hero til the end of the night. And he's got to be good and he's got to admit he's wrong and he's got to want to get me chocolate. I need a—"

Shayne's squealed and leapt for Annu. "Thank fuck. I was stuck in rock. Fucked up. Now you're safe, why the fuck did you go in here?"

Warning, warning, warning. Threat to revealing one's actual mistake close.

Annu peaked around Shayne's shoulders. "It's good to see you too. Ah, where are the kids?"

Shayne dug in her heels and glared. "Um, well, about that."

Oh sweet God. I missed this. Not.

Annu plastered a smile on his face and delved into the hall. "You're flarking kidding me right?"

Shayne plodded and exuded annoyance. "Yes, but no, but yes, but sort of. This time it really, really, wasn't my fault. It was the stone wall I mentioned."

Shame burned the back of Annu throat. "Fair enough."

Think of something. There's no point in her knowing the truth. No good will come of it. I better do the washing, cooking and dishes for the next six months.

"Why were you signing so loud?"

They turned into an identical tunnel, the portal no where in sight.

Shayne kissed his hand. "It scared a scary monster dog away."

Guilt added piled onto Annu's shame.

I'll make up for the lies later.

"Of course it did."

Shayne strode in front, her back straight. "I had a vision we blend our powers together to close this fucker."

Pain, my life is filled with pain. All brought on by myself.

Chapter 49
The Karma Bus is Coming, and Everybody's Running
Jupiter Galaxy and Yebu City, Yebu, Orion

The walls around Zeke and Erin lifted; Erin hunched over and heaved air. "I thought we were stuck like that. Even the hand thing didn't work right."
Zeke stroked her back and helped her upright. "Probably because we both freaked out."

This has been the craziest, mental, insane experience I'd never imagine. Ryan won't believe me, and Nathanial. Oh. I haven't thought about him for a while. It's been so nuts. What if I don't get home?

No. Don't think like that. Look how far I've come.

Erin finger combed her hair and ambled along. "I'm trying to break my panic habit among other things."

Zeke's voice boomed down the tunnel. "Hey, Shayne. Where are you?"

"After this is all over will you come and visit us on Earth sometime? Ryan will be thrilled to have another male around. Well besides his boyfriend, I mean. Oh and my fiancé."

Zeke scratched chin fuzz. "There's so much to learn about all of you. Ryan has a boyfriend and you're getting married?"

"Aha. They're pretty happy. You'll like Joey. He's a lovely—"

An unmistakable voice carried down the tunnel turned Erin into an instant child. "That's Mum. Mum. We're here."

Erin ran in her mind before the message reached her legs, she tumbled over her feet.

Zeke stopped her fall with one hand. "Someone's keen."

Erin brushed herself off and scoffed. "Whatever."

Mum turned the corner and flounced. "Mother fucking cock suckers. Every time we fuck things up people suffer. I've, we've, got a lot of growing to do. No offence darling but not using our powers for person stuff is not working—kids."

Erin met Mum halfway and encircled her. "All right. I'm not ready to be completely adult and without you yet."

Mum mumbled into Erin's neck. That's okay with me sweetheart."

Over Mum's shoulder, Zeke shoved Annu's shoulder. "What the flark dude? You flat out ignored me. Why?"

Mum released Erin and faced Annu. "We'd all like to know that."

Annu reddened and shuffled, an invisible wall erected around him. "It, ah, I, ah, someone said they knew who my father was and tricked me into going inside. I don't want to talk about it."

Zeke backstepped and shrugged. "I'm sorry. That sucks."

Shayne touched Annu's arm. "Oh darling. Those arseholes. Let me go back and sort them out."

Annu's clipped words created tension. "No. Just leave it."

Awkward. Poor guy. I'll change the subject and focus.

Erin pointed in each direction of the tunnel. "There's no portal anymore. It's disappeared, there's no obvious way out."

Mum faced Annu and flipped a hand. "We'll make our own. Do in reverse what we'll do outside?"

Annu clutched her hand and nodded. "Yeah."

A sense of safety blanketed Erin; she shuffled behind Annu and next to Zeke.

A combination of hand movements from Mum and blasts of energy from Annu and a portal appeared large enough for them to enter.

Mum held Erin's shoulder and Annu's waist, Annu crossed arms with Zeke and they stepped inside.

Erin landed lopsided on the sand meters from the original portal only a metre wide. "I'm really beginning to hate this freaky stuff. Are we done yet?"

Zeke plonked onto the ground beside her. "I need a minute."

Annu brushed himself off. "Sorry guys. Shayne and I aren't off the hook yet."

Mum cracked her neck, re-held Annu's hand and faced the portal.

Side by side they interlocked arms, Shayne engulfed in her blue aura and Annu reignited in flames.

Will I be that powerful one day? Do I want to be?

The black void folded in from the edges until nothing remained.

Annu walked over to Erin. "Listen, how about we do Earth first and drop you off at home? You're safe there. Zeke too if you want."

Home, bed, toilet, shower, quiet. Everything I've craved since I arrived. After all I've experienced how do I ever live a normal life again? How can I sleep when I know people are still dying?

Zeke turned and nudged Erin's shoulder. "What do you think?"

Erin pushed off the ground. "No. Whether I help or not, I'm not resting while this is going on."

Mum wrapped her arms around Erin's waist and snuggled. "What a courageous decision. We handle the big stuff. Okay?"

The virgin word's almost stuck on Erin's tongue. "Yes, Mum."

Annu's smile consumed his face. "I'll contact the Captain, tell him we're done and there's no need for them to pick us up. We'll wormhole it."

Annu tapped the communicator on his wrist and frowned. "There's no connection. Maybe being inside the portal screwed with it?"

Black smoke erupted in the distance, flying craft occupied the sky.

Shayne started into space. "Like I'd know why it didn't work. Anyway, you tried. He'll figure it out when he comes back and there's no more portal or us."

The creeps slid up Erin's legs, between her ears roared. "Something doesn't feel right anymore. Those craft over there—"

No it can't be? Can it? Apparently I can despite not believing what I'm seeing.

Bile burned the back of her throat. "Oh, hell. They look like Martian ships."

Annu's screwed up face offered little foresight into his thoughts. "Surely not."

He took off, flew towards to the ship, circled and came back, his eyes glazed. "You're right Erin. It is them. I don't understand. It's seems they've been here some time. There are Martian bases."

The atmosphere dropped from elation to devastation.

Erin stammered; her tongue thick. "But, but, how. We were gone maybe an hour or so."

Shayne slapped her cheeks. "We were much longer than we realised. Captain Being mentioned time is effected around the portal."

Shock and grief pummelled Erin, her mind cracked. "That means Nathanial, Ryan, Rosie, Sam, my friends and everyone else I love are gone. No. It can't be. It's too cruel. We did the right thing."

Please God, don't let it be true. Please. I've been good, I, I—

Erin suppressed sobs and clutched her chest. "How could you let this happen?"

Mum straightened and pursed her lips. "Before we all flip out and jump to conclusions let's be sure. We'll go from there."

Annu's somber demeanour cemented Erin's fear. "This never ends."

He's right. Are we in hell?

A wormhole formed before Mum, she offered her hand to Erin. "Let's see what the fuck is going on. There's a chance it's not that bad."

Please, please, God I beg you. Let it be okay. I won't lose it until I'm sure.

Annu raised an eyebrow at Mum. "Don't say that again. Every time you do, it's twenty times worse."

Mum's vocabulary reverted to default. "Fucking whatever. Like this is all my fault."

Great. What a family. I'm tired of all the cursing. Geez. It's adding to my stress.

Erin's teacher hackles raised. She took Mum's hand and stood beside her. "While we're working on things, can we talk about your swearing? I'm sure it's gotten worse."

Zeke scoffed behind Mum.

Mum's death stare at Zeke accompanied them into the wormhole.

Is it too late to change my mind about going home?

Chapter 50
The Karma Bus Crashed
Earth, Orion, Jupiter and repeat

I'm far from perfect, I'm a hypocrite and a liar, yet it's worth it. A slip, not a fall. I don't want them to lose confidence in me or doubt our relationship by knowing the truth of what I did and why.

Let alone I even considered for a second going back to my old life.

In Shayne's former kitchen, Annu wore self denial as cologne. "I can't fly far without being seen but it looks like they've been here for the same time. No idea on what damage has been caused elsewhere."

Shayne flipped between sad and angry—sangry. "And my fucking house is trashed. What the fuck?"

The opposite wall captivated Annu's attention. "Ah, yeah. The bastards. It needed renovations anyway."

Zeke paced the area where the pantry once stood and mumbled to himself.

Erin toppled on a three legged chair at the kitchen table. Earth's version of a hand held communicator trembled in her grasp. "Emergency services still work. News shows two weeks almost to the day have passed here since we walked into the void. The planet's been invaded, no place spared. Everyone's dead, captured or hiding. I've lost the almost everyone I loved and cared about," she bounced off the chair; it clunked to the floor and splintered with Annu's faith in himself, "no wedding. No love, no life."

Erin's cries amplified in the open space, Annu's soul ruptured. "How did you let this happen?"

Have I stuffed up that much? How bad could this be? I've done this to them. My loved ones. All for answers I no longer want. Flark, it's all my fault. I don't deserve them.

Shayne slumped next to Erin and rocked. "I feel sick. I've been so stupid and irresponsible. They were using me to win the war and take the Queen. Without me, they lost. Worst of all I created these problems and screwed them up a million times. Someone take away my abilities given to someone worthy. You kids for example."

Annu's chest tightened, guilt leaden his mind. "It will be okay. I'll correct this—somehow."

How does one exactly fix not a partial planet but universal genocide? It's me who's unworthy of the demigod title.

Annu denied emotions further access and manned up. "Shay, send me to Enki. Stay with the kids. The state of it, tells me all I there is to know. I'll send you a telepathic message when I'm done. It's possible—"

It's possible I haven't completely ruined everything.

Shayne stopped rocking, she blubbered. "What's the point?"

I'm so sorry. I won't tell you, but I'll show you. I'll return to the hero you think I am. I just don't know how yet.

Annu hunched down and hugged her. "I must be sure. Someone or something may help us."

Zeke strode to Annu and tugged his sleeve. "I'm coming. Even if it's shit there too, we'll get the Lexicon. There's answers in there. That's what it's for."

Annu struggled between common sense and parental duty. "I'd like bring you, but I need you to take care of these two while I'm gone. Great idea about the lexicon son, ah, how do you know that?"

Shayne flopped her arms. "Remember, you were there. He's been reading it with Jacob sometimes and apparently understands it no brain ache involved. I asked Jacob to keep him out of all this. Nice he listened."

Annu's nerves twanged like guitar strings. "I see your point, we'll address it later. Who knows it might work out in our favour. Any idea where it is?"

Shayne deflated and lay on the floor. "With Jacob, if he's alive. Dead, who knows. Yeah right. What good will that stupid fucking book do? Everything's gone to shit since we got it. Well, after our births really."

Zeke dipped his chin and spoke into his fist. "It's in my room."

Shayne cocked her head. "I didn't see it in there earlier. Where'd you hide it?"

Zeke's mouth dropped open. "What were you doing in my room?"

Annu's throat constricted; his collar bit into his skin. "This isn't productive. Zeke, where?"

"Under my pillow. There's a magazine there too but it's not mine."

Annu's shoulders pinched, his neck muscles tinged. "Thank you, Son. Blossom, please open a wormhole. It's something."

Shayne's blank face and limp wrist swish impaled Annu's heart. "There you go for what it's worth. I'll send one to you in half an hour, if you're still alive then."

Don't give up. Don't show them you're worried. They get their strength from you.

Annu faced the wormhole and willed courage. "I'll see you three soon."

At the ride's end, Annu hit dirt and tumbled amongst dead bushes in the house's rearyard facing the forest. "Can't blame her for being a little off."

Crouched down and covered in dirt, Annu turned, his heart fluttered. "I won't be finding a book in there anymore."

Either or both enemy turned their once magnificent home into a pile of ash, the gardens, outbuildings and all foliage resembled a desert.

No point grasping at hope, no renovations, total devastation. Nothing but dust.

Annu's guts roiled, a Martian craft flew in his direction; he ducked down and covered his head.

My, my, my. It's safe to say, here's flarked too. No point risking my butt checking elsewhere.

'Shay, please pick me up.'

The middle of Annu's brain tickled. *'Already? Fuck, fuck—'*

A wormhole opened, Annu's heart slugged against his ribs, he jumped in.

On the kitchen floor, Annu steamed himself. "I never get used to it."

Shayne rose and crossed her arms. "You weren't gone long. How'd know there's no book or help? Maybe you should check further."

Erin hugged herself in the corner, a blanket wrapped around her shoulder.

Fix it, fix it, fix it.

Annu sucked on his bottom lip and desperation. "Believe me, it didn't require looking far."

Shayne's cheeks hallowed, her demeanour slouched. "So are options are what?"

Any great ideas floating around up there feel free to hit me.

Zeke slapped his leg and jumped. "Hey. Even without the book I might have an idea. I don't remember exactly what the whole section said but you can time travel. It requires a lot of power dependent on how far you go back. By my calculations, a month in the past will suffice, right before they all acted on their plans. None of it's happened yet, but it's in progress. Only the participants recall the events prior to the time travel. The consequences are anyone's guess."

My son's flarking brilliant.

Annu grabbed Zeke by the shoulders and shook him. "Yes. Jacob mentioned it too. Let's do it."

Shayne spun around, her mouth agape. "I love you, kid. Annu, it's all over soon."

Erin livened. She shrugged off the blanket and rested on her knees. "Really? This can happen?"

Zeke's slipped under Annu's grasp. "Yeah, but there is one little problem."

Erin's sigh echoed Annu's. "What is it?"

Shayne's eye roll almost tipped her head back. "Fuck it. Of course there is."

Annu steeled himself and held his breath. "Spit it out, son. The worst is over."

Zeke clapped and folded his hands. "We have to go back into the portal you closed because I'm pretty sure that's where the main gateway to time and space is."

Yes it is. Not that I can say. Shit. How to keep Enlil from seeing my family.

Not travelling with one hip flask anymore. Three at least is the new standard. Enki, sometime soon, we're going to discuss this.

Chapter 51
Shayne: Let's Do The Time Warp Again
Rendelshem, South Australia, Australia, Earth

Moments ago grief tore Shayne's soul and engulfed her; collective and respective worlds forever altered, Erin's despair had tripled Shayne's. Now, inside the re-opened portal on Jupiter, Shayne's heart healed with a hope derived from more than a whim.

It's always the pain in the arse, difficult shit which works. I'm slow, but I'm getting it.

At the first junction in the tunnel, relief and anticipation danced along Shayne spine. "Which way? I paid no attention to anything last time."

A note book I carry around and make important reminders etc into is a great idea. Go brain.

Annu's Adam's Apple jiggled, sweat beaded on his forehead, he pointed right. "This way. I, ah, I believe I passed the room on way to you. Not sure about which mirror we use, something will give us a clue."

Is he having hot flashes too or just wigging out? I'm having trouble reading him since we reunited. I've so many relationship stuff to mend.

They entered another tunnel, no distinguishable features between one or another.

Zeke's walked with the unease of a new born giraffe, all arms and legs. "I didn't get that far into it. I'd only started the chapter a few days before."

Erin tugged Shayne's side, exhaustion painted Erin's eyes. "You get ready to sing if we so much as hear a hiss or howl."

Annu did a double take. "Did I hear you right?"

Shayne's fingers slicked over oily hair, her own body odour stung her eyes. "Ah, yes I am. Remember, it has monster deterring power."

The further down the tunnel, Annu's demeanour altered, his shoulders raised, and back straightened.

Something's bugging my man. We need time together so badly. Not fighting and killing, but loving and hugging. The good stuff.

Shayne followed Annu around a corner, metres ahead an open room occupied the tunnel's end.

Annu exhaled, his chest shrank. He slowed to Shayne's speed and held her hand. "There it is."

Shayne's brain undertook on the job training. "If it's at the end of a hallway how did you pass it on way to me?"

Annu stopped, faced her and turned away. "Ah, I, meant I'd come here when looking for you."

Duh. Like it matters. Ssh. You were doing so good.

Three quarters down the tunnel light flickered around the room reflected off mirrors of different styles along both walls.

Shayne rolled her neck and shoulders. "Ahhh, which disaster are we stopping first?"

I declare myself as a universal disaster. Fit for no man or beast. What the fuck does that even mean? Shit I'm tired.

Annu paused at the room's precipice, he stared at the ground. "Jupiter's last because of the portal, Mars is the biggest threat, followed by Orion, and Earth. When Erin finally goes safely home."

Erin shivered and hugged herself. "It'll feel like a nightmare. Strange and surreal."

Shayne passed Annu and wandered past the first few mirrors. "Sounds good to me. However, the details of how we'll achieve this are sketchy."

Zeke trailed beside her and wriggled a piece of paper. "I wrote the date down which coincides on the other planets, concentrate on it. Like I mentioned, it uses lots of power, it may permanently affect you."

At the end of this waits a huge block of chocolate and a pound of weed. Hell, weed covered chocolate while in a bubble bath. Mmm. I'll get so high Space Watch won't see me.

Part way down, Annu came up behind Shayne and hugged. "It doesn't matter. Are you two staying in here until we get out?"

Erin shook her head and grabbed Shayne's elbow. "No flipping way. I'm coming."

Zeke retrieved the piece of paper from Shayne's hand. "I'm not being by myself."

The concept of time itself boggled Shayne, let alone an altered one. "The family that time travels together stays together. Zeke, and Erin stand in the middle of us, you have a right to should remember what happened."

This is by far the strangest, most fucked up thing I've experienced yet. What the McFuck? We're a family of Donnie Darko's now?

Shayne turned a circle. "We're here. Which one?"

Annu's blank expression offered no assistance, he glanced each direction.

Shayne clicked her fingers in his face. "Hello. Now it's your turn to be the ditzy one."

Zeke tapped Annu on the shoulder and strode ahead. "I'll take a look then shall I?"

One foot ahead and Annu clutched Zeke's arm. "No need. I will. Just in case."

Mmm, okay.

Erin tapped her foot and huffed. "For the love of God. I'm about past caring."

Annu did a swift search of each mirror and reached a blank space on the wall at the end.

With his back turned, he moved something on the floor using his foot and returned. "It's up here. I suggest you sing for safety's sake."

Did we enter a parallel universe by accident?

Shayne stood akimbo and jabbed his chest. "All right. Now I know you've lost your freaking mind. I'm not taking anemone step unless you spit out what's—"

Mumble's emitted from the stuff Annu moved.

"What the?"

Panic flashed over Annu, he blocked their view.

Words spilled from his mouth like M & M's from a packet opened in the middle. "Fine. You're right. Earth's as evil as other planets, we're stronger together and I love everything about you. We'll form a stronger family unit, with all of us. From hereon, we're doing this godly stuff by the book, literally and sticking together."

Oh my God. I'm dead. I'm fucking dead and no one told me. I never thought I'd hear those glorious words.

"No wonder you seemed weird. That must have hurt like—"

Mumble, mumble, mumble.

Shayne peaked around Annu's waist. "Seriously, what is that?"

Annu steered Shayne to the right side of the room and stopped at a wooden framed mirror. "I didn't want to tell you in case you freaked out but it's some weird monster thing. Its stuck in the glass but if you want, sing your lovely voice and scare it away."

Shayne pinched herself.

Ouch. Maybe not.

And Erin, she winced. "Ouch. Mum?"

Followed by Zeke, he rubbed his arm. "Ouch. Flark."

Okay. Either I'm alive or you two are dead too. Here goes.

Shayne entered the portal first at full noise. "If you're lost you can book and you will find me. Time after time. If you fall I will batch you, I'll be waiting. Time after time."

Wait, what happens to our other selves after we go back to before? Oh ouch. Shut up brain.

On the other side, Shayne arrived onto and into a black void, nothing else existed. "Creepy. That's good for other people not me."

Annu, Zeke and Erin landed one after the other not far from Shayne.

Erin spun around and grasped Annu's arm. "What the cookies?"

Zeke rubbed his face. "The place between time and space."

Annu cocked his head at Zeke and patted Erin's hand. "We really should listen to you more."

Zeke's smile softened the harsh environment. "Yeah, you should."

Which reminds me. A little respect.

Shayne poked Zeke in the ribs. "While I think of it Zeke, surviving this whole ordeal in part because of me, must be catastrophic enough for you to consider being friends?"

Zeke's eyes twinkled. "It's a start but we'll see how it goes."

He shifted in front of Shayne, and positioned Erin behind him. "Grab Da's hands around us and concentrate on the date."

Shayne's arms extended, Annu grabbed her wrists. "Hi ho, hi ho, it's off to the past we go. Da da da da. blah, blah, blah."

Zeke cleared his throat and tapped his foot. "Any time now."

Eyes closed, Shayne focused on the date and her power. Energy surged from Annu to Shayne and circled back. Noise exploded around the void, with the date cast, Shayne peaked.

The day's events played out around them in slow motion, the connection between Annu and Shayne faltered, the images paused.

Shayne stamped her foot, she refocused on the date. "Shit. Come on."

A strand of Shayne's hair fell to the ground, she trembled.

Annu clutched his chest and let go of Shayne's hand. "Ah."

Shayne grabbed at him and missed. "Are you all right?"

Zeke spun on his heel. "Da?"

Erin bumped into Annu. "Sorry, you okay?"

The energy dwindled, Annu straightened and waved at them. "I'm fine. We're not quitting."

Annu found her hands and reconnected.

Shayne held tight and set aside frustration for later. "Of course you are. Whatever."

The power returned, one day passed by, the previous began and stopped.

Exhaustion weighted Shayne, irritation guided her. "For fuck's sake."

Zeke's hand replaced one of Annu's on hers and stood between them. "Should have done this first."

Parental responsibility slapped Shayne. "But, I don't want you guys involved in this. We're keeping you safe."

Annu frowned—a deep line marked his left cheek. "I, we, can't do this without them, Shay."

Zeke sneered and rolled his eyes. "Damned straight and it's way too late for staying out of it."

Erin held Shayne and Annu's other forming a circle. "Exactly. Too bad, Mum. We are in deep and happy about it. It's clear you need what we've got sometimes."

Shayne's heart swelled, pride slipped beside acceptance. "You're right. I'll shut up and go with it."

The power between them amplified a hundred fold, the events sped past, a collage of pain, suffering and despair.

I never, ever want to see or experience anything like this again.

Chapter 52
Highway to Redemption
Portal, Jupiter Country Side
Jupiter, and Mars

On the outskirts of Jupiter's main township, relief compensated for Annu's inner torment.

Too flarking close. I.D.I.O.T. Doesn't matter anymore. The damned things shut for good, we're sorted with the Jupling's and none of the stuff happened with he who shall not be named or anywhere else. Definitely worth it.

Shayne's diverted attention paid off hissy-fit wise; she'd not yet noticed her white hair. "The easy bit's done. Now for the tricky, unsticking of the undesirable."

For sanities sake, he'd begged Erin and Zeke not to mention the drastic change.

Annu probed his first wrinkles. "One way of putting it my love."

Shayne pointed and gasped. "You've got lines on your face."

It's nothing compared to the alternative.

"Had to happen sometime."

The kids appeared negative-consequence free, instead of wearing on them, it acted as a mini ascension.

The experience reinvigorated Erin, her steps bounced, her smile luminous. "I am strong, I am invincible, I am woman."

Once they'd closed the portal Zeke grew two inches in height and towered over Annu. "I like this new perspective. Let's have at it, Mars."

As for me, full God or not, holy and unholy shit, my humanity and arrogance need work. Keeping secrets however is a new one for—

A buzz trickled from Annu's head to his feet, he vibrated, old and new memories flooded his mind.

Annu hunched over and gripped his thighs. "Gods, what's going on?"

The wave ebbed, clarity returned, he rose and turned.

Shayne wobbled and held Erin's arm.

Annu rushed to Shayne's side and helped her up. "What happened?"

Zeke shook his arms and legs. "I'm guessing our old selves merged with our new selves."

Shayne paled and retched on the ground. "Glad it's over. It is isn't it?"

Zeke's nod provided some comfort. "Yep. We're all in one person again."

Annu's thoughts collided and smashed. "From here on my son, this stuff's your department."

Shayne's arm swirled, a light formed. "Fuck yes."

In a practised routine one by one they followed Annu and entered the wormhole.

Annu landed in an underground bustling military base full of purple pumpkin headed Martians.

Panic gripped him, the resemblance to DSI too close.

Not long enough ago, and we're back there soon.

Shayne stroked Annu's shoulder. "Hey. Are you okay?"

Zeke cleared his throat and tapped his foot. "You're not freaking out already are you?"

Erin exuded inner calm, her smile negated Annu's moment. "Of course he isn't. You're fine aren't you?"

Enough, it's not about me. Get a grip.

He shook himself and encircled Shayne's middle. "Yes. Very much so."

Now who's the liar, but I'm working on it.

Pilots climbed into their ships, workers loaded ammunition into craft. Several of the men turned in their direction. They stopped mid action and grabbed weapons.

Shayne instilled her aura. "This is only for our protection remember. We're not engaging in any warfare."

Annu ignited and raised a metre off the ground. "Gotcha."

Peace, love and glory, sans glory. It's a work in progress.

A group of armed men lead by a bald Martian formed in lines.

The bald man inched forward. "Halt. Who are you and what are you doing here?"

Shayne hovered, her assertiveness sent shivers up Annu's spine. "We're demigods from Orion, the planet you're about to invade and we're here to ensure it doesn't happen."

Annu spoke over his shoulder. "Erin, Zeke follow close behind me unless we need you."

Zeke slowed his stride and kept pace with Erin.

Annu joined Shayne, merged their auras and protected the kids. "We won't hurt you; we want peace that's all. You can restrain us, not our children, keep your weapons aimed if it makes you feel better and take us to your Queen."

Shayne whispered to Annu's ribs. "It makes no difference anymore."

Annu stroked her hair, his fingers stuck in a tangle. "As long as they think it does, it works."

I flarking adore you even when your hair is filthy and your personal hygiene's sketchy.

A draft wafted Annu's own odour his way.

Point taken.

A purple being against a ramp gained Shayne's attention. "Ja—

Annu glanced between the being and Shayne. "Who's he?"

Shayne allowed a Martian to cuff her hands. "A traitorous sort of friend for a while, they're not all killers either but never mind. It's in the past I guess."

Across a long landing strip filled with space craft, they entered a military building.

Recent memories filled Annu's mind, fear threatened his bravado.

Stay cool and collected.

On one side of the entry they approached an elevator, the Martians entered first.

This time, Shayne hesitated, she stayed the doors.

How much more damaged are we than before?

Annu filed his issues under TFTD: too flarked to deal. "Are you all right?"

Shayne swallowed, clutched Erin and jumped over the lip. "Oh yeah. Fucking tip top. You?"

Annu ushered Zeke inside, and joined them.

He rested his arm around Shayne's shoulder. "Not at all."

She stuck like glue to Erin's side and trembled. "I hear you."

We're going to need serious once it's over. And a long, long drinking binge.

The lift stopped on the highest level and opened into a pink, fluffy, over decorated section. In constant to the rest of the utilitarian facility, pillows and cushions covered every seat or couch; pink shaggy carpet softened the floor.

Annu's idea of decorating hell.

The aroma of cinnamon and strawberry irritated Annu's nose. "Argh."

Bald Martian knelt and dipped his head to the end of a chaise lounge buried by purple cushions. "I apologise for the intrusion you're Highness. I had no choice, two demigods and their children from Orion arrived in a ball of light seeking your audience. They have thus complied with our requests."

The middle cushion shifted, two skinny legs, one bandaged, popped out from under it. Two beady blue eyes appeared near the top. "What? The two demigods are where?"

The cushion is the queen. Not what I expected.

Shayne's slapped a hand over her mouth. "Get the fuck out of here. I could have sat on her until she squished and played nice."

Annu stifled a chuckle and refocused. "Later love, much later."

Queenie Cushion favoured the injured leg. She wriggled, squirmed, and rocked into a seated position. "I can't see them. Help me."

Bald Martian man rose, assisted Queenie Cushion upright, and motioned to Shayne and Annu. "Right there, my Queen."

On the edge of the chaise, Queenie tapped her chin. "I demand explanations. How dare you arrive unannounced and request to see me. I have plans for—"

Shayne raised her palm and waved. "Yeah I know. As to what Sham-man did in the past, we have no responsibility in that. Yes he did terrible things to a lot of planets, but no more innocent people need die because of it. It's time for a new age, a change in direction. In short your plans are permanently cancelled because if you don't we'll end it right here and now. However, if you agree to our terms, in exchange we'll repair your planet enabling you to live above ground once more, and allow you access to wormholes under a provisional basis. Any slip-ups and we'll rectify them however we must, which includes destroying you and Mars."

Annu's balls tingled, his sex drive returned from natural rather than torturous causes.

Damn woman, this is a side of you I want more of. Let's spend a whole day in bed re-acquainting ourselves. You're smell, taste, reactions to my touch. Nothing existing but us.

Queenie Cushion teetered on the edge; a range of expressions crossed her cushioned face.

Her voice rivalled Shayne's best singing. "It takes great courage to appear before one in these circumstances and speak in such a frank manner. I'd kill for less. However, you make an intriguing offer. Prove your ability to do so and I'll consider it further."

It might work. If we all keep our shit together this bodes well for the others.

Annu ignited his hands and pointed at the Queen's bandaged leg. "I'll heal you for a start. We have other, urgent matters we must fix and we swear we'll return directly after and do the same to Mars."

Shayne sat upon the end of a spare couch. "I second that."

Queenie's demeanour softened, she rubbed it. "No medical aid's helped and it worsens each day. They've said it's un-healable and soon I won't be able to use it at all. There's a possibility of amputation. I don't want to lose my leg."

We all have our demons and can learn to live with or work around them.

Annu knelt before the chaise and rubbed his hands together, and placed both on the Queen's leg, pink light covered the area.

Energy seeped from Annu into her leg, the pain on her face diminished. "Oh my. Oh my. It feels normal. It's hurt for such a long time."

Annu removed his hands and the bandage. "Happy to help."

I actually am.

The act of kindness replenished Annu's hope and faith.

The Queen jumped from the chaise onto both feet. "You did it. Thank you. Thank you, thank you."

A smile blessed Shayne's face and elevated Annu's confidence. "Are we all good then? We've got shit to do."

The Queen stretched her legs and clapped. "Yes."

Annu rose and embraced Shayne. "Excellent. Moving on."

He gathered his family ready for the next challenge.

Chapter 53
Begin Again McFinnigan
GC Head Quarters, Enki island, Orion

Shayne shuffled beside a computer bank, sneaking around the unattended office in the Grand Counsel gave her butterflies. "I'm like Nancy Drew or Jessica Fletcher. I could totally be a spy you know."

Erin tapped at various keyboards and stared at screens. "Then how come I'm doing all the work while mentally scanning for what Igra called his secret file."

"I'm more the hands on type. Besides your new mental abilities put you in the right direction."

And nothing to do with not knowing jack shit about any technological stuff. It's taken constant practice to work the wrist communicator thing.

Shayne faltered Erin's newfound serenity. "Have you found it yet?"

Erin gritted her teeth and fake smiled. "Mum, when I do, you'll know. Okay?"

Keep thinking of the huge joint and shares in cadbury's at the finish line. And if there's energy left, sex. Not full on but like a halfie, a revised sixty nine. A thirty-four point five.

Shayne tapped the computer top. "Aha. I hope the boys hurry up. How long does it take to destroy some machines anyway?"

Erin slapped the counter. "Yes. There it is. I'll email it to everyone in the building and then upload it to the main system."

Can't someone else think about this difficult shit for me? I'm not hurting my brain anymore thinking about it.

"Which means Maybe-Marg gets it too?"

Shayne ignored Erin's eye roll. "Seriously? Yes, and everyone on Orion sees it. They're—" Erin paused and faced Shayne, "you need to bring Annu and Zeke back."

In another life that would be just plain fucking creepy.

Shayne swished behind her without turning. "That's gonna come in handy kiddo."

Clump, clump.

The smell of her man preceded his arms around her. "All taken care of. We better get upstairs to see Marguerite before they arrest Igra. It's the perfect moment."

Shayne inhaled, released the embrace and slumped. "Fine, but we're taking this up again as soon as possible. I'm loving this extra affection side."

Zeke loped around them. "There are upsides to the bad crap before. This feels good."

Erin moved away from the keyboard and raised her arms. "And I'm done. Those courses paid off."

Shayne swirled, the light appeared. "Great."

Erin flipped her arm through it and pointed to their left. "Mum, there's stairs a metre or so away from us."

Shayne blinked and increased the wormhole. "Why bother. Besides no time to waste and all."

Fuck stairs. What's wrong with my daughter?

Their appearance in the hallway outside the offices guaranteed the immediate attention of Peace Officers and Guards.

Shayne's heart skipped, she poised her arms to freeze, Erin's hand stopped her.

Erin pointed in their direction and paused them mid action. "I don't know how long I can hold it, so be quick for once."

Zeke leaned against a wall and crossed his arms. "I'll wait."

Annu erected a wall of energy flames which blocked the other end. "Only until they know not to attack us."

At Maybe-Marg's door, Shayne smoothed down her clothes and regretted not brushing her teeth beforehand. "Not my best look or smell but it's also not my worst."

I remember a day not so many months ago I answered the door with a chocolate wrapper stuck on my head. Jesus.

Shayne opened the door and stepped inside, anticipation lodged her guts into her ribs. "Hello there. Don't freak out."

Annu hovered outside the doorway.

Maybe-Marg looked up from a communicator screen. "Who are you? What are you doing in here? How are you able to get this far and— "

Shayne broached closer to the desk. "I'm Shayne, this is Annu, we're demigods from Orion. Look, we haven't met yet, well we have. Ah, it's all very confusing. I need you to trust me anyway."

Maybe-Marg squinted and tapped a laser pen. "You seem familiar yet I can't place where. Hang on; this is about the explosive electronic message isn't it? You're the mentioned beings Igra wanted captured and ultimately killed."

Shayne's anxiety level lowered an iota. "Yes that's right. There's a lot to get through and now isn't right, just know we want to work with you peacefully once this part's over on two conditions, first,"

Ha, now who's making terms fuckers.

"we assume control over Orion's Space Watch, second, all wormholes and access to other planets are closed under peaceful agreements are made between them, and thirdly, we all work together for the good of fucking mankind, people kind, you know, beings and shit."

Maybe-Marg pressed something unseen behind a display. "Officer Ang, gather some men and come to my office. When you reach the hallway, tell the man in the middle of the hallway fire you're with me. There's an arrest to make and once you know who, order reinforcements. We'll get one shot at this."

Holy crap, it's GI Joe pre-promotion to the I.D.I.O.T.s.

Ang's voice reminded Shayne of post war days. "A man in fire ma'am?"

Maybe-Marg's confidence rubbed off. "Yes. You'll see when you get here.

Shayne relaxed her aura, her anticipation drowned. "You believe me then? I don't have to explain more or do magic tricks?"

Maybe-Marg raised and eyebrow, rose and came around the desk. "Yes and no. Something's eaten at me about changes he's discussed making in recent months. I've start lodging my concerns and he's rebuked all offers for further information. Honestly, there's a little of something I don't know what it is mixed in too and I'm listening for once."

She motioned to the door. "Would you like to witness history?"

Shayne followed Maybe-Marg out the door on autopilot.

Annu shifted aside and grabbed Shayne on the way out. "Everything's cleared up?"

Shayne nodded, her head lightened. "Aha. And it's revenge time."

Maybe-Marg spoke to the guards via the fire ring. "Officers, Guards, these people are not a threat. In fact, they're working beside us in the future. Lower your weapons and allow them access to where I go."

The officers dropped their guns; the guards reacted a second later.

Eyes closed, Zeke chin rested forwards. A soft hum came from his lips.

How can he sleep at a time like this?

Erin released her time hold on the other side's defences. "Thank cookies. I'm getting a headache."

Shayne erupted and poised, Annu engulfed.

Maybe-Marg rushed in front of them and raised her arms. "It's fine. They're with me."

Ang appeared through a parted bunch of unarmed security.

At sight of Shayne, Annu, Zeke and Erin he stepped back. "If I hadn't received that email too I'd be questioning your sanity. It's Igra then?"

Shayne clapped and bounced. "Yes it is. Hurry up. Shit. Can someone video this? I'll pay you."

Annu stormed over to Ang and shook his hand. "It's good to see you, man."

Ang looked at Annu's hand and Annu. "Yeah right. I'm sure it is."

He glanced at Maybe-Marg, she shrugged. "Later. Come on, follow me."

Shayne struggled keeping her feet on the ground. "I can't believe this. It's so fucking exciting."

Her bladder tingled, her stomach tickled.

Erin stood beside Zeke and yawned. "I'm not so much. It's all safe, I'll wait this one out. We've got more to do and this means more to you."

Shayne rocked on her heels. "You sure?"

Maybe-Marg turned and led Ang and his men down the hallway.

Shayne chased them and yelled over her shoulder. "I'll give you a play by play later."

Annu strode beside her down the hallway into another section. "Never thought I'd see things turn out like this. Hey, what do you think about offering Ang a job as a protector?"

Shayne maintained eye contact with Maybe-Marg's hair. "Yeah, yeah sure."

Maybe-Marg stopped before a double doored, end office ten times the size of the others.

Excitement flooded Shayne, her brain and mind danced, her skin buzzed. "Oh god, oh God, I might pee myself."

Annu pushed her onto her feet and held in her place. "Calm down. You'll pass out and miss it."

Shayne slipped ahead of Maybe-Marg. "Can I go in first please? Just let him think he's won for a minute?"

Annu touched Shayne's shoulder. "I'm coming with you then."

Shayne waved him off. "Nah. Not necessary. I got this."

Maybe-Marg's nod pushed Shayne into the room on air and enthusiasm.

Igra rose mouth agape, his turkey neck jiggled. "What the—how did you—you've got no right being in here. Guards—"

Shayne's blood boiled, icicles dripped on the floor. "Isn't this cozy and duplicitous. I bet I'm a big fat surprise for a big fat fucker."

Nimrod boomed from behind. "Hands in the air woman. You've made what's coming next a whole lot easier."

Iggy's pleasure gave Shayne the creeps, he cheered. "You're right. It does. You can't stop us. I know you're behind this electronic message, you little bitch."

Panic tickled Shayne. Nimrod, Lim Lim, and a handful of other recognisable I.D.I.O.T.s all armed and dangerous emerged from the shadows.

The black device from hell rested on a corner table, Nimrod moved towards it.

Nimrod's sneer infuriated Shayne; his light tone sealed the deal. "You're flarked."

Maybe-Marg appeared followed by bigger, larger Peace Officers.

A line of them filed in and formed an armed defence in front of Igra's desk.

Maybe-Marge became Shayne's best friend. "I don't think so. Put that down. Officers' arrest these men including the former Grand Counsellor for treason."

She crossed her arms and stood before Iggy. "You do remember the penalty for such an offence don't you, Igra?"

Igra's frozen image remained amongst Shayne's few recent, pleasant memories.

I should have killed you then.

His forehead broke out in sweat, he wrung his hands. "The message is all lies. You can't believe such rubbish from someone like her."

Maybe-Marg jabbed at his chest. "Their evidence trumps your bull shit, Igra. While I'm surprised at your connections to Shamesh in some ways, in others I'm not. It's time for the Counsel to wake up and take notice of what's really going on starting here."

Shayne flipped between them. "This is real-life reality TV. I fucking love it."

Iggy lunged at Maybe-Marg and wrapped his hands around her throat.

Shayne reacted, she froze him solid. "It feels just as good the second time. Ha, di, fucking ha."

Maybe-Marg pried at his frozen fingers, her face purple. "I, I, can't— breath."

Annu melted Igra's hands into puddles onto the floor. "It's all right. You're okay."

Shit, where was I on that one?

The colour returned to Maybe-Marg, she gulped in air. "Son of a bitch. Will he defrost?"

Igra's pompous arse positioned above the anti-power machine eating grapes reminded Shayne.

Oh yeah.

"Results vary and I'm no expert yet. If it's possible he'd be dealing with significant disabilities."

Fuck this. I'm not waiting to see if you come back.

She kicked his closest knee over and over, it shattered into pieces. Igra tipped to one side onto the ground, his midriff broke in half, his head chipped into parts.

Delight tickled Shayne's lower back. "Make that permanent ones."

Chapter 54
Changes, Choices and Flark You's
DSI Facility, Pine Gap, Earth

Stopped mid air, Annu's original hope for blood and devastation in DSI's demise evaporated. While a part of him yearned for the darker option, a deeper part embraced this version.

Start as I mean to go on.

Annu delivered one last fire ball to the Anti-Power and Tech building, it crumbled into pieces.

Shayne poked her head out of a wormhole next to him. "All righty then, all prisoners are released, agents and shit rounded up, I've sent the videos Zeke took to the news stations and they're sending correspondents out. No chance on anyone missing what went on here. I haven't seen the ones you described yet but there's a lot of beings coming out. Now what?"

Thank the Gods Ankor never did tell me back then who Enlil really was. I'd have flarked up beyond repair. It was a total distraction.

Annu scratched his chin. "I must be sure. I won't take chances on their safety. They helped me when no one did. It's the least I can do."

Where is she and Tony? Anything else doesn't matter anymore. Don't fixate on it.

Shayne pursed her lips and puffed her chest. "And the birdy lady is how to you again? Can I freeze her feathery arse?"

Annu hid his smirk with a hand. "No my love. It's not like that, it's a friendship."

Does she have— forget it.

"Good. I'm being about the peace shit but loving my man pushes my limits. And I'm not a fan of poultry."

Poof. Wormhole and future wife gone.

Crazy woman and she's mine.

Annu circled over the main area, a range of beings erupted from the buildings.

On one side of the yard Ankor stumbled into the open air supported by feline beings; on the other Dingle, Smith, Shooks, Tony and the female doctor joined a group of DSI workers under the guidance of three orange things floated above the ground.

Memories of torture and suffering returned, anger consumed Annu, he engulfed.

There's no guarantee of arrest or punishment by the Earth Government. Nothing to stop them doing this all over again somewhere else. Are they the only group like it? Ending them for good might deter others.

Ambient sound dulled, Annu flew over and floated meters above the area. His blood boiled, everything in him screamed destroy, ruin and kill. "In one blow I'll cleanse the planet of your scourge."

At the edge of the group, Zeke waved his arms and broke Annu's daze. "Hey, Da. Youhoo. What are you doing?"

Start as I mean to go on. This isn't the way. I know it.

Annu drifted to Zeke and bypassed Dingle and the others. "If I'd been in Enlil's life from birth, would I make him a better God or he make me an eviler one?"

How old am I? When did they get together? Another question filed for a better time.

Zeke crossed his arms and tapped his foot. "You seen somewhere else since we came to Jupiter. Is everything okay? The woman you're looking for is over there."

Annu turned his back on the enemy. "Not sure son. I'll let you know when I process—"

The sky rumbled, the ground shook, a bunch of Earth flying craft arrived on Annu's side of the clearing.

Unusual ships appeared in various parts of the sky, spot lights scanned the crowd below. A large ship cast a blue beam down on approximate place he'd spotted Ankor.

Earth craft landed, people holding equipment exited and hurried towards them.

Panic from a different source froze Annu. "I, I, I, shit."

Zeke steered Annu around the captured agents. "Not a fan of the public yet?"

No. Don't flark up. Be a good role model. Break the chain before another link's added.

Unless they attack me. Then all bets are off.

Annu regained control of his mental facilities. "I, ah, no. I'm not prepared for anything like it."

Someone bumped into Annu's side, he stumbled sideways. "That does it."

I want to burn you all so bad.

Annu spun around and engulfed.

Tony backed away from him. "I'm sorry. Please don't hurt me."

Annu's heart dropped, he diminished the flames. "I won't. You come with us."

Zeke nudged Annu's shoulder. "Why?"

"A rare good one here."

Tony licked his lips. "How do you know?"

This shit's hurting even my head.

Annu rolled his neck and held a deep breath. "I've got a sense about these things."

Men in black military garbed gathered the DSI members and ushered them into nondescript trucks.

In the middle of the group Dingle created a ruckus. "This is bull shit. They're the enemy not— "

A flock of raptor creatures swooped, one gripped Dingle in its claws and flew away, the rest picked up the majority of the DSI workers outside of the trucks.

Annu's chin dropped, he slapped Zeke's arm. "Flark, will you look at that. Ha. There's enough karma to go around for everyone."

Plasma bombs from a shimmered craft struck the trucks and Military men. It created no after shock.

All right. I might look them up. Bonus, the agents die and I don't pay for it. I'll live with it and sleep at night.

Annu clapped and gave Zeke another slap. "Hell yes."

Zeke rubbed his shoulder and motioned to the other side. "I got it, you're happy. What's happening with this guy and your friends about to leave?"

Thank the Gods one of us is with it.

Tony stared at the debris.

Annu peeled away from the site. "Can you bring him over to the news people? I'm sure he'd have plenty to tell them."

Zeke huffed and lead Tony towards reporters. "What am I your side kick now?"

Annu shot to Ankor, the blue beam lifted her off the ground.

He lunged at her and held her in place. "I, ah, wanted to make sure you're okay."

Ankor fluttered and blinked, Annu's mind tickled. *'You're Annu, one of the demigods who saved us. I'm Ankor, leader of the—'*

Annu's spine tingled, he nodded. *'Yes. I know. I've heard of you too.'*

She touched his hand, the blue light separated them. *'I must leave, but please stay in touch. I wish you both to join us. There's much we can learn from each other.'*

'We will. I'll see you—'

Ankor disappeared into the bottom of the craft and left behind regret.

I didn't say thank you for being the light and support. Without you I'm not sure I'd have seen another way out.

Shayne popped out of a wormhole in front of him. "Where have you been? Did you see the crazy shit over there?"

Zeke run over with Erin in his arms, he deposited her on her feet next to him. "We done here?"

Erin brushed off her pants. "Time for me to get home and do damage control. Technically I disappeared in the middle of class this morning. Nathanial's will have questions, then there's his parents. Ryan, setting Sam straight about you and Annu, oh, and a wedding to plan. There's the rest of the—"

Shayne jumped out of the wormhole and landed beside Annu. "Can do kiddo. Remember though, once we leave here the wormholes are only accessed through me. We can mentally chat now though and plan ahead."

Annu's thoughts drifted like tumbleweed and collided. "Hang on, what's with Sam and us?"

How much stuff do I miss? I'm paying more attention from now on. Should I worry about Sam? Does he want my woman?

Erin's wave and sigh didn't provide any clues. "Don't worry about it Annu, it's nothing. Silly stuff. You two are perfect for each other and Sam's feeling lonely. Anyway, Mum, home please."

I'm not convinced, yet leaving another thing for later.

Later's weighing up to be a huge day.

Shayne scrunched her nose. "Ah, yeah. Sorry, kiddo."

She gestured at Annu one handed and opened a wormhole. "I'll be back in a second to pick you two up and we're going home. Everything's fixed, sorted. Whoohoo."

The weight of responsibility on Annu lifted, a new beginning and his redemption waited.

I'm ready for you.

Chapter 55
Deja Vu
Erin & Nathanial's House
225 Sanderson Street, Beachport
South Australia, Australia, Earth

I didn't imagine a holding dinner with my in-laws and friends quite like this. Ever. I can do it. I've survived worse.

Erin shivered and concentrated on Nathaniel's hand in hers. "I know finding out like this comes as a shock to at least three quarters of you. There wasn't time for warning anyone before hand." She nodded at her mother in law at the opposite end of the table. "Marg, I'm not sure how it affects our future children, your potential grandchildren, but I assure you it won't matter and we'll learn through this together. It's definitely not usual dinner discussion is it."

Marg glanced at Ron, he nodded, she spoke. "No, you're right. It's a lot to take in, and I know I speak for Ron when I say our only concern is you both being happy with these big changes. If you are, then so are we. That won't ever change."

I'm so blessed. I didn't have to stress as much about tonight.

Nathanial squeezed Erin's hand and stroked her forearm. "I'm completely behind her on this. I find it exciting."

Marg's smile released the last of Erin's anxiety. "Then, we're supportive of you and Nathanial. We'll adjust in time. Don't worry about us. You've got much bigger things to concern yourself with."

Thank you, God. I won't waste this second chance.

A warm buzz tingled Erin's nape, calm enveloped her.

Ryan on Erin's other side blubbered. "Am I like the only one without powers in this family? I didn't get an invite or mention. Nothing."

Erin patted his knee and fake smiled. "Aw Ryan. Don't be like that. At the moment but it doesn't mean you aren't like us. Mum and Annu don't know if you will in the future."

Ryan's expression exuded disbelief. "Mmm. So she's Mum to you again too. Have you got a brain tumour? Did I enter the Twilight Zone?"

Nathanial's chuckle lowered the tension in the room. "I wondered the same thing for a while brother."

Erin leant against Ryan's shoulder and whispered. "I promise I'll tell you everything tomorrow. There's more to it. Trust me, it's not personal you weren't there. We'll get to know Zeke together."

Ryan's demeanour softened. "Sounds like a plan. Of course I trust you."

Sam cleared his throat and glowered from across the table. "You've changed your tune, Miss. Not so long ago you agreed with me and today you've done a complete one eighty. Seem's like a snap judgment to me."

I knew he'd be difficult. Perfect time to practice patience.

Erin used her 'be a good child not a pain' voice. "Sam, I don't make decisions willy nilly. You've known me for most of my life for goodness sake."

Sam clicked his tongue. "True, but I still don't get why Shayne and Annu aren't here too supporting you. Is he keeping her on again?"

Breathe, it's all news to him. He's being protective because he loves me. Difficult is as difficult does.

Erin ran her thumb over Nathanial's. "You of all people know no one can force my mother to do a thing unless she wants to. I explained there's a few things to tie up and it's not necessary for them to be here right now. I can handle this on my own."

Darn it. And I will without freaking out. Those days are gone.

Sam blinked in succession and raised an eyebrow. "Where is all this coming from? You're different, not the same Erin I knew yesterday."

Shame branded Erin's cheek; he'd chinked her happy armour. "Geez, Sam. Aren't I allowed to grow up? I'm not a little girl anymore. You're not being very nice."

Maybe not completely gone yet.

Ron rested his hands on the table and faced Sam. "Son, she's a capable young woman. I don't think you have much to worry about. You've all done a good job raising her."

It truly takes a village to raise a child.

Maternal pride enveloped Erin and hugged. "Mum did most of it believe me. I don't think I'd be as strong in her position. I judged her too harshly before and didn't rationally think about the situation. That's changing."

Ryan whispered in Erin's ear. "You've got brain cancer or something don't you? I'll help you through treatment."

Erin stopped a giggle and swatted her brother. "No I.D.I.O.T. I'm the best I've ever been."

Sam's stubbornness once worked against Shayne in Erin's favour, now she suppressed kicking him in the shins. "All right then big girl. How will you explain to the kids in your class this morning or the school why you disappeared into thin air? That's a quite a situation you created and you can't afford to lose your job over this."

Rosie clipped Sam's ear and frowned. "Sam, stop being an arsehole. What's with you lately? Kids adapt quickly, often faster than some adults. Our girls are happy. Everyone's fine. Let it go. This is all good news."

Thank God for Rosie, the moderator.

Sam huffed and puffed, his arms crossed. "I can't yet. Not until I make sure myself."

Erin embraced Rosie's confidence and ran. "Well you can't for a while. Only wormhole access is through Mum. You know you and Annu are a lot alike Sam. You'd probably like him given the opportunity."

Sam borrowed Erin's blush but wore it with less grace. "I hope you're all right but we'll see."

I'm not in the right frame of mind to deal with you tonight Sam. Once I've gotten myself sorted—

Erin's yawn encompassed her whole body, she relaxed into the chair. "Not tonight we won't. I love you all but I need some rest. It's been a huge few," *don't mess up,* "few hours. Thank you all for coming. I love you and I'll see some of you at the forthcoming Kitchen Tea."

Marg and Ron pushed off their chairs and came around to Erin.

Marg patted Erin's shoulder, her smile comforted Erin. "You're a clever girl, you'll figure this out. You know where we are if you need us. We look forward to getting to know your mum and her partner better."

Erin turned on the seat and held Marg's hand. "You'll get the chance soon. I can't thank you two enough for everything you've done from the beginning. It's in part because of you as much as anyone. Some people may not have reacted quite as nicely."

Nathanial rose and stood behind Erin. "They've got no choice. How can they not love you like I do? You're amazing and beautiful."

Erin's insides melted, her heart swelled, tears burned her eyes.

She faced him and squeezed his thigh. "This is why I'm marrying you. I love you too. You're so sweet."

Nathanial kissed her cheek, his breath brushed her ear. "Just don't turn me into a frog and we're all good."

Erin glowed, her entire being sang. "You better not leave wet towels on the bathroom floor anytime soon."

Ron tapped the table with his knuckles. "I think that's our cue to leave, Marg. We'll talk to you kids soon. Get some rest."

Nathanial walked around the back of the chair. "I'll walk you to the door."

He kissed Erin's other cheek. "Back in a few minutes."

In his absence Rosie stood before Erin. "Hey, gorgeous. I'm unbelievably happy to hear you've mended things with your mum. The other stuff's amazing too, but you know, that's always been a huge thing in your life."

Erin's energy resurged, she bounced off the chair. "This is why you're my Matron of Honour. Thank you, Rosie. Mum and I can't live without you. As soon as you can you've got to visit Orion. It's amazing."

Rosie cocked her head. "When did you go there?"

Oops. Great what do I say? I suck at lying.

Sam's bald head popped over Rosie's shoulder, the rest of him followed. "Hey kid. I'm sorry for being hard work. No promises but you've given me something to think about it."

Great diversion.

Erin wrapped her arms around Sam's middle. "I'm glad to hear it. Drive safe okay?"

He ruffled her hair. "Will do. I'll talk to you later. Rosie, tell the kids I'll call around for a visit soon. Thanks for the wake up call."

Erin's old and new lives began merging.

We all need those sometimes, though I'm not sure as catastrophic as mine.

Chapter 56
Ageing Sucks and So Does Life
Enki Island, Orion

At home on Enki, Shayne hobbled through the back door into the laundry, her joints ached. "Jacob, you there?"

It's finally fucking over. I'm here, and thanks to the Earth visit I'm in pain. I hate feeling like this and I'd forgotten about my whooha in all the hoo ha.

Annu removed his boots and a few top layers. "I'm having a shower before I see him or anyone else."

The sixty nine position won't work in the shower so a thirty-three point five it is.

Shayne's body pain and odour dulled the shine off their home coming. "I'll join you soon. I really want to set things straight between Jacob and I. Start fresh and take things seriously. I hope he doesn't have a heart attack."

I will keep an eye on him and his heart. Annu can make him a new one or something.

Zeke stormed past and down the hallway. "Food, shower and bed. Do not disturb. See you at breakfast, parentals."

Annu's socks stuck to the floor and crunched. "Right. Actually, I might get a drink first and check the news. It's not like another half hour of stink's going to matter."

Shayne rubbed her lower back and groaned. "I like your thinking. I'll start keeping an eye on it too. And the Earth news."

Annu's eyes twinkled, he wriggled his eyebrows. "First you and Zeke get along and now this, miracles do happen. Oh praise mighty Enki."

Shayne hobbled into the hallway on one and a bit feet. "Hail the island all you like darling. You smart arse."

"No I meant— never mind.

Annu slid into her side, his concern evident. "Are you all right? You seem in pain. Why?"

If it's the PSA shit, I have to pre warn him and give him a chance to absorb the information. See how he reacts. And it give him time to run or alternatively figure out how we live alongside it.

Nausea rolled over Shayne, she slumped against his side. "With everything going on it slipped my mind somehow. I've been feeling really off lately, worse after going to Earth. And before you say I exaggerate, I know but given my history with the whole autoimmune stuff I told you about, I have to be careful. The human side of me may be prone to illness."

The hallway lengthened each step.

Annu's hold lightened, his pace slowed. "Oh. Shit. You're right I might have said you were over reacting if you hadn't mentioned the other thing. How do we find out if that's it? What can I do to help? What does it mean for you?"

How is it you look more distinguished and handsome but with the same lines I'd look like a dehydrated ball sack?

Shayne's chest tightened, her throat constricted. "I'm calling the medical centre soon and booking in for a check up. If it is the autoimmune, we'll see what treatments may help or something. I don't know. Look, I understand if you want some space to think about this and our future. You didn't sign up for a sick wife."

Oh thank the Gods. I'm not going through it alone anymore. It's a huge relief and comfort.

Annu recoiled, and jutted his chin. "Why on Orion would I ask for space? How's being sick change my feelings for you? Woman, sometimes you hurt my head."

The fear of rejection Shayne refused access fled. "Just checking. You never know. I actually get what you mean about hurting your head. I'll work on that."

And a number of other things. Just call me WIP. Work in progress.

They reached the kitchen.

Zeke exited in a flurry of food and mumbles.

Shayne stepped aside and let him pass. "Is Jacob in there? Did you eat all the food?"

Zeke didn't turn around. "Mmmmdbhihbe."

"Okay thanks for that, step son."

Well the respect lasted all of five minutes. We better get some groceries ASAP.

Annu slipped into the kitchen. "No he's not in here."

Shayne followed at a slower speed and in Annu's wake. "I'm not sure putting off a shower is a great idea. I wonder where he is."

"Nah, doesn't matter. The couple who stinks together stays together."

The Lexicon lay closed on the end of the bench.

Annu loomed over it. "It's almost taunting us. After we rest, we're getting back into this. No excuses and no matter how boring Jacob makes the experience. Same for training. We can't always rely on our powers."

The T word. Sick or not, it's good for my muscles.

Shayne maintained a safe distance from the other bench. "Yeah I know. Argh. Stupid thing. What kind of moron made it difficult to understand yet so necessary for everything we do? Can't one thing go easy for us?"

Annu's socks crunched on the way to the glasses cupboard, he selected a massive one. "I'm going with no on that one my love."

Amber liquid filled the glass; he tapped the top of her grenberry tin. "You having a smoke? I thought you'd have already had two."

Shayne perched against the kitchen bench. "Yeah me too but I can't be stuffed."

"Want me to roll you one?"

It will relax me and stop things hurting for a while.

Shayne rested on her elbows, her stomach groaned. "Sure. Jacob's obviously not around the house. He'd have heard us. If he doesn't call in today, no doubt we'll see him tomorrow."

He slipped a paper between his fingers and rolled one handed. "Speaking of which, you need to call the medical centre. Let's not waste time of this and get whatever is going on sorted out. There's a lot ahead of us and I must have you by my side."

Shayne's socks left dirty marks on route to Annu. "As soon as I've eaten and gotten cleaned up I promise I will. The kids play a bigger part than we thought or liked. We've got stuff to learn from them as well."

Annu finished rolling the smoke and held it out. "It's a funny thing. I'm amazed by how well they dealt with it all let alone helped finish it."

She took the smoke and searched for a lighter. "Thank you."

Annu pulled one out of his pocket, lit the joint and refilled his empty glass. "A pleasure, like those I'll give you later."

Oooooohhhhh man. You're obviously still alive down there then.

"Fuck, I love you. Food first."

Shayne held the first drag and spoke smoke. "With other planets aware of us, someone might come forward with information about your father."

Annu paused mid sip, glanced around and sipped again. "Yeah maybe. Weren't you hungry?"

Weirdo. I swear anything to do with is father and he gets strange.

Shayne inhaled to the fridge, her reflection in the door caused her to exhale in splutter. "What the fuck's going on here?"

Annu spun on his heel, rum splashed over the lip. "What's wrong?"

She dropped the smoke, pulled a chunk of hair in front, and another three. The horror continued. "It's fucking white. My hair's white."

Shayne's stomach roiled, her pulse raced. "I look eight hundred years old. When did this happen?"

Annu paled and backed up against the bench. "Oh yes, that. After we went back in time. I didn't know how to tell you, and then I got used to it."

"You bastards. Why the fuck didn't you or the kids tell me?"

My family keeps life shattering information from me. Life hates me.

"I anticipated such a moment and I begged them not to. There's been enough shocks going on."

Tears poured down Shayne's cheeks, her life essence drained. "No. Just no. This isn't happening. It's cruelty of the highest degree."

Annu crunched to her side and hugged. "It's not such a huge deal, you'll dye over it won't you?"

Shayne grabbed the wall communicator beside the fridge and scrolled through the contacts. "Fucking bastards."

Annu rubbed her arms, his condescending tone tore shreds off Shayne's patience. "I don't think the doctors can help love."

"What? No, I'm calling the hair dressers first. No way I'm leaving the house like this."

There's always something to piss me off.

Chapter 57
All's Not Well That Ends Not Well
Enki Island, Orion

Outside the strong room, protectors carried out old equipment, Annu check each box on the way out and buried the previous night's bad dreams in activities.

There's bound to be some residual mental trauma after what we went through. We'll get back to normal, or whatever that is for us soon enough.

It's strange we haven't seen Jacob yet. No time to waste anymore.

Annu stopped a younger man at the doorway and peaked inside his haul. "Put it over there. I'd forgotten about those contraptions. I may need some of it one day."

Why does a fresh start mean throwing old stuff out? There's plenty of room to keep it. I do get Shayne's point about requiring a safe place in danger though.

Ang cleared his throat on the opposite side of the doorway. "That's the tenth box you've redirected. Only two have made it to the storage room. You wouldn't use even half of it in six lifetimes. Yours not mine of course."

Man it's good to see you alive in any respect. Your company's been a blessing too. I'm due a new friend.

Annu waved the next protector forwards. "Your opinion is duly noted."

A middle aged woman tipped a box his direction. "Your Grace."

Annu poked amongst the top section and pointed to the keep pile. "Over there beside the others. I'll get to it later."

I need another list than later.

Ang's chuckle lightened the mood. "You completely ignored what I said."

Annu dipped his head to the woman. "Still put it over there. No I listened to you. I just did what I wanted to anyway."

"Can't you pass time until Shayne gets out by a leisurely stroll rather than interfering with the job you gave me?"

Annu's chest tightened, an iota of doubt invaded his safe new world. "I'm helping. Everything else is under control at the moment."

Please Enki let Shave have anything but exhaustion wrong with her. I couldn't cope if it's terminal. Not after the mess we've survived. Doing that to me is tantamount to war.

Ang walked in front of the next protector and lead Annu by the arm into the yard. "I don't know what's going on with you, but I see you're worried about something. I'm here if you want to talk about it."

I made a good choice bringing you here.

Annu shrugged off Ang's arm and shook his hand. "I appreciate your concern. I'll be fine. Want to grab a drink tonight?"

Ang patted Annu's shoulder and walked away. "I'll message you. I'm in a new job and the boss gave me tonnes of things to take care of. Have a good one, boss."

Funny, funny, man. Things are looking up. We'd obviously headed in the wrong direction and needed turning around. In a major way.

An older protector, Bert crossed the yard.

Annu strode and stopped him halfway. "Morning Bert. You seen Jacob around?"

Bert's frowned niggled at Annu. "Who, my Grace?"

Annu crossed his arms and pushed aside frustration. "Jacob, from the Brotherhood of Orion, first protector of us and the Lexicon?"

Bert shuffled and scratched his beard. "I'm sorry my Grace. I don't know a Jacob or a Brotherhood of Orion."

What the flark?

Stay calm. There's a simple explanation other than Bert having dementia.

Annu uncrossed his arms. "Of course you do. He's been here since ascension. You and he were old friends."

Bert called over the older woman who'd carried the box before. "Kirst. Please come here?"

She stood akimbo aside Bert. "Is something wrong your Grace? Did I put the box in the wrong place?"

Annu deep breathed, his heart thumped. "No it's fine. Do you know who, and where Brother Jacob is? Bert's confused and has no idea who Jacob is."

Kirst looked between Annu and Bert. "I'm sorry, my Grace, I don't know any Brother Jacob either? Has he been here long?"

Unease crawled under Annu's skin. "Forget I said anything. I must have his name wrong or something."

Annu stumbled towards the medical centre away from them.

Oh shit. Did we accidentally delete him along the way? Flark. It's my fault.

Lexicon under his arm, Zeke jogged over and broke Annu's daze. "Da, I came across a few things which are a more than a bit concerning."

A chill invaded Annu's kidneys, he faced Zeke. "Lucky you're onto things, son. What's the problem?"

How much worse can this get? Why'd I even ask?

Zeke tapped the book and pointed at the Medical Centre. "It's paid off so far. There's Shayne. I'll chat to both of you on the way back to the house, which means walking not flying."

"Done."

Gives me thinking and stewing time.

Shayne sped to Annu's side and jabbed him in the ribs. "We'll get the results today sometime. In the meantime I'm not worrying about it. Hi Zeke."

Zeke rocked on his heels. "Hi, future stepmother."

Annu hugged Shayne and walked towards the lower island elevator. "Looks like you're feeling better. It's good to see. I'm concerned about you."

She wiggled her legs one after the other. "Well don't be. At least not until we're sure what's going on. He gave me this shot of something incredible which worked straight away. Which is perfect because I've got stuff to do at home before we meet Orion in a couple of days. Seen Jacob anywhere?"

Annu's blood pressure rose, his sanity lowered. "Ah no. Maybe he's on holidays."

If he still exists. It's add to my never ending list of concerns.

Zeke waved the book. "We've got stuff to discuss."

Annu lead the way beside Shayne and readied himself for the onslaught. "All right. As much as I don't want to ask, what'd you find?"

Zeke's solemn tone consolidated Annu's fears. "The biggest enemy I've come across is some guy named Enlil. The details are hazy, sketchy at best but despite the fact he's in prisoned somewhere he's a definite and immediate threat."

Shock and panic barrelled Annu.

No, no, no. I misheard.

Annu stumbled over his feet and let go of Shayne. "What?"

It can't be. Of all beings to mention, it's him.

Flarking hell. Literally. We fixed things. None of that happened. I'll make sure it doesn't again.

Zeke grabbed Annu under the elbow and steadied him. "You fly so much you forget how to walk?"

Play it cool. Easy.

Annu brushed himself off and ambled between them. "Clever son. No, I stepped the wrong way."

Shayne's sigh brushed by Annu's wrist. "What's the go with this Enlil? What's he after and what's it got to do with us?"

Stop saying his name people.

Annu concentrated on the ground ahead. "I appreciate the heads up Zeke, but we'll get back to it after we've gotten our public meeting out of the way."

It's not too late to take care of it. It's only a matter of letting the time lapse between now and his allotted escape slot, and stay well away from him.

Oh and if Jacob no longer exists get him back too. Easy.

Shayne relaxed into Annu's waist. "Good plan. I've had enough of bad guys for this week. What do you boys want for lunch?"

I'll be eating a crow pie with a side of crow in secret.

Annu leaned down to Shayne's ear. "You."

Her giggle pushed away the guilt and kept Annu focused.

Good choices, good outcomes from hereon. My DNA shall not define me.

Chapter 58
Let's Donnie Darko This Shit
Enki Island, Orion

Shayne finished the chocolate bar in one hand, pressed rewind with the other and peddled faster. "Dammit. I missed the time travel explanation again."

I really hope it never happens again, but just in case watching Donnie Darko a few times can't hurt.

The handmade dress slung over the couch slipped off and onto the floor.

Doing this must ensure I don't have a bulging belly in it. I don't want Orionion's thinking I'm a fat demigoddess. Thankfully a better smelling one though.

Sweat beaded across Shayne's forehead, she tossed the empty packet and toked on a nearby joint. "This is a hard workout. I'm gonna look fucking awesome."

Shayne exhaled, rested the smoke on the exercise bike's display and licked the chocolate off the remote control.

Annu appeared in the doorway and rested against it. "Woman, what are you doing?"

Shayne wiped her chin and sat the remote between her thighs. "I told you, multitasking. It's my new thing."

And I'm going to stick with it.

At least for today.

Annu strolled across the room and stood in front of the bike. "I thought you were cutting down on smoking and eating chocolate."

Shayne peered around him at the TV screen. "Yeah, it's only my second of each. The smoke makes it bearable."

"Since breakfast an hour ago?"

Way to flatten my enthusiasm. I'm not getting any headway here.

Shayne paused the actor's speech midway. "Hence I'm peddling extra hard. You're a real buzz kill today darling. What's wrong?"

Annu's yawn de-invigorated Shayne. "Marguerite and the rest of the Counsel are coming to the island later. Given the damage from the last two prior leaders I'm not sure we should trust these lot so easily on our own turf."

Shayne extracted herself from the bike and came around beside Annu. "Cheer up. I understand what you're saying but we've got the advantage. From what I've seen lately we can't assume everyone's bad. There's at least three non-related people who don't want us dead. For now anyway."

I need a personal assistant or something. One who works for free or for love.

"I can't believe I'm saying this but I miss Jacob. Aside from the Lexicon he offers moral support I didn't realise or appreciate."

Annu's thumb brushed her cheek, he gazed out the window. "Me too. I'm sure he'll turn up soon. He's never far away."

I love you and I know you love me but why does it feel like something isn't right with you. Perhaps because if there's nothing to worry about I'll create some.

No more.

Shayne blotted sweat with her sleeve. "Mmm. He better get back before we leave for Erin's wedding next week."

Annu's heart quickened against Shayne's cheek. "He'll be back by then. You bring up a relevant topic, Shay, when are we getting married?"

Marriage, shit. That takes even more organisation and time. I'm not sure I'm ready. Plus I'm going to have to wear make up and crap. I'm going to need to keep exercising for that too now. Boo. Hiss.

Shayne's appetite dragged from Annu, out of the room and down the hall. "There's no real rush is there? It's not like it's affecting us."

Annu followed Shane to the kitchen and plonked onto a seat at the bench. "On the same token nothings stopping us from doing it soon and I want to marry you. Be husband and wife forever."

Shayne's hangriness, 'hungry plus angry,' abated.

Aw. Bless you. This is what love is meant to feel like.

Shayne snuggled into him, stood on tip toes and kissed his cheek. "Done deal, but I thought you wanted your dad at the wedding and that's one of the reasons we're looking for him."

And I'm back to starving.

Annu's demeanour tensed, a wall went up around him. "I, I, I'm not waiting for anyone anymore. Let's drop that subject for now."

What the McFuck is up with him? Leave it. We've barely crawled out of the huge pile of cosmic crap dumped on us. Change of subject in order.

"All right. If we were getting married soon, where are you thinking of doing it? It means wormholing a few people here and a fuck load of organisation."

Annu's mood lifted, the wall vanished. "The back garden's a lovely spot and plenty of room for guests. We have to talk about what kind of food to serve and where people will stay the night if they wish. And alcohol of course."

Butterflies fluttered in Shayne's belly, her heart fluttered. "You already know what my vote for food will be. Alcohol I'll leave up to you, I know nothing much there. Before we work out where everyone's staying, we need a guest list and send out invites. People require notice so they can attend. After the festivities we're sneaking off to stay elsewhere for a few days."

Annu massed her shoulders and kissed her neck. "It sounds like you want to do this soon too."

I can't believe it, but yes I am.

Excitement tingled Shayne's spine. "Yes, let's do it. How soon are you talking?"

Annu traced his finger across her chest. "This weekend."

A ninety-ten vomit burp burned the back of Shayne's throat. "Honey that's four days away. It's not enough time to plan."

"Yes it is. I'll be doing half of it and some protectors will happily help. It's doable."

"I, ah, sure why the fuck not."

The wrist communicator buzzed, Nurse Sherryn's name flashed on the screen.

Annu tightened the embrace. "I forgot for a moment. Not so great timing but I'm here for you.

Shayne tapped the answer icon, her finger shook. "Here we go."

Nurse Sherryn appeared in full, her smile appeared forced. "Good day to you both."

Shayne's butthole constricted. "Yeah, hi. It was."

Fuck, fuck, fuck. What is wrong with me?

Annu's breath warmed her neck. "Stay calm. We've got this."

She took the seat next to him and gripped his hand. "Yeah, yeah."

May as well in case I drop.

Sherryn smiled at Annu. "I'm glad you're both there."

Annu perched on his knee, his concern eased anxiety. "Well? What's wrong with her?"

Goosebumbs covered Shayne's arms, her breath shallowed. "Please tell me is it that bad? Am I dying? Is it the autoimmune? Do I have to stop visiting Earth for a while?"

Sherryn's smile drooped, she look at a screen beside her. "I'm sorry. I'm working out the best way of telling you. I'm unsure how you'll react."

Shayne's bladder tingled, she double clenched.

Oh Gods, oh Gods, oh Gods.

"Start by letting the words out of your mouth."

Sherryn smoothed a hand over her face and straightened. "All right. Okay. Here goes the autoimmune is back mildly. We— "

Shayne relaxed against the bench. "That's not a big surprise. I expected it might be. Why were you worried about what I'd do?"

Sherryn pursed her lips and held a breath. "Because I haven't finished. Doc Ruc believes it's returned Shayne, due to you being without a doubt, pregnant."

Shayne's screech hurt her own ears. "Ha fucking ha. That's not funny Sherryn. It's been a fucking shit week. It's a cruel joke. Why are you being so mean?"

Annu flopped onto his butt. "Highly inappropriate given the gravity of the other condition, Sherryn."

Sherryn flushed as if Annu slapped her. "This is the reason I was reluctant to…oh, never mind. It's not a joke. Yes, it's a shock but you're pregnant, with child. Easily four to five months along. Come in tomorrow and we'll do scans to confirm your gestation and a delivery date."

Shayne squished into the corner, her chest rose and fell like sanity. "Delivery date? What am I ordering a pizza? Are you fucking kidding me? What did I ever do to you for you to be such an arsehole to us? I liked you."

We're not friends anymore. She's on the bad guy side of the new Christmas card list now.

Annu stopped blinking, he expressed enough dazed and confused for everyone. "Hang on. Wait, what?"

Sherryn released a deep breath. "Again, no I am not kidding, Get ready, there's one more thing and it's bigger. Here goes, your hormone levels suggest there's more than one baby in there. It's probable you're carrying twins."

Someone screamed, the tiles cooled Shayne's back but not her brain. "I, I, I, I."

Annu rocked on his arse and hugged his knees. "Huh? Babies. Our babies."

Shayne fanned herself, her iddilc life of two seconds ago shattered into little pieces.

I went through all of that pregnant? With two? No. No. Just no. It's not, it's just not. Oh my God.

Shayne rolled on her side and probed her face. "I think I've had a brain aneurysm. Is blood coming out my nose? Is my eye drooping?"

Annu snapped out of his daze, perched Shayne upright and held the communicator closer. "Huh?"

Sherryn's tone flattened with her demeanour. "You two make a great couple. Gods help us all. I repeat Shayne's pregnant with twins."

Annu slouched and lay beside Shayne. "Huh?"

Sherryn's features wavered.

Shayne reality shattered, she crushed the pieces under foot and poked her belly. "Me. No. Can't be. Fuck. No amount of bike riding's going to fix this roll."

Annu ended the call and dropped the communicator. "I'll let you both go so you can digest the news. The doctor wants to see Shayne again tomorrow. How's ten a.m. for—"

Annu wiggled his finger. "You're pregnant? We're having a baby, babies? How? When? Shit. I didn't expect, huh?"

Shayne threw the communicator at the opposite wall, it smashed into pieces.

Oxygen in the kitchen diminished. "Apparently. She seemed adamant she wasn't joking, and serious though insulting. The friendships over. Ah, yes, no, maybe, are we?" Shayne choked on shock lodged in her throat. "It's not just the PSA crap."

Annu poked her belly, it jiggled. A smile consumed him. "We're having babies." His colour and twinkle returned. "Holy shit. I can't believe it."

Poke, poke, jiggle, jiggle.

Shayne slapped his hand away and rolled on her back. "Quit it. I'm going to need new dresses. Oh fuck."

Annu pushed off the floor. "Yeah at least. Damned that explains the food bills and mood changes."

He lifted Shayne up by the arm, she paused halfway. "Fuck. The babies might be brain damaged from all the weed I smoke. Doesn't matter about the chocolate, they were coming out that colour anyway. Shit. I've been a terrible incubator."

"Don't worry about it, some women use Grenberry in labour here but with all the tests they'll run I'm sure they'll pick any issues up. Not that I expect any."

Shayne's blood pressure dropped, she clutched Annu's arm. "What do you mean?"

Annu put Shayne on her feet and beamed happy. "I'm in prime health and I have another normal kid despite my past questionable vices. We're definitely getting married this weekend. There's no way I'm having an illegitimate child. Holy shit. Holy shit. Holy shit."

Butterflies in Shayne's belly now held a different meaning. "Not gas. Babies. Fucking babies with all the vomit, poo, crying and wrinkle giving moments."

Annu supported Shayne's shoulders and dragged her along. "Did you hear me? We better get organised."

Zeke popped out his bedroom door. "Are you two seriously having twins and getting married? I'll get pushed aside for another reason. Well, good luck to you both. I'm not helping baby sit by the way."

Shayne flung a limp arm in his direction. "Oh yes you are. I'll need everyones help. I'm too old for this shit."

Annu appeared oblivious to Shayne's lack of desire to co-operate. He carried her like a rag doll and flopped her around for emphasis. "I'll make the wedding rings. We'll get Jacob to facilitate, do the ceremony. Oh, wait. Hell if he, ah, comes back. If not we'll get something else."

That's a bunch of adult stuff to deal with in one go.

Shayne's tongue numbed, her left side tingled. "Scratch the brain aneurysm, I think it's a tumour and I want lie down for like a long fucking time."

Holy fucking shit. How the fuck will we pull this off? Organised? Me? Us? My brain hurts. Babies, fucking babies.

Chapter 59
Enlil: The Sins of The Father
The Hell Realm - Enki Island, Orion

Memories returned to Enlil, his anger conflicted with the only good news since the initial incarceration—his discovered son Annu attempted to erase their meeting and Enlil's awareness of it.

Ann's his mother, there's no one else since. That sneaky bitch. They've hidden him all this time and turned him against me.

Enlil's hatred for humanity increased, he projected himself into his informant's communication system. "Tell me everything you know about Annu and quickly."

Marguerite flushed and looked around her office. "My Lord. How do you know about him?"

"I'm the reason you're on that damned board and the one who'll not only change it but flay the skin from your bones."

People mumbled in the background, and shuffled around.

Marguerite lowered her voice. "This isn't the best time. I'm about to start a Grand Counsel meeting. I'm the elected leader— "

Enlil's essence wriggled into her ear and brain. "I'm the reason you're on that damned board. Tell me what you know."

She rubbed her ear, her bottom lip trembled "He, he has a son Zeke, who has some powers, a fiancé Shayne, also a Demigod, and two stepchildren one of them has some powers too. Annu, Zeke and Shayne live on Enki Island. I'm scheduled there later, we're working together."

Enlil swallowed the bitter taste of disdain. "Excellent. You must take the Lexicon while you're there and keep it secure until I order you otherwise. Learn what you can about their weaknesses and report to me. Understand?"

If you won't listen to me, son, I've another way around you. Nothing or no one will get in the way of my last chance. Once out my power returns, no more physical form and finally able to exact revenge on Enki's creations.

Marguerite cheeks flushed, her bottom lip quivered. "Yes, my Lord."

Enlil ended the call and saved his sanity.

Anger festered Enlil's thoughts, his hatred of Enki increased. "Praise the unholy. As below as above brother. Fuck you. You'll pay for this."

I'm sick and tired of this depressing place.

Enlil grabbed a side table and hurled it at a wall. He tore at a cushioned seat, it melted on his touch. Enlil engulfed in flames and roared, the room burned.

Rationality interrupted his hissy fit.

Stop and think.

Enlil's ire and flames dwindled. "No, I can't lose it now. My temper only makes things worse. When Annu's before me if he doesn't see his rightful place is instead of me, I'll force him too."

The blessed sword shall slice his chest upon the portal and deliver my way out.

General Ralf of the Demonic Army burst into the chamber with his weapon close. "My Lord, are you all right? What happened?"

A smile threatened Enlil's facade, he cut it off.

Be careful. Don't give yourself away, I.D.I.O.T. You're too close to fuck this up.

"Yes. Nothing for your concern. I can handle it."

Ralf's blank expression accentuated his horrid features. "Can you? You should be aware there's talk about your lack of care and concern of late. Demons, guards and the like are turning to me for answers, and I've nothing to tell them."

Shit, they've noticed.

Ralf's demeanour chinked Enlil's confident armour, wariness replaced excitement.

I hope giving you power to fight the ancients war during my last attempt out doesn't come back and bite me. I have no intention of taking you too no matter what I said then.

Fear of failure sucked the air and joy out of the room. "I've had a few off years and they're already complaining? No one is ever fucking happy in this God forsaken place."

Ralf raised an eyebrow. "Isn't that the point to this place, my Lord?"

Tension tightened muscles either side of Enlil's spine. "Of course it is. I know that."

Shadow contorted half Ralf's grotesque features. "Yes my Lord. Before I leave, Greivence wanted a moment with you."

I finally have a pure blood spawn able to free me and no further use for that misguided, failed experiment. Curse the sixties on Earth.

"Tell my son later."

Ralf nodded, turned and exited the room.

Excitement consumed Enlil, his skin tingled.

No time like the present to get things under way.

'Annu it's Enlil, your father.'

The end.

Stay tuned for Shayne and Annu's next adventures in book 3 -
A demigoddesses guide to Inter-dimensional In-Laws.

BIOGRAPHY

R.L. Andrew

Along with being a great cook and gardener, R.L Andrew is a chronically ill Australian Author keen to inspire others or just make them laugh so hard they pee. Along with many short stories over different genres published in International Anthologies, R.L. was a long term contributor to the CrypticRock.com Website based in New York.

R.L's first book 'A Lunatic's Guide to Interplanetary Relationships' the first of eight in this series has been published by JaCol Publishing Inc. A Lunatic's Guide has received five star reviews on Amazon and Good Reads, and was an official selection of The New Apple 2017 Literary Awards.

R.L's third book – 'A Demigoddess's Guide to Interdimensional In-Law's' is in progress.

Keep up with R.L. Andrew via social media:

Amazon Author Page - http://www.amazon.com/-/e/B00R0OY14A

www.ingramcontent.com/pod-product-compliance
Lightning Source LLC
Chambersburg PA
CBHW070740190726
48292CB00002B/347